"To t
I
t
about any woman."

"What way?"

"Like a highland stag in rut and a besotted bridegroom combined. If I claimed you every time I thought about it, we'd be spending most of our time in bed."

He bent his head to kiss her. His wife possessed none of the prevailing inhibitions that afflicted most other women...she was irrepressively sensuous and completely honest in her reactions.

Releasing her lips, he chided her lightly, "Sweetheart, when you're in this mood, I don't trust you any more than I do myself. Unless you promise to let me set the pace, I'll not risk hurting you."

The declaration, however, was entirely rhetorical; Jolie was given no opportunity to agree or to protest. Instead her lips were claimed imperiously...

★   ★   ★

**"A GIFTED AUTHOR
WITH GIFTS OF INSIGHT."**
—*Barbara Critiques*

Bright Destiny

**Also by
Elizabeth Evelyn Allen**

Freedom Fire
Rebel
To Fortune Born
The Lady Anne
Witch Woman

**Published by
WARNER BOOKS**

Bright Destiny

Elizabeth Evelyn Allen

WARNER BOOKS

A Warner Communications Company

Cover design by Anne Twomey
Cover art by Pino
Cover type by Carl Dellacroce

Warner Books, Inc.
666 Fifth Avenue
New York, N.Y. 10103

 A Warner Communications Company

Printed in the United States of America

First Printing: June, 1990

10 9 8 7 6 5 4 3 2 1

Bright Destiny

1

While the piercing screams of a terrified child had gone unheeded for the better part of an hour, the report that a half-naked, red-haired woman was hanging from a remote wall of the sprawling Newcastle fortress brought people running. First to arrive at the ruins of the castle wing destroyed by Roundhead cannons fifty years before were a pair of groundskeepers who had been gathering wood in the brambly undergrowth that surrounded the derelict structure. Staring up over the debris of tumbled stones toward the inner side of the wall that had once surrounded the castle armory, the startled men saw the woman suspended by a rope eight feet from the top and thirty feet above the rubble. That she was there by design rather than accident was evident in her commanding shout to the astonished woodsmen.

"Don't just stand there gawking at me, monsieurs. One of you go for help while the other one pulls me to safety. There are injured children up here and an injured man. Run, monsieurs, it is an emergency."

Such was the authoritative power of the lightly accented voice that the older worker relayed an order to his gape-mouthed companion. "Hop to it, Jem, and locate Bailey, if you can. If he's in charge, won't no blame fall on us. Dunno who the woman up there is, but it's fair t'say she's

1

no serving wench—not with her fancy talk. Odds are she and the young'uns both b'long to the fancy nobs here fer the hunt and the duke's best wine.''

Had the young woman heard the groundskeeper's evaluation of her social status, she'd have been angered at being considered either a servant or a nob. Sister Jolie Campbell— the *sister* was her idea and not the accepted title for a soberly married woman—was a nurse, but not the common variety household retainer whose knowledge was limited to folk medicine. Jolie was a well-educated, medically competent practitioner who had been trained by an expert. Her income and that of her doctor husband was amply supplied by their efficient, modern infirmary in the town of Newcastle and by their most affluent patient, the town's powerful and wealthy duke.

The fact that the gardener, himself a lifelong servant, had identified her accurately as an aristocrat would have annoyed Jolie even more. While her French mother and Scottish father had belonged to noble families, Jolie had been raised as a foundling in a Sisters of Charity convent, and she was intensely proud of her unique childhood. Under the tutelage of a brilliant old nun, she'd learned to react swiftly to medical emergencies. And because of the excellence of that early training, she had responded automatically to the child's screams today without regard for her own safety.

Since she and her doctor husband, Rorke Campbell, could not leave the infirmary unattended, they visited Henry Cavendish, the duke of Newcastle, on alternate days, and Jolie had completed her visit an hour earlier. Under normal conditions, she would have left the castle through the main entry. In the ten months she had been living in Newcastle, she had been treated as a welcome guest in the duke's home. However, the arrival of the duke's daughter a fortnight ago had changed her status. The wife of a wealthy lord, Lady Marianne Cavendish Holles had decreed that Jolie was to be considered a servant. To maintain peace with his daughter and the thirty-odd guests she'd brought with her from London for the annual hunting season, and to protect Jolie from unkind remarks, the duke had ordered his full-time male nurse to show her out through a rarely used wing of the venerable fortress. On this day, as she and the young man she had trained as a nurse emerged from the remote doorway, they had heard the child's screams.

Although he had been a lifelong resident of the castle, it took Perry Tate almost half an hour after he had determined the location of the child to find the half-hidden entry into the abandoned tower. After he and Jolie used their combined strength to push the rusted gate open, Perry fingered the hasp lock that bore the scratches of recent usage.

"I never saw this gate open before. How do you suppose a child managed to unlock it?" he asked thoughtfully.

Jolie shook her head. She was staring at the flights of stone stairs that eventually reached the top of the wall forty feet upward. They wound past the destroyed flooring of three landings that had once served as sleeping quarters for soldiers.

"How could a child, or anyone else, climb these stairs?" she countered. "Over half of them are broken. There must be another way to get up there."

The renewed screams of the child made both of their questions academic; there was no time to search for a safer passage. Fastening her medical bag to her belt, Jolie began the slow ascent with cautious steps, gripping the uneven stones of the wall for added support. Curiously, her companion, a strong man several years her senior, made no effort to lead the way. Although his respect for her was obvious, it was the respect of a student for his teacher, and in no way bound by the rules of chivalry. During the months she had trained him in nursing, he'd watched her perform medical feats in surgery and exhibit a physical strength far greater than most women possessed. Perry was convinced that there was little she couldn't accomplish and was therefore content to follow her lead.

Those crumbling flights of stairs, however, taxed Jolie's physical skills to the limit; a dozen times she was forced to her knees to avoid falling down into the rubble-filled abyss.

Perry had been right, though, about her dexterity—she survived the frightening ordeal without a scratch. He reached the wide walkway on the top with his left leg badly sprained at both the ankle and knee. Had the screaming child, still thirty feet away, not been standing perilously close to a break in the low, protective wall of the rampart, Jolie would have turned instantly to help her injured companion. Instead, she reached the small boy's side in a swift dash that dislodged several more broken stones as she pulled him to safety. Even while his hysterical screams continued unabated, she carried him back to where Perry was awkwardly trying to stand.

"Perry," Jolie scolded him, "sit down before you fall down and hold this frightened child while I examine him. Do you know who he is?"

"Aye, he's John William," Perry muttered. "Most of the estate people know both him and his older brother. Twice last week Dr. Roxbury and I were routed out of bed to patch them up—once after they'd been thrown from a horse they had no business riding, and again to treat rat bites after they'd locked themselves in a storage shed."

Jolie, who was cleaning several raw abrasions on the child's arms and legs, frowned. "Doesn't anyone watch out for them? *Ma foi*, this one is still an infant."

"The governess is the one who sent for us. According to her, their uncle is supposed to supervise them, but he's an avid hunter, so he's seldom around."

"Perry, are they related to the duke?"

"No, but they're the sons of one of the lords whom Lady Holles brought with her, so I'm glad we found the lad safe and sound. With the duke confined to the sickroom, the staff's as jumpy as fleas about this pack of guests. Sister Jolie, have you given any thought about how we're going to get down from here? I don't think John William and I will be able to use those stairs."

Again Jolie studied the boy, whose cries were reduced to gulping whimpers but whose eyes still reflected his terror. Leaning toward him with the confiding smile that had made her a successful nurse even when she was only a thirteen-year-old in the convent infirmary, she asked softly, "John William, did your brother come up here with you and then go for help when you hurt your leg?"

Jolie's smile faded as the child buried his face against Perry's broad chest. "What's the brother's name?" she demanded sharply.

"Francis," the man replied, "but he wouldn't have left John up here alone."

Ignoring the protest, Jolie addressed the boy more forcefully. "John William, look at me and tell me where Francis is."

Obediently, the child raised his head and pointed his finger at a break in the opposite wall. "Holy mother of God," Jolie muttered through stiffened lips. The premonition that had assailed her for a moment before was more than likely true—the older brother had fallen over the edge! Cautiously she crossed the walkway and peered down, gasping in fear at the sight below. Eight feet down, a narrow crevice had formed when an eight-foot-wide chimney had pulled away from the original wall. The chimney was now leaning outward pressing against the body of a young boy Jolie estimated to be seven years old. Wedged tightly, he seemed lifeless, and Jolie could detect no sign of breathing.

A moment later she was racing back toward the crumbling stairway. Only if she could lower herself enough to turn the boy's head away from the wall would he have any chance at all. His nose had been pressed tightly enough against the stones to smother him, if his precarious position had not already done so. Halfway up those stairs, near the rotted second landing, Jolie had seen a coil of rope. Praying that it wasn't a century-old discard, she started cautiously downward, only to lurch to a jolting stop when she almost tripped over the full skirt of her robelike uniform.

Muttering the French expletive "*Peste!*" with mounting impatience, she returned to the walkway and stripped off her robe, underdress, and wimple, until she stood in only her pantaloons and shift. Having been a hard-working nurse for more than seven years, she'd learned to meet emergencies without any stultifying self-consciousness. The life of a child was at stake; she reacted automatically and without false modesty. Her knowledge of ropes, too, was a matter of experience. During her dramatic escape from persecution by the French Inquisitionists, she and the Scottish doctor she'd been forced to wed had spent several months aboard a ship on the Rhine River where ropes often provided the only margin of safety. Now that her own life would be at risk, she hoped she could remember the knots she'd watched the deckhands tie with such swift efficiency.

Thoughts of future danger fled from her mind as she edged her way down the stairs with her back pushed against the protective wall. Climbing upward had been frightening enough, but nothing compared to the challenge of descending when her eyes were fixed on the deadly, littered floor far below. But the rope proved to be worthy; its hempen strands were still flexible to the touch, and there was only small evidence of fraying. Placing the coil over her head and under one shoulder so that her arms would be unfettered, she climbed the stairs again. Twice she paused in raw fear when the tread she'd just left broke loose from its anchor and crashed into the dark pit below.

Once again on the stone ramparts, she wasted little time in explaining her plans to Perry. Instead, she spoke directly to John William, who was staring at the break in the wall.

"Your brother has hurt himself, John, and I'm going to see if I can make him more comfortable. What I want you to do is to stay right here with Perry and watch the rope. You're not to leave this spot, even if I'm down there a long time. Will you promise me that you won't move?"

With belated gallantry, Perry offered to be the one to help the older brother. "I looked over the edge while you were fetching the rope. 'Tis doubtful there's much use, but I could probably pry him loose more easily than you can."

Already measuring out the rope and knotting one end around a stone merlon on the undamaged outer wall, Jolie dismissed Perry's offer, since he was too badly injured. Stubbornly, however, Perry insisted on playing out the rope as she descended the opposite wall, letting her down slowly until her shoulders were level with the injured boy's head. For the next few minutes, Jolie forgot all about her own precarious position as she strained to ease the victim's breathing. Able to fit only one of her slender arms at a time into the narrow crevasse, she succeeded in pushing the child's head up only an inch or so—just enough to free his nose. More than that she dared not do without expert help!

The situation was even worse than she had anticipated. Because the boy was lying on his side, one arm and leg were wedged too deeply to allow a pole to be inserted beneath his body. An even worse horror was the condition of the chimney itself—the front section had already fallen and the rear wall was cracked at half the mortar joints. Any undue pressure could bring the hundred-weight stones crashing downward. Ignoring the pain of the rope cutting into her underarm flesh, Jolie began to reclimb the short distance of wall by using the chimney as a prop. She had succeeded in lifting herself only two feet before she stopped in dawning horror and stared upward at the hewn stone a foot above her head. Although she'd exerted no pressure on that particular stone, it had begun to sway dramatically. Then it slowly toppled outward and shattered below them. Jolie breathed a sigh of relief; had it fallen in the other direction, she and the boy could have had their skulls crushed.

For a moment Jolie could not hear Perry's cry of alarm, asking if she were all right; she was listening to a voice from her youth—to the sister superior who'd raised her. "Learn to look before you leap, young lady," her beloved guardian had often warned her.

It was sound advice, but Jolie had a history of forgetting her own safety in an emergency. When she had been charged with helping Huguenots during Louis XIV's unholy crusade against them, she'd dared to strike a monseigneur of the church, and fortunately, was able to outrun her pursuers. Even more recklessly, in an attempt to cross the Rhine River, she had risked her own life to save that of her husband's cousin, who had turned out to be more dangerous than the monseigneur. In Edinburgh, armed only with a surgical knife, she had once fought off an attacking soldier.

Hanging from a decaying wall now with only one of her feet supported in the narrow crevasse, she looked cautiously down and felt more frightened than she had during any of her earlier brushes with death. The child was breathing more easily, but she still had not saved his life, or her own. "I'm all right," she called back to Perry, "but I'll have to stay here with Francis until help comes." Stoically she wiggled her foot into a more comfortable position and waited. In the unnatural quiet, the sound of axes striking wood was suddenly audible. There were groundskeepers nearby. Small John William joined his voice to those of Perry and Jolie to cry for help.

While Jolie had endured the earlier discomfort and fear with equanimity, she became morbidly impatient as she waited for rescue. As the minutes ticked by without any action, her hope dwindled and her conviction grew that the woodsmen had decided not to become involved. Then she again heard the sound of axes, but coming from above this time, rather than from below. Not until she had been pulled up from her precarious perch did she learn that there had been a second way to scale the wall from the castle proper, through barricaded entrances and stairs. Only one minor mishap accompanied her rescue—as she yanked her foot from the overly narrow crevasse, it twisted painfully. But in the excitement of greeting the capable man who had taken charge of the more complex rescue attempt, Jolie forgot her sprained ankle.

Bailiff Wickham was not a typical estate manager who had been trained for the post of chief administrator of a sprawling complex that included ten productive farms and more than six hundred employees. Until the preceding spring, he had been a deck officer aboard a ship whose captain had befriended Jolie and Rorke Campbell long before the duke of Newcastle had. As a result of that earlier friendship, the new bailiff had become one of Jolie's favorites among the castle retainers. After a quick glance that assured him Jolie was more disheveled than hurt, the bailiff turned his attention to the problem at hand—a problem he'd been wrestling with even before the young groundskeeper, Jem, had located him. An hour before, their distraught governess, Betsey, had reported the two Somerton boys missing, and Wickham had promptly organized a search party.

"So, you finally got yourself into a pickle you can't get shut of, young Lord Somerton," Wickham said irritably as he peered down at the boy. "Third time you and the caterwauler have upset castle folk. But by the look of you, you'll be keeping out of mischief for a week or two, at least!"

Turning toward Jolie, the bailiff was once again the efficient ship's officer marshaling his deckhands to meet an emergency at sea. "Best you tell me everything you learned when you went over the side, Sister Jolie," he told her. "I don't much like the look of that chimney wall, and I've an idea the lad is wedged in as tight as ship's caulking."

Jolie gave him a quick, concise report and concluded, "Monsieur Wickham, you'll need two men who aren't afraid to dangle like a pair of fish on a pole, and you'll need a third man strong enough to lift the child at least six inches. *Ma foi*, I could scarcely squeeze my arm in far enough to move his head so he could breathe."

Nodding in understanding, the bailiff issued a string of sharp orders to four of the groundskeepers. One was to fetch the most experienced of the castle roofers and the equipment needed for a sling hoist. The others were sent to take the younger Somerton child to his governess, to locate two wagons and drivers, and to notify the duke. When Jolie protested this final order, Wickham insisted.

"Henry Cavendish may be dying, lass, but 'tis still his bailiwick, and we'd be fools not to seek his protection. That's a rum pack of titled London wastrels his daughter brought with her. Last time we rescued this pair of young devils, Lady Holles tongue-lashed me for not watching out for them, as if I had naught to do but play nursemaid."

"Perry says she also tongue-lashed the duke when he told her that he'd permit no hunting until after the harvest was complete."

"She was told months ago not to bring her parasite friends with her this year," Wickham complained sourly. "What in the devil's wrong with women like her?"

Jolie's shrug was an eloquent testimonial to her contempt for most of the wealthy women she had met thus far in England. "They are of no use even to themselves," she admitted candidly. "This one worries only that her rich husband will not be able to inherit the duke's estate and title."

"I wish that rich husband had come with her this time. According to the captain, he's a sensible man who keeps his wife and her friends from acting the fools. Important man, too—one of the king's privy counselors."

Cynically distrustful of still another English lord, regardless of his qualifications, Jolie turned her attention to the captain the bailiff had mentioned, a man she did trust. "I'd much prefer that Captain Huntington were here, Monsieur Wickham."

"Aye, lass, so would I. Lady Holles would not be acting the shrew with him around. Captain has a way about him."

"She doesn't know that he's a German baron, does she?"

"Nay, lass, there's few in England who do, and he's grateful that you and your husband have kept the secret."

"But it is for our safety, too, monsieur, and the main villains are my husband's relatives."

Only because Captain Huntington and the duke of Newcastle had come to their assistance had Jolie and her husband enjoyed a peaceful sanctuary here for almost a year. Uneasily, she reminded herself that their safety was by no means guaranteed, and hastily returned the conversation to the more immediate problem of the child's survival.

"Will the men you sent for be able to brace the chimney until we have the child out?"

Repressing the smile that momentarily softened his craggy, weather-beaten face, Bailiff Wickham glanced at Jolie again. Hunkered down on the uneven stone walkway and incongruously clad in sooty undergarments only partially concealed by her uniform cloak, she looked more like a street urchin than the aristocratic beauty he knew she was. Her red-gold hair was windblown and her lightly tanned cheeks were streaked with dirt, but her bright blue eyes regarded him with a sharp intelligence. God's blood, she had already displayed the courage of a lioness during this unfortunate mishap, he reflected with admiration, and she had analyzed the problems involved as shrewdly as a man. His response to her question, therefore, was a serious consideration rather than a peremptory *no*, as he would have given any other woman.

"The less we touch those stones, lass, the longer they'll hold together. 'Twill be speed that decides the issue; the lad's been unconscious an ungodly long time as is." Jolie nodded in silent agreement.

Upon the arrival of the workers, some of her pessimism dissipated. These men were not confused servants or over-cautious groundskeepers; they were the bold repairmen who defied gravity and danger in their daily labor of keeping the vast roofs and spires of Newcastle fortress in good repair. Within minutes their rigging was well anchored and two of the men were lowered slowly down the wall. Standing a distance away from the men concentrating on the crucial job of controlling the ropes holding the suspended men in a stationary position, Jolie watched with tense anticipation as one of them tried to push a long, slender pole underneath the boy. Despite her earlier conviction of failure, she felt a despairing urgency when the man called up, " 'Tis no use, Bailey. I'd smash him up worse'n he already is."

"Is he still alive?" Wickham demanded.

"Aye, he's breathin', but not by much."

"Can you pull him out from your side?"

"Not likely. Only thing I can reach is his head. He'll need raisin' afore we can shove the pole twixt him and the stone."

Jolie watched with increasing anxiety as Wickham strapped

a wide canvas belt around a heavy-shouldered man before
he was lowered headfirst into the narrow crevasse with one
arm straining downward in a futile attempt to reach the
stricken child. Earlier, when Jolie had offered to make the
attempt, the bailiff had fobbed her off. " 'Tis a job for
professionals, and you've already done more than your
share. Besides, lass, if you were injured, I'd have to answer
to both His Grace and your husband, and I've no liking for
either prospect."

At such moments of frustration over blockheaded mascu-
linity, Jolie remembered her convent years when there had
been no men to remind her of the limitations of womankind.
Under Soeur Marguerite's tutelage, she had learned a doctor's kind of medicine out of necessity, since French physicians seldom offered poor people their lofty services. As the
trained assistant to her crippled teacher, Jolie had developed
a resourceful mind and resilient muscles in the process.
Never had Marguerite allowed her favorite pupil the luxury
of pleading helplessness. "Use the brain God gave you,
child!" had been her incessant command. Only on the eve
of Jolie's departure from France had the old nun modified
her advice. "Use the brain God gave you, but don't let men
see you do it."

Now, as Jolie watched a second man fail to reach the
child, she listened to his words of defeat with frustrated
impatience.

" 'Tis only a pint-sized chimney sweep what'd fit down
there," the begrimed man muttered defensively. "And nary
a one of them puny runts would have the strength t'pull the
lad out. What's more, Bailey, the whole bloody chimney's
loose and like to tumble any minute."

Not daring to reconsider the danger, Jolie leaned over
toward Perry as he dozed from the pinch of laudanum she
had given him to ease the pain of his mangled leg. "I need
your shirt, Perry," she whispered urgently.

Obediently, he removed the garment, then blinked in
confusion when Jolie hastily donned it and bound her hair
peasant-style with her wimple. Gingerly, so as not to further

injure her sprained ankle, she edged her way to the scowling bailiff's side.

"If we're going to save the child, you'd better let me try, monsieur," she volunteered quietly.

As he had scores of times aboard ship when decisions had to be made, regardless of the gamble, Wickham nodded brusquely. "Aye, lass, you could be right; we've no time left to experiment. As long as you know there's danger involved, I'll let you have a go at it."

Looking over the wall at the two roofers who had been suspended in air for half an hour or more, Jolie smiled at the frustrated bailiff. "It will be no more dangerous for me than for them, but you did not warn them. I am willing to take the same chances, monsieur."

Laced into the canvas safety belt, and with a second rope tied around her ankles, Jolie was lowered cautiously into the crevasse at a spot just above the boy's head and chest. Closing her eyes tightly in an attempt to repress the fear that assailed her, she stretched her arm downward and groped about until she succeeded in grabbing a handful of the victim's clothing. Exerting the whole of her strength, she gave a hard yank and felt the small body move upward an inch, and then two, before she was pulled back to the safety of the ledge.

" 'Tis a minute at a time only I'll allow you to work upside down, mistress," Wickham cautioned her. "Watched a seaman die once when we didn't right him quickly enough, and I'll not risk that happening to you."

Three times more Jolie was lowered. During the second and third descents, she raised the unconscious child enough to allow a pole to be shoved beneath him; and in the final one, she managed to tie the limp body to the supporting pole. So fiercely had she concentrated on each immediate goal, she hadn't felt the increased swelling of her ankle; the bruises on her shoulders and hip, acquired when she had been momentarily trapped; or the numerous cuts, inflicted by jagged pieces of mortar. Still immune to pain when she was hauled up for the last time, she watched breathlessly as

arms reached out to lift the injured child to safety, and she
gasped in horror as the chimney broke loose seconds before
the roofers reached the landing and one of them screamed in
pain.

As she knelt beside the small, still body, she was suddenly aware of the sharp spasms of pain now shooting from her
own ankle, hip, and shoulder. Resolutely, she ignored them
as she examined him.

"Did we save him, Sister Jolie, or just prolong his
suffering?" Wickham asked softly.

"I don't know," she said tiredly. "He's alive, but he
won't be for long unless he gets help. His leg and arm are
broken and he's having trouble breathing. I think his ribs are
broken and—"

"Aye, and mayhap his lungs punctured. Is it your plan to
take him to your infirmary, so your husband can operate?"

Jolie nodded her head impatiently. Her voice was sharp
with fear. "Yes, but we must hurry. Even my husband
cannot help him if we delay any more. Can you take us
there, Monsieur Wickham?"

"I've wagons below the wall waiting for you, and a
bosun's sling ready to lower you over the side. But, lass,
think for a moment. Will your husband be wanting to take
the risk? 'Tis no tradesman's son we have here; 'tis the heir
to a lord—a damnably arrogant man with a hotheaded
brother who fancies himself a swordsman. Mayhap we
should wait until we have the father's permission."

"*Ma foi*, what stupidity! If I were the papa, I'd want my
son alive!"

Surrendering to her unassailable logic, Wickham directed
the use of the efficiently rigged bosun's sling that carried the
injured down to the waiting wagons. As practical and
single-minded as Jolie once he'd decided on a course of
action, he issued a series of orders that got the wagons
under way with a minimum of delay and jarring, resealed
the tower and the stairway leading into the castle proper,
and warned all the men involved to maintain silence until
the incident was officially announced.

As Wickham left the scene to report directly to his employer, his mind was busy with defensive speculation. One of the duties he'd been ordered to perform by both Captain Huntington and the duke was the protection of the two Campbells. And since this unfortunate episode could conceivably put them in jeopardy, Wickham was convinced that only the duke could control his daughter and her irresponsible friends. The bailiff had another, more puzzling aspect to report. Both of the children had been clutching coins in their hands—shiny copper and silver coins—and the bailiff himself had located an untarnished penny. What the devil, he asked himself, was recently minted money doing on the top of a locked-off, decaying castle wall? Damn, he felt like a fish out of water already, and the suspense had only just begun!

The slow half hour's drive into Newcastle ended in front of the Campbell infirmary when the first of two hay-padded wagons was pulled to a gentle stop. Already alerted by a messenger, Rorke Campbell rushed out to greet his wife. When he worriedly tried to examine her, she brushed him aside.

"Rorke," she protested, "there's nothing wrong with me that a good scrubbing and a few bandages won't cure. The child is the one who needs your skill. I'll see that the other nurses take care of Perry and the roofer." Not until the unconscious Somerton boy had been taken into the surgery did Jolie climb painfully down from the wagon bed and order the drivers to carry the injured men inside.

2

Despite his failing health and his deliberate isolation from his daughter and her friends, Henry Cavendish, the duke of Newcastle, was still master in his own house. Even before he had received the bailiff's message about the latest problem with the Somerton children, Henry had known that something was amiss. Perry Tate had not returned on schedule, and any event that made the conscientious attendant nurse even a minute late must be catastrophic in nature. Without waiting to learn the outcome of the potentially tragic situation, the duke summoned his secretary, who in turn summoned the most recently arrived of the castle guests, a nobleman whose far-flung interests kept him too busy for the frivolities of hunting and gaming. Lord Thomas Pelham was in Newcastle at Henry's invitation despite his newly established relationship with the duke's daughter.

The friendship between Cavendish and Pelham had been twenty years and a dozen clandestine conspiracies in the making. In his nearly fifty years, Pelham had amassed a fortune and gained a political power far beyond the title of *lord*. No stranger to intrigue, he had been one of the aristocrats who had helped the duke of Newcastle gain revenge against the unscrupulous Scottish politician John Campbell, earl of Breadalbane. After William III had wrested the British crown from James II, the Scottish Catholics had threatened civil war. With money supplied by these English aristocrats, William had commissioned Breadalbane to bribe the rebellious Highlanders into submission. Instead, John Campbell had lied to the rebels and appropriated the fortune for his own use. To recoup the money they had lost, a dozen English aristocrats had conspired to kidnap the earl's illegitimate son, Tavis. At the time, the plot had seemed justified, since the young rapscallion had not been harmed, but unfortunately, a pair of innocent bystanders had been endangered. Because the kidnap victim had proved as vicious as his father, he had blamed his cousin, Rorke Campbell, for the kidnapping, and later had attempted to murder him.

Having taken no part in the physical aspects of the plot, Pelham knew nothing of Rorke or Jolie Campbell or of the other details of the kidnapping for almost a year until his friend, Henry Cavendish, had once again requested his help. For the past two months Pelham had been working on behalf of the duke in London, but his visit to the northern port of Newcastle was the first time he had seen the older man in ten months. As he followed the secretary into the private sitting room, Pelham noted with dismay the physical deterioration in his old friend, but was relieved by his cheerful smile of welcome.

Henry had long since come to terms with his failing heart. His greeting was an eager question: "Did Ramsey Huntington deliver my message to you?"

"Yes, he did, and I'm sorry as hell about your health."

With a negligent wave of his hand, Henry brushed aside the expression of condolence. "'Tis no longer of importance. I've accomplished my fair share. But you, my friend, have just taken a new lease on life. Congratulations on your marriage to my son-in-law's sister. She is one of my favorite people."

"Grace returns your regards full measure, Henry, and even professes to be grateful for your part in the matchmaking."

'' 'Twas a selfish move on my part, Thomas. My daughter seems to be barren; but if I succeed in convincing King William to name my son-in-law my legal heir, John will be able to name any son you and Grace produce as his heir.''

Pelham shook his head. " 'Tis but a pleasant dream, Henry. Our Dutch king will never permit an estate this wealthy to escape his clutches. He'll loot it of all assets, then sell the title and land to the highest bidder.''

"More than likely, Thomas, but there's none in all of England or Holland who'll be able to outbid you and John combined. And the estate will still be worth ten times whatever it costs you! But that matter is not the reason I sent for you. Did Ramsey tell you what happened at his home in Germany last year?''

"That he did, and I damn near choked on my wine when he informed me that he was only a part-time Englishman. How the devil could he ever succeed in posing as a German baron for six months of the year?''

"Because he *is* a German baron—has been for more than twenty years. He was exiled from England, as most of us were, almost fifty years ago, after his father was killed. The family estate was confiscated by the cursed Roundheads. In Germany he lived with the former Baron Wallmond and was adopted after he married a Wallmond niece; eventually, he inherited the estate and title. 'Twas quite a lovely fairy tale at the time, but when his English estates were finally returned, Ramsey decided to divide his life into two discrete and secret parts.''

"Then 'twas a secret that was well kept—I'd known him for ten years and never suspected. As a point of interest, how did you persuade him to kidnap Breadalbane's bastard son?''

"He dislikes Breadalbane as much as we do. Did he tell you how Rorke and Jolie Campbell became involved?''

"Yes, but he didn't explain why he took them into his confidence.''

"To avoid killing innocent people. Rorke Campbell was

no stranger to violence. For five years he'd been working for William of Orange, bringing William's French Huguenot friends safely out of France. On Rorke's last mission there, Breadalbane sent his bastard along to give the appearance of helping Rorke and to reap some of the rewards Rorke had been promised by William. Because he'd been sworn to protect his cousin Tavis, as well as the Huguenots, Dr. Campbell and a handful of his soldiers tried to storm the Wallmond castle to get Tavis back. Ramsey had to tell him; he'd agreed to commit a harmless kidnapping, but not murder! Moreover, he thought he could keep Breadalbane from holding Rorke responsible. In that goal, he failed miserably. Breadalbane tried to have Rorke arrested in Holland, and then his bastard son tried to kill him in Edinburgh.''

"Huntington said the young fool Tavis was determined to have the doctor's wife.''

"I know, and that's the real reason both he and his father want Rorke dead. Has Breadalbane made any public accusations since I left London?''

" 'Tis not his style to accuse openly, Henry. John Campbell is sly enough to whisper his mischief into the king's ear only. Besides, the Scottish fox has no one to accuse at the moment. Huntington covered his tracks well, and your illness deflected any suspicion from you. The rest of us agreed to the kidnapping, but we didn't know a damn thing about how it was carried out. To be honest with you, I'm sorry you thought it necessary for me to be told about it even now.''

" 'Twas a simple matter of justice, Thomas. I don't want to go to my grave leaving someone else to pay for my sins, and I've an idea that will keep us all in the clear, providing you'll agree to present another petition to our king in full view of the entire court.''

A shrewd businessman who had learned, to his dismay, that sentiment was no basis for wisdom, Pelham asked dryly, "What petition, Henry?''

" 'Tis a petition for the establishment of infirmaries.

You'll see one in operation today if you decide to humor me—'tis the most efficient one to be opened in England since we drove the Catholic nuns and nurses from the land. Dr. Campbell and his remarkable wife have established this one in Newcastle, and the town has reaped a benefit far beyond the cost. 'Tis my wish to leave my personal fortune in the care of Rorke Campbell, with the proviso that he and Sister Jolie set up similar infirmaries in other English cities.''

"Then donate the money now, Henry, and hire Dr. Campbell to carry out your wishes. You don't need the king's permission to accomplish your goal.''

"No, but I want Rorke Campbell and his wife under the king's personal protection. Only if William agrees publicly will he take enough of an interest in the enterprise to keep my young friends safe from Breadalbane and his bastard. Nine months ago in Edinburgh, Tavis Campbell tried to murder Rorke and kidnap Jolie; they barely escaped with their lives. Without mentioning my own name or identifying any of the other conspirators, I made certain the king heard of the incident, but obviously Breadalbane was able to convince William of his son's innocence. Will you present the petition, Thomas?''

"I doubt it will be granted but I'll try, Henry. After three years, William has not even considered your request to name your son-in-law, John Holles, as your heir, and he'll not accede to this one because he needs all the money he can beg, borrow, or steal to fight his damnable war against Louis XIV. There are times when I regret our part in deposing King James.''

"Had we not done so, Thomas, we'd have had a civil war over the Catholic issue in England and Scotland. At least William has spared us that catastrophe, and his frequent absences from England have allowed Parliament to take over the reins of government. If I thought Parliament could protect my favorite doctor and nurse, I'd ask you to deliver the petition there. But an English Parliament would have no control over a Scottish politician; only the king has that power."

"This Dr. Campbell," Pelham probed cautiously, "is he really enough of a physician to undertake such an assignment? From what you said, he sounds rather more like an adventurer than a man of science."

"Thomas, ten months ago, two expensive London physicians gave me but a few weeks to live. I was in such pain I almost welcomed their diagnosis, but now I consider them ignorant fools. Even poor old Oliver Roxbury, who has been our family doctor for fifty years, is not as stupid; he at least admits his education is now too ancient to be useful. A week after I arrived home, Rorke Campbell returned from Edinburgh University, where he'd been studying the latest in medicine. No, he didn't cure my worn-out heart, but he knew of medicines that eased the pain and have allowed me to live very comfortably and pleasantly. Since those early weeks, he and his remarkable wife have performed medical miracles and have won the respect of almost everyone in town."

For the first time during the reunion with his old friend, Pelham appeared uncomfortable, having just repressed the words, "But not that of the local aristocrats!" Instead, he probed for answers by a more circuitous route. "Tell me about this remarkable wife, Henry. Is she a red-haired Frenchwoman as Huntington said, and an heiress, as well?"

"She's all of those things and more, since she is doubly an heiress. Her French grandfather, Count Arnaud de Laurent, has already provided her with a substantial dowry, and there is a second fortune from her long-dead father waiting for her in Scotland."

With his previous skepticism replaced by confusion, Pelham asked bluntly, "Does the local gentry know about her background?"

"Every bit of it!"

"Then, how in hell did that damned rumor about her start?"

Henry Cavendish smiled in tired understanding. He had wondered why Thomas had seemed so stiffly formal; now he knew. The ugly gossip that he and Jolie Campbell were far more than nurse and patient had spread far beyond his daughter's circle of dissolute London friends. When Marianne had first arrived, she had condemned him nastily without bothering to determine the truth of the whispered scandal. Contrarily, after learning the name of the local aristocrat who had spread the lie, Henry had not bothered to correct his daughter's misinformation.

"You mean the one spread by Lord Mayhew's young wife, Dorothea, accusing Jolie of being my mistress? As you can plainly see, Thomas, even if I were the old lecher my daughter considers me, I've not the strength for such nonsense. Nor do I have the courage to inform the Campbells of the rumor. They're in love with each other, and together or singly, they're well able to defend themselves."

"God's blood, Henry. I've little enough use for Howard Mayhew—he's always seemed the bumbling ass to me—but I never thought he'd stoop so low."

"I doubt Howard knows a word of it. 'Twas his undisciplined wife who wrote letters to all her old London friends."

"In God's name, why?"

"Female bitchery, I suspect. To an extent, I guess it was my fault. Jolie's grandfather requested my help in introducing her to English society, and I complied out of mischief as much as anything else. The women here are a dull, gossipy lot, and Sister Jolie—she prefers the title—is a social rebel with opinions as sharp as her medical skills. The fact that she is damnably pretty added to the female spite against her. By omitting the facts that Jolie is a beautiful, wealthy, and happily married woman, Lady Mayhew manufactured a libelous story that'll be hard to disprove. So far, I haven't even succeeded in disabusing my own daughter of the notion, and I'm hoping that you—"

Henry's hope was cut short midsentence. With only the most cursory of knocks on the outer door, the ducal secretary entered the room in a flurry of motion, followed closely by the bustling, determined bailiff. That their arrival had been expected was evident in the duke's sigh of anxiety.

"Is it finished, then?" he demanded.

"Aye, 'tis, Your Grace," Bailiff Wickham responded. "Leastwise, the lad's on his way to the Campbell infirmary. There was naught we could do here at the castle. I took the precaution of having Dr. Roxbury look at him, to spare you the blame if the boy dies."

"How did you get him out of that deadly trap, Bailiff? When I heard the report earlier, I thought it a hopeless situation; that old chimney should have fallen four decades ago."

With an economy of words, Wickham told him about the wall-top rescue and about the oddities he'd observed. "I've no use for that pair of Somerton scamps, as I reported the last time they turned the castle topsy-turvy; but this time, I don't know. First off, there's the gate—unlocked it was and shoved open as if it wasn't as rusty as the strongbox of an ancient shipwreck. Then there's the coins—newly minted ones, and scattered in so odd a place. And one more item, easily overlooked—a castle rope missing from storage, found in an ancient tower."

The duke nodded in speculation rather than agreement, making no comment about the "oddities." He reverted instead to an earlier statement. "You said Sister Jolie was limping. Did she have any other injuries?"

"Aye, Your Grace. I suspect she's aching in every joint, the same as the others who went over that cursed wall, but I don't think a one of them regrets trying to help. Leastwise, the lad has a chance now. Sir, I've no call to interfere, but I think 'twould be best if we delay telling the parents. Neither one is overburdened with common sense, and the brother lacks any sense at all."

"Even so, Bailiff, they have to be notified," Henry cautioned sternly. "But tell your messenger to travel by cart. 'Twill take twice as long that way and keep our guests on Mayhew property an hour longer."

"Aye, and 'twill give me time to post guards so as to keep them away from our crops. Will there be anything else, Your Grace?"

"Not at the moment, Bailiff. You can take your ease after a job well done." With his patient secretary, who knew as much about castle activities as the duke himself, Henry was less in command.

"Damn me, Charles. I'd thought to give Doctor Roxbury a permanent rest, but I doubt that either of the Campbells will be available to tend me until this confounded idiocy is resolved. You'd best tell Oliver to locate another strong lad to replace Perry, and you'd best do it quickly. I still don't want my daughter to know the extent of my illness."

Charles Garnett nodded in cynical agreement; he'd known Lady Holles all her life. Once she learned the truth, she would become hysterically concerned, not so much for her father's fate, but rather because her husband had not yet been named the next duke of Newcastle. There were times when the middle-aged secretary was grateful that he'd lived and would die as a commoner bachelor, without the bother-ation of estate or heirs. Repressing a vague sense of disloy-alty to the nobleman he had served for thirty years, Garnett added still another unlamented lack in his own life—he had never possessed the power or wealth to develop annoying idiosyncrasies!

Two weeks ago, he had overheard the jealous, self-centered Lady Holles accuse her father of playing the fool with young Jolie Campbell. At the time, Garnett had expected the duke to make an angry denial; instead, he asked only who had started the rumor, and never did he really deny the charge. Garnett's sense of outrage stemmed from a variety of sources. Months of observing her behavior at ducal receptions had convinced him that Lady Mayhew, who had spread the rumor, was naught but a highborn courtesan. Even in his own private ruminations, Garnett avoided using the blunter word, *whore*, although he didn't cavil at using the words *malicious* and *vindictive* to describe the duke's daughter, Lady Holles. Dr. Campbell and Sister Jolie, he felt, did not deserve to be insulted by false gossip, even temporarily; they had worked too hard to establish an excellent reputation with the townspeople to have a pair of useless women destroy it. Never did Garnett really doubt the duke's intentions; however it was not Henry Cavendish's habit to hurt the people who served him. But on occasion, he allowed his whimsical sense of humor to overrule common sense.

At the moment, however, the duke had little cause for humor of any kind. A child had been injured, perhaps fatally, on his estate, and he had no doubt that the parents would attempt to blame everyone but themselves. Henry did not mind for himself, and his power was sufficient to protect all of his own people, but he could do very little to shield the Campbells. Regardless of her remarkable heroism, Jolie would be exposed to still more ugly rumor, and Rorke to the accusation of incompetence if the child should die in surgery. Even more ominous was a second possibility. Rorke Campbell was not a mild-tempered scientist, like most of his counterparts. If he thought his wife endangered, he would be furiously vengeful!

"God's blood!" Henry said to Thomas Pelham. "What damnably unlucky timing! Someone will have to ride into town to prevent Lord Somerton from tangling with Dr. Campbell. The fool will be damned fortunate to survive if he's reckless enough to blame either Rorke or Jolie."

"How so?" Pelham demanded. "You told me that Campbell is the finest doctor in Newcastle."

"He is that, but he's no more a magician than poor old Dr. Roxbury. If the child was mortally wounded, no one can save him, but 'twill take a cool head to keep the peace. If Percy Somerton threatens any physical action, he'll receive the shock of his life. In addition to being an excellent doctor, Rorke is one of the deadliest swordsmen in Northern England. Twice a week he fences with my guard captains, and from what I've heard, no three of them combined could bring him down in a genuine duel."

"An unusual skill for a doctor," Pelham murmured

dryly. " 'Twould be interesting to know how he acquired it.''

"Breadalbane sent him on bloody raids under the leadership of brutal Campbell soldiers when he was only a fourteen-year-old boy. What he didn't learn in those desperate years, he learned during the five years he spent in France, rescuing Huguenots for King William. I think before you meet either Rorke or his wife, you'd best read the reports my secretary has compiled on the pair of them. You'll find their histories as remarkable as they are.''

"They sound too remarkable already, Henry—I feel the dullard by comparison. Do you still want me to maintain the fiction that your Sister Jolie is little more than a servant?''

"Aye, if 'tis at all possible. That pack of parasites and my unmannered daughter need lessoning, and I've a plan to squelch that ugly rumor the Mayhew woman started so that there'll be no doubt of Sister Jolie's worth. Humor me in this request, Thomas, and inform Dr. Campbell that I'll expect both him and his wife to attend the hunt ball as my guests.

"Since you'll be returning to London long before that event, I'll keep you informed about the outcome. In the meantime, I'm praying that today's misadventure will have a happy enough ending to enhance the success of the petition you'll be presenting to royal ears within the fortnight. But, as a precaution, in case the news is bad, you're to take several of my guards into town with you. Captain Paxton is a good man in an emergency, and he'll be able to help you with another matter as well. I want to know how a pair of puny children ever gained access to that locked wing of my castle.''

Irritated by an assignment that would involve him with two foreigners he didn't know and with a pair of aristocratic Englishmen he didn't respect, Thomas Pelham read the secretary's reports of Jolie and Rorke Campbell with growing interest. Henry hadn't exaggerated; they were interesting and talented people. Choosing to make the short trip to the infirmary by carriage rather than on horseback, Pelham asked Captain Paxton to ride with him inside the cab. By the time they reached the outskirts of town, the Londoner had been regaled with a dozen laudatory stories about Dr. Campbell's skills and with as many derogatory reports about Lady Holles's friends.

"I know that not all of them are the fools they seem. Some even are officers in the king's army who are home on leave from Flanders. But," Paxton volunteered candidly, "without His Grace about to keep them in check, even the ladies gamble far into the night, overindulge in wine, and mayhap participate in other unseemly pursuits, as well. On days when there is no organized hunt, the lot of them race across country as if—"

Paxton stopped in midsentence when the wagon was pulled to a jarring halt. The veteran soldier pushed the door open, craned his neck outward, and peered at the confusion on the narrow street ahead. He dismounted swiftly, then turned around to address his companion.

"This time 'twould seem the pack of them raced across town, milord. They're crowded in front of the infirmary, and from the look of them, they've come directly from the hunt."

Repressing his irritation at the prospect of having to greet and perhaps discipline a crowd of his peers—one of whom, at least, outranked him—Pelham dismounted heavily and stared at the scene just ahead. While the two-story Tudor infirmary building retained its somber dignity—no one inside disturbed the sedately curtained windows by peering out in rude curiosity—the aristocrats on the street looked like a band of lawless gypsies. For the first time in his circumspect life, Pelham was ashamed to be a member of the ruling class of English citizenry. They were making a circus out of what might well become a tragedy. The women, in particular, disgusted him. In their extravagant hunt clothing, they were as frivolously out of place on the staid commercial street as barroom strumpets would have

been. Their unguarded comments contrasted garishly with
the sober conversation usually voiced outside a hospital.

"Lud, I'm parched," one titled lady complained peevishly.
"I don't suppose there's anyone around here civilized enough
to offer us a decent cup of wine."

"M'dear, you'd be risking your life if you drank anything
that came from a place like this," her friend responded in a
strident denunciation. "The hospital in London is naught
but a charnel house run by diseased prostitutes, so you can
imagine how much worse the one in this godforsaken town
will be. 'Twould be a wonder if Percival's heir hasn't
already been butchered into a corpse."

Overhearing this last comment, Thomas Pelham turned
hastily toward Captain Paxton. "Do you know Dr. Campbell
well enough to warn him that his infirmary is about to be
invaded?"

Paxton looked with disdain at the milling crowd of
aristocrats. "Not likely, Lord Pelham! Dr. Campbell employs a pair of guards who'd prove more than a match for
this lot—used to be castle soldiers, so they're no raw
country brawlers."

"God's blood, Captain, we're here to prevent violence,
not encourage it."

"Then you'd better tell these people to leave, Lord
Pelham, and warn them to walk the horses. I doubt that His
Grace would appreciate having his finest stock damaged any
more than they already are."

"Is there a decent inn here in town where they can wait
until there's news?"

Again the officer's eyes gleamed with thinly disguised
insolence. "Aye, milord, there's the Crown and Thistle,
where common folk aren't welcome. Even Lady Holles will
approve, since she frequently entertained her friends there
when His Grace was away on business. While you're
talking to her ladyship, I'll see the carriage off the street and
ask the other soldiers to help the ladies remount."

Suppressing his annoyance at Paxton's rude humor, Pelham

approached his sister-in-law, whose expression changed from
startled surprise to sour contempt as she greeted him.

"Well, well, Thomas, so my precious father sent for his
favorite sycophant to salvage his own reputation. How
clever of him. Or were you sent here to defend his mistress?
'Twill do you no good. Lord Somerton has every right to
protect his child!"

Tiredly, Pelham shook his head. Lady Holles was an
unpleasant woman he avoided as much as possible, but in
this present emergency, she was somewhat essential. Masking
his repugnance with a diplomatic dryness, he asked casually,
"How did you get here so quickly? Your father—"

" 'Twas no thanks to him that we found out. My escort
and I were taking a shortcut during the hunt—William
Somerton knows his way around the Cavendish and Mayhew
estates better than I do. 'Twas our third such roundabout
when we met a group of father's groundskeepers. Believe
me, those men will be harshly punished because they
refused to answer William's questions, but they could not
refuse me. As soon as we learned that Percy's son was
injured, we rejoined the hunt and everyone rode directly
into town."

"Your father's bailiff told those men to hold their tongues,
Marianne. 'Twas he who sent the boy here to the infirmary."

"I don't trust Wickham any more than I do my father;
both are to blame for allowing that arrogant Frenchwoman
to take over, instead of leaving the child with Dr. Roxbury.
Well, Thomas, are you going to help us get the boy safely
back to the castle, or not?"

While Pelham's voice remained calm, it now rang with a
steely edge.

"No, and neither are you, Marianne. According to your
father, Dr. Campbell is the finest surgeon in town. Why
don't you take these people to the Crown and Thistle while
Percival Somerton and I go inside and make inquiries? Your
father asked me to keep the peace, Marianne."

"More likely, he asked you to protect his new friends.
God knows he's been insulting enough to mine throughout

this visit; he hasn't even bothered to come downstairs to greet them.''

''Marianne, we're blocking traffic. Do you mind if we discuss your father at some future time? I suggest you take Lady Somerton with you. I think everyone here would appreciate being well supplied with wine before she succumbs to her first attack of motherhood in several weeks.''

''What a prude you've become since you married my saintly sister-in-law, Thomas.''

''Only ashamed, my dear. You were all off chasing some pitiful fox to ground while Sister Jolie and the others you referred to with such contempt were risking their lives to save the child. Yet you seem concerned only with the negligent parents, who allowed their offspring to play without supervision on a strange estate. And I think you'll find most of the others far more interested in that wine than in the survival of Percival's heir.''

As he watched the eager acceptance of the Lady Holles's suggestion about the Crown and Thistle, Lord Pelham displayed an older man's intolerance of the young and frivolous. These were the pampered sons and daughters of the English cavaliers who'd lost the civil war and been forced into penurious exile. Only the miracle of a restored monarchy had returned their abused parents to wealth and power in 1660—just in time to produce the most self-indulgent generation in English history. Lady Somerton had allowed herself to be remounted without protest; and only because Lord Somerton demanded his attendance did the younger Somerton brother remain behind with him.

That the guards inside the infirmary had been listening as avidly as Lord Pelham was evident by the speed with which they opened the doors as soon as the rest of the hunt party had departed. Once inside, the three men were seated courteously in the office and served cups of wine by a neatly uniformed nurse. While the Somerton men accepted the wine with scant courtesy, Thomas Pelham performed the introductions and inquired about the condition of the injured child.

The nurse shook her head. "We do not yet know his fate, Lord Pelham. The doctor is still in surgery with him."

Having finished his reviving draught of wine, Lord Somerton regained his authority and his truculence. "Then we'll damn well find out for ourselves, madam. Tell your doctor I wish to speak to him."

Again the nurse shook her head. "That is impossible, sir. The doctor cannot be disturbed until he has completed his work."

"The hell you say, madam! 'Tis my son, and I gave no one permission to touch him! Now show me the way to your damned surgery."

Intimidated by the blustering anger of the father, but too well trained to break infirmary rules, the nurse stood her ground. "You cannot go there, Lord Somerton; 'tis not permitted. If you will wait here, I will ask Sister Jolie to speak to you. She knows more about your son's injuries than I do." With a hurried curtsy, the flustered nurse fled from the room.

The woman who was helped into the room by one of the guards a moment later had obviously been eavesdropping in the entry. Her voice vibrated with barely controlled anger.

"Your son, Monsieur Somerton, was barely alive when we reached the infirmary. In addition to a broken arm and leg, he had sustained head injuries, chest injuries, and hip injuries. I assure you that if you interrupt Dr. Campbell, your son will die, and two men and I will have been injured for nothing. Now, resume your seat, please, and stop badgering Sister Mercia. As soon as the operations are completed, the doctor will see you."

Giving the disconcerted father no chance to sputter a protest, Jolie turned toward the eldest of the three men. "Captain Paxton reported that you're the one who dispersed the others, Monsieur Pelham. We are most grateful. It would have been embarrassing had we been forced to summon the *gendarmerie* to arrest them for trespassing. *Ma foi*, how stupid of them to come here."

As she was talking, Pelham studied her animated face

with deep interest. Sister Jolie was every bit as remarkable
as Henry Cavendish had claimed, and far more than merely
pretty. Despite a bandage swaddling her bright golden-red
hair and part of her face, she looked beautiful as her blue
eyes sparked with indignation, and her facile lips articulated
a mixture of French and English that was succinct in
meaning and delivered with spirit. Pelham had been impressed
by her subtle warning about the constables; he had no doubt
that she would have sent for them, regardless of the social
rank of the trespassers. She possessed an air of subtle
authenticity that left no doubt of her identity; but she was a
woman of rare courage, regardless of her bloodlines. Vaguely disappointed as she limped from the room on the arm of
the fiercely protective guard, Pelham smiled openly when
Lord Somerton exploded into speech.

"Who in blazes was that?"

"That, my friend, was Sister Jolie—the woman who
pulled your son to safety just before the chimney collapsed."

"She's damnably arrogant, even for a Frenchwoman! 'Tis
always a mistake to give a servant ideas above her station."

Lord Pelham shook his head in disbelief. Only a fool
could have overlooked the aristocratic self-assurance of the
woman whose command of language reflected a finer education than Somerton's own. A moment later, Pelham's amusement changed to concern when the younger brother broke
his silence.

"I say, big brother," the youthful Sir William said,
"since you're going to dismiss old Betsey for letting your
monsters run loose, why not offer Sister Jolie the job?
'Twould be a reward for her and a damned pleasant prospect
for me. I can understand why old Henry has been chasing
her around his bedroom for the past six months. She'd be a
lively addition to any household, especially at the medieval
monstrosity where I'm currently residing as your prisoner."

"Stop being a melodramatic ass, William. You're not the
first Englishman to earn a king's displeasure and lose your
estate through royal confiscation. I'm certain Thomas has

heard all about your misfortune and knows you're no more a prisoner than I am.''

Maintaining the bland expression of indifference required whenever someone else's skeletons were being rattled, Thomas Pelham noted Lord Somerton's descriptive skill in making his brother's ''misfortune'' sound like nothing more serious than a youthful peccadillo. Although he'd never heard the specifics of the scandal, Thomas knew that the charges against the younger Somerton had been the serious ones of cowardice in battle and cheating at private gaming tables. He suspected that, in addition to confiscating his small, almost bankrupt estate, the king had exiled the culprit to his brother's ancestral home. With a carefully veiled interest, Thomas listened to the continuing argument.

''Aye, big brother, he knows I'm not chained to a tower wall or buried in the stench of Newgate Prison. But this is the first time in two years I've been allowed away from Edgemont, while you and your precious Eleanor have spent only six weeks in the gloomy old castle where you and I endured our miserable childhood.''

'' 'Twas your choice, William, to manage that estate instead of the one in Jamaica, and to tend to the welfare of my sons when their mother and I were otherwise engaged. And that reminds me that you promised Eleanor you'd remain with them today. Had you done so, they would have been safe, and we wouldn't be in this awkward position.''

''I had no choice in the matter, Percy,'' William Somerton protested earnestly. ''Lady Holles asked me to ride escort for her today, so I turned Francis and John over to their governess. As usual, they tricked her. They need someone younger and livelier than old Betsy, big brother, and I still say this Sister Jolie would solve all our problems—especially mine.''

''You're a fool, William. Didn't you hear what she said? That insolent baggage threatened to send for the constable and have us arrested. And just what do you think Henry Cavendish would do if you walked off with his favorite nurse? We don't need any more problems in our lives right now. God's blood, I hate waiting around for news."

Unable to decide which of the brothers he considered the more contemptible, Thomas Pelham stirred restlessly in his chair, resenting his involvement in another family's complicated affairs. The prospect of spending additional hours bottled up in this small, utilitarian office depressed him, too. Impulsively, out of desperation rather than sympathy, he leaned forward and addressed his companions.

"Percival, there's naught any of us can do here until the doctor finishes his work. I imagine by this time your wife is frantic. Why don't you and your brother go to the inn and offer her what reassurance you can? From everything I've been told, Dr. Campbell is the finest surgeon in town. Since I have other business at the infirmary, I'll send a messenger to you the minute there's any news."

To Pelham's surprise, it was the younger brother who protested. " 'Tis more fitting that I be the one to wait, Percy. I'd like Francis to see someone he knows when he awakens. Besides, 'twill be easier for me to move him back to the castle as soon as the doctor finishes whatever he's doing. Strangers would frighten him, but he's used to me."

Despite the fond regard implicit in the words, Pelham regarded the younger Somerton with disbelief. If Sister Jolie had been even half right about the extent of the child's injuries, it would be days before he could be safely moved. Abruptly, Pelham remembered the duke's warning about Rorke Campbell's temper and intervened once again.

"I still say you'd be more comfortable at the inn. It could be hours yet before there's any news." To Pelham's relief, the older Somerton nodded in agreement and ordered his brother to fetch their horses. As he watched the pair ride off with precipitous haste, Pelham reflected that William had some cause for his complaints. Percival treated his younger brother with little more respect than he would have given a servant.

Within the hour, Thomas Pelham's momentary interest in the sordid problems of the Somertons had been replaced by

genuine admiration for Rorke and Jolie Campbell and for
the remarkable infirmary they had established. He had been
given a tour of the premises by one of the guards, and had
noted the efficiency of the kitchen and washrooms, the
locked pharmacy, and the cheerful wards. From the male
nurse, Perry, and the wounded roofer, he had learned the
extent of Jolie's participation in the rescue; and from the
soft-spoken Sister Mercia, he had received a comprehensive
accounting of the infirmary's financial success. By the end
of the tour, he had changed his mind about the duke's
proposal to establish similar infirmaries in other cities. It
was not merely a gesture of gratitude to the Campbells; it
was a sound business venture of enormous humanitarian
potential for common people. Pelham was again seated in
the office, contemplating the best way to present the proposal to a nonhumanitarian king, when Rorke Campbell
strode into the room and looked around.

"I'd expected to see the boy's father, Lord Pelham," he
announced brusquely.

"He's waiting at the Crown and Thistle with the others,
Doctor."

"What others?"

"The entire hunt party, I'm afraid."

"Good God!"

"How is the lad, Doctor?"

"He's still alive."

"Was your wife correct in her diagnosis of his injuries?"

"She usually is. When did you talk with her?"

"She came in here to prevent Lord Somerton from
invading your surgery."

Rorke's lips tightened angrily, and Thomas received his
first intimation of temper as the Scotsman's piercingly
direct blue eyes raked over the aristocrat's face. "She was
told to remain abed," Rorke snapped.

Smiling with a diplomat's humor, Pelham asserted gently,
"Pardon my rudeness, Doctor, but if I read her character
accurately, she didn't seem the type of woman to yield

tamely in the face of trouble. She was extremely effective in her reprimand to Lord Somerton and his brother.''

"My wife still doesn't believe such men can be danger-ous, Lord Pelham.''

"Sit down, Doctor, and share the wine your Sister Mercia kindly brought me. You look tired to death. I didn't come here out of idle curiosity; the duke asked me to deliver a message to you.''

"Aye, His Grace mentioned your name some time ago, and Captain Paxton identified you for me. 'Tis why I recognized you, Lord Pelham.''

"I'm sorry I can't say the same for you, Doctor. After the way Henry and Dr. Roxbury praised your work, I'd expected a much older man, and the description Captain Huntington gave me during his last stopover in London was somewhat vague.'' Ramsey Huntington hadn't mentioned the fact that Rorke Campbell was a somberly handsome man, far taller than most Scots, with a shock of dark brown hair and a tanned complexion that made him look more English than Celt. But all of Pelham's informants had been accurate about the doctor's intelligence.

"Have you known Ramsey Huntington long?'' Rorke asked blandly.

"I've known the sea captain Huntington for years, but I'll admit I was astounded when both he and Henry informed me that he was also the German Baron Wallmond who helped us in the kidnapping of Earl Breadalbane's son. You needn't frown, Doctor; the secret is entirely safe with me. Mine would be one of the first heads to roll if King William ever learned that I'd plotted against his favorite Scottish nobleman. When Henry confided in me, he was hoping that I might be able to help you and your wife avoid any future trouble with Breadalbane. His Grace is worried that after his death—''

"He told you he was dying?''

"He told *me,* but none of the others—not even his daughter or his son-in-law. Henry is convinced that you'll be safe only if you're under the direct protection of the king himself. I'm to present a petition in open court requesting that you be granted royal permission to establish infirmaries like this one in other English cities. Henry would like to dedicate his personal fortune to the cause. My mission today is to ask if you would be agreeable to such a proposal. But before you answer, Doctor, perhaps you should send Captain Paxton to the Crown and Thistle. Despite their foolishness, I suspect the Somertons are worried."

As Rorke left the office, his thoughts were seething with alarm. After almost ten months of safety, he had hoped that Breadalbane would have forgotten his limited part in Tavis Campbell's kidnapping. Not that he'd ever been one of the conspirators, only that he had failed to rescue his cousin after Baron Wallmond had carried out the kidnapping. During that abortive rescue attempt, he had met the German-Englishman and learned the entirety of the plot. Two months later in Holland, he had learned that Breadalbane held him responsible and had arranged to have him arrested. And long after the ransom had been paid, the kidnap victim had tried to murder him. Only in Newcastle, under the protective wing of Henry Cavendish, had he and Jolie been safe, but once the duke was dead, that protection would be at an end.

Reflecting on the proposal Lord Pelham had just made, Rorke was cynically gloomy. By the time he returned to the office, he had decided not to rely upon a king who hadn't protected him in the past—not even after five years of dangerous service in France.

"I think I'll take my chances on remaining hidden in Newcastle," he told the waiting aristocrat. "I don't imagine much gossip about this unimportant town ever reaches London or Edinburgh."

For a moment, Pelham hesitated to reveal the rest of what Cavendish had told him, but eventually, his innate sense of justice prevailed. "I'm afraid there's already been gossip, Doctor," he admitted bluntly. "A very prejudiced and deliberately contrived scandal about your wife."

Rorke's abruptly stony expression revealed little of his

inner agitation. "A scandal about what?" he asked with a deceptive calm.

"In the letter I read, you were not mentioned, nor was your marriage or your wife's family background. She was described as a red-haired French nurse with whom Henry had become infatuated."

"My God! Did anyone really believe that about His Grace—at his age and in his state of health?"

"Not his friends and not the queen, but there are those who thrive on scandal. Have you met Lady Holles yet?"

"The duke's daughter? Yes, she accosted me several times outside his room, but her questions were about his health, not his morals."

"The letter she received in London is the main reason for her current visit here."

Rorke stared moodily out of the window. He knew the answer before he asked the question. "Did the duke deny the charges and defend my wife?"

"No, but he learned the identity of the letter writer. Would Lady Dorothea Mayhew have any special reason to dislike your wife?"

"The damned bitch!"

"I quite agree with your choice of epithets, Doctor. Like my wife, Lady Mayhew is married to an older man—in her case, to a man ten years my senior. She is spoiled and childish and thoroughly disliked by Mayhew's grown sons. She is also extremely vain about her attractiveness to men, and unfortunately, Mayhew is too besotted to discipline her. I think Henry intends to do it for him, as soon as he learns the reason for her vicious attack on your wife and himself."

"Jolie had nothing to do with her. I was the one who insulted the—"

"Was the insult accidental or intentional?"

"After a month of refusing her invitations to become her personal physician, I declined to partner her during a dance at one of the ducal receptions. When she became abusive, I told her that she'd have better luck with her husband's stable boys—that they were quite used to female animals in heat."

Repressing an inclination to smile, Pelham studied the younger man. Even slouched tiredly in a chair with his face darkened by a thundercloud of anger, Rorke Campbell was an undeniably handsome man who possessed the brooding look of reserve that seemed to fascinate women.

"I assume Lady Mayhew didn't take your marriage any more seriously than she does her own," Pelham commented mildly. "You must have been quite a shock to her. From what I've heard, Dorothea has acquired the reputation of being a highly successful flirt."

"Women like her don't flirt with their social inferiors, Lord Pelham; they demand the obedient attendance of a trained dog."

Even though he admitted the truth of the doctor's scathing criticism, the aristocrat felt compelled to protest. "I wonder if you'd feel this degree of hatred for titled people had your grandfather's estate not been destroyed forty-odd years ago. If I remember the details of the history that Henry compiled when he was plotting revenge against Breadalbane, your grandfather was a wealthy vassal of the Campbell earl of Argyll until the Glencoe MacDonalds ravaged his land and killed everyone except your father. Tell me, why didn't your father rebuild the estate? He still owned the land."

"He was in France at the time of the massacre—a fifteen-year-old scholar who was forced to earn a living as tutor to the sons of wealthy Englishmen. When he returned to Scotland ten years later, Breadalbane had taken control of the land and arranged for my father to marry his cousin. One of the few undamaged structures left standing on the property was a caretaker's cottage near the burned-out manor. That was the home Breadalbane allotted to my parents—that and a small portion of the rental money."

"Why didn't the earl of Argyll take over? Technically, your father was an Argyll vassal—I believe the term you Scots use is tacksman."

"That particular earl was in the process of having his head chopped off by Charles II. Fifteen years later, his son did reclaim my father's allegiance by giving him a commission in his private army, but my father, who was untrained, didn't survive his first battle. A month after his death, my mother turned the estate over to her beloved cousin, and I became an unpaid Breadalbane clansman.''

''Was that when you learned to fight? Henry said that you were a superb swordsman.''

''That was when I learned to survive, Lord Pelham.''

''The report stated that Breadalbane had paid for your medical education.''

''And charged me double what it cost. For three years after I returned from Edinburgh, I practiced medicine in the old armory of Kilchurn Castle and received no recompense for my work. It was during those years that I met a dozen women like your Lady Mayhew and learned to despise them. I also refused all of the forty-year-old widows Breadalbane tried to arrange for me to marry—widows whose fortunes he already controlled.''

''How did you escape his domination?''

''He was an early supporter of King William, and he offered my services to win favor for himself. My father had taught me the necessary foreign languages, so I was well qualified to rescue Huguenots from their French persecutors. But I was still an unpaid servant to Breadalbane and still in debt to him.''

''I recall some mention of that debt. Has it ever been paid?''

''Since the duke of Newcastle has seen fit to make my past history a public matter, you might as well know the details. The old nuns in my wife's girlhood convent left her a small dowry—enough to pay all my debts.''

''I thought it was a French grandfather who'd given her a fortune.''

''Arnaud de Laurent didn't know who she was until after we'd left France. His younger daughter had deserted my wife as an infant, leaving the older sister who headed the nunnery to raise the child as a foundling.''

''Did your wife know about her MacDonald blood? More

to the point, did you know that she was the granddaughter of the man who'd destroyed your family?''

"My wife didn't know anything about her Scottish family until we were married, but I did.''

"And you agreed?''

"I was offered no choice. She'd become an embarrassment to a vicious pair of brothers who controlled the local French Inquisition—Monseigneur François de Guise and Colonel Henri de Guise. Mercifully, neither of them knew that Henri's wife was Jolie's mother. Their persecution of my wife stemmed from the fact that she had helped me tend my wounded soldiers. Through stupidity on my part, she and my cousin were captured during an escape attempt when both Tavis and Colonel de Guise were badly injured. Jolie saved their lives by operating on them at night in a crude riverside camp.''

"God's blood—a remarkable medical skill for a woman!''

"The nun who educated my wife was the daughter of one of the finest physicians in France, and both she and my wife are more doctor than nurse. It was my wife who organized this infirmary, Lord Pelham; and, in truth, she performs the simpler operations as well as I do. Now can you understand why I resent useless, malicious women like Lady Mayhew?''

"I never doubted the reason for your anger, Doctor, but I think you must realize that the gossip in London may already have revealed your location to Breadalbane's spies. If he is still as determined to have you killed as he was in Edinburgh—''

Despite his lifelong hatred of the Scottish earl, Rorke's innate honesty compelled him to correct Pelham's misinformation.

"I'm not certain that he engineered that attempt on my life; it was his undisciplined bastard who tried to kill me there. Tavis has wanted Jolie for himself since he first met her.''

"Then, wouldn't both of you be safer under the king's protection?''

"Do you really think our Dutch king will agree to spend

money on Englishmen, Lord Pelham—money he has not yet secured?''

"Henry has powerful friends. If the petition receives a public hearing, King William may be persuaded by political pressure. 'Tis at least a fair gamble.''

"Then I suppose I have little choice in the matter; I want Jolie protected. In all honesty, the appointment would offer a challenging career for both of us.''

For a moment, Pelham regarded Rorke with a quizzical expression. As impressed as he had been by Jolie's medical skills, the idea of a woman having a public career would create a worse scandal than the one Dorothea Mayhew had manufactured.

"Are you certain your wife will want the responsibility?''

"She'll insist. Jolie has no social ambitions, Lord Pelham; she has attended the duke's parties more as a nurse than as a guest. She has none of the social skills that women like your wife learned in girlhood. I have to insist that she wear the ball gowns her grandfather gave her rather than the uniforms she cherishes. If she were ever required to attend a hunt, she would probably attempt to protect the fox; and the only dancing she knows are the folk dances she learned at harvest time on her aunt's farm in Strasbourg. In Edinburgh, she studied the same books I did with as much or more comprehension; and without my permission, she worked in the hospitals there. Jolie is twelve years younger than I am, but I've yet to win a serious argument with her about our medical careers.''

"I would have thought that, with her family background—''

"When her grandfather visited us in Holland, she was amused by his insistence that she become a lady. And she has refused to meet her Scottish uncle, Lord Alasdair MacDonald.''

"Does she know it was her clan that destroyed the social position you would have inherited?''

"She knows all about that sordid history, but her affection for me is not based on my Highland heredity. My wife has little family loyalty except to the two nuns who raised her, and both of them ignored all the social laws pertaining to women. Her Aunt Charlotte was widowed when her Bourbon husband was executed for heresy; her sons were given to a relative, the duc d'Orleans; and she was forced to join the Sisters of Charity. By using the only inheritance left her, she became one of the most successful vintners and farmers in the Strasbourg area and one of the most respected sister superiors in France. The other nun was the doctor-nurse I mentioned earlier—a sharp-witted cripple whom my wife quotes endlessly. Because of them, Jolie is a social and intellectual rebel who has as little respect for masculine authority as she has for her religion.''

''No wonder Henry is so fond of her; he's an intellectual rebel himself. Incidentally, he insists that both you and your wife attend the hunt ball.''

Rorke's jaws clamped shut with irritation and he shook his head in disapproval. ''He is in no condition to attend any social affair. As for my wife—''

''He doesn't plan to stay long, and he's given his assurance that neither of you will be embarrassed. You're hardly in a position to refuse this request, Doctor. Henry has expended considerable effort to assure your future success.''

''I'm quite aware of my obligations, Lord Pelham, but I don't want the words *crippled* and *disfigured* added to the current description of my wife. Being labeled a red-haired French harlot is insult enough. We will attend the ball only if she has recovered sufficiently.''

Throughout the blunt conversation, Pelham had tried to suppress the vague resentment the younger man aroused in him. Like others of the growing numbers of commoners who were succeeding in the professions and in business, Rorke Campbell reflected a contempt for the aristocracy, and even more dangerously, for the monarchy itself. England had not yet recovered from its last attempt at a commonwealth, when a king had been beheaded and most noblemen driven into exile. Pelham was no longer certain that he wanted to place a potential rebel in as powerful a position as the one Henry Cavendish proposed.

"Doctor, have you ever contemplated emigrating abroad to the Colonies? You'd be safer there than in England, Scotland, or Holland under our present king."

" 'Twas once my only ambition, Lord Pelham. Had I not been declared a criminal in France, I might still be tempted to settle on one of my wife's properties on Martinique or in Quebec."

"Just how were you trapped in France? My information was that you'd been highly successful in avoiding capture on your previous missions there."

"One of the last people I brought out of France was a special friend of King William—a Huguenot minister named Abelard Darrell, who insisted on preaching noisily in French streets. My men and I were forced to expose ourselves when we tried to protect the fool."

"God's blood! Are you the one who delivered that Calvinist zealot to our king? Not only has he become the worst troublemaker in the royal court, he influences every decision the king makes. I can't help wishing that you'd dumped him overboard into the Rhine River."

"I considered it on several occasions. He almost cost me my life, and he was insufferably rude to my wife. If ever I do migrate to the colonies, I'd want to be certain they aren't dominated by his kind of fanatic. But 'tis nonsense to talk about the colonies; I doubt His Majesty would grant permission for us to leave England. Besides, we're tied to Newcastle as long as the duke has need of our services.

"In the meantime, Lord Pelham, I'd appreciate your seeing the Somerton boy, so you can assure his parents that I didn't hack him to pieces. Afterward, you can tell the father that I'll expect him to pay for all four patients before he leaves Newcastle. I'm not yet certain about the extent of their injuries, but you might warn him that this is not a charitable institution and that our costs run high."

Pelham was less than encouraging. "The Somertons of the world do not consider such debts of critical importance, Doctor. You may have to wait years for your money."

Rorke smiled with a cynical grimness. "I know his kind

very well. Among our patients, the local gentry are the slowest to pay and the most contentious about the amount. 'Tis why we don't seek their patronage, but 'tis also why we no longer hesitate to use both Constable Langford and unpleasant publicity to collect our bills. I can assure you that our less exalted patients have been delighted with the equality of payment.''

When Pelham left the infirmary a short time later, his thoughts vacillated between admiration and irritation. He no longer had any doubts about Rorke's medical skills—the surgery room had been the cleanest and most efficient one he'd ever seen, and the small boy, bandaged almost like an Egyptian mummy, was sleeping peacefully. But God's truth, the doctor was an arrogant rogue!

The haste with which Rorke had encouraged Lord Pelham to leave the infirmary had not been inspired by arrogance or by personal animosity. As much as he could trust any aristocrat, he respected this one to the extent of answering all his intrusive questions with candid honesty. But halfway through the prolonged interview, he had become increasingly anxious about Jolie's injuries. He had intended to examine her immediately after finishing with the child, but she had already been put to bed in their private quarters upstairs. Now, as he ordered the infirmary locked and barred against any additional intrusions, he fretted about her reckless disregard for her own safety.

Since the day he had met her, it seemed to him in retrospect, she had been prone to taking chances with her life. During that first escape effort, Jolie could have reached safety had she not remained with Tavis to treat his wounds. During an outbreak of dysentery aboard ship on the Rhine River, she had risked her life to treat the refugees, and hadn't told him until long afterward that she had been ill herself, with both the disease and with a miscarriage. In Edinburgh, she had exposed herself to danger every day. And on the night they had been forced to flee from the inn after Tavis' murderous attack, she had been the one to fight off the pursuing Campbell soldiers, armed only with a surgical knife. And today, she had hung upside down on a damned castle wall and pulled the son of a worthless pair of aristocrats to safety. God in heaven, when was she ever going to learn the limitations of womanhood?

Determined to voice his disapproval of her dangerous heroics, Rorke entered their bedroom and stopped short in silent consternation. While he had recovered from the injuries Tavis had inflicted on him, Jolie had slept on a pallet on the floor next to his bed. Tonight she lay on the same pallet, looking vulnerably childlike, with her head and arms bandaged and a livid bruise visible on her bare shoulder. Gently Rorke lifted her in his arms and settled her on the big, comfortably cushioned bed; it was his turn to use the pallet. As he looked down on the relaxed face of his sedated wife, he wondered if he would ever fully understand the generous, courageous girl he had married. Even though she must have been in pain, she had still seen to his comfort—his supper was waiting for him, and there was hot water for washing on the fireplace hearth.

The following morning, however, when he examined her numerous bruises and contusions more closely, his mood was not nearly as sentimental. One ankle was badly sprained, three of the cuts needed stitching, one large abrasion on her hip was angrily red, and another on her shoulder was painfully swollen.

"You said you hadn't been hurt," he remonstrated sternly after he had completed his examination and repaired much of the damage, adding even more disapprovingly, "You also assured me that you would let the other nurses treat Perry and the roofer. But this morning, they reported that you had insisted on doing most of the work yourself."

"Joe Foss was hurt worse than I'd thought. Are he and Perry all right?"

"They'll recover sooner than you will."

"And the boy?"

"If we can keep him quiet, he'll recover, but you're the one I'm worried about. You're not leaving this bed until I say so. Is that understood?"

"I'll stay in a bed, Rorke, but not up here during the day where it would be difficult for the nurses to wait on me. I'll remain in the room with our little patient and keep him content. In Strasbourg, Soeur Marguerite always put children in rooms with other patients so they would not be so frightened. *Ma foi*, this one was terrified yesterday."

Looking down at her animated face, Rorke asked curiously, "How about you, Jolie? Weren't you frightened, too?"

"I was too busy to be afraid; there was no time for delay. Besides, I wasn't in any real danger—Monsieur Wickham was most careful to keep me safe. He pulled me up so often, I felt like a bucket in a well."

Despite his resolve not to be cajoled into a tolerant humor, Rorke smiled involuntarily. She had always had that effect on him with her honesty and her ability to strip away pretense. Moreover, there was no real reason for him to be angry; she had done nothing that wasn't in her nature to do. She had always possessed the necessary courage; it had been that courage and her lack of feminine wiles that had first won his admiration and respect. His love for her had developed only after he had discovered that she was as uninhibited in lovemaking as she was in living; and that notwithstanding her nun's robe and shaven head, she was a uniquely beautiful woman.

He bent over, kissed her with a caressing tenderness, and made his peace. "Sweetheart, being you, you didn't have any choice; but I'll be damned glad when we're both finished with daily servitude at the castle and can plan our own future. I don't like being dependent on other people."

"But we are dependent, Rorke; the duke is the one who has kept us safe. When he is dead, I do not think we should stay in Newcastle."

"Where would you want to go, Jolie?"

Her response was prompt and decisive. "Where there are no people like the *cochon* Breadalbane and his bastard son, or anyone like Monseigneur de Guise and his murderous brother."

"We'll have to remain in England, sweetheart. I doubt

that King William would let us leave the country without his permission.''

"We left Holland without his permission.''

"We can't risk a two-month voyage across the Atlantic in a smuggler's boat; we scarcely survived a nine-day trip across the Zuider Zee and North Sea. So until we're able to leave legally, it will have to be an English town where no one knows us. In the meantime, I have to go to work. I don't imagine yesterday's excitement did the duke any good—not with that crowd of jackals worrying him.''

Jolie's first morning as an invalid was spent in and out of a bed in the small private room where the Somerton boy was recovering. Dressed in a uniform with a white wimple covering her bandaged head, she alternated her time between lying on the bed and learning to walk on crutches. Pointedly, she ignored her fellow patient until the child roused enough to request her companionship. His first mumbled words were an acknowledgment of recognition.

"Did you break a leg yesterday, same as me?''

"No, I just sprained mine.''

"My name is Francis Percival. Someday I'll be Lord Somerton.''

"You won't be anything if you keep trying to climb broken walls in old castles, *petit* Francis.''

"You're the one they call Sister Jolie, aren't you?''

"Yes.''

"And you pulled me out of that place.''

"There were many of us who pulled you to safety, Francis.''

"Are you going stay here with me until I can walk on one of them things like you were doing?''

"Only part of the time. I help the doctor manage this infirmary, so I'll have to do some work.''

"That's not what old Betsey said.''

"Who is old Betsey, Francis?''

"She's John William's governess—used to be mine before I got a tutor. She said you were a servant at the castle who'd gotten too uppish for your own good."

Slowly, Jolie sat up and looked across at the small occupant of the other bed. "How old are you, Francis Percival?" she asked quietly.

"I'm nine, most on to ten."

Jolie's eyebrow rose. He was undersized for his age, but she wasn't really surprised. His language and his youthful arrogance had reflected a greater sophistication than that of the seven-year-old she'd thought him to be initially.

"Then you're old enough to learn good manners," she counseled him sternly. "I am a nurse, not a servant, and I am not the kind of nurse you had when you were an infant. And for your information, young Francis, you're not the only one who can boast about a title. My *grandpère* is the comte de Laurent, my uncle is a lord in Scotland, and my husband is the doctor who saved your life. So you can tell your old Betsey that if I'm 'uppish,' I have a right to be."

Pausing long enough to note the boy's startled expression, Jolie relented. He had only repeated what gossipy adults had told him—adults such as old Betsey, Lady Holles, and the newcomers at the castle. For the first time in the months she had known the duke of Newcastle, Jolie doubted his sincerity. He knew everything that went on in his household, yet he hadn't bothered to correct his daughter's misinformation. Not once since her arrival had he invited either of the Campbells to a social function at the castle, whereas before, he had insisted on their attendance every week.

Regretting the reprimand she'd just delivered to the injured child, Jolie made an effort to reestablish their rapport. "I'm sorry I lost my temper, Francis. *Ma foi*, I must have sounded worse than old Betsey, and over nothing."

The future Lord Somerton, however, had not been overly intimidated. "Her eyes don't shine like yours do, and she doesn't look pretty when she talks. But how come you have to work if you're all the things you say?"

Jolie smiled in resignation and murmured the Latin phrase

that Soeur Marguerite had inscribed on every wall of the Strasbourg infirmary: *"Labor ipse voluptas."*

"What's that mean?"

"Don't you recognize Latin when you hear it? I thought that every future English lord had to learn Latin."

"Reckon not. Uncle William says I don't have a head for it. What did you say?"

"That work is fun."

"How come you know Latin?"

"I learned it when I was young, and so did two other nurses here. You could, too, if you spent your time studying, rather than looking for the kind of trouble you got into yesterday."

"We weren't looking for trouble yesterday, Sister Jolie. We were trying to find the money Uncle William had lost; he said we could keep it if we did."

Remembering the sallow-faced young man who had leered at her so rudely in the office, Jolie asked cautiously, "How did you and your brother get up on that wall? All the passages from the main castle had been locked and barred."

"Uncle William showed us the old gate at the bottom of the tower, and he undid the lock for us."

"Did he take you up to the wall?"

"No, he said the old stairs were too crumbly for him, but they were strong enough for John and me. 'Sides, he said he'd been up there the day before."

Before she realized the full implication of the boy's admissions, Jolie demanded impulsively, "Did your uncle often suggest such dangerous places for you and your brother to play?"

"Once he let us go on a boat by ourselves, but it turned over and we almost drowned."

"Was he the one who rescued you that time?"

"Not hardly. 'Twas a pair of poachers who pulled us out."

"What did your parents say about that boat ride, Francis?"

"They were in London—that's where they are, mostly.

Only Uncle William lives with us permanently, and he made sure those poachers paid for stealing our fish."

Not since Edinburgh had Jolie experienced any fear of another human being, but William Somerton sounded too much like Tavis Campbell for her to ignore. He was another aristocratic young scoundrel whose criminality was condoned by a society that punished commoners harshly. While Tavis had gone unpunished for his cowardly attempt to murder Rorke, the landlord at the Edinburgh inn had gone to prison. While Uncle William had tried to murder his nephews, the men who had saved their lives had been punished for stealing fish from an English river.

Restlessly, Jolie reached for her crutch and stood up. "Weren't you even grateful to those fishermen for saving your life, Francis?"

"Reckon so, Sister Jolie, but Uncle William says lawbreakers are best off in prison. Where are you going?"

"I have to see to the safety of the men who rescued you this time. I don't want your Uncle William to accuse them or me of a crime."

Her face was grimly set as she made her way awkwardly to the front of the infirmary. In Rorke's absence, she wanted to be the one to greet all visitors, especially if one of them proved to be William Somerton. But the man seated calmly on a bench in the entry was not from the castle; he was Constable Langford of the Newcastle police, and his expression was as grim as Jolie's.

"There's been trouble in town, Sister," he announced heavily, "and I may be needing your husband. Right now, I'm waiting for him and Lord Mayhew. The lord's youngest son is one of those involved in roistering through the town on horseback after a night of carousing at the Crown and Thistle."

"Was anyone injured, Monsieur Langford?"

"Aye, a collier was horse-stomped when his cart overturned, and a pair of sailors were threatened when they tried to stop one rider."

"Have you apprehended the criminals yet, monsieur?"

Instantly the official's anger was replaced by caution, and his words were admonishing. "I wouldn't call them criminals, Sister Jolie—young blades sowing their wild oats is more like. Besides, 'twas only one who did the damage; t'other two stayed to help the collier. 'Tis the third man who's still missing—a young lord who's guest to His Grace the duke. Can't say there'll be any charges laid against him other than paying for the damage done. 'Twill be up to the magistrate, Lord Mayhew, to decide the outcome. I just want the young buck under control before he—"

Whatever it was the constable intended to say was never completed. Simultaneously, he and Jolie heard a child's shrill scream of pain.

3

Even handicapped by a crutch, Jolie was first to reach the small room she had left only minutes before. Her shriek of outrage brought every other infirmary worker there on the run. Leaning over the bandaged body of his nephew, William Somerton was attempting to untie the cloth bonds that had kept the boy immobile. At Jolie's strident outcry, he straightened up and turned to face her, relaxing noticeably when he saw that she was momentarily alone.

"You saved me the trouble of searching you out, pretty nursemaid," he claimed with an arrogant confidence that changed into smiling cajolery as Constable Langford and several nurses appeared. "I'm glad you people are here; I'll need help in getting Francis ready to travel. Since my brother has agreed to hire sister Jolie to take care of this lad and his brother from now on, she'll be going with us."

"You *cochon imbécile*," Jolie sputtered as she propelled herself across the room and then used her crutch as a hard-driven prod to move the man away from the bed. "*Bon dieu*," she gasped as she knelt down and stared with horror at the widening spot of blood soaking through the bandages swaddling the boy's chest.

As swift to defend himself as Jolie had been to attack, Somerton blustered, "All I did was try to lift him. How was I to know you butchers had tied him up like a market pig?"

Instantly aware of the antagonism emanating from his silent audience, he underwent a second emotional metamorphosis, from belligerence to wheedling persuasion. "I'm only following my brother's orders. Lord Somerton wants his son returned to the castle, where he can be looked after properly, and not just tied to a bed in an empty room. My nephew was unconscious when I got here, and I have done nothing to—"

Frightened for the child's life and furious at the villainous uncle, Jolie interrupted shrilly, "He is a liar, Constable. He was trying to kill his nephew. He was told yesterday that the child could not be moved, and until he came, Francis was recovering. I want him out of here, and I want him charged with murder. The *canaille* has reopened the chest wound!"

In a voice no longer under control, Somerton screamed, "You bitch—you damned French slut. I'll have you flogged for that insult!"

Accompanying his vocal insults was a physical blow from his doubled fist, which missed Jolie's head and landed heavily on her sore shoulder. A moment later, the constable and one of the soldier guards ended the violence by dragging him from the room, leaving Jolie and two of the nurses on their knees, attempting to undo the damage he had done to his nephew.

Ignoring the throbbing pain in her shoulder, Jolie focused her attention on recalling everything she had learned in Edinburgh about stopping hemorrhage. For half an hour she and Sisters Mercia and Esther worked with silent desperation to save the child. So intense was Jolie's concentration, she barely felt the strong arms that lifted her to her feet and carried her to the other bed.

"I'll take over now," Rorke asserted with professional calm. "You've stopped the bleeding, lass, and the danger is past."

Late that afternoon, while young Francis Somerton slept under the heavy sedation of laudanum, Rorke carried his wife into the infirmary office in response to an official summons issued by the Newcastle magistrate, Lord Mayhew.

Lord Pelham and Constable Langford both stood and inquired solicitously about Jolie's well-being, but Mayhew remained seated.

"Mistress Campbell," he began heavily, "Constable Langford reported the serious accusation you made against the Honorable William Somerton. Unless you have sufficient evidence to support the grave charge of attempted murder, I have been instructed by Lord Somerton to accuse you of criminal libel. The young man admits he may have made a mistake in trying to move his nephew, but he insists that his motives were entirely innocent of any evil intent. He also admits that his judgment may have been impaired by a night of unwise carousing with friends and by the unfortunate accident he suffered during an ill-advised race through city streets early this morning. Since Lord Somerton has agreed to pay for the damage his brother caused, there will be no official charges against him in that matter. But your accusation cannot be so easily put aside, since it threatens the whole family's reputation. Now, will you kindly explain why you acted as impulsively as you did?"

"Did your *honorable* Monsieur Somerton explain how he got into this infirmary?" she demanded. "He did not have permission to be here."

Mayhew nodded impatiently. "He admits that he forced his way through a rear door to avoid meeting the constable, but he insists that one of your nurses assured him that his nephew was sufficiently recovered to be returned to his parents."

"He is a liar, Monsieur Mayhew. He intended that the child should die before he could tell anyone that his Uncle William had deliberately caused yesterday's accident. Then your *honorable* Monsieur Somerton would have only the younger child to murder in another accident tomorrow or the next day. This morning, Francis told me that his uncle had unlocked the gate to the tower and ordered his nephews to look for money he had lost there. He also told me about the time his uncle put them into a small boat on the river near their home. Their lives were saved by fishermen that time."

Regarding Jolie with a veiled contempt that hinted that he believed his wife's slander, Mayhew drawled sarcastically, "Either you are a most inventive liar, Mistress Campbell, or the child is highly imaginative. William Somerton has been his nephews' caretaker guardian for several years. If what you claim is true, he would have succeeded a long time ago."

Before Jolie could defend herself, Thomas Pelham cleared his throat noisily. "Mistress Campbell's conclusion is the same as mine, milord magistrate," he asserted. "Yesterday, His Grace asked me to investigate, and my findings are in complete agreement with hers. I am convinced we're dealing with an attempted murder. The tower gate could not have been opened by a child under any circumstances, and one of the groundskeepers reported seeing the suspect wandering around the tower the day before the accident he arranged so neatly. And Bailiff Wickham reported finding new coins on the top of the wall."

"I'll tell you what I told the woman, Thomas," Mayhew countered tartly. " 'Tis not logical that the man would choose a strange estate for such mischief."

"Then I suggest you talk to the governess, Howard. She and the other family retainers have suspected his intentions from the beginning, and have watched out for the children. At the duke's estate, he had only one elderly governess to worry about. You might also talk to the younger child; he's very much afraid of his Uncle William. And for what the testimony of a six-year-old is worth, he claims his uncle did unlock that gate, and that several days before, his uncle had locked the brothers in a shed."

"God's blood, Thomas, do you realize what you're saying? 'Tis understandable for hysterical women and undisciplined children to make such accusations, but you're a man of the world. How the devil do you intend to prove any of this in a court of law?"

"I don't, but His Grace expects you to solve the problem so that there is no further danger to the children and no additional public scandal. Lord Somerton shouldn't be too difficult to convince that his sons would be safer if their uncle were permanently exiled to the family estate in Jamaica. He knows that his brother is a problem, if not a scoundrel, and that the only possible inheritance left for William is the Somerton fortune itself. Unfortunately, younger brothers can inherit only if there are no direct heirs, hence the need for William to dispose of his older brother's sons.''

"Does Henry believe this remarkable theory of yours, Thomas?'' Mayhew asked with the snappishness of an irritated man.

"Yes, and he wants you to handle both this case and the street accident with discretion.''

"Why don't you continue being his errand boy, Thomas, and take care of the matter yourself?'' Mayhew muttered sarcastically.

"Not my bailiwick, Howard. My only personal interest is to make certain the Campbells are paid in full for their services and for the inconvenience we've caused them. Now I think we should leave them alone. God knows they must be sick to death of all of us by this time.''

Rising stiffly to his feet, Rorke spoke for the first time since the brief interrogation had begun. "Lord Pelham, tell His Grace that I'll be remaining at the infirmary until the—the suspect has left the area or is under restraint. Please inform Lord Somerton that if his brother threatens my wife or enters these premises again, I won't hesitate to defend my home.''

None of the departing men, not even the irritated Lord Mayhew, added a cautionary warning to Rorke's blunt declaration; but his threat of lethal defense was heeded, nonetheless. For the following two days, no one from the castle visited the infirmary, and it was a subdued Lord Somerton who appeared on the third morning to pay his bill and to see his injured son. Because Francis was still unresponsive much of the time, the visit with his father was of brief duration. For another three days, infirmary life was undisturbed. Not until the problem of William Somerton had been completely resolved were Rorke and Jolie notified; and the notification was delivered by the ducal secretary, rather than by Lord Pelham.

As knowledgeable about the duke's affairs as Henry himself, Charles Garnett had known Rorke's and Jolie's histories long before their arrival in Newcastle and had sympathized with their predicament. On the duke's orders, he had undertaken the responsibility of the Campbells' correspondence—sending the monthly allowance to Rorke's mother, Edina, and infrequent letters to Jolie's relatives in France. His other services to them had been equally discreet— he had made sure that they were well paid for their work at the castle and that a carriage was always available for their use. Garnett had been kept busy throughout the unfortunate Somerton affair. He was relieved that it was over and that castle routine would return to normal immediately after the hunt ball in a few days' time.

His greeting to Rorke in the infirmary office was explosively partisan toward his employer and the Campbells. "You can come out of hiding now, Doctor. His Grace finally persuaded the others to ship that murderer to Jamaica. This morning I watched the ship sail with him aboard, locked in a cabin."

"As a criminal indentured?" Rorke demanded sharply.

Garnett's shrug was a mutely eloquent testimonial to the inequity of English justice. "Lord Mayhew ruled the street accident as unavoidable—incidentally, the injured collier died."

"And the attempt on the child's life?" Rorke prompted.

"Mayhew called it unprovable, but the duke thought otherwise and convinced Lord Somerton to ship his brother abroad."

"For how long?"

"Permanently. Lord Somerton was not a complete fool; he believed what both his children and the governess told him. However, he did insist that there be no publicity. Not even his wife was told, nor any of the other guests. The rest of us were sworn to secrecy—even Constable Langford—

and His Grace agreed. He could see no reason for adding to the children's nightmare.''

''I'll have to tell my wife, Charles. I don't want her having any nightmares about the scoundrel.''

''Your wife was the reason His Grace insisted on Jamaica. William Somerton was quite violent about what he called 'that libelous, lying nursemaid.' If she hadn't won the older lad's confidence, there'd have been no case at all.''

''Not even with Lord Pelham's testimony?''

''Lord Pelham returned to London before the hearing began. His Grace doesn't want any more court gossip about your wife before the king has ruled on the infirmary petition. Odd thing, Doctor. I've never known His Grace to be as keen on any other project.''

More cynical than ever about the prospect of gaining King William's approval, Rorke asked the secretary, ''How do you rate our chances, Charles?''

''I think His Grace is a century ahead of the times. The aristocracy still isn't willing to share medical advances with the common people. They still want doctors to be their personal servants, just as they were in medieval times—just as poor old Roxbury still is.''

Recalling the three years he had worked as a doctor without pay for the earl of Breadalbane, Rorke nodded in agreement, but fairness compelled him to admit that the duke of Newcastle was very different from most of his peers.

''I'm grateful for the help Henry Cavendish has given my wife and me,'' he murmured.

''Aye, Doctor,'' Garnett concurred readily, ''but 'tis my opinion that he needs your help now more than you need his. If you're free this afternoon, I'd appreciate your seeing him; and if young Perry is well enough, we'll take him with us. This morning, His Grace was too weak to leave his bed.''

When Jolie learned that William Somerton was no longer a threat, she uttered a heartfelt ''thank God!'' and bid her

husband a relieved good-bye. For days he'd hovered over
her with a brooding intensity, and he'd worn his sword even
in surgery. Equally on edge, the nurses and attendants had
watched over her and the boy Francis like keyed-up guard
dogs. While the guests at the castle had not been told about
the attempted murder, the infirmary people had witnessed
the near tragedy. Jolie was eager to be free from locked
doors, barred windows, and nurses who jerked nervously at
every noise.

She also wanted to restore patient morale without the
interference of an overprotective doctor. Joe Foss, the roofer
who had broken his leg, had not yet learned to walk on
crutches; and Francis Percival, the future Lord Somerton,
had regained none of his earlier resilience or spirit. During
his father's visit, he'd answered one or two questions with a
bleak apathy and continued to stare fearfully at the door; nor
had he responded to any subsequent efforts to reassure him.

As she entered the familiar small room where Rorke had
insisted she remain in bed during the crisis, Jolie remembered
another of the rules Soeur Marguerite had rigidly enforced
at the Strasbourg infirmary. The crusty old nun had never
allowed her recuperating patients to brood. To the extent of
their ability, the women had been put to work mending
clothing or cutting bandages, and the children had been
given lessons to learn. If Sister Mercia would agree to be
the teacher, Jolie decided, this young patient was going to
learn Latin.

Her voice was briskly cheerful as she addressed the boy
whose eyes still held the apprehensive look of fear. "Francis,
your Uncle William isn't going to come through that door or
any other door for the rest of your life. He can't ever return
to England, so you're quite safe."

"Why did he want to hurt me? Papa said he really didn't
mean to."

Jolie shrugged impatiently. Why did adults try to protect
children from the truth with foolish lies that wouldn't
convince an imbecile, much less a bright boy like this one?

"But you know better, don't you, Francis? Your father

loves his younger brother just as you do yours; but your Uncle William is a villain all the same, and a very stupid one. But now you're to forget him and think about something useful. How would you like to learn some Latin?''

''My tutor says I can't.''

''Your tutor is another stupid man. Any boy who will be a lord some day has to know Latin.''

''Will you teach me?''

''Sister Mercia is a better teacher than I am, but I'll be the one to scold you if you don't try and if you don't eat the food that will help you get well.''

''I don't like to be fed like a baby; I want to sit up and feed myself. I've still got one arm that works.''

Jolie smiled in triumph; it was the first sign of rebellion he had displayed in days. ''The doctor will untie you as soon as your chest heals,'' she promised. ''By that time, if you concentrate, you'll know at least fifty Latin words. Will you promise to try?''

Although his assent wasn't enthusiastic, Jolie congratulated herself on achieving even minimal cooperation. She had almost reached the door when his childish voice stopped her.

''Sister Jolie?''

''Yes, Francis?''

''Did you ever have someone like Uncle William in your family?''

Reluctantly, she focused her thoughts on Henri de Guise, who would have been her repressive stepfather had he known who she was, and on Tavis Campbell, who was more violently murderous than William Somerton. ''Almost everyone does, Francis,'' she said slowly. ''The best thing to do is to forget about them.''

Unable to take her own advice, Jolie felt a surge of envy as she left the room. None of the villains in her life had been punished as decisively as the boy's uncle. The French colonel was still tormenting unlucky Huguenots; the earl of Breadalbane was still the king's favorite; and Tavis Campbell was still a pampered and protected *canaille*. For a fleeting moment she experienced again the fierce emotion that had driven her to desperate savagery during her last night in Edinburgh. Seated in the rear of the death wagon, she had vowed to protect her sword-slashed husband with her life. When the door of the wagon had been yanked open by a Breadalbane soldier, she had struck out wildly with a sharp surgical knife and had felt no remorse that she had deliberately injured another human being. The anger she had felt for William Somerton had been fleeting compared to the enduring hatred she held for Tavis Campbell and his vicious soldiers for threatening her husband!

Although Rorke had told her nothing about the duke's plan to establish infirmaries in other cities, Jolie knew that when Henry Cavendish died, Newcastle would no longer be a secure hiding place. She doubted that she and Rorke would be safe anyplace in England—only powerful lords were protected from other powerful lords. Even when the earl of Breadalbane had been with the king in faraway London, she and Rorke hadn't been safe in Edinburgh. Jolie still shuddered when she remembered her meeting with Rorke's mother and with Lady Alanna Fairleigh, the Scotswoman Rorke had been expected to marry. Rorke's mother was the one who had betrayed them that time; she had been the one who had led Tavis Campbell to their inn and precipitated that night of horror. Surprisingly, it had been the beautiful widow Fairleigh who had privately warned Jolie to leave Edinburgh as quickly as possible.

Ever since that narrow escape, Jolie had tried to anticipate trouble, and she had deliberately avoided attracting unnecessary notice at the castle and in town. Until she had been forced by circumstances to help in the rescue of Lord Somerton's son, she thought she had succeeded. But when the young boy had called her a servant "who'd gotten too uppish for her own good," Jolie knew that there was yet another enemy seeking to harm her, and that untrue stories about her had spread as far as London. Her first reaction had been one of foolish pride—she had been angry over the appellation of *servant* when her family bloodlines were as

aristocratic as any of the guests now visiting the duke of
Newcastle. A moment later, the common sense she had
acquired during her eighteen years as a nameless foundling
in a French convent pushed all such trivia from her mind.
The only real hope she and Rorke had of achieving anything
approaching permanent security was to avoid all titled people in the future—English, Scottish, and French. And the
only place such avoidance would be possible was in the
New World, where titles did not exist and where men were
measured by their accomplishments, rather than by their
inheritance.

That afternoon, as she resumed her infirmary duties, her
thoughts reverted frequently to the practical problems involved in reaching a world thousands of miles from England.
It had been so easy for a criminal English aristocrat to be
shipped to faraway Jamaica. Why should it be any more
difficult for a Scottish doctor and his French wife? Still
vague about geography, but no longer completely ignorant,
Jolie reasoned that with a vast ocean separating them from
England, they would be free from the earl of Breadalbane
and his bastard son Tavis, at least. The probability that their
flight would have neither the king's blessing nor permission
did not disturb Jolie's increasingly elastic conscience.
Numbered among the friends she had made during her
sixteen months of married life were a dozen sea captains,
but only one of them met her requirements for this most
demanding voyage. Only the Baron Wallmond, Captain
Ramsey Huntington, possessed both the ships and the necessary disregard for King William's laws to smuggle her and
Rorke to one of the American colonies.

At present, Captain Huntington was in his fortress home
on the banks of the Rhine River; but if he returned to
Newcastle in time, Jolie wouldn't hesitate to enlist his help.
Since he had been the one who had involved Rorke in the
kidnapping of Tavis Campbell, it seemed a reasonable
request. Safely stored in the vaults of the best goldsmith in
Newcastle was most of the fortune her grandfather had
given her and the money she and Rorke had earned. Rather

than live in constant fear for Rorke's safety, Jolie vowed to spend the entire amount for ship's passage, even if the captain were a smuggler like the Dutchman, Henrik de Voort, who had brought them from Amsterdam to England.

Having spent the afternoon worrying about the future, Jolie almost forgot that the present was also uncertain until Rorke failed to return from the castle by suppertime. Knowing that only an extreme emergency could have detained him, she prepared herself mentally for the news that would alter their lives immediately. On a more practical level, she prepared the amenities needed for the comfort of a tired and possibly demoralized husband. Rorke still considered death the enemy, whereas Jolie's childhood experience with old and sick nuns had taught her that it was often a merciful friend. If Henry Cavendish were dead, she would be saddened by losing a good friend, but she would not grieve or wish it otherwise. He would be free of pain and fear he had suffered for a long time.

Sometime before midnight she heard the coach pull to a stop on the street below her bedroom window, and minutes later she listened to her husband's footsteps on the stairs. After bracing herself for a dire announcement, she giggled in relief when she received an irritable scolding instead.

"Jolie, I expressly asked you to remain in bed this afternoon, but I have just been informed that you have been working steadily. What am I going to do with—?"

"First of all, *mon amour*, you're going to eat your supper and then come to bed. *Ma foi*, you look worse than I do."

Because she had taken special pains with her own appearance and knew she looked pretty, Jolie was smiling as she helped him undress and put on a fire-warmed robe before she shoved him gently into a chair and poured him a cup of wine. But not until he had eaten most of the supper she had kept warm for him did she ask about the duke's health.

"Perry and I almost lost him today," he admitted heavily.

"What happened?"

"His Grace has been in power too long to retire gracefully. He didn't trust Mayhew to deal firmly enough with that scoundrel Somerton, so he conducted the hearings himself. And because he didn't want the townspeople to know how ill he was, he walked up and down those damn flights of stairs, instead of letting the servants carry him in a sedan chair as I'd ordered. If those stupidities weren't enough to kill him, Dr. Roxbury and that damn substitute nurse were; they overdosed him with the medicine I'd prescribed.''

"Is he all right now?"

"He's alive, but he won't be much longer, and he still insists on attending that accursed hunt ball next Saturday."

"Then give him your blessing, Rorke; there's nothing else you can do for him. A few weeks won't matter, so let him enjoy his one last soiree."

" 'Twill mean you and I will have to be there, too, sweetheart.''

Instantly, Jolie's philosophical acceptance of life's vicissitudes vanished, and her lips curled in rebellion. "*Peste*! I don't want to supply the amusement for those people. Some of them already think I'm nothing but a servant."

Resisting the impulse to reveal the source of that rumor, Rorke tried to reassure her. "I'm certain the duke will have told all his guests about you by that time. Now, let's go to bed and get some sleep. I want you off that ankle before it starts swelling again."

Jolie was smiling as she turned back to covers. She hadn't thought he had even noticed that her slender ankles were once again a matching pair. But, as always, his sharp eyes had taken a thorough inventory of her—almost as thorough as the one his questing hands made as she nestled next to him beneath the fire-warmed blankets. Gently, he shoved her away from him.

"You invited me back into your bed too soon, lass. Your shoulder is still swollen, and the bruise on your hip is still tender," he murmured regretfully.

Jolie's response was a soft giggle and an instant return into his arms. Although he didn't push her away this time, he was slow to accept the uninhibited invitation she was offering him.

"Sweetheart, 'tis too soon," he cautioned her again, but less forcefully.

"How absurd! You did not think so after you'd been injured, *mon amour*. You could not even lift the arm your *cochon* cousin had slashed. And we required but a small adjustment to—"

" 'Tis different with a man," Rorke interrupted her unabashed reminder. "Our bodies are not so delicate, and we're taught to tolerate pain."

Again she laughed. While she had been training the other nurses, he had been convalescing from the sword wound, and he had been the most difficult and demanding patient she had ever tended. Not until she had finally succumbed to his insistence that she join him in bed had his recuperation really accelerated. Now, with the situation reversed, it was her own sense of urgency that drove her. For weeks, their lives had been dominated by other people and by problems not of their making, and Rorke's reaction had been a return to the secretive distrust that had once been habitual. During the early months of their marriage, he had rarely confided in her; she had learned about the unhappy circumstances of his life from other people. From a veteran Scottish soldier, she had learned that her own MacDonald clan was responsible for her husband's poverty. From Tavis, she had learned that Rorke had been slated for permanent indenture to the earl of Breadalbane, and that he was to be tricked into marriage to a widow whose fortune the earl already controlled.

A practical woman whose youth had been molded by Soeur Marguerite's stern dictum that God helps those who help themselves, Jolie had already acquired sufficient sophistication to trust her own judgment. She had known for a week that Rorke was worried about something far more threatening than William Somerton. But since he hadn't as yet confided in her, and since, at the moment, she could do little to safeguard their future, she had decided to reestablish the normal routine of their marriage, regardless of his predictable objections. A passionately eager husband, for the most part, he had developed only one irritating flaw in regard to his young wife—he was overzealous about tending to her health. After she had suffered a miscarriage, he had waited weeks before he'd touched her, and then he had insisted that she be fitted with a pessary to prevent future pregnancies. Jolie smiled as she recalled her first experience with the pessary—the ancient contraceptive gold button that free-thinking Dutch doctors had brought into modern usage. Because she had insisted that they bring a supply of them to England, Jolie had helped eight other Newcastle women avoid unwanted motherhood.

Cuddled next to her husband after sleeping alone for two weeks, she remembered warmly what he had told her in Holland—that he wanted to spend his life with her, not with the child she might leave behind. On that occasion, for the first time, she had been confident that he loved her as much as she did him. For both of them, that domestic crisis marked the beginning of a happily democratic marriage in which neither of them dominated—at least in bed. Unaware that she was far less inhibited about marital intimacy than most women, Jolie often initiated their lovemaking, with Rorke's full approval. Tonight, however, the tension of the past week and Rorke's bitter conviction that he and Jolie had already been betrayed had intensified his medical concern for her recovery.

"Don't bedevil me, lass," he chided her. "It has been almost a fortnight, and I've had trouble enough keeping away from you."

"The same for me," she murmured, then added, "but that part of me was not injured, *mon amour*. If I were to remain on top, as I did when your arm was still healing—"

" 'Twould have to be very different this time, sweetheart. I'd have to hold you so you couldn't move your hip—'tis just now healing properly, and I'd not want you permanently scarred."

Jolie's triumphant smile was hidden beneath the covers. She hadn't misjudged his mood; he'd already devised a workable method. She felt his body relax as she reached her hand downward, only to pull it back hastily to the safety of his chest and arms. He didn't need any added stimulation; he was already fully aroused.

Laughing in tacit admission of the fact, Rorke whispered huskily, "I tried to warn you. Now you'll be lucky to get to sleep by dawn."

The totality and speed of his transformation from a soberly professional doctor to an impassioned lover still could take Jolie by surprise. When she had first learned there had been other women in his life, she had felt jealous enough to ask if he had reacted in the same way to them. His denial had been a bluntly worded avowal of love.

"To tell you true, lass, I never expected to feel this way about any woman."

"What way?"

"Like a Highland stag in rut and a besotted bridegroom combined. If I claimed you every time I thought about it, we'd be spending most of our time in bed."

His lovemaking tonight reflected the same earthy humor. As he bent his head to kiss her, he murmured with an apologetic chuckle, "God's truth, I feel as if we've been apart for years instead of weeks." His chuckle deepened into satisfied laughter when his sensitive, questing fingers determined that her degree of readiness equaled his. His wife possessed none of the prevailing inhibitions that afflicted most other women. Having known few frustrated wives during her youth, she was irrepressively sensuous and completely honest in her reactions. She could also be as athletic as a gymnast, he reminded himself wryly, and now was not the time for a redislocated shoulder or a resprained hip or ankle.

Releasing her lips, he chided her lightly, "Sweetheart, when you're in this mood, I don't trust you any more than I do myself. You and I are not timid or reluctant lovers, and unless you promise to let me set the pace, I'll not risk hurting you."

The declaration, however, was entirely rhetorical; Jolie was given no opportunity to agree or protest. Instead, her lips were reclaimed imperiously, and she was lifted by two strong hands cupping the rounded globes of her buttocks, deposited on top of her husband's body, and held there immobile by an inflexible arm. Without any pause in his swift tempo of lovemaking, Rorke's free hand continued its purposeful caresses and his kisses deepened in intensity. Again without warning and with a dexterity that eliminated all but minimal discomfort to her, he thrust into her body, only to remain motionless until his throbbing readiness calmed. A more knowledgeable lover than most men, especially about the mercurial emotions of the sensuous girl he had married, Rorke had always before been able to control his own rioting passion long enough to assure that her needs were equally satisfied. Handicapped this time by the immobility he deemed necessary for her, he gambled that he could still arouse her to climax before he lost control.

As he began the slow, hypnotic rhythm, his hands held her pressed tightly to him, as if she were an unconscious body without willpower or emotion. That her lack of physical participation indicated a corresponding absence of sensual pleasure, however, was an illusion. Jolie felt breathlessly alive; her mind and senses were focused intently on the poignant sensations she was experiencing. Because her body had responded instinctively, even during her chaotic initiation into womanhood, she had thought the physical violence an essential preparation for the culmination of climax. But as she forced herself to remain motionless, the excitement built with a breathless speed, and she felt the vibrating thrill of approaching ecstasy more sharply than she ever had before. And as if Rorke had been waiting for her signal, her first gasping moan brought an instant reaction. Holding her even more tightly, he thrust one last time before the pulsing explosion became a shared experience that obliterated all conscious thought for both of them. Rorke was the first to regain his humor.

"Your countryman was right," he asserted softly.

Still mentally enmeshed in the uniqueness of the moment, Jolie was slow to comprehend his reference. "What countryman?" she mumbled.

"The French doctor I've told you about often enough—
the one who taught me about childbirth, lovemaking, and
women. He said that the drive for love was as much mental
as physical, and sweetheart, I could all but feel your
thoughts that time."

Aroused by a sharp disagreement with the concept, Jolie
blurted, "He is an imbecile, your doctor, and he knows
nothing about love. It is not a lesson you learn in a book; it
is a gift from God."

Amused by her vehemence, Rorke asked lightly, "What
happened to your claim that you were not religious, my
once-upon-a-time nun?"

Shrugging her one good shoulder to indicate the contempt
such a frivolous question deserved, Jolie relaxed comfortably against her husband's strong, protective body. "You
don't have to be a *religieuse* to know what is true," she
defended herself confidently. "We didn't plan to fall in love
with each other. *Ma foi*, you didn't want to fall in love with
anyone, and I didn't know what love was. But now I could
never be happy without you, *mon amour*. It was God who
made our love possible, not our foolish thoughts."

Rorke's smile was a surrender to her irrefutable logic.
Not since his father's death had he believed in divine grace,
but the term "gift from God" was as good an explanation
as any other for the love that now bound him to this woman.
The French doctor may have understood the most effective
mechanics of physical lovemaking, but nothing in his scholarly notes had defined the fierce emotion Rorke felt for the
girl he had been forced to wed by the Catholic zealot,
Monseigneur François de Guise. Ruefully, Rorke admitted
that the warm possessiveness he felt was more spiritual than
physical, and more primitive than intellectual. Before he
drifted off to sleep, he remembered the whole of her defense
and nodded silently in agreement. His happiness was as
dependent upon her as hers was on him.

Hours later, just after dawn, when he heard her cry out in
her sleep, he was jarred instantly into full awareness. He
had never known her to have nightmares before—not even

during the frightening months on the Rhine River—and only on rare occasions had she been a restless sleeper. But now, she was moving her head from side to side and straining her body with desperate strength. Gently Rorke shook her awake and pushed her tumbled hair away from her face, noting that the tendrils were damp with perspiration.

"What were you dreaming about, lass?" he asked softly.

For a moment she stared at him blankly and shook her head. "I couldn't find you," she admitted finally.

"Then 'twas but a foolish dream, sweetheart. I've not left your side, nor could I abide a future without you. I know you're half Scot, lass, and 'twould be a temptation to believe you'd inherited second sight from some remote ancestress. But 'tis just an old wive's tale that Scotswomen can predict the future; the ones who claim the skill are often as daft as village idiots. More likely your dream was caused by your concern for the duke and the parasites you'll be meeting at Saturday's ball."

As Jolie listened to his murmurs, she gradually relaxed, but her eyes retained the look of shock. Whatever her dream had been, its emotional impact lingered. Rorke himself had suffered nightmares after his mother had made the ruthless earl of Breadalbane his guardian, and he reacted with a swift understanding. He knew from experience that only an abrupt change in mental focus could dispel the gloom. Displaying less concern for her injured shoulder and hip, he began the ritual of seduction with demanding hands and a lilting language that reverted to his early childhood, before his scholarly father taught him to speak English as crisply as an Englishman.

"Ne'er forget, Jolie lass, tha' ye're my ain true love and tha' I canna be glae wi' ou' ye."

Having heard the same lyrically accented words on other occasions, Jolie relaxed even more, but still she gave no indication of responding to his overtures. It was his next, less sentimental words that brought a giggle to her lips and roused her to action, as soon as she'd interpreted their meaning.

"I dinna wa' t' complain like an auld monnie, lass, bu' 'tis daft I am t' be makin' love alone. I'm thinkin' I've naught bu' a wee bairn in my arms and no' the lusty wench I wed."

Not for the next demanding hour did Jolie remember her sore hip or shoulder, or the dream that had jarred both of them awake. In Holland, after her sober, serious husband had first revealed the streak of pixie humor that surfaced only during their hours of intimate isolation in the bedroom, Jolie had lost the last vestiges of the inhibiting reverence that had made her a follower rather than a partner in love. After that initiation, she had given free rein to her own irreverent humor, which had rarely been suppressed during her unconventional childhood. Despite her insistence that their love was a "gift from God," there was nothing religious about her appreciation of Rorke's earthy humor or her response to it. The reminder that she had reacted childishly to a mere dream was all that she needed to ignite the hot pride that was the core of her fire. She was still giggling as she fitted her body more closely to his and returned his kiss with an attentive fervor that slowly warmed to passion. Rorke welcomed her into his arms with relief.

Jolie's reluctance to attend the hunt ball was dissipated by the news that Captain Ramsey Huntington's magnificent ship *Lorelei* had arrived in harbor. The English sea captain had promised to bring letters to her from her French family. Although she had no desire to return to her girlhood home, she longed for news from her aunt and grandfather. Most important, however, the captain was a lifelong friend of the duke of Newcastle, and as preoccupied as Jolie was about the future she and Rorke faced, she wanted the dying nobleman to garner as much happiness as possible during his few remaining months.

With Captain Huntington in attendance, even a misbegotten hunt ball would be a success. Before he had returned to Germany, the captain had dominated every one of the duke's parties with a subtle authority, and Jolie doubted that even Lady Holles would dare challenge him. Ironically, although these title-proud aristocrats knew him only as a commoner sea captain, they treated him with a cautious respect. It was this realization that hardened Jolie's own resolve to make sure that no one in England would ever again mistake her for a servant, as Lord and Lady Somerton obviously had.

For days, Jolie had threatened to wear her nurse's uniform to the ball, but now she chose the costliest dress in her clothespress without hesitation—an elaborate formal gown she had refused to consider on earlier occasions. When her cousin, Paul Arnaud, had first shown it to her in Holland, he had labeled it fit for a princess, but Jolie had been appalled by its opulence. French in fabric and style, the overdress was cream-colored brocade covered by brilliant red and orange flowers, each one vividly outlined in gold thread. In place of flowers, the exposed front panel of the cream silk underdress was so heavily embroidered with gold it needed no additional stiffening. Matching spool-heeled shoes and a delicate gold net snood for her hair completed the lavish outfit.

Its cost, however, was not the only notable aspect of this particular dress. Both the comte de Laurent and his grandson Paul possessed a keen appreciation for Jolie's unique coloring and potential beauty. The bodice fit her like a second skin, revealing enough throat and rounded breast to be daring, while the woven flowers of the widely belled skirt blended dramatically with the ruddy gold of her hair. When Rorke glanced up from his own complicated dressing, he dropped the shoe he was holding and his lips formed a silent whistle, but his praise was oddly reserved.

" 'Tis a beautiful dress, but mayhap 'twould be better saved for another time," he suggested.

"Why? You've urged me to wear it often enough."

"I didn't realize the neckline was so low or that it would fit you so snugly," he murmured, but his protest lacked conviction. Rorke was experiencing the same vague rejection he felt every time he was reminded of his wife's French family. Both the grandfather and grandson had been Rorke's friends and co-conspirators in helping Huguenot refugees, long before the two aristocrats had learned they were related to Jolie. Ironically, Paul Arnaud had been half in love with the girl he'd thought a nameless foundling. Only after she had been forced to marry the foreign doctor had either comte de Laurent or Paul learned her identity, and both of them had traveled overland to Holland so that they could greet their newfound relative when she and Rorke arrived. In addition to an inheritance of almost twenty thousand gold guineas, her grandfather had ordered expensive wardrobes for both Jolie and Rorke—costly dresses suitable for society, and elegant suits Rorke could never have afforded on a doctor's income. Every time Jolie had reluctantly worn one of the opulent dresses, Rorke had been reminded that other men had chosen them for her.

"Jolie, since we don't know most of these people," he began more determinedly, "I think you should wear something less challenging. There won't be a woman there tonight with a dress as magnificent and regal as this one."

Shrugging her shoulders disdainfully, she retorted sharply, "Then perhaps Madame Holles will stop calling me a servant, and Madame Mayhew will know I am not stupid. I shall also wear *Grandpère*'s medallion tonight, and if I had a gold crown, I would wear that, too," she concluded defiantly.

Rorke nodded in abrupt understanding. She might not know the specifics of the gossip about her, but she knew the two logical perpetrators and was reacting according to her own bold temperament. The fact that she was wearing the medallion indicated her resolve to outface her enemies. Centuries old, the heavy round gold ornament was engraved with the de Laurent family motto: *fortes fortune juvat*— "fortune favors the brave." With a wry smile, Rorke recalled Jolie's scornful words on the only other occasion she had worn the necklace.

"*Quelle absurdité*! Cowardly kings and criminals like your Breadalbane will always be richer than brave men."

With a cynicism based on personal experience, Rorke had agreed with her. Tonight, he wished he had a similar amulet to wear. Just for once, it would be gratifying to outrank the gilded, useless wastrels who were born to fortune. A moment later, he wondered if it might not be more appropriate to wear his sword. Never before had Jolie looked so glitteringly beautiful or so arrogantly aristocratic. The months of exercising authority over nurses and patients had stamped her face with a self-assurance that not even the overbearing Lady Holles could match, and her vivid blue eyes sparked with a determined challenge.

Silently, Rorke followed her as she led him through the room where their youngest patient was still bedridden. Predictably, Francis Somerton's eyes widened in awed appreciation of the woman who had saved his life twice. Unpredictably, his first compliment was a proudly blurted Latin phrase Sister Mercia had taught him: "*Prima inter pares!*" More in keeping with his not-quite-ten-year-old mentality, however, were the giggled words that followed: "Reckon you're prettier than 'most anyone else, 'specially old Betsey."

As Rorke helped Jolie into the carriage the duke had sent for their use, he soberly echoed the boy's praise. "Reckon you *will* be first among the women there tonight, sweetheart, but don't forget the French fairy tale about Cinderella. At midnight you'll become my wife again."

Ironically, Rorke's words were almost prophetic. Not until he and Jolie were homeward bound five hours later could they exchange confidences about the remarkable evening that had brought changes to both of their lives. Since Jolie had been the stellar attraction during the most memorable incident of the ball itself, she had been too distracted at the time to appreciate the honor that had been paid her. But from the beginning, the hunt ball had been a unique experience for her. Even their arrival had contained an element of drama. As the carriage had pulled to a halt before the great doors of the castle proper, the two uniformed footmen lifted her from the coach and placed her gently in a sedan chair.

"His Grace insists, Mistress Campbell," the majordomo informed her with a firm politeness before he turned toward Rorke. "Doctor, His Grace has also requested your services for one of the guests. If you'll follow the torch boy, I'll escort your wife to the ballroom."

"I'll go with my husband to assist," Jolie said hastily, but her protest went unheeded as she was carried through the entry, past the ancient great hall, and up the broad stairs to the second floor. Feeling ridiculously conspicuous, she was carried into the candlelit ballroom, where a hundred guests stared at her with expressions that varied from amusement to shock; however, she was vastly relieved that she had been spared the usual ordeal of a public introduction. Instead, she was carried directly to a fire-warmed alcove, where she was allowed to dismount before she was greeted by her host, who had insisted on standing up.

"M'dear," Henry Cavendish murmured gallantly, "I expected you to be as pale as a wraith after your ordeal, but you look ravishing. Your gown is the most beautiful to grace this room in many a year, and you, m'dear, are singularly lovely tonight. Your husband has kept me informed about your recovery, but I confess that I had an even more accurate source of information: the Somerton boy has talked of little else to his father. I regret to say, however, that he did somewhat spoil a surprise I had planned. When the lad told his father that you were a lady and not an available serving wench, the jackanapes informed the other guests."

Silently blessing her youngest patient, Jolie sought the security of a professional interest in her oldest one. Having already noted the signs of deterioration in the nobleman— the bluish tinge of his lips, the gaunt thinness of his neck, and the transparent skin of his weakened hands, she scolded the duke earnestly. "Monsieur, you must sit down and conserve your strength."

Henry's wan smile projected just a hint of a gambler's resignation. "You and I have no need for pretense, m'dear. We both know 'tis of no real importance whether I stand or sit, but mayhap you're right. Most likely, our guests will be less agitated if we both sit." Jolie noted with trepidation that the chair he indicated for her was next to his own. In the past, she had always sat facing him, with her back to the main body of guests.

"Tonight is an occasion, m'dear," the duke informed her confidentially once they were both seated. " 'Twill be my last time to play lord of the manor. The state of my health is now public gossip, and I'm afraid there are more than several awaiting my death with impatient anticipation."

Knowing that any attempt at consolation would be futile, Jolie was similarly candid. "Then we will keep them waiting as long as possible," she promised him determinedly.

Her reward was another smile and a barely perceptible wink of one faded brown eye before Henry Cavendish nodded to the majordomo who had been standing at attention in the nearby entry. Jolie winced as he tapped his staff on the marble floor and began to speak in the stentorian voice of a town crier.

"Ladies and gentlemen, His Grace has asked me to make an announcement. In keeping with a three-hundred-year-old Cavendish tradition of publicly recognizing courage, His Grace is making the first such presentation of his adminis-tration. In the past, the recipient has always been a soldier whose bravery saved the lives of his fellows. This time, the honoree is a woman whose bravery saved the life of a child."

Jolie listened with increasing horror as she was identified with a biographer's thoroughness. Her relatives were named with reverence for their titles and importance, her nursing career in Newcastle was lavishly lauded, and her actions during the rescue were praised. But not even that unsought indignity could compete with the carefully planned travesty that followed. In his efforts to compensate for the damage the malicious gossip had done to Jolie's reputation, Henry had requested that his daughter make the presentation, as a punishment for her gullible participation. Since the slander about the duke and his French nurse had been discredited by Lord Somerton's report that Jolie was both a married wom-

an and an aristocrat, Lady Holles had merely changed the
nature of her prejudice, broadening it to include Dr. Campbell,
as well as his wife. That metamorphosis in her distrust of
the couple, whom she considered to be fortune-hunting
interlopers, had occurred the day before Thomas Pelham
had departed for London. On the duke's instruction, Pelham
had informed his sister-in-law that her father planned to
leave his personal fortune in the care of Dr. Campbell, to be
used to establish infirmaries for the poor.

Outraged by the prospect of a much-reduced inheritance,
and furious that outsiders would reap the benefit of her
father's industry, Marianne Holles had consented to present
the despised Frenchwoman with the award, only because her
father had insisted with abruptly harsh authority. However,
she was an accomplished enough actress to carry out the
hated assignment with a gracious flourish. Only Jolie heard
the softly spoken threat as Lady Holles placed a second
heavy gold medallion around the younger woman's neck.
"Englishmen do not tolerate foreign thieves, Mistress
Campbell. Please warn your husband not to rob my foolish
father any more than he already has."

Giving her victim no chance to respond, Lady Holles
rearranged her lips into a vapidly social smile and moved
swiftly away. Jolie would not have known what to say
anyway; she had been told nothing about the duke's plans
for her and Rorke's future, and she was shocked by the
notion that Englishmen might consider her husband either a
thief or a foreigner. He had seemed far more a foreigner in
Edinburgh than in his adopted country. Had Jolie been alone
with the duke, she would have demanded that he explain his
daughter's accusations. When Rorke's reputation was at
stake, Annette Marguerite MacDonald Campbell could be as
ruthless a fighter as Marianne Holles, and a more resourceful one.

Unfortunately, His Grace was occupied in being His
Grace to half a dozen men demanding his attention, while
an elegantly uniformed army officer approached Jolie with a
determined step and an appreciative smile. As he bent over

to kiss her hand, she heard the words, "The Honorable Gordon something-or-other at your service, beautiful heroine." Jolie would have been surprised to know that this friendly soldier was the youngest son of the unfriendly Lord Mayhew, and that he knew about his stepmother's roving ways from firsthand experience. She would have been chagrined to know that the duke had appointed Gordon Mayhew as her escort during Rorke's unavoidable absence. It was Gordon's own sense of justice that prompted him to tell her about Dorothea Mayhew's crime and punishment. After hearing that the woman who had tried to destroy her had been forbidden to attend the ball, in addition to being exiled from Queen Mary's court for a year, Jolie asked only one question: "Did my husband know about the gossip?"

"Lord Pelham may have told him, but I don't think he was surprised. I imagine he's known other women like my—like Dorothea. God's truth, he's handsome enough to tempt even decent women." Smiling at Jolie with the assurance of a male Dorothea, Gordon Mayhew confided brashly, " 'Tis why I was so eager to meet you. I wondered what kind of woman could make a husband give the heave-to to a highborn courtesan who's seduced more than one erstwhile faithful husband. Now that I've seen you, there's no mystery, and your magnificent French gown would turn half the women here tonight into willing thieves if they thought they'd look as good as you do in it. As for the medal His Grace gave you, there isn't a man here who wouldn't do nip-ups to earn one like it. What does it say?"

Having not yet had time to read it, Jolie twisted the medallion around and grimaced as she read the words inscribed beneath the Newcastle crest: "*Soeur Jolie—une femme courageuse.*"

"It exaggerates, just as you do, monsieur," she demurred unenthusiastically. "There were others on that wall who took a greater risk than I did."

That Gordon Mayhew was shrewder than his earlier raillery indicated was evident in his smooth rejoinder. "I suspect the courage referred to was your getting rid of

murderous Uncle William. Poor old Percival doesn't know
that Thomas Pelham needed my sturdy sword arm to help
him take the blackguard Willy to the waiting ship. And
speaking of poor old Percival, here he comes. I imagine
he's been told to express his gratitude to you very publicly—
he and his wife both—but you needn't expect any thanks
from her. She's one of our unfortunate crackbrains who
much prefers gossip to truth.''

His description of Lady Somerton was entirely accurate.
Without spilling her goblet of wine, she nodded her head
after Gordon performed the introduction and stared avidly at
Jolie's dress. But Somerton seemed sincere in his praise and
genuinely interested in his son's recovery. Ironically, he was
particularly curious about Francis's embryonic mastery of
Latin. Assuring the ill-at-ease father that his son was intelligent enough to acquire a good education, Jolie ended the
awkward interview with a suggestion that he talk to Sister
Mercia. To her consternation immediately after the Somertons
had left her, she discovered that they hadn't been the only
ones ordered to pay their respects to the guest of honor.
With Gordon performing the introductions, Jolie was forced
to speak to thirty or more people during the following hour.
Acutely conscious that many of the women were as uninter-
ested in her as she was in them, she made no attempt to
prolong any of the conversations.

By the end of the embarrassing ordeal, she was eager to
leave the ballroom and to locate her husband. Noting that
the duke of Newcastle was momentarily alone, she asked if
he minded her leaving. To her relief, his own slender
reserve of strength had been exhausted and he acquiesced
willingly. While they were waiting for the sedan chairs—the
duke refused to allow her to walk the distance to his private
quarters—Jolie learned that Captain Huntington, the one
person she had expressly wanted to see during the party, was
the injured man Rorke had been summoned to tend. Because
she had childishly thought him indestructible, she felt a
brief premonition of fear. ''How was he injured?'' she asked
hesitantly.

"A shipboard accident of some kind or other," Cavendish responded vaguely.

"Don't you believe it, Your Grace," Gordon Mayhew volunteered boldly. "I was watching when his crewmen carried him from the coach. After a year on and off the battlefield, sir, I've learned to recognize the different types of injuries, and 'tis my guess that Captain Huntington was suffering from a bullet wound."

4

Within an hour of leaving the ballroom, Jolie had abandoned her plans of asking Ramsey Huntington for transportation out of England. He would be lucky if he could get himself and his ships safely away. When she and Henry Cavendish arrived in his quarters, they found the heavily drugged captain asleep in a room adjoining the ducal bedroom and four tired men drinking wine around a table in the anteroom. Three of them—Rorke, Dr. Roxbury, and Perry—had completed the demanding operation of removing a bullet from the swollen leg of a sixty-two-year-old man. The lead musket ball had already been spreading its festering poison for four critical days.

"The danger now is gangrene," Rorke announced tersely. "Dr. Roxbury and I will repeat the debridement tomorrow and as long as necessary, but at the moment, we think we can avoid amputation."

"How did it happen?" Cavendish asked tiredly.

The fourth man at the table—the discreet, hard-working ducal secretary, Charles Garnett—cleared his throat fussily and reported the information it had taken half a day to accumulate. "During the three months Captain Huntington has been in Germany, King William issued another of his royal directives that made it a treasonable crime for an English ship to bring French products into England. On this trip, the *Lorelei*'s cargo was French wine and wrought iron from the de Laurent foundry. Both consignments had been ordered by Englishmen when such commerce was still legal. Had Captain Huntington told the London port authorities that his ship was also German-registered, there would have been no trouble; but for obvious reasons, he didn't want that fact to become public knowledge. When one of the inspectors threatened to confiscate his ship, Captain Huntington decided to make a run for it. He was shot just as he was reboarding his ship."

Without pause, Garnett continued his report with his dry, expressionless precision. Huntington had come to Newcastle to warn his other captains and to obtain medical help for himself. Both of those captains would leave Newcastle on the morning tide bound for Germany. The *Lorelei*'s cargo was being transferred to wagons for an overland delivery to its purchasers, and Garnett himself had dispatched letters to the duke's Parliamentary friends. Because of the need for secrecy, the secretary estimated it would take those men several months to clear Huntington of the charges. In the meantime, the *Lorelei* would remain in hiding just offshore until the captain was well enough to rejoin his crew.

When Garnett finished with his report, there was a brief silence as the members of his small audience related the news to their own problems. Henry Cavendish was the first to speak. "As always, Charles, you anticipate my wishes. Were you able to find out if Ramsey completed that errand in London we had discussed earlier?"

"The matter has been resolved and the delivery already made, Your Grace."

"What delivery, Charles, other than a letter?"

"The earl of Argyll, Sir Archibald Campbell, sent a sword engraved with the boar's-head crest of his clan, as well as the letter stating his willing acceptance of Dr. Campbell as the heir to his grandfather's estate and to his grandfather's title as an Argyll tacksman."

At Jolie's gasp, the duke smiled sardonically. "'Tis an old English custom to set a thief to catch a thief, m'dear.

Last spring, Ramsey and I decided to ask Argyll to protect
Dr. Campbell and you from his cousin Breadalbane. I'll
admit I didn't expect this degree of generosity, and I'm as
curious as a cat to know what your husband's reaction will
be. Is the sword an honorary ornament or a weapon,
Doctor?''

Rorke's responsive smile was caustically cynical. '' 'Tis a
superb weapon, Your Grace, and the earl of Argyll will
expect me to fight a damn superb war with it. That patch of
land is now covered with a hundred Breadalbane crofter
farms, and John Campbell will fight to the death of every
one of those crofters and all of their relatives before he'll
give up one foot of land. And the only help I'd get from
Archibald Campbell would be a handful of volunteers. He
won't dare risk the king's displeasure by attacking Breadalbane
openly, since he doesn't want to suffer the same fate as his
father and grandfather. They were beheaded by Charles II
and James II, respectively.''

"You don't wish to take your entitled place in Scottish
society?" Cavendish asked quietly.

"No, Your Grace. I've no desire to become a medieval
warlord. Scotland is a primitive country compared to England."

"Still," Cavendish concluded with satisfaction, "Argyll
has now been apprised of your existence and would undoubtedly offer you his protection should you require it.
However, as you must know, I much prefer the solution I
have arranged for your future. According to Thomas Pelham,
you're equally agreeable."

Aware that Jolie was staring at him with inquisitive eyes,
Rorke responded cautiously, '' 'Tis a generous offer, Your
Grace, and I thank you for it. But—''

"But you don't think William III is any more divine in
his judgment than his predecessors," Cavendish asserted
with a tired smile. "You and your wife are singularly
difficult to honor, Doctor. She was quite certain I'd lost
what little sense I had when she received her award tonight."

Embarrassed that her lack of gratitude had been so apparent, Jolie tried to explain. "I am not a Jeanne d'Arc. I am

grateful for the medallion, but I did not earn it, and I feel as if I'm intruding into your family."

"My daughter is not a gracious woman, m'dear, but believe me, you are most welcome to share Cavendish honor. So I'd appreciate your wearing it on occasion as a reminder of the delightful hours you guarded my health and entertained me. But now 'tis time for me to take responsibility for my own well-being and seek my bed." As everyone at the table automatically rose to assist the duke, he shook his head. "Perry is quite competent to see to my needs, and I've yet an assignment or two for the others of you."

To his aged family doctor, Cavendish nodded companionably. "Oliver, I'd appreciate your sleeping in the same room as Ramsey. He hasn't as yet acquired my patience with infirmity and might become obstreperous if he awakens before morning." To his secretary, the duke was more precise. "Charles, I want you to devise a cock-and-bull story that will keep that young scapegrace, Gordon Mayhew, from talking. He knows Ramsey was shot, but I don't want him to know the particulars, and I particularly don't want him snooping into Ramsey's private life. One more errand, Charles—you're to take the doctor and his wife to supper. Part of the *raison d'être* for that abomination of a ball tonight was to put an end to all the scurrilous canard about them. So perhaps you can make their entrance into the ballroom a memorable one."

Contrary to expectation, the memorability of that entrance had nothing to do with the gossip or gossipers or with Jolie's insistence on leaving the sedan chair in the hallway and walking into the ballroom unaided, thus displaying the magnificence of her gown for the second time. It was the sheathed sword Rorke was carrying in his hand that attracted the instant attention of the young officer friend of Gordon Mayhew. Like every man present who had spent his youth learning the art of sword fighting, George Redmond had acquired a love for the soon-to-be-obsolete weapon. Moreover, Redmond's sharp eye had recognized the sword as the classic product of the most exclusive of London armorers.

Within minutes both the sword and Rorke were surrounded by a dozen male guests, who actually listened with interest to Charles Garnett's explanation of Rorke's connection to the earl of Argyll. Even more respect was engendered a few minutes later when Captain Paxton and two of the household guards described the Scottish doctor's prowess in the use of a sword.

As mindlessly as a gaggle of geese—the dignified Scottish doctor included—the men drifted toward the momentarily empty end of the ballroom, and for the better part of an hour, dancing and dining were ignored in favor of the age-old sport of sword practice. The grudging admiration Rorke had earned as a skilled physician and surgeon paled in comparison to his instant acceptance as a premier sword fighter and a potential member of the Scottish aristocracy.

Left alone with the secretary and Gordon Mayhew, whose curiosity about Captain Huntington outweighed his interest in athletic competition, Jolie was amused by Garnett's easy persuasion of the younger man. "You were right about Huntington's bullet wound, Gordon," the secretary admitted candidly, "but the duke would appreciate your silence on the matter. The captain is embarrassed enough about the incident without any more public exposure. When he was attempting to instruct several of his crew in the use of firearms, he shot himself with his own pistol. I don't suppose he'd mind your talking if the action had been heroic, but as it is, he's an old man whose pride has been hurt. And now I suggest we get Mistress Campbell some wine and take her to supper before she tires of our company."

In the adjoining hall set aside for the munificent buffet supper, Jolie enthusiastically accepted Garnett's invitation, eating sparingly enough but exceeding her usually spartan allotment of wine several times over. By the time Rorke announced they were leaving, she light-headedly refused to use the sedan chair, walked without a limp or twinge to the carriage, and punctuated her nonstop conversation with giggles throughout the homeward drive. Walking up the stairs to their bedroom, she tripped only once and smiled at her husband without apology when he steadied her. Since he had overindulged a few times in the past, Rorke was tolerantly amused. The only effect the wine seemed to have had on her was to increase her enjoyment of a party situation she had found inhibiting in the past. She had charmed the brash young Mayhew and the dignified middle-aged secretary equally; and with an uncharacteristic tolerance, she'd exchanged friendly comments with some of the other women.

In the bedroom, her behavior differed even more from her normal routine. Usually meticulously neat about the care of her clothing, she left the separate parts of tonight's costume in untidy piles on the floor, and giggled irrepressibly as she dropped the two priceless medallions carelessly on the table.

"Those are valuable pieces of jewelry," Rorke scolded her.

Pulling off the last of her undergarments, Jolie shrugged indifferently. "They are useless ornaments, and your pretty new sword is almost as bad. You are not an Argyll and I am not a Cavendish or a de Laurent, except for my *grandpère*. *Ma foi*, when I wear those foolish things, I feel like a duck pretending to be a swan." Without a backward glance at her grinning husband, she pulled back the covers and climbed into bed.

"Aren't you going to put on your robe?" he asked with amusement. "Or warm the bed with the fire bricks?"

"I am already warm enough," she insisted airily.

"What you are is intoxicated, my inexperienced young wife, and what you're going to be tomorrow is damned sorry you let that young whippersnapper keep your goblet full of wine. Furthermore, you'll be blessed lucky if your ankle isn't swollen again and your hip as stiff as a board."

To Rorke's not-so-slight irritation, it was his head that was throbbing the next morning and his muscles that felt cramped and sore. An hour-long fencing exhibition after a difficult two-hour operation had taxed his strength more than Jolie's injudicious drinking spree had hers. And that strain had been further compounded by a passionate hour of lovemaking that had left him drenched in perspiration. When he had joined her in bed after shoving all the flannel-wrapped fire bricks beneath the covers, he'd thought his wife sound asleep, but she had quickly roused to that state wherein conscious thought is suppressed to a primitive level. His own desire, already well stirred by the sight of her slender, unclad body, surfaced in an automatic response he no longer questioned.

As Rorke pulled her to him, she kissed him with sleepy relaxation and pressed her body against his with soft insistence. When she began the sinuous movements of lovemaking, he worried only briefly about her injured shoulder and hip. At the moment, she seemed oblivious to all sensation other than the fire that was steadily building within her. Tonight her rhythm was languorously sensual, as if the wine had altered her inner clock to slow the tempo without reducing the passion. Women had a curiously different reaction to alcohol than men, Rorke reflected irrelevantly with the small part of his mind that was still objective. Wine might increase a man's desire, but it limited his performance, whereas a woman's performance seemed to be enhanced. Whimsically, he wondered if Jolie would remember. He knew he would—never before had he exerted this much control, and never had the buildup soared to such heights. When the rolling, hypnotic waves of ecstasy began for her, Rorke released his control and let the pulsing emotion fuse their bodies together. During the moments of peaceful void that followed, he remembered Jolie's words—"a gift from God."

Rorke's first waking impression was a flash of blue whisking industriously about the room. Reluctantly forcing his eyes open to check the empty space next to his own, he smiled at his wife with a grudging appreciation. She was already dressed in her working uniform, the room had been tidied, and she was not displaying a hint of distress. He checked the pattern of the late October sunlight on the wall and pushed himself out of bed with annoyed frustration. He was already late for his appointment at the castle. "Why didn't you wake me earlier?" he demanded.

"There was no need," Jolie responded calmly. "Dr. Roxbury sent word that Captain Huntington was sleeping peacefully and that you would not be needed until late afternoon."

"Damnation, Jolie, Roxbury can't tell the difference between natural and drugged sleep, and he still hasn't the vaguest understanding about the danger of lead poisoning."

"That is why I told the driver to return early, and also why I'll assist you in the debridement of the captain's wound. Now, eat your breakfast, *mon cher*, while I check on our other patients."

Next to his bowl of stirabout oatmeal and his hot cup of coffee, Rorke found a spoonful of powder he recognized as Soeur Marguerite's cure for headaches. Grimacing as he swallowed the bitter dosage, he wondered how much Jolie had taken to calm her own head. He had expected her to be groaning from her first encounter with the penalty of overindulgence; instead, she had awakened first and organized the day's activities for both of them. There were times, he reflected without any of the sentiment he had lavished on her the night before, that he wished she possessed more of the weaknesses common to other females and that her beloved Soeur Marguerite had not installed such a devotion to duty in her. Two hours later he was damned glad the crippled old nun had trained her favorite pupil so thoroughly.

Even with a healthy stomach, the recleansing of Captain Huntington's wound was a queasy task, but Jolie did not flinch throughout the painstaking process. Afterward, while Rorke responded to a summons from Charles Garnett, she volunteered to take Perry's place with the duke for an hour. By the time Rorke reached the secretary's office, his appreciation of his wife was once again intact. It grew steadily when Garnett handed him a letter, the contents of which described the most recent actions of Rorke's mother.

"How reliable is the man who wrote this letter?" Rorke asked dully.

"Alan Murray occupies the same position in a Scottish lord's household as I do in this one. He's well-educated, discreet, and honest to a fault. I know 'tis harsh to be told that one's mother can't be trusted with secrets, but I suspect you already know that about yours. And I don't suppose you're too shocked to learn she is frequently visited by Breadalbane's agents. Are you going to take Murray's offer to ship your mother here to avoid even more trouble in the uncertain future?"

"Even if I wanted her here—which I assuredly do not—she'd refuse to leave Scotland. 'Tis something only a Scot can understand, Charles. She's a clanswoman, and her loyalty's always been greater to Breadalbane than to me."

"Then a word of warning, Doctor. If you ever try to contact your mother directly, instead of sending her monthly allowance through Murray, don't be too trusting of His Majesty's postal service. 'Tis said that many of the coach drivers carry more news on their tongues than in the mail sacks, and that some of them are not above pilfering."

"Will this Murray fellow continue the service even after—?"

"That His Grace will soon be dead is hard for both of us to admit, Doctor, and afterward, I can give you no guarantees. Political loyalties are always too flexible to predict, particularly between England and Scotland."

"Then I'll make other arrangements as soon as possible. I imagine your life will be in greater upheaval than mine."

The secretary stared out at the small stretch of treed landscape visible through his narrow window. "I've been with His Grace for almost thirty years, and the prospect of starting over with someone else is quite terrifying."

Sitting alongside his wife on the homebound ride, Rorke felt a fortunate man compared to the middle-aged secretary; not even his concern for his mother's latest troublemaking weighed too heavily on his spirits. However, the packet of letters that had been delivered to the infirmary by one of the *Lorelei*'s officers destroyed all peace of mind for both him and Jolie. From the letters written by the members of Jolie's family in Strasbourg, Rorke learned officially that he had been condemned to death for what King Louis XIV called "treacherous espionage against the Crown." After sixteen months, the threat he'd thought long dead had been revived to add to Jolie's and his trouble, and all because of a pair of French brothers—the priest who had married them and the army colonel who had never been told that he was Jolie's stepfather.

"Henri de Guise was spiteful enough to blame you for his own failure to capture that last group of Huguenots you spirited out of France," Arnaud de Laurent had written, "and he still broods about losing what he calls the insolent foundling's fortune. *Mon dieu*, if he ever learns that my daughter is Jolie's mother, I could be forced to join you in exile. In the meantime, you may have worse problems than playing host to a gouty old man. I am afraid, *mon ami*, that both Henri's meddlesome brother François and I are equally the villains in this case. He notified Jolie's Scottish uncle of her marriage to you, and I was foolish enough to write to Lord MacDonald of my relationship to her. *Ma foi*, I wish you had told me not to mention the name MacDonald to the devious Breadalbane! After what that despicable villain did to you in Holland by accusing you of being one of the kidnappers, and after his scoundrel son tried to murder you in Edinburgh, I'd sooner have cut out my tongue than have caused you more trouble.

"The letter Breadalbane sent me starts out harmlessly enough by thanking me for delivering the ransom money to Baron Wallmond, but you'll note that most of it is devoted to trying to enlist my help in locating you and Jolie. A short time later, I received a letter from Alasdair MacDonald with the same request. I'm sending both letters to you so you can determine for yourself what action to take in the possible advent that my granddaughter needs protection from your dangerous relatives."

With a sense of dread, Rorke read Breadalbane's letter first. In the florid language of a politician, the earl had written fulsomely of his gratitude to Arnaud, and of his satisfaction that Rorke had married into so illustrious a

French family. Rorke's lips curled in contempt; the Grey
Fox had undoubtedly learned the exact extent of de Laurent
wealth.

"While I was in Flanders with King William," Breadalbane's letter continued, "I reminded His Majesty of the
debt of gratitude we owe to you and to Rorke for securing
the freedom of his Huguenot friends. It might please you to
know that the Reverend Abelard Darrell is now with the
king, lending his spiritual support to both His Majesty and
the soldiers. But of more immediate import, I am concerned
for the welfare of Rorke and your granddaughter. It grieves
me that he has lost the trust he once held for me and that he
removed his mother from my home without my knowledge.
I suspect by this time you may have received an account of
an incident that occurred last winter in Edinburgh, but I can
assure you that Rorke completely misunderstood my grandson's intentions. Tavis was merely attempting to persuade
his cousin to return to Kilchurn Castle and to tend to some
family business concerning his own estate. I regret to say
that Rorke has always been a bit hotheaded."

After Jolie read her grandfather's and Breadalbane's letters, her pithy comments echoed Rorke's sentiments. "My
grandpère talks too much, but your earl is a hypocrite and a
liar."

The letter from Alasdair MacDonald, heavily inked as if
written by a hand more accustomed to the sword than to the
pen, was both informative and cordial. In it, he stated that
he would welcome another Campbell into his family. His
son, Alasdair Og, had married a Campbell woman some
years before. He expressed no doubt about the identity of
Annette Marguerite MacDonald, since he'd known of her
existence for nineteen years. Her father had been Alasdair's
foster brother, the only son of his own father's dead brother.
Niall Angus and Alasdair had been raised together and
educated in France. But while Alasdair had been forced to
leave France when his father died, Niall had lived there
most of the following seventeen years and had embraced the
Protestant faith, in opposition to MacDonald tradition. At

his death, his estate had been set aside for his daughter, who need only to return to Glencoe to reclaim her birthright and to take her place as an honored member of the clan. Her husband, too, would be most welcome, since physicians were always needed in the Highlands.

Jolie's reaction to this letter was an explosive denial of that "birthright" and a succinct observation that all clan leaders sounded like medieval warlords. "We'd be as much prisoner in his Glencoe as we'd be at Breadalbane's Kilchurn Castle," she complained. Vaguely disappointed that her father had been an older man and not the romantic young adventurer she'd secretly pictured, Jolie felt more alienated from her Scottish relatives than before.

Not even the letters from the Strasbourg infirmary gave her any comfort. Charlotte expressed a fervent relief that Jolie was happily married and far away from France and the discipline of the church.

Marguerite's sharp wit, however, had not been dulled or silenced. "The fools threatened to declare my medicines heretic poison until the holy mother arrived with her annual bout of ulcerated carbuncles. After I let her suffer for three days, she declared my special wine to be a blessed sacrament. How I envy the freedom you and your husband have to practice medicine unhampered by religious pygmies."

Jolie sighed as she handed these letters to Rorke. Despite the love expressed by the two women who had been her guardians, their messages had been explicit—she could never again return to the infirmary, not even for a visit in the distant future.

Rorke's concern was more immediate; it dealt with the uncertain present. Breadalbane's vague promise to return the estate he had stolen was nothing but a lure. Like the earl of Argyll, he would promise the world, but deliver nothing in the way of a reward for a lowly doctor who had defied him. John Campbell's intentions were the same as they had been since he had first learned of Jolie's connection to the MacDonald clan: he was determined to achieve a clan victory through her. Rorke experienced a chilling apprehension at the thought.

Although MacDonald's letter had contained no threats, Rorke knew that the six-foot, seven-inch giant who ruled the Glencoe clan was as sly and acquisitive as Breadalbane. If he decided that he wanted Jolie under his control, Alasdair MacDonald wouldn't hesitate to use violence to gain that end. But of the two clan leaders, Rorke would sooner trust the son of the man who had destroyed Rorke's own family. A thief he might be, and a murderer on occasion if he followed his clan's tradition, but at least Alasdair MacDonald did not have any reason to harm Jolie or to murder her husband.

During the ensuing weeks, tension at the infirmary and the castle increased daily. The first major disruption in Jolie's and Rorke's professional lives was the departure of their two most valued nurses. Imperfectly concealing his impatience to return to London, Lord Somerton visited his son every day; and in the process, he learned to appreciate the talents of the educated sisters, Mercia and Esther. While the women were reluctant to leave, the salaries offered were too generous to refuse. Both Rorke and Jolie encouraged them to accept Lord Somerton's offer to care for and tutor his sons.

With a reduced staff and with the increased demands of their two patients at the castle, Rorke and Jolie were forced to limit their practice within the community, but no one in Newcastle voiced any complaints. The residents were nervously aware of the tense drama being played. While they dreaded the prospect of having the king appoint a new duke who might be indifferent to their needs, the rumors about Captain Huntington were far more disturbing. Like any port city where captains and their ships supplied the lifelines of commerce, the threat of still more government control frightened even the most successful of the mariners. The rumor that the king, whom few townspeople really trusted, had ordered his men to confiscate the entire fleet of Ramsey

Huntington, the richest and most powerful captain among them, had an electrifying effect. And on the day an armed frigate of His Majesty's royal navy sailed into Newcastle Harbor, a messenger was on his way to the castle even before the vessel dropped anchor.

Henry Cavendish's response was an instantaneous defense of his oldest friend, and his solution to the problem involved Rorke and Jolie in still another crisis not of their making. They were asked to escort the recuperating Huntington on the eight-mile overland trip to the coast and to enlist the aid of the smuggler who had ensured their own safe entry into England almost a year earlier. The smuggler, in turn, would locate the *Lorelei* and arrange for the captain to be taken aboard his ship without arousing suspicion. For two days the doctor and nurse tended their patient in the crowded quarters of the smuggler's home, as relieved as Huntington himself when the ship was finally sighted.

During the last few hours, the Campbells refused Huntington's invitation to accompany them to his home in Germany. "I don't have Henry's sublime faith in the generosity of kings," he warned them. "Henry believes the king will approve of the infirmaries; I stopped trying to predict what kings would do many years ago. I'd not be able to return you to England until my own altercation with the English throne is resolved and my son can safely resume his life in Newcastle. But you'd be most welcome in my home, and your professional services would be greatly appreciated."

Rorke shook his head regretfully. The arrival of the royal ship had refocused his own attention on the uncertain future, but he was not yet willing to become a homeless refugee. "Jolie and I are already committed to remaining with His Grace as long as necessary. Besides, our need is for a permanent solution, not for another temporary hiding place. If we're unlucky about the infirmaries and we still have reason to fear Breadalbane's further interference in our lives, we'll relocate in a less obvious part of England."

Jolie's farewell to the urbane German-Englishman held a note of sadness; he'd been as much a friend to her as to

Rorke. "*Au revoir*, Monsieur Huntington. I wish we could
go with you, but it is not meant to be. Perhaps in the future,
we'll be able to help each other again." Unable to repress
the unaccustomed tears that blurred her eyes, she mumbled
more softly, "You must not worry about the duke—he will
know how you feel."

Ramsey Huntington's thoughts as he was helped aboard
the *Lorelei* were about the young Frenchwoman waving to
him from the shore. In the past, she'd both challenged and
amused him with her candor and her rebellious determination to have an unhampered career in medicine. Despite his
condescension to women in general, he had learned to
respect her courage and her obvious ability; and throughout
his own painful recovery, he had appreciated her as a skilled
nurse. But today, she had revealed a sensitive understanding
far beyond her tender years. She had known that he was
already grieving for a friend who would soon be lost to him.

Rorke's decision to return to the infirmary instead of to
the castle kept him from learning the ironic truth about the
mission of the royal ship for forty-eight hours. By the time
he notified Henry Cavendish that Captain Huntington had
escaped safely, the naval frigate had pulled anchor and
sailed from Newcastle Harbor, leaving four Flemish envoys
of William III and half a dozen dignitaries from the English
Parliament behind. The pending death of one of the king's
privy council members, once it was officially known, was
never a private matter. The news that the second duke of
Newcastle was terminally ill held great interest for the
Parliamentarians because there were no bloodline heirs and
because few of these ruling aristocrats trusted the new king
to deal fairly in awarding the estate.

When Rorke arrived at the castle, he knew nothing about
these investigators or their purpose in coming to Newcastle.
Like the other townsmen, he still thought Huntington had
been the target. Just outside the duke's bedroom, an exhausted
Dr. Roxbury informed him that Huntington had not been
mentioned and that the "flock of vultures" had known

nothing about him. "But 'tis better anyway," the aged family retainer added, "that the good captain is safely away. His Grace did not want his friend to be here at the end to witness the indignity."

"How is the duke?" Rorke asked quietly.

"He collapsed within an hour of the captain's departure and has not left his bed since. I've not let the vultures in to talk to him."

"Does he know why they're here?"

"Aye. He's always known that no king could resist such an easy plunder. 'Tis why he proposed what he did to you and why he wanted young Lord Holles to be named his heir."

"Did the king agree to either proposal?" Even as he asked the question, Rorke was dismally skeptical.

"Mr. Garnett has been in conference with the king's envoys every day since they arrived, but as yet, they've answered neither question."

"Where are they staying, Oliver?"

"Here at the castle," the old man blurted with pent-up bitterness. "Their kind wouldn't spend their own brass for public accommodations—not when there's free lodging for the taking. 'Tis why I've not left these quarters—for fear one of them would shove Perry aside and add still more misery to His Grace's burden. Will you see him now, Rorke? I doubt you can fan the spark of life by much, but 'twill be a comfort to him anyway."

In a voice that was little more than a breathy whisper, the duke asked about his friend even before Rorke reached the bed, and expressed his gratitude with a tired smile. But when the Scottish doctor attempted an examination, the duke of Newcastle shook his head. " 'Twill do no good, Doctor, I've need only for your friendship now." With the gentle acceptance of someone who no longer fears death, the nobleman closed his eyes and drifted into sleep.

That the activities of everyone in the castle were being carefully monitored by the Flemish envoys who had taken charge was instantly apparent to Rorke as he stepped outside the duke's room. The soldier who brusquely ordered him to report to the library wore the uniform of the king's guard and spoke heavily accented English. When the man insisted on following him, Rorke felt as he had in France, when he had been declared a criminal and relentlessly hunted by the special dragonades of Louis XIV. Whether by accident or design, upon his arrival in a library crowded with grim-faced men, Rorke was greeted in the Flemishly accented Dutch language and handed a scroll sealed with the royal signet.

Even before Rorke had finished reading the document, the harsh voice of one of the Parliamentarians broke the tense silence. "What does His Royal Majesty say about the infirmaries, Dr. Campbell?"

"Nothing," Rorke snapped with a bitterness that was just beginning to twist his insides. "Nothing at all about the infirmaries. Instead, when these gentlemen make the order official, I will travel overland to the port of Hull and board a troop transport ship that will take me to the battlefields of Flanders, where my medical skills will be put to use. It would seem, gentlemen, that the king's polyglot army has suffered additional losses and is facing another winter in the cold, wet Lowlands. On the advice of his most trusted followers, the king has decreed—"

"Which advisers?" the same Parliamentarian demanded.

"The first one mentioned is Reverend Abelard Darrell, a Huguenot minister I brought out of France on my last mission there. Because I escorted him and his followers only as far as Holland, he has accused me of dereliction of duty. At the time, my life was being threatened by—"

"Aye, we know the story and we detest the troublemaking preacher," the man interrupted impatiently. "Who was the other adviser?"

"The man who threatened to send me back into danger by ordering me to lead his private army in the rescue of his grandson, and who has threatened my life ever since—the earl of Breadalbane. For five years, gentlemen, even before William became king, I served the Crown in a capacity far more dangerous than battlefield surgery. I had hoped I was finished with—"

This time it was another of the Flemish envoys who interrupted. "Dr. Campbell, we do not like either the Pastor Darrell or the Scotsman Breadalbane any more than you do. It is the king's orders we must obey, just as you must. You have ten days in which to settle your affairs and prepare yourself for the discomfort of the battlefield. In the meantime, we suggest you do not risk the danger of having the charge of treason added to the one of dereliction of duty, however falsely it was earned."

Rorke's thoughts were the violent ones of open defiance as he made his way out of the library, which was now the scene of an angry debate. The promises being made by the furious Parliamentarians that they would soon strip the king of the power to waste English money and men in a Flemish war was of little comfort to the doctor who had just lost his freedom. Instead of offering him the position that would have guaranteed him a secure career, the king had ordered him once again into danger. Instead of heeding the advice of an English nobleman whose family had served the crown far beyond the call of duty, William had chosen to listen to the self-seeking Breadalbane, whose loyalty was always to whichever side promised the greater reward, and to a religious fanatic who had almost cost Rorke his life in France.

The regard Rorke had once held for the monarch England had chosen plummeted to contempt. A loyal Dutchman despite his royal English mother and wife, William cared little for his English and Scottish subjects, except as soldiers who could help him win back the Flemish territories he had lost to Louis XIV. Physically, the austere prince of Orange had always repulsed Rorke, who had developed a keen distrust of leaders who seemed more partial to pretty men than to beautiful women. On the two occasions the Scottish doctor had seen the king, William had lavished honors on youthful aristocrats who had done little to earn them, but he had been coldly arrogant about demanding sacrificial services from those less favored. Rorke did not look forward to serving such a despot again.

As much as he hated the thought of rendering battlefield service to an incompetent military leader, Rorke's greatest worry concerned Jolie's safety. While he had contemplated a hundred other potential dangers when the duke of Newcastle could no longer protect them, not once had he considered the possibility that he would be sent to war, leaving a vulnerable young wife behind. When a terse voice interrupted his stormy thoughts, Rorke spun around to confront an angrily sympathetic Charles Garnett.

"The foreign devils wouldn't answer any of my questions, so I couldn't give you warning. Had we not rushed to get Captain Huntington safely away, you could have gone to Germany with him," the secretary commiserated.

"No, the Rhine River is still patrolled by French gunboats. Neither Jolie nor I would have been safe, even aboard the *Lorelei*."

"You can't leave her in Newcastle, Rorke. All too obviously, Breadalbane schemed to separate you. Have you thought about sending her to the earl of Argyll? He sounded willing enough to help in the letter that accompanied the gift of your sword."

"I don't know the man, other than by reputation, and I can't risk Jolie's life by sending her to a stranger—particularly to a Campbell who's related to Breadalbane. There's only one man in England or Scotland who can keep her safe, Charles—the head of her own family clan, Alasdair MacDonald. But damn, I've only ten days, and I've no way of getting even a message to a remote valley in the Highlands, much less getting Jolie there."

" 'Twould be no problem about the message, Rorke, and if you supply the money for their transportation, I'm certain MacDonald will send enough soldiers to give her safe escort."

"Where can you find an English messenger who knows enough about the geography of the Scottish Highlands to avoid getting himself killed?"

"This man's not English, Rorke. He's a Scotsman, like yourself, and he hates Breadalbane equally. He's a MacGregor whose clan was exterminated by your greedy relative. Two years ago, we hired him to seek out information about John Campbell, and he's worked for His Grace ever since. 'Twas he who located Breadalbane's oldest son, Duncan, who'd been disinherited over some trifling dispute and who vowed vengeance. 'Twas this MacGregor and Duncan Campbell who proved that Tavis was Breadalbane's son, rather than a grandson. And 'twas he who—"

Interrupting the uncharacteristically verbose explanation, Rorke asked impatiently, "How soon can this man be ready to leave?"

"By afternoon, if you'll allow me to write the letter while you secure the money you think necessary."

Jolie's reception of the news was explosively negative, and her rebellious mind quickly devised alternatives. Rorke shook his head in rejection at each of her suggestions, trying not to add to her fear. "If we flee to another English town or city, or even to a distant English colony, I would be labeled a traitor and hunted down. Nor would we be any safer in Holland or in France, where there are already warrants for my arrest," he argued firmly.

"Then I'll stay right here and operate the infirmary," she declared stubbornly.

"Nay, sweetheart. Aside from the fact that the other doctors would condemn you for practicing medicine, you'd be without any protection against Breadalbane. Tomorrow we'll close the infirmary."

"What about our equipment and our people?" she demanded.

"Our present lease has another year to run, and the goldsmith will renew it for us if necessary. I've already hired Hugh and Turner to stay on as caretakers, and Charles Garnett is helping the others to find positions. As of this moment, sweetheart, we're out of the infirmary business."

"It will seem empty without patients."

"We won't be here to notice. I've been ordered to remain at the castle, and you'll be staying with me. I don't suppose we'll have much privacy; 'tis as crowded there as a London inn during a coronation. But at least we'll be together, and you'll be staying on there after I've gone."

Those last eight days together were the saddened ones of a deathwatch, and what private time they had in the crowded fortress was spent in the bittersweet regret of parting lovers, as uncertain of the future as they'd been sixteen months earlier when they'd been forced into marriage. Of the pair, Jolie was the more cheerful, her resignation of the day before replaced by still another plan. Lacking Rorke's knowledge of Highland terrain and clan isolation, she'd already determined to return to Newcastle and reopen the infirmary for women patients only should she find Glencoe too repressive. With a flexible conscience, she reasoned that until her husband's return, she owed obedience to no one but herself.

When Jolie had moved their baggage into the small room allotted to them at the castle, now crowded by an ever-increasing army of the duke's friends, she had discovered that Rorke's prediction of limited privacy was an understatement. They would be sharing the room with the two young officers she had met at the hunt ball. Both Gordon Mayhew and George Redmond had been recalled to the Flanders battlefield, much to the angry consternation of their aristocratic parents. And both men were more than willing to tell Jolie about their earlier experiences in the king's service. All Rorke had told her was that, as a doctor, he'd be in no danger.

"The French have pushed our forces over half of Flanders, so who knows where 'twill be safe," Redmond said disconsolately.

"Most of the time the camps are no safer than the fields. French cannon could pick us off any place their cannoneers aimed them," Mayhew added.

"David against Goliath," Redmond obliquely criticized

the new king. "Only our David doesn't know how to use a slingshot."

"The only ones who are safe are those lucky enough to be assigned to guard our beloved monarch, but 'twas not a job to my liking," Mayhew confessed with a sly wink to his friend. "King William's not a coward," he added hastily, "but he and his preachers don't believe in taking any chances with their own lives."

Thus fortified with firsthand information, Jolie resolved to make her farewell to her husband a memorable one. Unashamedly, she joined him in bed whether the time be morning, noon, or night. With small regard for the sensibilities of servants and other guests, who might think such activities inappropriate in a house of approaching death, she boldly initiated the caresses that forced her husband to forget his natural inclination to shun intimacy in a somewhat public situation.

" 'Tis not private enough, sweetheart," he had protested the first time. "Remember that we share this room with our two young warriors."

"They will not disturb us," she responded airily. "And they promised to keep the others away when I explained to them that it is to be our first time apart."

Laughing helplessly at her lack of inhibition, a character trait he had gradually learned to accept, Rorke capitulated and followed her lead. She was so vitally alive and so essential to his peace of mind, he wasn't sure he could endure the horrors of battle-injured men without her by his side. Before her entry into his life, and even during the problem-plagued Rhine River voyage, he had accepted the realities of a violent world with philosophical resignation. But happiness had destroyed much of his old courage, and he dreaded a separation from her as much as he feared for her safety.

During their last hours together, just before his departure, Jolie was unrestrainedly passionate in both word and deed. She stripped her uniform off with speed and stood before him slimly and gracefully nude.

"I do not want you to forget me, *mon amour*," she asserted firmly. "I do not think that plump Dutch women will be so pretty, but they are there and I will not be."

Even as Rorke's lips curved widely into a smile of appreciation, his dark blue eyes glowed with the inner fire she aroused in him. She still didn't know how beautiful and alluring she was with her tawny-russet curls freed from restraint, her piquant face alive with challenge, and her slim, muscular body boldly displayed.

"I'll not forget you," he promised solemnly, adding silently as he opened his arms to her, "as if I ever could."

"Then I will try not to hate your King William, who is, I think, an idiot without honor," she declared softly, completing her thought with a flash of impudent humor. "Perhaps, if you purge him often enough with wormwood and castor oil, he will not be so eager to separate us again."

Rorke was laughing as he bent to kiss her. She'd never be easily conquered—not even by the fierce Alasdair MacDonald, whose very name aroused fear in most Scots. She had enough of the same MacDonald fire to bow to no man, and to retaliate with action should words fail.

The minutes ticked by swiftly as their bodies welded together with a poignant intensity. They were both aware of the impending wrench of separation, and determined to make these moments of parting memorable. Not once but twice they climaxed together in a unity that was as much spiritual as physical, and they sought no other expression of farewell when the appointed hour of departure arrived.

Although Jolie did not collapse into hopeless tears, she felt a desolation that numbed her. For the first time since she had left Strasbourg, she fled into the sanctuary of a church— the stone chapel within the castle. What prayers she mumbled there were private ones and not the ritualistic chants she had learned during childhood. Curiously, it was the odd sensation that she was not alone that gave her solace, and she wondered how many other women through the centuries had come here to pray when their men had gone to war. She closed her mind to the shadowy question of how many had come to weep when their husbands and sons had not returned. True to her self-reliant nature, Jolie vowed that the months of separation from her husband would not be wasted. Straightening her uniform, she walked with a brisk step toward the duke's sickroom.

5

A week later Sister Jolie was holding Henry Cavendish's hand when he died quietly. His last words had been a whispery expression of gratitude for her care. In the days following Rorke's departure, Jolie had found a curious solace in tending the sick nobleman. Seated close enough to his bed to hear the occasional requests of her undemanding patient had reminded her of the early years at the Strasbourg infirmary. Even as a child, she had felt no fear of death and no revulsion for the old nuns who had come to the infirmary to die. Perhaps it had been their calm acceptance of the inevitable that had given the impressionable young girl a measure of tolerance many of the other nurses had lacked. Jolie hadn't minded that Soeur Claire had been childish or that Soeur Felicia's face had been hideously disfigured by cancerous sores. Performing the simple chores Soeur Marguerite had assigned, the child Jolie had remained by the bedside as long as the dying women requested her attendance. Those hours had not been wasted ones; the young nurse had acquired the comforting philosophy that death was not always the enemy, to be fought with medicine and surgery. Although she never fully understood the concept of immortality or the reasons for the priestly rituals of extreme unction, she gradually developed the simple faith that for sick old people, death was a merciful release offered by a merciful God.

More than any of the others who tended him or who sought to confer with him, Henry Cavendish had been most grateful to Sister Jolie, who had been a source of entertainment for all of the ten months he had known her. She was the only one who spoke in a formal voice rather than the depressingly sepulchral tones usually reserved for the tomb. While Dr. Roxbury, who had accompanied the Campbell family into exile, looked funereally sad to be losing the last male member of the once large family, Sister Jolie was invariably cheerful. After her husband's departure—Henry had experienced a sharp pang of guilt when he had learned of the king's perfidious action in ignoring his petition to establish small hospitals—he had expected her to be tearfully sad. But when she visited him several hours later, she had sparked with a treasonable disapproval of all kings.

"It is not *le bon dieu* who gives them the right to make war—it is the stupid men who make such imbeciles into kings."

Lacking sufficient energy to laugh, Henry had smiled wanly in agreement. He had been one of those fools who had deposed the Catholic James, only to burden England with a Dutchman who had as little regard for English common law as the most despotic of the Stuarts. But his irrepressible nurse had not allowed him to brood about national affairs he could no longer direct. She had read to him from the lighthearted comedies his own brilliant father had written after the Restoration, and from the escapist essays his remarkable stepmother had composed. To his shame, Henry had never had the inclination to read them for himself. As he'd listened to her pleasantly accented voice as she read from them, he drifted backward into a happier time in his life. She also read and reread the several letters Ramsey Huntington had written just before he had left England—letters about the escapades and adventures the two men had shared during their youth.

Only after his death did Jolie learn that the duke of

Newcastle's gratitude was more concrete than the mumbled words he had spoken. Even as the official dignitaries were organizing the state funeral, and the Flemish envoys were taking inventory of the Newcastle estate, Charles Garnett was doing his best to fulfill the promise he had made to Rorke to protect Jolie until the MacDonald soldiers arrived. Unfortunately Lady Holles, who had reached Newcastle just hours before her father's death, had ordered the secretary to remove the Frenchwoman from the castle as quickly as possible. In a hasty conference with Bailiff Wickham and Captain Paxton, it was decided that Sister Jolie would be safer if she stayed in her own infirmary. There were too many strangers moving in and out of the castle and more arriving daily; any one of them could be a Breadalbane agent. With a heavy heart, Garnett escorted her to a waiting carriage and handed her the small chest he had concealed beneath his robe. Jolie opened it and stared at the gold coins. She whispered an awed, "*Ma foi!*"

"His Grace didn't trust the vultures to reward his friends properly," the secretary explained with sad candor. "Take care, mistress. 'Twill not be as safe a world as it was."

Jolie was thoughtful as she ordered the driver to take her into the shopping center of town and to wait for her while she completed some errands. Three blocks away from where the carriage was parked, she stepped into the recessed entry of Nathan Morris's goldsmith shop and pulled the bell rope. When Rorke had first brought her here, she had thought that the private entry, barred windows, and locked door were exaggerated precautions, but now she appreciated the security. The substantial sum of money she and Rorke had stored in the vaults would be safe from grasping hands as long as need be.

An unsmiling man, the goldsmith himself opened the door for her and escorted her politely into the counting room before he spoke.

" 'Tis over then, Mistress Campbell?"

"He died three hours ago, Monsieur Morris."

"Aye." The goldsmith sighed heavily. "I thought as

much. 'Twas just slightly later that the king's envoys were here to close out the duke's accounts. I trust you've not come on a similar mission concerning your own money.''

Jolie shook her head and removed the small chest from its concealment. Gravely, the merchant counted the coins and nodded in approval.

''He was a generous man, our duke, and he wanted his friends to share his fortune. At least this way, some of it will escape the death taxes our needy king demands. Will you be putting all of it into my keeping?''

''All except a few coins, monsieur.''

''Will you be going to Scotland, as your husband said?''

Glumly, Jolie nodded. ''Only if I must. Did my husband tell you to keep our money safe until we return?''

''Aye, he told me, and he told me of his problems with the earl of Breadalbane. Your fortune will be safe; I never betray the confidence of a client. How much of the coin will you be needing?''

''Fifty guineas, monsieur. Are these the same coins that are used in the Scottish Highlands?''

''They have some of their own, but gold is always accepted by merchants.''

''I was thinking of ships' captains, not merchants,'' she murmured. On a sudden impulse she pulled the two medallions from beneath her robe. ''Would they also take these in payment, monsieur?''

Inspecting the ornaments with an expert's eye, the goldsmith nodded. ''The one from His Grace the duke I cast myself, so I know its worth. And as I told you when I first saw it, the other one is even more valuable. Either one of them would pay for a ship's passage to the distant colonies and back, so take care you're not cheated.''

''I won't be,'' Jolie promised grimly.

''Then until there's need, you'll be wise to keep them hidden. 'Tis a small fortune you're wearing about your neck, and there are thieves aplenty in Scotland with few enforcers to regulate their trafficking. 'Tis not like England, where there are gibbets waiting to punish the scoundrels.''

Jolie remembered the goldsmith's gloomy words as she visited the baker's and butcher's shops on her way to the carriage. She recalled them even more vividly when she walked into the infirmary and found four strangers waiting for her.

Rorke's lack of enthusiasm for military service had not gone unnoticed, and the most officious of the Flemish envoys had taken steps to prevent his desertion by assigning Lieutenants Mayhew and Redmond as his escort. Since both men were career officers in the royal national army, their loyalty to King William was unquestioned despite their grumbling. Lacking any such assurance about Dr. Campbell, whose presence at the battlefront had been the more urgently requested, the envoy had made certain that the doctor and his pretty wife did not leave the castle surreptitiously and disappear into the still-unpatrolled areas of northern England.

On the morning of departure, the envoy himself rode with them to the boundary of Newcastle lands and watched as the small procession headed south on the main highway. That precaution had resulted from an unpleasant scene in the castle library the night before, when Lord Mayhew and Sir Redmond had loudly protested their sons' premature return to battle. The resentment of the two fathers had been particularly acute when they had been told that their lieutenant sons had been needed to perform escort duty for Dr. Campbell. Fearful that the two English aristocrats might try to countermand the orders, the chief envoy had overseen the farewells at the castle and been vastly relived that his fears had been groundless.

Throughout the incident, the envoy had avoided arousing Rorke's suspicion by telling the young officers that they were the doctor's protectors, not his prison wardens. Amused by that polite fiction, since Rorke was far more experienced in weaponry than they were, Gordon Mayhew and George Redmond had performed their duty lightheartedly, despite their envy that they lacked the consolation of wives as pretty as Mistress Campbell. As they bid farewell to their respective fathers, they were relieved that the waiting was over, and they began the trip with a reckless sense of adventure. Neither of them noticed that their companion's face was grimly set. Rorke was a veteran of five years of dangerous missions, and he lacked the youthful exuberance of the younger men.

During the first five days of the six-day overland trip from Newcastle to Kingston-upon-Hull, Rorke and his two companions had maintained a steady pace, despite the blustery winds and rain squalls of late fall. The officers were expert horsemen who knew the coastal roads and the available inns along the way. Since he hadn't ridden a horse in almost a year and a half, Rorke would have preferred shipboard travel. But Newcastle was not one of the designated ports of troop muster, and he lacked the papers necessary to travel aboard a civilian ship. Moreover, the horses would be needed for transportation in Flanders.

Mounted astride one horse and leading two others burdened with his luggage, Rorke ignored his aching muscles and concentrated on keeping up with his companions. Each night he spent an hour soaking in the hot bath he cajoled every landlord into supplying him. It was during these hours alone that he remembered Jolie most vividly, and missed her with a sense of irreparable loss. He had no illusions about what lay ahead for him—the prince of Orange had a twenty-year history of losing his battles against the forces of Louis XIV. This year he'd lost the fortress town of Mons and been defeated in every skirmish since, yet still he persisted in remaining in the country of his birth. The only use he had for England and Scotland at the moment was the acquisition of money to support his war and soldiers to fight in it.

That he was successful in securing soldiers was evident by the numbers Rorke and his companions passed along the way, all headed for the port of Hull. There had been a hundred-man mounted troop supplied by the duke of Northumbria, a two-hundred-strong cavalry contingent from the Campbell earl of Argyll, and smaller groups of straggling foot soldiers called up by individual towns and shires.

With that reservoir of manpower, Rorke reflected gloomily, the war could last for years, and he'd be trapped in the middle of it without hope of reprieve. He thought of the fate he had decreed for his spirited and rebellious wife—perhaps years of being a cosseted prisoner in the Highland stronghold of the Glencoe MacDonalds—and shuddered with foreboding. God alone knew if they would ever again share the challenging future they'd planned so carefully.

A few hours' ride from the diked port city of Kingston-upon-Hull on the seventh day of travel, Rorke was suddenly faced with the probability that for him, there might not be a future of any kind. Riding hard to reach their destination before nightfall, the three men were halfway through a stretch of forest roadway when they were ambushed. So swiftly were they surrounded by a mixture of men on horseback and on foot that neither Rorke nor the two officers had the time to draw a sword or pistol. They were pulled from their horses and disarmed in seconds, their hands secured behind them and their mouths gagged with lengths of dirty cloth. Minutes later they were led deeper into the concealing underbrush beneath a cover of oak and beech trees.

Although none of them had been harmed thus far, Rorke felt a chilling fear as he watched the practiced efficiency of the captors. They inspected the contents of the various pieces of luggage with the expert appraisal of shopkeepers before piling each container on the bed of a wagon. After exchanging the fine leather saddles on the three captive riding horses with motley ones from their own mounts, they led those and the nervous pack animals deeper into the woodland, away from the main body of men. What occurred next both terrified and puzzled the captive prisoners. Within clear sight of the road, three separate piles of loose dirt were hastily molded into oblong mounds two feet wide and six feet long, and the captured swords were driven into the ends of each mound. Rorke watched with a sense of doom as his prized sword, bearing the Argyll crest, was ignominiously plunged into the dirt.

As grimly silent as they had been throughout, the brigands untied their victims' hands long enough to strip their clothing off and to force the shivering captives to don the coarse garb of common seamen. Immediately after, the prisoners were bound hand and foot, lifted onto the bed of the wagon, and covered with an odorous, tar-impregnated tarpaulin. With barely enough air to sustain life, Rorke and the two officers lay in abject terror, listening to the sounds around them. They never saw the powerfully muscled man who had watched the proceedings on horseback, but they heard his harsh voice clearly when he rode over to the wagon.

"Dr. Campbell, if ye value yer own life and those of yer mates, ye'll not move or make a sound. If ye're lucky, ye'll be spendin' the next few years aboard ship, if the captain decides ye'll be of use. If ye're unlucky, ye'll be fillin' those mock graves in truth."

In the Stygian darkness that had descended on them when the tarpaulin had been lashed down, the prisoners struggled to control their terror. For Rorke, the fear was mingled with a burning hatred. Someone had paid to have him murdered; otherwise, the brigand leader could not have known his name. Ten minutes later he knew the identity of his would-be killer—the man who had paid highway cutthroats to do the job for him. Like his companions, Rorke lay rigidly still when they heard the sound of a hard-ridden horse approach the camp, and they listened tensely to the belligerent voice, heavily burred with a Scottish accent, that berated the brigand leader.

"Damn ye t' hell, Scully! I dinna want him buried. I told ye I wanted his body found, so there'd be no doubt of his death."

The man thus addressed responded with equal belligerence. "Ye're the fool, Campbell. There are wild animals in these parts that would strip the bones clean by morning and drag the remains into their burrows. I'll see the graves well marked with papers and such before we leave. Now, pay the money ye promised, Scotsman; 'tis not healthy to be seen near new-dug graves along this road.''

" 'Nothing was said about my paying for the other two. Ye should ha' let the pair of them escape.''

"Ye bloody ass, they were officers in the royal army. If we had let them go free, they would have alerted the whole of Hull and trapped the lot of us. Ye'll pay me for all three, or ye'll join them in the ground, and there'll be four graves for yer skirted soldiers from Scotland to find when they pass this way tomorrow.''

Raising his voice to a sharp command, the man called Scully shouted, "Get the wagon moving, mates. We're yet twenty miles from safety, with only three hours of daylight left.''

Just before the wagon began to move, Rorke heard one more exchange of dialogue. "Ye're a villainous scoundrel, Scully, and ye'll be hanging from a gibbet wi'in a month,'' the Scotsman shouted.

"Aye, with ye hangin' beside me. I'm just the executioner— ye're the cowardly murderer. But since ye've paid yer dues, begone with ye and leave us to finish the bloody job.''

Not for an agonizing hour of travel did Rorke analyze the oddities of Scully's words and realize that the brigands were naught but a skilled impressment gang who supplied ships' captains with crews. This time the ship would be pirate or smuggler instead of merchant or royal navy, since the port of Hull was twenty-two miles inland, where illegal ships dared not go. Instead, they anchored along the Hull River, twenty miles closer to the North Sea; hence the longer wagon trip Scully had mentioned.

Before his mind had begun to function logically, Rorke's thoughts had been the seething ones of raw hatred. He had recognized the voice of the murderous Giles Campbell, but his hot fury had been directed more toward the masters than toward the slavish servant. In Edinburgh, Giles had waited outside the room where Tavis had tried to murder Rorke; only if he had been ordered to assist in the killing would he have dared. In the present instance, he lacked both the brains to have contrived such a complicated plot or the will to have executed it without permission from Tavis Campbell or his father, the Grey Fox of Glenorchy—Sir John Campbell, the earl of Breadalbane. Giles Campbell was nothing but a distantly related clansman who had served as a Breadalbane soldier since his boyhood thirty years before. He had been the one who had first taught Rorke to use a sword, and he had led murderous raids against enemy clans whenever the earl had so ordered, but he had never initiated the action himself.

With a desperate hopelessness, Rorke wondered if Tavis had been hiding in the forest, watching as his henchman had cold-bloodedly ascertained the murder of three men, two of whom were sacrificial strangers without any ties to the Campbell clan. The sweat that beaded Rorke's face despite the numbing cold was not caused by fear of his own life; it came from the sick realization that Jolie would pay an even greater price because of his careless stupidity in not watching the road more closely. The thought of Tavis waiting until he was sure Rorke was dead before he went to Newcastle to kidnap the woman he had considered his property since the day he had met her twisted Rorke's gut until he felt physically ill. What a sanctimonious fool he'd been! When Jolie had suggested they employ another smuggler to transport them to the distant colonies, he had blathered some idiot drivel about not wanting to risk their lives by leaving England illegally. God's blood, they would have been safer crossing the North Sea in a rowboat than they were now!

Rorke's bitter self-recrimination vanished instantly as the wagon came to a halt. By force of habit, he focused his mind on the ordeal he sensed was only minutes away. His companions, too, were attempting to overcome the demoralizing terror of the brutal capture. More arrogant and less inhibited than his friend Redmond, Gordon Mayhew rasped the question with a biting resentment, "Who the bloody hell are these people, Campbell?"

Knowing that he had already been condemned as the Judas goat, Rorke responded with terse brevity. "The Scot is a killer named Giles Campbell, but the man responsible is the earl of Breadalbane—the same thieving nobleman who convinced King William to send for me."

"I meant the devils who are holding us now," Gordon snapped.

"You heard the same information I did, Mayhew. They're an impressment gang, and we're about to become crew members aboard some ship—a smuggler, or one of the other illegals, would be my guess—although 'tis the way most English ships gain their deck swabs. Any captain in need of crew replacements sends the word out, and criminals like Scully oblige by kidnapping unwary highway travelers and drunken farm workers."

"Then if it is only money these criminals want," Mayhew blurted with renewed hope, "my father would pay triple the price."

"Mention your father or Redmond's father, and you'll be tossed into the river like a sackful of unwanted kits," Rorke advised harshly. "Your fathers are aristocrats and magistrates. If common gossip holds true, English criminals hate both equally."

"They already know who we are," Mayhew insisted. "Our family crests were on our swords, and our names were written on the papers the bastards stole from us."

"The Scullys of the world can't read, Lieutenant, and 'tis doubtful they know one crest from another—or from the brainless scratching of a chicken," Rorke added in an inaudible mutter. His own sword had borne the crest of the Argyll Campbells, yet the earl of Argyll didn't know him, and more than likely wouldn't claim him as a clansman if it came to paying ransom. Painfully he tried to exercise his hands and feet, numbed both from the penetrating chill of early December and from the tight thongs that bound him. Momentarily he forgot the discomfort and his own despair when the more thoughtful George Redmond spoke softly.

"Do you think there's any chance for an escape, Dr. Campbell?"

Rorke's dismal "No" was lost in the abruptly noisy

activities of the captors as the protective tarp was yanked off and rough, callused hands pulled the prisoners from the wagon. Unable to stand on feet whose circulation had been cut off, Rorke leaned weakly against the wagon side and stared toward the pinpoints of lantern light that moved in a rhythmic pattern a hundred feet away. Only when his ears identified the lapping sound of water did he realize that the lanterns were hanging from the masts of a ship. A rough estimation of the size of the vessel made Rorke shudder with a cold apprehension that had nothing to do with the damp chill of the night air. It was a three-masted, double-decked frigate that seemed larger than any ship he'd ever seen before—the kind of ship built to house men and cargo on voyages to places on the other side of the globe. The full horror of his predicament crashed into Rorke's consciousness like an unrestrained bull: if he were imprisoned aboard that floating fortress, he could be at sea for a year with no hope of escape, no chance to send a message to Jolie that he was still alive.

Abruptly, for the second time in minutes, Rorke was forced to refocus his attention. Fifty feet away, the door to a small land structure was flung open, and the coarse, grating voice of the English criminal Scully broke the silence. "Bring the lads in, mates, and watch t' see they don't give ye the slip. Ye'll be deck swabs yerselves if e'en one of them gets away, and 'twill be a damn bloody search the night through to locate the bastard before he sounds an alarm."

As threatening as Scully's words were, it was the voice of an unseen man waiting within the small frame building that increased Rorke's apprehension. The voice was cultured, and the Dutch-accented words suggested an assured power far beyond that of most captains. "Dammit, Scully, I hired you to find me a doctor—no one else. Get rid of the others! I've no wish to do battle with a British frigate in her own waters."

As she walked into the receiving room of the infirmary, Jolie's first tremor of fear was accompanied by a hot flush of anger when she noted the livid bruises on the face of the older caretaker. Before any of the four strangers could speak, she demanded in a strident voice that belied both her slender form and her aristocratic forebears, "What murderous *cochon* did that to you, Hugh?"

Giving the cowed servant no time to reply, the only one of the intruders dressed as a gentleman with buckled shoes and white hose, rose precipitously from his chair and responded in the unctuous tones of self-assured authority.

"We were forced to reprimand the fool when he refused to assist us in our efforts to protect your wealth, Mistress Campbell," he murmured smoothly. "He stupidly pretended ignorance about the location of your strongbox."

There was no conciliatory relaxation of Jolie's defensive stance. "You are the imbecile, monsieur. We have no *strongbox* here. And who are you to dare such a search of my home?" she demanded.

"Allow me to introduce myself, mistress. I am Colin Carwhin, law agent to my laird, Alasdair MacDonald of Glencoe. I was sent here to give you safe escort to Scotland."

"Why didn't your Laird MacDonald come himself?"

For a moment, Carwhin studied the suspicious face of the woman he'd been told was a naive young girl. There was an alert intelligence in her eyes that made him cautious.

"Your uncle would not be safe in England, mistress," he explained apologetically.

"Did Laird MacDonald tell you he was my uncle, Monsieur Carwhin?"

Carefully the lawyer amended his earlier words, thankful that he'd had the foresight to do a little research about the woman's father. "The title *uncle* is a courtesy one, mistress. I'm sure you know that your father was only a cousin to Alasdair MacDonald."

Still vaguely suspicious, Jolie continued her questions. "Are you a MacDonald, monsieur?"

Again Carwhin hesitated, then answered evasively, "Most of us in Edinburgh no longer claim clan membership."

Gazing briefly at the three silent men standing behind the seated lawyer—men with the stolidly expressionless faces of professional soldiers, and whose dark leather trews and jackets bore no clan insignia—Jolie demanded, "Are these men MacDonalds?"

"Aye," Carwhin replied briefly.

"Why aren't they wearing anything to identify them?"

"'Twould not be safe in—" Abruptly the lawyer's explanation was interrupted by the arrival of the Newcastle carriage driver, burdened with the luggage Jolie had brought from the castle.

In the expressionless voice of a well-trained English servant, he asked politely, "Where do you want them stored, Mistress Campbell?"

That innocent question was never to be answered, and in the next few minutes, Jolie's distrust of Carwhin proved more than justified.

"Search those bundles," the lawyer ordered one of the soldiers, "and restrain the driver and the caretakers. No use arousing the local authorities before we're safely away. We'll release them an hour or so outside of town."

Carwhin's expression was no longer amiable as he returned his attention to Jolie. "Enough of foolish games, mistress. The Laird MacDonald wants your money safely stored under his supervision. Where have you hidden your hoard? The only coins we found were the ones your servant claimed as household funds. Now we want the rest."

With the same bravado she had employed long ago with the French dragonades on the river beach after Tavis Campbell had been shot and she'd been captured, Jolie resorted to subtle insolence. "That money you *stole* from my caretaker, monsieur, is all you'll find. My husband had the sense to store the rest with a goldsmith."

"There are four goldsmiths here in Newcastle, Mistress Campbell. Which one is it?"

"My husband never told me, Monsieur Carwhin."

Long expert at eliciting the truth from reluctant witnesses, the lawyer turned to the Newcastle driver. "Did you drive

Mistress Campbell to a goldsmith's shop on the way here? 'Twas four hours ago that the church bells announced your master's death; she had time for any number of errands in town.''

The frightened man nodded, but the only responses he gave were vague mumblings about a baker and a butcher. Silently Jolie blessed the subterfuge Rorke had taught her of never revealing the location of their money, even to loyal servants. Just as silently, she offered the bundles she was still holding to the lawyer. As he reached out to accept them, she opened the cloth covering to reveal a loaf of bread and a cut of meat.

"My supper, monsieur," she murmured.

Defeated by what he was certain was a trick, Carwhin asked more casually, "Is your jewelry also hidden at the goldsmith's?''

Even as she remembered the costly medallions hidden beneath her uniform robe, Jolie shook her head. "I have no jewelry, monsieur, except my cross and rosary. Since Laird MacDonald is as Catholic as I am, perhaps he will allow me to keep *them*—or were you told to steal everything of value?''

"As I told you before, he is interested only in protecting your wealth from English thieves.''

"Well, then, since I do not have any wealth to bring him, he might be happier that I do not come at all.''

"Nay, mistress, my laird wants you safe in Scotland. We'll find a legal means of securing your fortune at a later date. Right now, you'll order your servants to pack what belongings you wish to take. 'Twill be a long and miserable drive to Edinburgh.''

6

Of all the clandestine and often illegal acts he'd been required to perform as law agent to the earl of Breadalbane, Colin Campbell of Carwhin quickly discovered that the most nerve-racking was the abduction of Annette MacDonald Campbell. Having made careful preparations that included every possible exigency he could conceive, he had expected no complications in such a simple assignment. He had known almost to the day when Rorke Campbell would leave Newcastle for Flanders. Breadalbane had taken no chances that the king might change his mind about sending for Rorke; he'd convinced William to let him arrange for the delivery of the royal summons in Newcastle.

Ironically, before the duke of Newcastle had petitioned the king to permit Dr. Campbell to establish infirmaries in English cities, Breadalbane had not been entirely certain about Rorke's location. The gossip he'd heard in London about Henry Cavendish and a red-haired Frenchwoman had not been specific enough, but there was no doubt about the petition. All Breadalbane had to do was bribe one of the Flemish envoys to deliver the summons to the fugitive doctor promptly and then wait for the powerful English nobleman's death before carrying out his own private plans. Carwhin's part in the scheme had been the relatively simple task of delivering the royal summons to the king's personal envoys when the men arrived in Newcastle, and of kidnapping the doctor's wife. Between the time of delivery and the mournful ringing of the church bells, the lawyer had remained in his rooms at a discreet Newcastle inn while the men he had brought with him had taken turns watching the castle from a distant vantage point. Carwhin had been told when the doctor and two companions had left, and again this morning when the woman had been taken into town. All that had remained to be done was to drive the large coach Breadalbane had supplied for him to the infirmary and to secret it in the mews at the rear of the building.

While he had been questioning the caretakers about the money, he had inadvertently learned that the woman was expecting the arrival of her MacDonald relatives. Always the alert opportunist, Carwhin decided his task would be easier if she believed that he and his men were the expected MacDonalds. Unfortunately, she had no more trust or respect for her own relatives than she had for Campbell's. Although he was certain she had accepted his claim, her distrust for him personally had increased with each unpleasant mile of the overland journey from Newcastle to Edinburgh. Not that she was a shrewish woman or a complaining traveler; she'd borne the discomfort of winter travel along muddy roads better than he had. But as large and well-equipped as Breadalbane's private coach was, it had been an unsettling experience for him to remain within touching distance of the damnable woman.

It was the same vigilant suspicion she'd displayed at the infirmary that irritated him most. She'd outwitted him about the fortune he'd been ordered to bring to Breadalbane—he was positive she knew the identity of the goldsmith. She'd stubbornly insisted on packing a trunk of medicine; she'd adamantly refused to pack any of the conventional dresses hanging in her clothespress; and most aggravating of all, she'd worn a damn nun's robe with a cross and rosary, the cursed symbols of Catholicism that she hadn't dared display in Protestant Newcastle.

Five miles outside of town, when he'd decided it was safe to release the servants and the ducal coachman, the insolent woman had shoved past him and jumped down from the raised body of the carriage without the aid of a step. After giving the one she had called Hugh a handful of gold coins she had hidden on her person, she had climbed back into the coach and warned Carwhin that if he stole that money, she would not travel another mile. The lawyer had been forced to order two of the mounted soldiers to ride alongside the coach to prevent her escaping his vigilance again.

Mercifully, there had been no need for such measures at night since they stayed at the small, well-guarded castles of lesser aristocrats like himself. Such men, borderland English or Scottish, may have had no personal liking for the earl of Breadalbane, but they dared not offer an insult to any of the king's advisers. Moreover, many of them owed favors to the powerful earl, whose monetary interests were far-reaching, and like all isolated men, they were eager for news from Scotland and Flanders. In the privacy of libraries, Carwhin supplied them liberally with well-edited accounts of both. With thousands of new troops joining him, King William was expected to turn defeat into victory. In Scotland, the dissident Jacobites, except for the MacDonalds and MacLeans, had been brought to heel by Breadalbane's successful negotiations. While most of these recruited hosts remained skeptical about Flanders, they welcomed the news that many of the Jacobites had been pacified. Two years earlier, several of them had almost lost their lives when the savage Highlanders had defeated the king's forces at the battle of Killiecrankie.

Prudently, Carwhin did not reveal that Breadalbane had been publicly accused of being both Royalist and Jacobite, and had narrowly avoided imprisonment. Nor did the lawyer mention the thousands of pounds of the king's money that the earl had failed to pay the clan leaders, or the fact that the agreement those leaders had signed was not the one the king had dictated. Since his own fortunes rose and fell with Breadalbane's, Carwhin had developed remarkable skills in duplicity and in convincing people that the earl was an honest politician, despite the mounting evidence to the contrary.

In response to his hosts' questions about the oddity of his female traveling companion, Carwhin had been equally untruthful. She was, he declared earnestly, a refugee from France who would become Lady Breadalbane's companion and nurse. Because she was a frightened foreigner, he requested that no one speak to her. At each separate keep, he'd asked that she be locked in a tower room with an ample supper and with the annoying hot bath she demanded every night. He had to admit, though, that physically she was an inoffensive traveler since she was immaculately clean and completely free of the cloying scent of French perfume. He also had to admit that she entertained herself and didn't bother him with questions about the MacDonalds—questions he'd have been hard-pressed to answer civilly, since he hated the Glencoe clan with a long-ingrained passion.

Although the arrogant, glibly tongued lawyer would have denied the charge, part of the fear he felt for the fierce and bloody Alasdair MacDonald had transferred itself to the slender woman. Whenever she was angry, her blue eyes blazed with the same fiery defiance Carwhin had seen in the chieftain's eyes during one of his rare visits to the Scottish Parliament. On his way home from his last appearance there, MacDonald had led his clan soldiers on a destructive raid upon Breadalbane's land. Whenever Carwhin spied a lock of his unwilling companion's red-gold hair that had slipped from its cowled restraint, he was again reminded of the MacDonald chief whose flaming red hair, atop his gigantic height, had made him the most feared warrior in the Highlands.

For a self-assured man who had never considered women of any importance except for their dowries and for the male heirs they produced, it was disquieting to watch a young woman reading a complicated medical book. Since his own eyesight did not permit him to read aboard a swaying coach, Carwhin had peevishly questioned her during their second day of travel and learned that she understood both the contents and the Latin text of the book. It was at that moment that he began to have doubts about Breadalbane's wisdom in ordering her abduction. Granted, the ransom money, if MacDonald paid it, would replace recently lost income, but the lawyer's inquisitive mind pried busily into the less attractive alternatives. The MacDonalds might well decide to ravage Breadalbane land again, and Carwhin's own estate might be the first one hit with fire and sword.

An even more disturbing possibility slowly began to form in Carwhin's fertile brain. Once Rorke Campbell learned that Breadalbane had engineered his return into the king's dangerous service, he would seek vengeance. The earl might still consider the well-educated doctor a tame servant, but the lawyer knew better. He'd been the one who had interviewed the Huguenots and soldiers upon their arrival from France. Rorke Campbell was no longer a reserved young doctor; he'd become a fierce fighter and a resourceful leader—a man highly protective of his young wife.

Carwhin knew Breadalbane was hoping that Rorke would not survive the Flanders battlefields. The lawyer was certain that not only would the man survive, but that he would win enough royal support to return to Scotland and to reclaim both his wife and her fortune. The reminder that he had not yet secured that fortune for his clan leader added to the lawyer's growing disquiet; his own future as law agent might very well be forfeit. He had already failed miserably in an assignment he'd been given earlier in the year.

Over ten months ago, when Tavis Campbell had been returned to Scotland, Carwhin had inadvertently learned another reason for the earl's interest in the granddaughter of a wealthy French count. During one of his visits to Kilchurn Castle, the lawyer had overheard the drunken Tavis shouting at Breadalbane that the French heiress was his by right. Having known the true relationship between the two men from the beginning, Carwhin had never understood the father's preference for the sly young wastrel he called his grandson. The earl had two families of legitimate children and another bastard or two by wealthy mistresses, but he never paid much attention to any of them other than Tavis. He had actually disliked his oldest son enough to label him a half-wit and to request royal permission to disinherit him. But as far as the observant lawyer knew, Breadalbane had never disciplined Tavis or denied him anything.

Two weeks after he had overheard that unpleasant scene, Carwhin had been told to find an heiress wife for Tavis. To his enduring frustration, the law agent had not located a single wealthy aristocrat in Scotland or England who would accept the offer. Not even the more successful of the tradesmen had been interested. While Breadalbane's reputation for usurious business dealings had been responsible for most of the failure, Tavis himself had contributed with his excesses in gambling and drinking. Despite his occasional boyish charm, he was essentially a vicious weakling.

Having failed to locate an appropriate wife, Carwhin had done the next best thing. Five months ago, through bribery and persuasion, he had secured a commission for Tavis in the earl of Argyll's proud, red-uniformed regiment. Since the regiment was scheduled to report to Flanders, he had thought the problem permanently solved. But again, Breadalbane had prevailed upon his distant Campbell relative to let Tavis remain at Edinburgh Castle as a member of a smaller battalion, providentially captained by Breadalbane's nephew, Sir Robert Campbell of Glenlyon.

Glancing over at the intent face of the woman who had told him days earlier that she preferred to be called Sister Jolie rather than Mistress Campbell, Carwhin shuddered with apprehension. If the earl had decided to give her to his scoundrel bastard as a plaything to infuriate Alasdair MacDonald still more, all of the Jacobite clans would respond with violence, and the fragile peace would be destroyed.

Late in the evening of the sixth day of the arduous trip, as the tired horses pulled the coach into the bailey court of Stair Castle on the Lowlands near Edinburgh, Carwhin breathed a sigh of relief that the problem was no longer his to solve. In comparison to the powerful men awaiting his arrival in the vastness of the estate, he was merely a well-paid servant. As he turned to help his traveling companion descend from the coach, he was told he was something quite different, as well. Attempting a long-delayed gallantry in a few conventional words of apology, he murmured, "I'm sorry the trip was not enjoyable for you. Usually I am more congenial company."

Looking at the pompous, untidy man whose elaborately curled wig was now a shapeless mass, Jolie responded with candid honesty, "You are a disagreeable pig—you do not bathe often enough. *Ma foi*, it was unpleasant to sit so close to you, Monsieur Colin Campbell!"

As he watched her turn away and follow a servant up the broad stairs and into Stair Castle, Colin Campbell of Carwhin was silently outraged, but not about the physical indelicacy of her insult, which only the crudest of women would dare voice. He was furious that she had discovered his deception in names and successfully concealed the fact. How in bloody hell had the insolent bitch beaten him at his own game? Recalling the rest of her brash words, the lawyer decided he would request a bath before he reported to Breadalbane. While he experienced no embarrassment at having offended the woman, it would not be politic to risk a repetition with two of the most important men in Scotland.

While Jolie trudged tiredly after the silent servant who led her down endless corridors to yet another tower room prison, her brief flash of spirit faded into dismal apathy. She had known since her second night in captivity the name of her captor and the identity of the Scottish laird he served. While she had been allowed to speak to no one of importance at the castles where they had stayed, she had questioned the servants freely. One brash young footman had been both knowledgeable and talkative after she had given him one of her last gold guineas. The news had not taken her completely by surprise; one of the soldier guards had stared at her cross and rosary as if they were symbols of some foul evil. A Catholic MacDonald would have known their meaning and respected them. Her first reaction had been relief that her own kin had not attempted to rob her; her second had been a rash confidence in her ability to escape.

Increasingly frustrated during the successive days, she had learned that her captors could not be eluded easily, if at all. The rooms she occupied each night were in drafty towers with slitted openings instead of windows; and once underway, the coach stopped only to rest the horses on deserted stretches of muddy roads, never at public inns, where she might have been able to hide. Once when she had been granted permission to relieve herself behind a screen of roadside shrubbery, she had contemplated running across the open countryside. But there had been no concealing vineyards, and no farmhouse in sight to give her shelter.

Resigning herself to the inevitability of finally meeting the dreaded earl of Breadalbane had not been easy, and the calm demeanor that had so irritated the Campbell lawyer had been nothing more than a desperate resolve to conceal her fear. For the first time since childhood, her interest in medicine had been minimal. Her thoughts kept reverting to her earlier visit to Edinburgh and to the Campbell soldiers who had threatened her and Rorke. Until she'd learned that Tavis had been leading those soldiers, she hadn't really believed that they had intended physical harm—only that they had been ordered to return her husband to the man who had once controlled his life.

Now, on the eve of meeting that man, Jolie was no longer as optimistic or as naive. Breadalbane had known all about Rorke's summons to return to the king's service; and at great expense, he had arranged for her abduction. But she disagreed with Rorke's belief that she would be held for ransom. Why should Alasdair MacDonald care about a second cousin he had never seen? The only explanation that seemed logical to her was the most unpleasant one—Tavis Campbell still wanted her! Jolie shuddered at the thought, but some of her fear was replaced by defiant resolution. Remembering the contents of the chest of medicine she had packed and the fact that Tavis was addicted to wine, she decided that his health would suffer a painful relapse if he attempted an attack.

That night, in a room as prisonlike as the others, despite its more comfortable furnishings, Jolie studied her medical books with a purposeful dedication until the candle guttered out. In the morning, she sponge-bathed with cold water and donned the same Sisters of Charity robe she'd worn for six days, calming her seething emotions by counting all one hundred ninety-five beads of her rosary. Many of her prayers, though, would have appalled the gentle old nun who had given it to her.

When the summons came in the early afternoon and she was led into a fire-warmed library, Jolie's face was as devoutly serene as the most religious of the nuns she had known in Strasbourg. Not even her dramatic introduction to the two men seated near the sculptured fireplace destroyed her composure.

"God's blood, John Campbell," one of the men exploded into disapproving speech. "Why the devil didn't you tell me the woman was a cursed nun? I'd not have polluted my home had I known."

Repressing her anger at the insult, Jolie studied the speaker's handsome, humorless face, framed by a massive wig of long, gray curls, and wondered about his identity. She had expected to meet only the one enemy she knew about, not another aristocrat whose anti-Catholic prejudice was as vindictive as Reverend Abelard Darrell's had been. That he was powerful and wealthy, she hadn't a doubt. His castle was almost as imposing as the duke of Newcastle's, and his richly furred velvet coat was more expensive than anything she had seen in England.

Abruptly, her attention was refocused when the second man spoke. At first she thought him a twin of the first one, so similar were their disapproving expressions. But on closer examination, she determined they had little else in common. Although he was older, the earl of Breadalbane's wig was brown and even more elaborately curled, and his eyes were set in a face that seemed more like a mask than human flesh.

Unlike his companion's, his lips barely moved as he spoke, and his speech was devoid of emotion.

"I believe our young guest is play-acting, Dalrymple. Unless Carwhin brought us the wrong woman, Mistress Campbell has been a wife for more than a year, and according to her grandfather, she has never been a nun. However, I think we'd best satisfy ourselves about her identity before we continue."

Without moving his cold, speculative eyes from Jolie's face, he nodded slightly to a servant standing near the double-doored entry and continued his speech with only the briefest interruption.

"Do you know who I am, mistress?"

"*Oui*, monsieur."

"You will speak English, Mistress Campbell. My lawyer has informed me that you're quite fluent in its usage. Did Carwhin tell you the name of your host?"

"*Non*, monsieur."

"Your response, madam, should have been 'Nay, Sir Campbell.' You will address me so in the future, and you will address my friend as Sir Dalrymple. We share in common the first name of John. What is it you call yourself?"

"Sister Jolie. I do not like the name of Campbell."

"Your grandfather neglected to warn me about your insolent tendencies, mistress. But no matter, you will soon learn to adjust."

"Why am I here, monsieur, and how long am I to be held prisoner?"

No trace of annoyance crossed Breadalbane's face as his eyes moved toward the door and the woman who entered. He waited impassively until the newcomer was in a position to see Jolie's face.

"Is this your daughter by marriage, Edina?" he asked blandly.

Jolie heard the biting acrimony in her mother-in-law's voice, but she gave no sign of recognition. Edina Campbell's self-control was considerably less.

"Aye, 'tis the popish French jade my foolish son wed,"

she blurted. "If you'll tell her to take off that abomination she's wearing on her head, you'll find her hair as red as a fox's and her tongue as sharp as a shrew's. But where ha' you put Rorke, Cousin John. You promised he'd be brought here, same as her."

"Your son was recalled into the king's service, Edina. At present, he's on his way to Flanders," Breadalbane responded smoothly.

"You lied to me, John Campbell! Could you no' ha' kept my son as safe as you keep your own? You were wi' the king but a few weeks ago. Could you no' ha' protected my Rorke from the greedy man?"

The earl's voice remained calm, but Jolie noted that his nostrils flared in anger at Edina's shrill accusation.

"I've warned you before, madam, about your careless choice of words. I had naught to do with the king's decision. Rather, I think, 'twas the English duke of Newcastle who overboasted about your son's abilities. Had Rorke not been so foolish as to flee from Edinburgh, I could have hidden him from the king's notice at Kilchurn."

A flood of outraged denials pounded in Jolie's head, but she held her silence. The less she admitted to this dangerous man, the safer she would be. Fortunately, she was given no time to interrupt Edina's bitter reaction to Breadalbane's lie.

"Then why did you no' have the decency to gi' him a kindly invitation, John, instead of sending your jackal, Giles Campbell, to hound my lad. 'Twas not Rorke who defied you in Edinburgh; 'twas his rebellious wife."

"I am quite aware that I underestimated Mistress Campbell on that occasion, Edina, but I'll not make the same mistake twice." Turning to look directly at the younger woman, he demanded sternly, "Remove your cowl, mistress. I want the others to know how much more Scot you are than French. Your father's family would be proud of your defiance; you're much alike in spirit to Alasdair MacDonald himself."

A faint smile touched his lips as he watched Jolie's bright curls tumble free of the restraining cowl. " 'Tis more gold in color than his was in youth, and your skin is not as

ruddy," he murmured judiciously. "But Laird MacDonald
could never deny you, mistress. Mayhap in time, he'll
welcome you to Glencoe. In the meantime, you'll remain
under my protection until the small matter of your money
has been addressed. Carwhin informed me of your foolish
lack of cooperation in that respect, but you'll find I have
little fear of goldsmiths. I have always found them most
cooperative after a small bit of persuasion."

Jolie ignored Edina Campbell's gasp of outrage when she
heard the MacDonald name and watched instead the flare of
irritation that had replaced Dalrymple's cynical arrogance.

"You invited a MacDonald into my home, as well as a
Catholic?" he asked Breadalbane. " 'Tis a reckless game
you could be playing, John. Why couldn't you have waited
another month to settle your family problems?"

"She'll be here only a few more days, Dalrymple, and
I'll see she doesn't strain your hospitality. But I think you'll
find this 'game' will prove to be a lively addition to the
more important one you're playing."

"The game *we're* playing, John Campbell," Dalrymple
amended sharply. "I've not forgotten 'twas your idea at the
start. Now, get these women from my sight. I dislike
shrews, and I've no more trust in this sly MacDonald than
you do."

To Jolie's horror, half an hour later, after she'd been
returned to her prison chamber, she discovered that Edina
had been domiciled in the small anteroom adjacent to her
own, and that the locked door imprisoned her mother-in-law
as securely as it did her. Controlling her agitation at the
prospect of the unwanted companionship, she indicated the
small dining table set for two and issued an ungracious
invitation.

"We might as well eat, madame." Halfway through the
awkward meal, she discovered that Edina was not as blindly
loyal to Breadalbane as she'd seemed.

"Di' you know this English duke, mistress?"

"I was with him when he died, and it was not he who

asked the king to send Rorke into battle. My husband believed your cousin was to blame."

"You heard John deny that charge."

"Yes, I heard, but I do not believe him, and I do not think you do, either. Your Breadalbane does not care that your son was always in danger from the dragonades in France; he was worried only about his *cochon* Tavis. Did he tell you that Tavis tried to murder Rorke in Edinburgh?"

For a brief moment Edina's eyes blazed with a hot anger, then her shoulders sagged in defeat. "I dinna believe John would play me false again. Di' Rorke ha' the sense to put his money where 'tis safe?"

"Quite safe, madame. The people in Newcastle do not like your cousin any more than Rorke does. Do you think he really intends to hold me for ransom?"

"Nay, I dinna think he'll be that daft. Your MacDonalds are savage killers that 'tis best not to rile."

"I wouldn't know. I've never met a MacDonald."

The gloomy night and following morning passed slowly for both women. While Edina paced the floor in restless agitation, Jolie tried to concentrate on reading. When a summons came for them in midafternoon, they welcomed it with relief. They had been dressed and waiting for hours, but neither would have merited any praise for her choice of costume. Edina wore the same dark dress, with the Breadalbane Campbell tartan draped diagonally across one shoulder and fastened at the waist. The only concession Jolie had made was to change into a clean robe, identical to the one she had worn earlier but without the cowl, and to brush her hair. Halfway down the corridor, she slipped her cross and rosary into the pocket of her robe, determined not to antagonize the earl and the disapproving master of Stair any more than she could avoid.

"Don't be afraid to bow your head, Jolie, child," Soeur Marguerite had frequently advised her, "especially when you think you can gain from it." *I have my freedom to gain*, Jolie thought as she assumed a pleasantly composed expression.

Ablaze with illumination from a dozen more oil lamps

than on the previous day, the library was still an intimidating place. Watching her as she entered were six additional people—three men in brilliant red coats bearing the Argyll regimental insignia, and three women in gowns as colorfully elegant as the ones Jolie had left in Newcastle. Before she could single out her main adversary, one of the officers detached himself from the group, replaced his own cup of wine with fresh ones from the heavily embossed salver, and walked toward the two women still standing in the wide entry.

Fascinated by the unusual appearance of the officer, Jolie studied his face covertly. His colorless, tightly curled hair fanned out to cover his shoulders, and his complexion was so pinkly tinged, she thought at first that his face was smeared with cosmetics. She was still staring at him as he nodded to Edina and handed her a cup of wine. As he turned his attention to the younger woman and bowed deeply, Jolie saw the hidden signs of age. Despite his dramatically youthful coloring, he was as old as Breadalbane, and his eyes held the same fixed look as the old Frenchmen who had frequented the winery near the Strasbourg infirmary and spent the afternoon drinking. Although Jolie was repulsed by his bizarre appearance, she smiled faintly at his gallant words. As practiced and insincere as they were, they were the first friendly greeting she had heard in eight oppressive days.

"I was told you were fair, mistress, but the telling did not do you justice—you are entirely beautiful. I am Robert Campbell of Glenlyon, at your service, mistress."

That service lasted throughout the hour Jolie remained at the party, and it smoothed over the shock of meeting Tavis Campbell for the first time in seventeen months. She hadn't recognized him from across the room; the dramatic red uniform coat had made him look indistinguishable from the other young officer. Oddly enough, he had reminded her of William Somerton at first, but on closer inspection, she decided that his face had changed. His expression was now one of hardened confidence rather than angrily petulant immaturity. There was also a new breadth to his once-slender frame, and his straw-colored hair was attractively curled. Unerringly, Jolie's eyes riveted on the side of his head that had been gashed open by a French musket ball.

"The scar your stitchery left no longer shows, Soeur Jolie, and my leg is strong enough for a day's march and a night's merrymaking," Tavis bantered with a poise Jolie found more disturbing than his improved appearance.

Relieved that his interest in her seemed as impersonal as the casual smile he bent upon the richly clad woman at his side as he performed a negligently graceful introduction, Jolie tried to repress the hatred and fear she felt. With an impulsive courage, she asked bluntly, "What am I doing here, Tavis?"

" 'Tis where you should have been from the beginning, Jolie MacDonald. But now that you've no husband to protect you, 'tis where you'll be safest."

"I've not been safe so far," she demurred in a deceptively soft voice. "I've been kidnapped, lied to, and kept a prisoner. Why was I not allowed to go to my father's family?"

"You'd find 'twould be a worse prison there without me to protect you."

"I do not think so. Lord MacDonald even offered my husband a safe home, and that is something you would never do, would you?"

"Rorke knew the risk he was taking when he stole what was mine. You've yet to learn that I'm not a man to accept defeat, pretty Jolie."

As she stepped backward into the protective arm Robert Campbell extended toward her, Jolie experienced a chill foreboding. For just a moment, Tavis's pale eyes had held the same cold authority as Breadalbane's darker ones. More cautiously, she submitted to the rest of the introductions until she was courteously seated on a small bench facing the earl.

"I'm pleased to note you treated my grandson civilly, mistress. I was afraid you might have believed the villainous lies the criminal Baron Wallmond spread about. I'd have been more pleased, however, if you'd worn a gown becoming to your station, but you at least had the sense to discard your religious flummery. Now, if you'll smile and relax your look of guarded suspicion, you'll make my nephew Robert a happier man. He wouldn't appreciate having his gallantry go for naught.''

"You've left me little to be happy about, Sir Campbell,'' Jolie retorted brusquely before she remembered her resolve to be conciliatory.

"Well, then, since you've no choice in the matter, 'twill be to your advantage to surrender gracefully.''

Before she could stay her tongue, Jolie demanded hotly, "Surrender to what, monsieur?''

His response held a cold finality. "To whatever I decide, madam; you have no one else to champion your cause.''

"Then I'll champion my own!'' she declared with a desperate bravado as she stood abruptly and walked across the room to where Edina was seated. In obedience to Breadalbane's curt nod, Robert Campbell shrugged gracefully and followed her.

Almost as unbearable as the earl's veiled threat for the distraught young woman was the icy reception a tight-lipped Edina gave her.

"It dinna take you long to forget you already ha' a husband,'' her mother-in-law rasped.

With a tired smile that reflected his growing boredom, Robert Campbell murmured peaceably, "You're overset, Edina. 'Tis not the lass who's to blame; 'tis the oddity of John's humor and the short time he has left to complete the king's work with the Highland clans.''

Edina's breathy snort of disbelief was audible throughout the room, as were her rash words. "'Tis no' John's humor that sickens me, Robert of Glenlyon; 'tis the care wi' which he protects you and the whelp Tavis. You're safe in Scotland, as always, while my son is sent to be the sacrificial lamb again.''

As Jolie watched the silent exchange between Breadalbane

and his nephew—a jerk of his head on the earl's part and brief, responsive nod by Robert Campbell—she rose to her feet and asked softly, "Is it permitted that I return to my room, monsieur? I've no wish to intrude."

The first flicker of sincere admiration shone briefly in the man's eyes. "You're quick-witted, mistress. 'Tis a gift that's always eluded me. Come along, Edina, the party is over for you."

Jolie didn't look back as Robert escorted her and Edina to the door and signaled the two uniformed soldiers standing guard. Listening to the cadence of their marching feet echoing hollowly on the stone floor as they followed the silent women, Jolie shivered uncontrollably.

Edina's silence lasted only until the outside bar of their prison rooms was slid into place before she exploded into speech.

"He dinna take his eyes off you!"

In the process of lighting candles with a splinter of wood from the fireplace, Jolie jerked nervously. "Who didn't?" she muttered.

"The Tavis devil, that's who—him with his grand airs and sly ways. Di' you find him so attractive when you saved his life? 'Twould ha' been better if you'd ha' let the French kill him—you'd still ha' a husband wi' you who'd no' be in danger of murder again."

Aroused to alertness by the gloomy words, Jolie asked curiously, "Did you know Tavis before he went to France with Rorke?"

"Aye, and hated him."

"Is he really the earl's grandson?"

"Nay, 'tis more likely he's John's own bastard. 'Tis what the lady Breadalbane believes."

"Did you know about Tavis's abduction before he was returned?"

"Aye, the lot of us could no' help but know. 'Twas the whelp's fortune John used to pay the ransom. Now that the scoundrel has no money, John wasted months to find a woman wealthy enough to support the dim-witted booby, but none will ha' him. Poor as my son was, he had offers aplenty. If he hadn't lost his head and wed you, I'd no' be a pauper, and I'd no' ha' been cast out of Kilchurn Castle.''

"What kind of place is it?''

" 'Tis John's birthright home, the grandest in the Highlands, except for Argyll's Inveraray.''

Recalling the sword Argyll had given Rorke, Jolie asked, but without much hope, "What kind of man is this Lord Argyll?''

"The present laird, Archibald, is the only one of the last three Argyll chiefs to keep his head from the chopping block.''

"Is he a friend of your cousin?''

"Confederate is more likely; there's no love lost 'twixt them. But you'll find no comfort from him—Argyll hates the MacDonalds, the same as the rest of us.''

"Have you ever met any MacDonalds?''

"Nay, I've ne'er seen the devils, no' e'en from a distance, but they ruined Rorke's family just the same. In recent times, they've fair beggared Robert of Glenlyon, his castle being close enow for easy raiding.''

Jolie's heart was beating with excitement as she asked softly, "Is Glencoe that close to Breadalbane land?''

"Aye, only twenty miles and a range of mountains north, but the thieves roam farther afield than that. Rorke's grandfather was an Argyll tacksman—a vassal lord, kin to Argyll himself, before the old MacIain killed him and burned the castle down.''

"Who is MacIain?''

" 'Tis the name the savage MacDonalds gi' their chief. Dinna you know anything about your own kin?''

"I never heard of them until the day Rorke and I were married. I didn't know anything about my French *grandpère* either; I thought I was a foundling.''

"Di' my son wed you wi'out knowing you had money?''

"He knew that the nuns had given me some over the years.''

"You were ne'er a nun yourself?''

Jolie shook her head slowly, not out of regret for a lost career, but because her mind was still spinning from the information that Glencoe was close to Kilchurn Castle. Suddenly, she didn't want her mother-in-law to stop talking; there was still much to learn. Shrewdly, she cast about for a means of winning at least a small measure of trust, and decided that Tavis Campbell was the only villain they both agreed upon.

"I was trained as a nurse, but now I wish I had not been so good a one. If Tavis had died, I would no longer be afraid of him. He is the reason Rorke and I will never live in Scotland."

"The whelp claims you promised yourself to him before you wed my son."

"No, madame, I hated him!"

By nightfall, Jolie knew many things about Kilchurn and the land around. She knew about the soldiers stationed there and how they defended the castle. She learned that Breadalbane did not plan to return there until spring, and that Lady Breadalbane had already taken the youngest children to spend the winter at Caithness Castle in the north of Scotland. Interspersed with these vital pieces of information had been an outpouring from Edina's well-stocked reservoir of Breadalbane history and scandals, of John Campbell's loveless marriages, and of Rorke's childhood. Jolie had listened to these rambling stories with polite attention, but without much faith in their accuracy. Except when asked a direct question, Edina tended to confuse her embittered opinion with fact. Still and all, Jolie had gained her first glimmer of hope—a hope that was to be crushed into desolation two days later.

During those two days, while Jolie had struggled to control her mounting impatience, Edina had lapsed into an apathetic melancholia. On the first morning, one of the guards had remained inside the rooms as the servants cleaned them. When Edina tried to insist that she be allowed to leave since she was a warden, not a prisoner, the soldier had laughed.

"The laird said naught about ye, save to keep ye under lock, same as t' other. And under lock ye'll stay, old woman!''

Jolie had attempted to offer sympathy, but her mother-in-law had remained secluded in the anteroom, emerging only long enough to eat small portions of the increasingly dreary meals. At one of these awkward sessions, Jolie had asked if Edina had received the money Rorke had sent her.

"Aye, the last time he wrote he said 'twas enow for two years, but I wanted my son, no' his money. 'Tis what John promised me.''

"Do you think your cousin will let you return to your Edinburgh home?''

For a moment, the Scotswoman looked bleakly unsure of herself, then her jaw firmed with a crafty determination. "He'll no' dare do otherwise; I've papers aplenty in my rooms there tha' he'd no' want made public. Di' you think me the complete fool?''

Shaking her head, Jolie lapsed into a momentary silence. Edina hadn't needed her sympathy; she was enough like her cousin to know the rules of the games he played. Morosely, the younger woman finished eating and returned to her solitary reading without asking if Edina's part in this game had been to contribute to the destruction of her despised daughter-in-law. Until she'd learned her son had been sent to war, she had been shrewishly vindictive.

Late in the afternoon of the second day, Jolie was ordered to report to the library without Edina. Having donned two robes that morning to ward off the damp, penetrating chill, she felt dismally unattractive, but the impatient soldier who had delivered the message gave her no time to do other than brush her hair. On an impulse, she slipped on her small cross and buried it beneath the folds of fabric.

The dimly lit library seemed even more crowded than on the day of the unpleasant party, but this time there were only men present. Breadalbane and Dalrymple occupied their usual chairs near the fire, with another man standing between them facing the door. Although younger, he was more commanding in appearance, and his face was less forbidding in expression. Remembering Edina's description, Jolie identified him as the earl of Argyll, the most trusted of King William's Scottish adherents. It was he who offered her a chair, rather than the small bench Breadalbane had supplied her on the previous occasions. Glancing nervously around the room, she nodded tersely to Robert Campbell, stared briefly at the unsmiling young officer standing next to him, and sucked in her breath with a painful rush when she recognized the sixth man in the room. She'd seen him only once before and at a distance, but his face was unmistakably that of Giles Campbell, the man Rorke had been most afraid of in Edinburgh. Jolie's apprehension turned into dread.

"Mistress Campbell," the earl of Argyll began gently, only to be interrupted by Breadalbane's harsh command.

"Give her the letter, Archibald—the woman can read for herself. And nothing you say will change its contents."

Jolie accepted the folded paper, whose seal had already been broken, and opened it with stiff fingers, her eyes focusing slowly on the fateful words.

To our beloved earl of Argyll, written five miles west of Kingston-upon-Hull, England, on December 3, 1691.

It is my sad duty to inform you that on this day, the regiment came upon three roadside graves, freshly dug and marked with the swords of men who had been murdered by highway brigands. I dispatched messengers to notify the English families of the two dead officers identified by the crests on their swords, and by the embarkation papers the murderer had left behind. The third man, though, was someone I knew personally and had spoken with only two days earlier, when he passed me on the road from Newcastle. His sword bore the Argyll crest, and I believe his father had been an Argyll clansman. His name was Rorke Campbell, a doctor of some repute and a fine man. He told me that he had a wife about whom he was deeply concerned. I hope you will be able to locate her and break the news more gently.

Because we are due aboard ship within the day, we will not disturb the graves, but instead, have hired a local woodsman to guard them until a more fitting entombment can be arranged by the families. I am sending Lieutenant James Campbell with this letter and the sword. He will rejoin the regiment in Flanders upon completion of this assignment.

> Respectfully, your humble servant,
> Captain Ian MacCallum
> Argyll Regiment on Horse

The letter slipped unnoticed from Jolie's hands as she reached up to clutch her small cross. No tears gushed to her eyes to break the spell of paralyzing shock. She stared into the fire without seeing the flames, and she heard nothing of the low-spoken comments being exchanged among the men. Gradually, her mind focused on one part of the letter— "murdered by highway brigands"—and her stiff lips articulated the word "No!" Rorke hadn't been murdered by strangers; his death had been ordered by the same man who had tormented him for years—the calculating earl of Breadalbane, the coldly arrogant aristocrat who had told her three days earlier that she had no one else but him to champion her cause. He had known then that Rorke was dead!

As if the realization of his villainy was a caustic poison coursing through her blood, Jolie's grief was momentarily replaced by an uncontrollable fury. She rose shakily to her feet and glared at him with a hatred that swept aside all caution. "You murdered my husband," she accused in a shrill voice strident enough to penetrate into every corner of the room. "You ordered him murdered, just as you ordered me kidnapped!"

"Take her back to her room, Giles," Breadalbane commanded swiftly before any of the other men could react.

"She's overwrought and doesn't know what she is saying," he added more blandly after Giles Campbell had wrapped a sinewy arm around Jolie's waist and clamped a hand over her mouth as he propelled her toward the door. "As Dalrymple can attest, she is an insolent Frenchwoman without the sense to guard her tongue," Breadalbane added calmly.

While Dalrymple and Robert Campbell accepted Breadalbane's explanation in silence, the earl of Argyll was not so easily cowed.

"She looked more like a MacDonald than any Frenchwoman I've ever seen," he asserted speculatively. "You did tell me she was niece to Alasdair MacIain, did you not? 'Tis an odd coincidence your holding her prisoner at such a time—an odder coincidence even than your man finding mine so easily on a distant English road."

"Giles was on other business entirely, Archibald."

"What business, John?"

"He was there to collect a debt Rorke Campbell owed me and had promised to pay. Needless to say, I didn't receive my money, since Rorke had already left the city by the time Giles arrived."

"If that be so, why did he try to convince me that the woman was naught of my concern?"

Shrugging his shoulders with an artful indifference, Breadalbane countered diplomatically, "Why should you concern yourself with a woman you'd never heard about before this day? When my men found her alone in Newcastle after her husband's departure, they brought her here so that I could protect her during her husband's absence. Rorke Campbell had been one of my clansmen for twenty years."

"And his ancestors before him were my loyal tacksmen for two hundred," Argyll countered, thoughtfully. "I like it not, John Campbell. Nor did I like the way your man dragged her from this room. I think 'twill be wiser if I take her into my custody, at least until the Glencoe MacDonalds swear loyalty to King William. Then I will turn her over to the MacIain."

"You're welcome to her, Archibald; but I warn you, she's a troublesome piece of baggage."

Listening to the veiled acrimony that existed between the two opposing Campbell leaders, Dalrymple concealed his contempt behind an expression of cynical boredom. Like most Scottish Lowlanders, he distrusted all of the Highland clans, and dealt with them only when necessary. In this instance, he knew that Breadalbane would be the winner. The Grey Fox would never permit a chance for added power and money to slip through his grasp—not after the trouble he'd undergone to secure the woman. That he had ordered her husband's murder, Dalrymple hadn't a doubt. How else could he gain an heiress wife for his rapscallion bastard?

As Jolie was half carried, half dragged down an unfamiliar corridor in Stair Castle, she knew she would never see her room there again or her mother-in-law. Emerging into a rear courtyard near the stables, she shivered from the sudden blast of icy air that struck her face, but she felt no surprise at seeing mounted men waiting beside the same carriage that had brought her here. She was shoved roughly inside the cab by Giles Campbell, and noted with apathetic relief that her luggage occupied the seat opposite the one covered by a fur robe and pillows. At least they didn't mean to freeze her to death, she thought uncaringly—only to keep her captive until they reached a more secure prison. And this time she'd not be sharing the cab with a jailer or be forced to use the roadside for essential relief—a covered chamber pot occupied one corner of the floor between the seats. Grateful for the privacy, Jolie buried her face in a pillow and wept.

For five days and nights the routine of travel didn't vary for the grief-stricken woman held prisoner in the cab of a speeding coach. At night, she was led from the carriage and locked in a room of still another gloomy keep. Only if she overheard the soldiers talking did she even know the names of the villages or towns of the Lowlands. Only when the road bed angled upward into the hills was the speed of travel slowed by the increasing amounts of snow. Looking out over the white fields, Jolie wept unrestrainedly. Her memories of the winter walks she and Rorke had taken in the snow-covered parks of Utrecht in Holland were poignantly vivid. Had they but remained there, she thought despairingly, he would still be alive. Huddled beneath the fur robe, she felt alone and dehumanized.

On the fifth night, in a drafty castle near the village of Tyndrum, Jolie's grief was momentarily held in abeyance, and she learned that friendship, even with clannish people who spoke an alien language, was possible. She was prodded awake just after she'd fallen into exhausted sleep and was asked to look at a sick child—an infant suffering from convulsions that the resident leech had been unable to calm. Alienated by the suspicious looks she received from the people crowded outside the room, she was tempted to plead ignorance until she realized that medicine was the only life she had left. As unsure of the cause of the child's violent illness as the poorly educated leech, she began a systematic examination as she'd seen her husband do at their infirmary.

An hour later, with the permission of the castle owner, she performed a circumcision and began the delicate task of cleansing the pus-filled sores that had blocked the child's urinary tract. When the bottled-up infected liquid gushed out, she felt a faint thrill of victory. The joy of love might be gone from her life, but the challenge of a nursing career remained.

By dawn the child was calm enough to nurse at his mother's breast, and Jolie was no longer treated as a stranger. She'd learned, however, that if she were to escape from these confining Highlands, she would have to learn the lilting Highland language. Only a few of the castle residents had spoken English. At the breakfast she was allowed to share with the servants, she acquired a small vocabulary of the names of foods and utensils. During the following day of travel, she learned still more by asking questions of the escort soldiers who spoke both languages.

Jolie did not have to be told the name of the castle that

loomed ahead late in the afternoon of that same day. The huge, forbidding structure was much as her mother-in-law had described it. Nestled at the foot of the towering, bleak mountain Edina had called Ben Cruachan, and overlooking Loch Awe, Kilchurn Castle was the most forbidding fortress of all the ones Jolie had seen during the past unhappy weeks. She shivered with dread as the iron-gated portcullis clanged shut after the coach had been driven into the stone-paved court and pulled to a halt in front of the iron-studded doors of the entry. As she dismounted, she looked up at the towering walls to the crenellated defenses on the castle's roof and shuddered again. Kilchurn, she reflected bitterly, was a fitting home for the man who owned it—inhospitable and brooding. She wondered dully if anyone had ever succeeded in escaping from it.

Expecting to be locked in still another tower prison, she gasped in shock when she was led up two flights of stairs to a gracious fire-warmed room with windows that overlooked an inner court and garden. Most welcome of all was the sight of a wooden tub already filled with steaming water. Even before the silent woman servant had left the room, Jolie was stripping off the robes she had worn throughout the trip. As she reached for the jar of stavesacre salve, her eyes filled with tears. A lifetime ago, in the tunnel at Chateau Laurent, she and Rorke had argued about stavesacre's potency as a treatment for lice.

In the morning Jolie discovered still another aspect of her new prison—pale rays of mid-December sunshine streamed in through the east-facing windows. For a drowsy moment, she thought, she was back in Strasbourg, where winter was only an occasional visitor. But the sound that greeted her was not the impatient command of Soeur Marguerite; it was the modulated, lilting voice of Alanna Fairleigh.

"I didn't disturb you last night because I thought you needed sleep more than conversation and food. I'm hoping you're ready for both this morning."

Sitting bolt upright in bed, Jolie looked warily around the room. "Isn't this Kilchurn Castle?" she blurted.

"Aye, 'tis Kilchurn; there could hardly be two such monstrosities, even in Scotland. The present Lady Campbell had the windows installed when she married the earl; otherwise, we'd be sitting in darkness."

"I thought you lived at—"

"At Fairleigh Manor? I do, except when the earl asks me to serve as his hostess, when his wife is staying at her former home in the far north. 'Tis not as unusual an arrangement as it sounds. My late husband was one of the earl's tacksmen. I inherited the post and all the responsibility it entails. I'm afraid that Highland customs are still hopelessly medieval."

"Are you to be my warden while I'm being held prisoner at Kilchurn, madame?"

Avoiding any answer to the blunt question, Alanna murmured soothingly, "I think 'twill be more bearable for both of us if we call each other by our given names. I was sorry to hear about your husband's tragic death. I wish I could tell you that you will forget in time, but you won't. 'Twill just become a little easier to bear."

"When did you hear about my husband's death, Alanna?"

"Two days ago, when Giles Campbell came to my home and order—requested that I come here to be company to you during your period of grief. The earl thought I might be of help, since I've also lost a beloved husband."

Looking at her hostess with eyes that sparked with anger, despite their glistening sheen of unshed tears, Jolie demanded harshly, "Did the earl of Breadalbane murder your husband, as he did mine?"

Visibly shocked, Alanna stared at the vivid face of the younger woman. "Dear God, Jolie, 'tis not safe to make such an accusation about John Campbell. Whatever else he may be, he is not a murderer."

"Then how did he know about Rorke's death before the earl of Argyll brought the official letter? And why was Giles Campbell in England at the same time and in the same place as my husband's murder? If he is so innocent, how did your *cochon* Breadalbane know I would be alone when he sent his devil lawyer to kidnap me?"

Despite her earlier defense of the man she herself had just cause to hate, Alanna was shaken by the volley of hotly delivered questions.

"Is your French grandfather a wealthy enough man to pay a large ransom for you, Jolie?" she asked slowly.

"My *grandpère* will not be the one. They will demand the money from Alasdair MacDonald."

"God's blood! Are you related to the Glencoe MacIain?"

"In a letter to my *grandpère*, he said my father was his cousin and a tacksman, I think, like your husband. He said there was an estate that he has kept for me. Now do you understand why I am so certain that Breadalbane ordered my husband killed?"

"But he could have held you for ransom without killing your—" Alanna began, and stopped abruptly before she completed the thought. She knew all about the unsuccessful search for an heiress rich enough to satisfy Tavis Campbell. Only with Jolie's husband gone could the earl force her to marry his unlovable bastard and then claim part of MacDonald land for his own. Hastily, the older woman changed the dangerous subject. Until she could achieve her own escape from Breadalbane's domination, it would be wiser not to meddle.

Choosing a more immediate problem to address, she warned Jolie sternly, "While you're here, you must not mention the MacDonald name to anyone—especially not to the crofter tenants living in the outlying villages. They have good reason to be afraid of all Glencoe people."

Swiftly, Jolie seized the opportunity. "Will I be allowed to meet those tenants, Alanna?"

"As a matter of fact, you may meet more of them than you'll like. Lady Campbell always takes the Kilchurn physician with her when she goes to Caithness, so the crofters are left without any medical assistance. The earl thought that you might volunteer to help some of them while you're here. After we breakfast, I'll take you up to the ramparts and point out the different villages for you."

During the hour-long walk around the crenellated rooftop defenses of Kilchurn Castle, Jolie saw many things besides the several small clusters of cottages. Despite the foot of snow that covered the floor of the valley, there were still Campbell soldiers posted at regular intervals in small guardhouses on the rooftop ramparts. No one entering or leaving the castle during daylight hours could hope to escape their notice. As she shivered in the chill wind and wiggled her icy toes in the warmest of her Holland boots, she realized she'd have to acquire a fur-lined cloak and a pair of fur-lined boots like the ones the soldiers were wearing. As she looked down at the few workers who left the castle to walk across the fields, she noticed that they were wearing something in addition to boots on their feet.

"What are those things the people down there have on?" she asked her companion.

"Snowshoes, Jolie. Fifty years ago, someone brought a pair of them back from the American colonies. Since then, Highlanders have made their own."

"Have you ever worn them?"

"Occasionally for sport, but never for serious travel. 'Tis said that only a few experts can use them on mountains, but most people find them useful in walking over meadow snow."

Reminded that Edina had told her about the mountains surrounding Glencoe Valley, Jolie asked casually, "Are those the Glencoe Mountains north of here?"

Alanna smiled sadly and shook her head. "Jolie, what you are contemplating would be impossible even in summer. Unless you know the secret passes in that series of mountain ranges north of Black Mount, you'd never reach Glencoe. 'Tis why your father's clan has been protected from attack for hundreds of years. The only way anyone from here could get into that valley would be to cross the width of Argyll land to the west and to travel northward by boat on Loch Linnhe."

"Could I find shelter along the way?" Jolie asked boldly.

" 'Tis one of the few civilized customs we practice in the Highlands—no one is turned away during the winter months. But I'm afraid that the Argyll tacksmen would feel honor bound to return you to Kilchurn; I imagine most of them know all about you by this time."

"What about the crofters? Would they know about me?"

"Probably not, and they'd give you shelter, but they'd expect some payment for food. Many of them have scarce enough for their own families. Jolie, 'tis nonsense we're talking. Such a trip is an impossibility for you. Few crofters speak any English, and the trails and roads are already buried in snow. You'd be lost within hours of leaving Kilchurn. Come, let's go below before we freeze to death. I'd like you to meet my son and forget your troubles for a bit."

Even as she nodded her agreement, Jolie turned around to stare once more toward the forbidding mountains to the north and again toward the west, where Alanna had said the way was possible. It was no longer so important that she survive; it was important only that Breadalbane not profit from his cowardly murder of her husband. As she brushed away the flakes of snow that had begun to fall, her face hardened with determination.

7

Throughout her protected youth, Jolie's spirit had been tempered into morally flexible steel by Soeur Marguerite's stern philosophy: "Don't let the villains and the fools of the world see you weep, child. You'll rob them of their victory. If you have to admit defeat, do it without showing the hurt." Although the enduring old nun had been equally adamant about owning up to fault with humility, Jolie had developed a stubborn reluctance to admit either defeat or fault.

Despite Alanna Fairleigh's continuing sympathy, she gave way to her grief only in the privacy of her room, and she retired there only after she reached a point of exhaustion. She had achieved the healing miracle of work just after Alanna had informed the castle bailiff that Mistress Campbell— Sister Jolie—had the earl's permission to tend all medical complaints. Led down flights of stairs to the armory where Rorke had begun his medical career, she and the English-speaking bailiff had achieved a prompt understanding. A crafty survivor who'd long served his penurious laird, Griogair Rowan readily agreed that she be paid for her services to the household people, but in goods rather than coin. During his years of servitude, Rowan had found that while household money was audited regularly, his occasional pilfering from the supplies stored happenstance throughout the cellars that had once supported a population four times the present number had never been detected.

Thus, in her first week of lancing boils, relieving chilblained feet, stitching up the cuts the soldiers received in their off-duty brawling, and issuing doses of emetics, tonics, and cathartics to those who complained of stomach ailments, Jolie had amassed enough pelts of coarse, long-haired fur for a hooded cloak, two pairs of fur-lined boots, and a pair of snowshoes. When the suspicious bailiff had asked her reason for wanting these particular items, she had responded glibly, "The earl has instructed me to treat the crofters at their homes, instead of here. He does not want their diseases to infect the castle people."

Although Alanna knew that Breadalbane had intended no such liberty for the prisoner, his letter of instruction had been a vague order to keep Mistress Campbell too busy to become moody or hysterical. Reluctantly, during the second week, when a crofter's wife had come to the castle with the report that her husband was too ill to leave the cottage, Alanna had agreed to Jolie's first medical mission beyond Kilchurn walls. Accompanied by a pair of soldiers, Jolie had been driven to a distant croft where she remained for two days, saving the life of a man who had been attacked by a wild boar a week earlier. While the worried family watched in the outer room of the small cottage, Jolie had performed a complicated debridement. Remembering Rorke's obsessive instructions about the prevention of gangrene, she had removed putrid flesh, cleaned out the pockets of infection and the clotted remains of the primitive medication the wife had used, and stitched the lacerated flesh together.

A day later, after an all-night vigil, the man's fever broke, and Jolie received a jug of the potent brew the natives called *usquebaugh*. Back at the castle, the bailiff assured her that the drink was the coin of the Highlands.

" 'Tis considered a mark of approval if ye're paid with it."

"I'd prefer money," Jolie protested.

"Scotland's a poor land, mistress. Only the lairds ha' the

gold. The rest of us are lucky to possess a small hoard of silver, and only the soldiers are paid much of that. If ye're planning to sell yer usquebaugh, our lads will be eager t' pay ye for it, and I'll see they dinna cheat ye.''

Within the week, Jolie had made three more outside calls and been paid a jug of the popular brew for each one. To her surprise, since she'd tasted it and decided the human body could not survive its regular usage, the soldiers now competed for the dubious honor of accompanying her. Each jug had been sold within minutes of her receiving it, and she'd amassed a handful of silver coins. Knowing that she was as prepared as she would ever be, she packed a scant supply of clothing, medicine, and soap into a leather backpack and waited for the weather to clear. To her horror, she waited a day too many to avoid a terrifying scene with Tavis Campbell.

Ten days past the new year, he arrived at Kilchurn, accompanied by Giles Campbell and the same four Breadalbane guards who had escorted her from Newcastle. In a jubilant mood, Tavis announced to Alanna that he had come to claim his promised wife. As was her wont each afternoon she was not on an outside call, Jolie was in the armory attending to complaints from castle workers. When a frightened Alanna entered the gloomy stone cavern and dismissed the waiting servants, Jolie knew the news would be unwelcome. Lady Fairleigh had always before shunned contact with sick people and anything medical.

"You cannot avoid having dinner with the man," she warned a stricken Jolie after she had identified the newly arrived visitors. "You wouldn't get a hundred yards from the castle if you were foolish enough to attempt an escape tonight. Wait until morning, Jolie. I'll try to help you then and so will the bailiff. Don't look so shocked, my friend. He has kept me informed about your preparations, and he hates Tavis Campbell as much as you do."

Except for Tavis's caustic humor when Jolie entered the guest hall looking as nunlike as she had in France, the dinner hour passed without any unpleasant disruptions. After the table had been cleared and the men were sipping the brandy they'd been served, Alanna asked about news from Edinburgh and Flanders.

Smiling as he had for much of the evening, Tavis responded promptly, " 'Tis good news all around—the king has finally agreed to a united Scotland. In six weeks, there'll be a permanent peace twixt the Campbells and MacDonalds.''

Leaning forward, Alanna asked with an eager intent, "Did Alasdair MacDonald sign the king's amnesty?''

Tavis smiled more broadly, but it was an alert Giles Campbell who answered Alanna's question. " 'Tis only rumor, Lady Fairleigh; no one knows the way of it yet.''

Having paid scant attention to the earlier conversation, Jolie had experienced renewed apprehension when Tavis mentioned the MacDonald name. Her sensitive ears had also detected the undercurrent of warning in Giles's evasive comment to Alanna. Now, as Tavis turned to face her directly, Jolie's apprehension turned into raw fear.

"At least there'll be peace between one Campbell bridegroom and his MacDonald bride,'' he boasted lightly. "My beautiful French nun and I are to be wed within the fortnight. Are you finally resigned to your fate, pretty Jolie? 'Twas what should have happened when first we met, before my unlucky cousin interfered.''

Pulling away swiftly to avoid the hand he stretched out toward her, Jolie broke her silence as she rose abruptly from her chair. "You are mistaken, Monsieur Campbell. There will be no marriage between us and no peace. I will never consent to be related to you or your father. I do not forget or forgive what you and he have done.''

Gasping in shock, Alanna stared at the younger woman, who seemed alien to the composed nurse of the past weeks. For a moment, Jolie had looked as fierce as the most savage Highland warrior, her blue eyes cold and defiant, and her refusal deliberately insulting. Fearfully, Alanna watched the angry flush that reddened Tavis's cheeks, and waited for the inevitable explosion of his temper.

"Do you think I'll give you a choice, you French slut?'' he rasped furiously. "If I could avoid it, do you really believe I'd wed a secondhand jade with the manners and looks of a kitchen slattern?''

With her lips curling in contempt, Jolie retorted recklessly, ''Now you sound like the old Tavis, and just as stupid.'' Her voice was still tense as she addressed Alanna. ''*Pardon*, madame, but I have work to complete.'' Without waiting for a dismissal, she fled from the room. As Tavis started to follow, Giles Campbell restrained him.

''Ye were told to guard yer tongue and not upset the damned woman,'' he said harshly. ''Let her be now until ye cool off; she'll be just as available tomorrow. Lady Fairleigh, I'll check the posting of the guards before I retire. 'Twas hard riding we did today.''

To Alanna's dismay, the brusque captain strode from the hall, leaving her alone with the more difficult guest whose earlier calm had been replaced by surly loquacity.

''Is she using her dead husband's old dungeon for her work?'' he asked.

''Yes, but don't disturb her tonight, Tavis; she's too upset.''

''Why the hell should she be?''

''You were not very flattering.''

''Neither was she!''

''She believes she has good reason. She is convinced—'' Alanna's voice trailed off as she watched him down a goblet of brandy and pour himself another. Disdainful of drunkenness even among the decent men of Scotland, she hoped this self-indulgent popinjay would drink himself into a stupor quickly so that she could be relieved of his company. But thus far, his tongue seemed unaffected.

''Finish what you were going to say, Alanna; I've other questions to ask,'' he commanded harshly.

Shrugging her shoulders in defeat, she replied curtly, ''Jolie is convinced the earl contrived her husband's death.''

Reacting with a sly smile, Tavis asked mildly, ''Has she ever mentioned my name in that regard?''

''We have never discussed you at all.''

"She didn't even tell you what her cursed husband did to me in Germany?"

"Not a word."

"He was the trickster who helped the German bastard."

"Your grandfather doesn't think so."

"Why do you think the earl schemed to get the fool shipped to Flanders?"

"I wouldn't know."

"Then I'll tell you, fair Alanna; 'tis not right you should miss the fun. He'd planned to make old Alasdair MacDonald pay a ransom larger than mine, but now 'twill not be necessary. The MacDonald laird has accepted me as Jolie's husband and agreed to have me take over her father's estate as one of his tacksmen. 'Tis where we'll be taking the hot-tempered termagant in a week, and the wedding will be held just after we arrive."

"How fortunate for you," Alanna murmured through stiff lips, shuddering when Tavis burst into laughter that was shrill with excitement. In a voice that now slipped and slurred over a rush of words, he began to talk with a half-sly, half-wild exuberance. Fifteen minutes later Alanna sat unmoving as she watched him walk unsteadily from the room. She knew she should try to warn Jolie, but her mind was too preoccupied with her own safety and that of her infant son. God's blood, what a fool she'd been! Now her only chance to regain her estate and perhaps her life was to take the protective asylum the earl of Argyll had offered her when the marriage to Rorke Campbell had failed to materialize. She shivered when she remembered the cost of Argyll's asylum—marriage to a homely, battle-scarred Argyll tacksman who would publicly claim her son as his own and make Fairleigh Manor a part of Argyll land instead of Breadalbane. As repugnant as the prospect was, Alanna knew she had no other choice. If John Campbell ever learned that his bastard son had told her about a plot so violently obscene that his reputation as a politician would be permanently ruined, he would be merciless in his need to silence her. Alanna's lips twisted into a grimace that was both bitter and vengeful as she thought of the earl's other bastard son—her own beautiful Alexander—who would soon become the son of an Argyll Campbell.

Rising stiffly from her chair, she walked slowly to her distant apartment to pack a small bundle of infant clothing and to inform her son's nurse that they would be leaving early the next morning. Except for the money in her purse, she warned the servant, they would take nothing else.

"'Tis why we've been taking daily sleigh rides for sport," she explained. "So there'd be no questions asked if 'twas needful we leave here in a hurry."

Not once during a sleepless night did Alanna remember that the young woman she'd been ordered to guard faced an even more dangerous future. The instinct for self-preservation that had kept her safe throughout three years of being the unwilling mistress of the powerful man she feared was too deeply ingrained to leave any room for compassionate concern about a woman she hardly knew. As friendly as she'd been toward Jolie when her own safety had not been threatened, Alanna was too entrenched an aristocrat not to consider her own survival the more important.

When Jolie had fled from the great hall, she raced not to her bedroom or to the armory, but to the bailiff's office. In a voice tense with fear, she gambled on Alanna's report that he had cause to hate Tavis, and blurted out her plan of escape and the reasons necessitating it.

With his shrewd face knotted in thought, he nodded his agreement to help her. "But 'twill not be easy, mistress," he warned her. "The blackguard captain the villain brought wi' him will be hard to avoid, and the bastard himself is no' easy to fool even when he's drunk. I've seen him outdrink a room full of soldiers and still be fit enow to do mischief. Was he drinking brandy tonight or usquebaugh?"

"Brandy, I think, monsieur."

"Di' ye know anything about drugging brandy, lass?"

Despite her shock, Jolie nodded grimly.

"Enow to keep him under 'til late morning wi' ou' killing him?" the bailiff persisted.

"The drug won't last that long, but he'll probably sleep that late naturally."

"Then 'tis best we tend to that business now, before he comes looking for ye. 'Tis a shame to waste the whole bottle, but he'd be as cautious as an old vixen if I brought him one only half full."

Jolie's hand shook as she measured the white powder into the brandy bottle the bailiff uncorked carefully. She wasn't certain which sin she was committing. While the relief of pain was blessed, this usage probably ranked close to the "thou shalt not kill" commandment. A half hour later, she almost wished the dosage had been lethal.

Tavis had located her quickly after he'd left Alanna in the great hall. As he strode into the dimly lit armory, he accosted the bailiff with an uncivil greeting.

"So this is where my grandfather hid you, Griogair Rowan, after you'd become violent at the MacTavish keep. 'Twas generous of him to appoint you a bailiff over such a trifling complaint. But now, you can earn your office by bringing me a bottle of something to drink and by leaving us alone. I have words to say to my future wife."

Tavis seated himself on the opposite side of the table and leaned toward her. Perspiring from fear, Jolie prayed helplessly that the bailiff would bring the brandy quickly, before Tavis demanded they return to the warmer quarters upstairs. Thus far, though, he seemed immune to the penetrating cold, and his speech was one of amused cajolery.

"We were foolish to argue over trifles, pretty Jolie. 'Twill be more pleasant if we forget the past. 'Twas not the truth when I said I didn't want you; I've thought of no one else since the day we met."

"I cannot forget the past, monsieur." From beneath her lowered eyelids, she watched his fist clench on the table and reflected nervously that his earlier fury was not yet under control.

"Then remember what you will, mistress, but not while

you're with me. I'll not abide a weeping woman, or one who hides herself behind the flummery of pills and nostrums. You'll be tending to more suitable pursuits once we're married." With the alert awareness wealthy people seemed to possess whenever a servant is close by, Tavis paused when the bailiff entered, carrying a bottle and single goblet.

" 'Tis the bottle ye ordered, sir," Bailiff Rowan intoned.

Waving his hand, Tavis indicated the table and ordered peremptorily, "Bring another goblet. I'd like my betrothed to join me in a toast."

"I do not drink brandy, monsieur," Jolie protested in dismay, adding with a burbling fluster, "but I will drink wine if Monsieur Rowan will bring me some."

Peering at her abruptly with calculating shrewdness, Tavis commented sharply, " 'Twould be interesting to know how a convent-raised woman recognized a brandy bottle."

Realizing her mistake, Jolie resorted to angry bravado. "The infirmary was in the middle of a vineyard, monsieur. All of us had to work at harvest and in the winery."

Tavis watched as the ruddy flush receded slowly from her face before he asked with ill-concealed contempt, "Did you really stomp grapes like the other peasants?"

"It was an easier job than picking them," Jolie gushed in relief, "but I hated the odors when I had to help with the bottling of wine and brandy."

"With all that temptation around, 'tis a wonder you didn't become a winepot."

"We were allowed to drink only watered wine with our meals, monsieur."

"My name is Tavis, as you well know, my stubborn wife-to-be. You can stop this inane pretense that we're strangers. You remember as well as I do that we were once good friends. Why else would you have saved my life and nursed me for all those weeks?"

Alarmed by his continued abstinence and angry that he considered her such a fool, she retorted brashly, "How could I have been a friend to you? You didn't think I was anything but a *coquine stupide*."

"If you'd told me the truth, I'd have acted the gentleman. How was I to know that you were related to the comte de Laurent? I thought you were a runaway nun looking for excitement. What did my saintly cousin do when he learned that you were doubly the heiress?"

"My husband was not impressed, monsieur."

"The hell he wasn't! He used your money fast enough to pay his debts."

"That was his right."

" 'Twill be my right before long, so we'll not argue the point now. Alanna said you blamed my grandfather for the good doctor's death."

"For his murder!"

"I'm not saying he wasn't pleased by the news, but he had nothing to do with it. 'Twas English highwaymen, just as the Argyll's letter said."

"When did you read that letter?"

"I didn't have to read it. I was waiting at the Edinburgh barracks when Giles brought me the good news."

Jolie sat frozen in her chair as the meaning behind those words penetrated her consciousness. She didn't look up when the bailiff brought the bottle of wine, nor did she speak when Tavis poured a cup of it and filled his own goblet with brandy. Her hands were shaking as she lifted her cup and drank deeply; she needed the warmth of the wine to ease the icy chill that had settled in the pit of her stomach. As she watched him sip his brandy, though, she felt an overwhelming urgency to know the whole truth and end the agony of doubt.

"Did you know what Giles's message would be before he returned?" she asked slowly.

There was a smile of triumph on his lips and a glitter of excitement in his eyes as he swirled the brandy around in his goblet. "Aye, I knew," he boasted, "but 'twas better than I'd hoped to have a company of Highlanders bear witness. That was just lucky chance, but the rest—"

"Was planned," Jolie interrupted in a whisper.

"And why not? Once I learned you were well-blooded enough to be my wife, how else could I gain that end? After I'd failed in Edinburgh, 'twas necessary to try again. This time 'twas a simple matter to plan once my grandfather learned where you were and had Rorke recalled to the king's service. There are thugs aplenty all over England eager for hire, and Giles knew enough to hire the best of them."

Numb with horror, Jolie listened to the increasing recklessness in his voice as Rorke's murderer continued to boast of his own cleverness, sipping his brandy in quick gulps so as not to interrupt himself. But her thoughts were no longer concentrated on his words or his increasingly slurred speech. She was remembering the contents of a small crock marked with a death's head she'd discovered the week before on a dusty shelf of the armory. She had no idea what disease either Rorke or the later physician had treated with the small dried berries, but she knew what they would do if they were powdered and put into brandy. Belladonna, the fruit of the dreaded nightshade plant, was as fatal as hemlock. From now on, it would be her protection against this monstrous killer who had announced so casually that he had murdered Rorke in order to marry her himself. With a hatred as intense as any Scot's for a clan enemy, Jolie watched Tavis Campbell slump slowly in his chair and fall asleep with his head on the table.

Out of breath from running, the bailiff was at her side in a minute. "God's wounds," he muttered, "I was afraid the murderous villain would talk forever. We've no time to waste, mistress."

Still concentrating on her unconscious enemy, Jolie asked curiously, "Why do you hate him, Monsieur Rowan?"

"A sordid story, mistress. Six years ago I was the head warden in the castle where this unholy bastard was raised. My daughter was his first victim; she died in childbirth when she was thirteen years old. But 'tis ancient history, and we've yer safety to consider now."

"What about your own safety?"

"He'll not dare accuse me, not with a castle full of soldiers who are my friends."

Nodding her head in relief, Jolie walked around the table with calm deliberation and removed the heavy sporran from around Tavis's kilted waist. After counting out twenty gold guineas—the sum the lawyer Carwhin had stolen from her in Newcastle—she returned the sporran and pocketed the money. At least in this small measure, the Campbells would repay the debt they owed her.

After a moment's hesitation, the bailiff took a like amount, but he pocketed only half the coins; the rest he kept in his hand.

"I've an idea that will get ye safe to Ballachulish, mistress, and a stone's throw from the entrance to Glencoe. There's a stable lad who's eager to rejoin his mother there, and he knows the Argyll countryside. Aye, and he's horseman enow to ride ye double until ye reach the Argyll boundary. 'Twill gi' ye the start ye need to avoid being overtaken if the villains decide to follow. The beast will return here on its own. I'll rouse the lad and pay him his due while ye get yer things together. The sooner ye're off, the sooner I can get that drunken clod into his bed."

An hour after dark, a shaggy plow horse carrying two riders and an assortment of bundles plodded through the main gate and headed west, its hoofprints in the snow indistinguishable from those made earlier by the sleek mounts of Tavis and his guards. Five hours later the great beast returned and was admitted by the same two smiling guards. For this night's work and for the mendacious report they were to make the next morning that they'd merely followed orders to let the nurse leave Kilchurn whenever a sick crofter summoned her, the soldiers had received a pair of shiny guineas each—the equivalent of two months' wages.

When the bailiff sounded the alarm late the following morning, it was not for Jolie and a missing stable boy; it was out of a genuine fear that Lady Fairleigh, her son, and his nurse had suffered an accident during their regular horse-drawn sleigh ride across the Kilchurn fields. Hours later, the hastily assembled troop of hunters could report only that the sleigh tracks led westward to Argyll land, where Breadalbane soldiers could not follow without permission. It was midafternoon before the other fugitives were missed, and a furious Giles Campbell roused Tavis from his bed.

Recalling at the last minute that his own future safety was dependent upon the temperamental younger man, Giles muted his anger when he reported the two women missing.

"I know the Frenchwoman dinna need an excuse, but di' ye say anything to upset Lady Fairleigh? 'Tis no' like her to take alarm."

Groggy and headache-ridden, Tavis glared at his comrade in crime. "I don't give a damn about Alanna. Let the earl take care of his own problem women," he declared sulkily. "'Tis the other bitch you have to find."

"How?" Giles asked in frustration. "Ye were told to hold yer peace about yer marriage to her until the earl ga' ye permission. Now 'twill be impossible to look for her. The earl of Argyll is already suspicious of me, so I canna go on his land with only four soldiers at my back to search her out. We'd best return to Edinburgh as soon as ye're up to hard riding. 'Tis no' a safe fix we're in, my lad, if ye were too drunk to know what ye were sayin' last night."

Having never been forced to accept blame, Tavis exploded into denial. "I didn't say a damn thing, and even if I had, 'twill make no difference. Since the bitch has probably headed for Glencoe, we'll be wed on schedule anyway."

Alanna's sleigh ride lasted only five hours—only until she was admitted into the small fortress that guarded the boundary between Breadalbane and Argyll lands just west of Fairleigh Manor. Escorted immediately into the owner's library, she announced without preamble, "I've come to accept your offer, if 'tis still available, Aillin Sloan Campbell. But until we're wed and my estate and son are legally under your protection, I'll not be returning to my home."

Shrewdly, the startled bridegroom asked no questions.

After two childless marriages, he considered himself a
fortunate man to gain a beautiful wife and a handsome heir
so easily. His only concern was the practical one of defense.
He summoned his sergeant-at-arms and ordered the watch
doubled. As an added precaution, he sent word out to the
closest of the other Argyll tacksmen to stand ready to assist
him should it prove necessary to repel an invasion by the
Grey Fox of Breadalbane.

As she listened to his efficient expediencies, Alanna
smiled wanly with relief, and the distaste with which she'd
always regarded him changed into respect. He was the only
one with the determination and the military prowess to
defend her, should John Campbell attempt to reclaim her
son. Thankful she'd been completely honest with her soon-
to-be husband about Alexander's parentage, she was assured
that Aillin Sloan would outshout Breadalbane even on the
floor of the Scottish Parliament that the child was his
through handfast. As much for his protection as for her
own, Alanna didn't tell him about Tavis's final boast that
there would be a Campbell laird in possession of the whole
of Glencoe in less than two months. Instead, she exerted her
considerable charm to guarantee herself and her son a
pleasant, secure future.

Jolie would never forget any detail of her five-day ordeal
on Argyll land, from her first night in a smoky, one-room
cottage already overfull with the crofter's family, to the final
morning, when she boarded a boat at the junction of Loch
Linnhe and Loch Leven. Miraculously, that boat had been
operated by Highlanders wearing the blue and green tartans
of the MacDonald clan.

Her remarkable companion, Quinn, whose lice she would
share within the first hours, was a short, fourteen-year-old
lad whose sinewy muscles had already acquired the strength
of a man's. Speaking not a word in English, he issued his
commands to her in Gaelic, cannily chose only humble,
outlying crofts, and paid the cost sparingly from Jolie's
meager hoard of silver coins. On the trail, when he'd

bounded from the horse and pulled the bundles off before he helped her down, he'd laced up her snowshoes efficiently, even though she could see almost nothing in the dark. After he'd put on his own, he tied a rope around her waist and started walking. Two hours later, he'd pounded on the door of a cottage that Jolie had seen only as a shapeless blob in the dim moonlight.

She didn't know or care what explanation Quinn gave to the hulking man who opened the door, nor did she make any protest when she and her guide were forced to share the same pallet on the floor. In the morning she'd devoured the heavy oatmeal cakes and fatty haggis sausages with an appetite that astounded her. That day her painful muscles had gradually hardened to the demanding exertion of walking on snowshoes at a pace that covered seven miles before Quinn located his next targeted lodging.

Although she knew she could not have survived without him, Jolie did not realize how fond she'd become of her young companion until they reached Ballachulish. There, in another cottage, she watched Quinn hand his mother the six gold guineas the Kilchurn bailiff had given him. As his mother's expression changed from disbelief to joy, Jolie realized with a shock that those few coins represented a fortune to the poor people of the Highlands. Yet a wastrel like Tavis Campbell could carry a pouch full of them that need only be spent on frivolities. She wished now that she'd emptied his purse.

The next day, when Quinn took her to the lake and paid for her ferryboat passage with the last of her silver coins, Jolie learned another lesson. Even the most lowly born of Highlanders were proud. With an unpretentious dignity, Quinn had refused to take the additional gold coins she'd offered him. From aboard the small craft, she watched him staring out over the water, and waved to him. As he returned the gesture, she felt a surge of humility. In spite of her tragic bereavement and the problems she still faced, her life was so much richer than his could ever be. With an abrupt determination to make her life a useful one, she pulled her rosary and cross from beneath her robe and arranged them neatly in place.

Ironically, that small gesture attracted the attention she had hoped to avoid. Before she had untied the bulky fur cloak, she had appeared much like the winter-clad peasant women of the Highlands. Not even the boatmen had paid her much notice, despite the oddity of a woman carrying snowshoes and traveling alone to Glencoe. But two of the passengers now peering at her closely had recognized the cowled headdress beneath the furry hood, and as Catholics, they'd understood the significance of the displayed rosary and cross.

Jolie would have been embarrassed by the degree of their automatic respect had she known. Although she'd tried to remove some of the filth that morning when Quinn's mother had handed her a bucket of warm water and pointed to a closed alcove in the yard, she still felt dirty and unkempt. It had been too cold to remove enough clothing for anything but a scant sponge bath and a vigorous brushing of her hair and uniform robe. She could only hope that her appearance did not offend these well-dressed, confident-looking men who wore their MacDonald tartans so proudly. Had she realized that one of them had already guessed her identity and would be responsible for the reception she'd receive after she'd been put ashore on Glencoe land, she might have become too suspicious to leave the boat.

Engrossed in her first sight of her father's homeland, Jolie didn't notice the other passengers who alighted with her or the one who was driven away in a sledge pulled by two horses. She was too appalled by the sight of the barren, towering hills that guarded the narrow entrance of the glen to pay any attention to much else. Expecting the hills to be as heavily forested as those in Breadalbane's Glenorchy Valley had been, she felt alienated by the bleakness of the landscape, which seemed nothing more than one steep, snow-covered hill after another. Fearing to enter the glen that might prove a more formidable prison than Kilchurn Castle, Jolie was slow to lace up her snowshoes and to adjust her backpack. As she watched the boat pull away from shore, she was tempted to recall it and inquire about a sea passage to England. But already she had waited too long; the boatmen were too far away to hear her.

Taking a deep breath to bolster her sagging courage, she began the long walk backward into her MacDonald father's past, rather than her own. How she wished Quinn were still with her to lead the way! A mile into the glen, her fears turned to puzzlement. The only buildings she had seen were the familiar farm crofts and shielings for the animals, and an occasional business establishment. There had been a roofed smithy where a man was shoeing a horse; a weaver's barn with lengths of heavy, coarse wool cloth hung on lines outside; and a small foundry whose snow-covered, outdoor furnaces looked as primitive as the bakers' ovens in France. Even the black cattle huddled in small shielings looked lean and hungry. Disappointed that Glencoe homes appeared as destitute as those in which she and Quinn had lodged, Jolie continued her steady plodding and stared anxiously into the distance, hoping to locate some sign of a castle, but so far there had been no structure of any great size.

She stepped away from the road to allow a large sledge to pass, and gulped nervously when it stopped beside her and two men dismounted. To her astonishment, one was a priest wearing a fur jacket over his heavy brown robe. Not expecting to find a priest in so sparsely populated a place, Jolie was further unnerved when he identified himself as Father Andrew and asked her name.

Too flustered to think coherently, she responded, "I am Sister Jolie from the Sisters of Charity Infirmary near Strasbourg."

Frowning in confusion, Father Andrew challenged her claim. "I wasn't aware that your order of nuns had any chapters outside of France, Sister Jolie."

As Jolie listened to the stern, familiar, admonishing tone of voice that had been typical of all the priests she'd met, she experienced an overwhelming sense of fate, and her vague thoughts of becoming a nun crystallized. Since the

day she had learned of Rorke's death, she had known that
her only chance to regain any permanent peace of mind
would be as a Sisters of Charity nurse. But now, she felt an
additional urgency—the only way a Catholic woman could
avoid being forced into a marriage she did not want was to
join an order of nuns.

"Father Andrew, could I speak with you privately in your
church?" she asked, her earlier embarrassment forgotten.

"If you like, Sister Jolie, but I think my home will be
more comfortable. During the winter months, Saint Munda
Chapel tends to be an icy tomb."

Seated beside the priest aboard the sledge, Jolie learned
more about her father's people during the twenty-minute
drive than she had in the year and a half she had known she
was a MacDonald. The Glencoe clan was only one of
several MacDonald clans, and the small valley's population
numbered less than five hundred, with only a hundred fifty
soldiers for its defense. When she had first heard of the fear
Alasdair MacIain aroused in his neighbors, she had thought
he would have thousands of fierce warriors at his command.
As the sledge was driven over a bridge spanning the half-
frozen Coe River, she received another shock as Father
Andrew pointed out a large two-story house with whitewashed
stone walls and a blue slate roof.

"That's Carnock House, Laird MacIain's home, Sister
Jolie."

"But it is not a castle," she gasped.

"There are no castles in Glencoe," the priest assured her.
"The mountains have always been protection enough."

"*Ma foi*, Father Andrew, there are a dozen fortresses in
Glenorchy, and the earl of Breadalbane is said to have
thousands of soldiers. Why is he so afraid of Glencoe, and
why does he hate Alasdair MacDonald so much?"

As he listened to her impassioned question, Father Andrew's
confusion vanished. This young woman was not a nun at
all; she was the widow he had been told to expect. He had
been puzzled earlier because he'd been told she would be
escorted by her Campbell betrothed, but no nun from France

could possibly know so much about the Grey Fox of Breadalbane or about such things as castles and soldiers. Frowning in disapproval, he responded to her urgent questions.

" 'Tis an ancient feud that's existed between the MacDonalds and Campbells for centuries. No one outside the Highlands can be expected to understand the depth of hatred.''

"Are you a MacDonald clansman, Father?''

"Aye, a Glengarry one from the clan just north of Glencoe, but I no longer approve of the feud or the hatred or the religious persecution. I saw enough of that during the fifteen years I studied for the priesthood in France. I suppose I could have gone elsewhere for my ministry, but I preferred to return to my home and work for peace here and in Glengarry. I pray that I may finally have succeeded. Just after Christ Mass, Laird MacIain left Glencoe to sign the papers of amnesty.''

Recalling what she had overheard John Dalrymple and Breadalbane say when she had been a prisoner at Stair Castle, and what Edina had told her later, Jolie shook her head in confusion.

"I was told that none of the MacDonalds would sign unless King James gave them permission. Did he?''

"I'm afraid kings are too self-centered to care what happens to their subjects. The MacDonald chiefs were forced to sign to save their clansmen. Glengarry signed first, then MacIain, and Keppoch will sign as soon as he is well enough. Hopefully now, the bloodshed will finally be over and the clans will be at peace with each other.''

As the sledge stopped in front of a stone house, larger and more attractive than most of its neighbors, Father Andrew alighted and waited for Jolie to follow him along a path that had been cleared of snow. His only additional comment before he was admitted into the house by a servant was to point out the nearby chapel and complain that like all Catholic structures left standing in Scotland, it was in need of repairs.

The house, however, Jolie quickly discovered was not! It

was furnished with thick carpets spread over polished wood floors and with beautifully carved tables and chairs.

"Some of the spoils from MacDonald raids on their neighbors," the priest explained. "Even today some of my parishioners consider clan thievery a profession rather than a crime. Most of these things were donated to former priests. In my time, I have refused all gifts, and I've worked hard to discourage the—"

Unwilling to listen to any more clan history, Jolie interrupted brashly, "Father Andrew, I need your help."

"Aye, and my spiritual guidance, as well," he scolded her brusquely. "You've not been honest with me. Now, remove your cloak and that pretension on your head, and tell me why the niece of Alasdair MacIain calls herself Sister Jolie instead of Annette MacDonald Campbell, and why she is disguised as a Sister of Charity."

Relieved that her pretense had been detected without having to undergo the tedium of confession, Jolie responded candidly. "Because for eighteen years I lived with Sisters of Charity, and I expected to become one. That is why I need your help now. I want you to hear my vows and certify me as an active member of the order."

Father Andrew stared at her thoughtfully before he shook his head. "Such an action on my part is impossible," he stated firmly.

"Why? Sisters of Charity are not like other nuns. We are allowed to choose the length of time we serve, and even our superiors can administer the vows."

"I know the rules that govern your order, Mistress Campbell, but I do not approve of them. Nuns should be lifetime servants of the church, not merely temporary members."

"Some of those temporary members are better nurses," Jolie demurred, adding the placating declaration, "There is no need for us to argue, Father. I am not interested in temporary vows; I wish to take a permanent one."

"As I told you before, such an action is impossible in your case. Your uncle, Laird MacIain, has made other plans for you."

"He is not my uncle—he is only a second cousin," Jolie amended sharply, "and he has no authority to arrange my life. What was it he planned for me?"

Studying the face of the woman now freed from the concealment of a coif, Father Andrew experienced abrupt trepidation. She wasn't the helpless woman he'd expected. There was a look of temper in her eyes as fierce as Alasdair's own, and the fiery tint of red in her hair marked her as another stubborn MacDonald. Still and all, he reflected, he would have to hear her out; his allegiance to the church must take precedence over all other considerations. If she was a qualified applicant and he refused her, she looked capable of stirring up a hornet's nest with his Franciscan superiors in France, particularly if MacIain's information was correct, that her grandfather was a French count of some importance.

"I prefer the laird tell you his plans himself; he should return in a day or two. In the meantime, I suppose I must consider your request. I know you have been recently widowed, and 'tis frequently grief that drives women to seek the safety of a convent. But I do not think it a wise choice until a year or more has passed, and I doubt that many of them would be interested then. Do you have any reason other than widowhood?"

Jolie's impassioned answer was an accounting of her twenty years of life—an untroubled childhood, a turbulently happy marriage, and six weeks of villainous treatment at the hands of her husband's murderer and his scheming father. Father Andrew flinched visibly as she described Rorke's cruel death.

"I was told only that your husband had died, not the circumstances," he admitted. *Mother of God*, he agonized silently, *how can I tell her that MacIain has already promised her in marriage to that same murderer?*"

"What else were you told about my husband and me, Father?"

"That he was a Campbell doctor, and that you had already inherited a fortune from your French grandfather and would soon inherit the one your MacDonald father left you.''

"I don't want my father's estate. I already have enough money to build the infirmary I'll need.''

"Here in Glencoe?''

"No, and not in France either, but in Martinique or Montreal, on property my mother has given me.''

"I don't understand. Why did you come to Glencoe at all, then?''

"My husband thought I'd be safe while he was away—'' Jolie paused to steady her voice and to blot out the poignant memories of Rorke's concern for her. "When the soldiers came for me in Newcastle,'' she continued shakily, "they said they were the MacDonalds I was expecting.''

"The MacIain did send three men to fetch you, but they reported that you'd already left.''

"I'd been abducted by Campbells. Now, tell me, what does your MacIain have planned for me?''

Struggling against the feeling of inescapable entrapment, Father Andrew rose from his chair and walked across the room to stare out of a fancifully leaded window with his back toward his disturbing guest. As a servant of the church, he knew what his decision should be. The Sisters of Charity order had been created for women just such as this one—unfortunate victims whose gratitude often enriched the church. As a parish priest who had ministered to the MacDonalds of Glencoe and Glengarry for twenty years, Father Andrew could not endanger his people. He had labored too long to convince the MacDonald chieftains to accept the amnesty regardless of King James, whose own stupidity had cost him the throne. After the battle of Dunkeld sixteen months ago, the deposed king had been hiding safely in France. Father Andrew had been the one who had had to tell a hundred MacDonald women that their husbands and sons had been killed in another futile battle.

When the news had arrived in the Highlands that the new king, William, was threatening to declare fire and sword against the rebels, Father Andrew was not deceived. In twenty years, he'd learned that the real rulers of Scotland were the two Campbell chiefs and the ambitious, zealously Calvinist Lowlander, John Dalrymple, master of Stair. These were the real enemies of the MacDonald clans; and both Dalrymple and Breadalbane were ruthless men who conquered by stealth. If an interfering priest prevented the marriage that Breadalbane had arranged through murder and kidnapping, all MacDonalds would be in danger, despite the amnesty granted by a faraway king.

Turning around to face the woman staring at him with eyes that were already stricken with a dawning suspicion, Father Andrew announced heavily, "MacIain has signed a wedding contract with the earl of Breadalbane that will unite you and—"

"My husband's murderer," Jolie interrupted in a lifeless voice.

Encouraged by her lack of hysteria, the priest became more expansive. "Other women have survived such marriages, and Alasdair will see that you're safe enough. He made the earl agree that you and his grandson—"

"His bastard son," Jolie interrupted again.

"That you and the young man will live here on your estate in Glencoe under the clan's protective eye."

"You're wrong, Father Andrew. I'll be leaving Glencoe long before Alasdair MacIain returns." With hands that trembled from shock and exhaustion, Jolie picked up her cowl and refastened it around her head before she stood up and walked toward the entry where her equipment was stored.

"In God's name, mistress, you can't leave Glencoe," the priest exclaimed in agitation. "By this time, the entire glen knows of your arrival."

"Do you plan to tell them who I am, Father?"

He didn't have to meet her steady gaze to realize his defeat. It was one thing for a priest to deny a request; it was unthinkable for him to betray an innocent woman.

"What I am going to do right now, mistress, is to see to

your dinner and lodging. Afterward we'll find a way out of this dilemma.''

By the end of that dinner—a meal of delicately roasted venison and dried berry cake—Father Andrew and Jolie had agreed to a compromise. The following morning after she'd bathed in the priest's private tub, a neatly uniformed Jolie was escorted to the chapel by two men who would act as witnesses. Kneeling on the icy floor before a fully robed Father Andrew, she took her first vow as a Sister of Charity, a vow that might keep her safe from a forced marriage for one year, a vow promising that she would remain in Glencoe for the same period of time.

Immediately afterward, Jolie accompanied the priest to the shore of Loch Leven, where the signed document was handed to a boatman to begin its long trip to church officials in Paris. For the three days following, Jolie remained at the priest's home while Father Andrew stayed at Carnock with MacIain's wife and her sons' families.

On the second day of Jolie's seclusion, Laird Alasdair MacDonald returned to Glencoe with his sons and tacksmen. In a mood as violent as a thundercloud, the Glencoe chief told of the insulting treatment he had received when he had tried to sign the amnesty. After being refused at Fort William, he'd begun the harsh trip to Inveraray, the stronghold of the earl of Argyll. Along the way at another Argyll castle, he had been arrested and imprisoned for a full day. At Inveraray, he'd been prevented from signing for five days and treated like a criminal rather than a respected clan chieftain.

"But you did finally sign?" Father Andrew persisted anxiously.

"Aye, I signed."

"Was your signing witnessed and recorded?"

"Aye, by a pack of Campbell jackals."

"Then your clan is safe, Alasdair," the priest exclaimed in relief; but his relief was short-lived. MacIain had been told of Jolie's arrival the minute he'd stepped off the boat onto his own land.

"Aye, the clan's safe," he agreed gloomily, "but the MacDonald name has been disgraced, and within the month, I'll be forced to accept a cursed Campbell as a tacksman. Did you tell my niece she'll be wed to a weakling cub whom the evil Breadalbane claims as a grandson?"

Long familiar with Alasdair's unpredictable temper, Father Andrew had hoped to avoid any mention of the marriage until the clan chief recovered from his demoralizing defeat. But there was no way he could avoid answering so direct a question.

"There will be no Campbell tacksman in Glencoe for at least a year," he declared firmly. "The woman has already taken her vows as a Sister of Charity."

As the priest explained the circumstances that had prompted his interference in clan business, MacIain's anger against Breadalbane increased steadily; but so did his suspicions about the reliability of his unknown niece.

"You say she escaped from Kilchurn Castle and walked across the whole of Argyll land in the dead of winter?" he demanded skeptically.

"You'll find her a remarkable young woman, Alasdair," the priest murmured soothingly. "I used the only means possible to convince her to remain in Glencoe, else she would have walked out of here as determinedly as she walked in. Remember, she has better reasons than you do to hate Breadalbane and the young Campbell. Do you want me to write the letter informing them of her change in status?"

Bleakly, the laird of Glencoe shook his head. "As much as I admire her courage, the wedding will take place as scheduled. I've given my word. You're to destroy the record of those vows, Andrew; the cursed Campbells would pay no attention to them anyway."

"That record is on its way to Paris, Alasdair. I, too, have given my word that she'll be spared for at least a year. If you force her against her will, you'll be punished by the church, and she will be excommunicated. Think, man; at least in part, your rebellion over the past twenty years has been for the right to remain Catholic in a land of fanatic

Covenanters. Not even clan safety could justify your disobedience to the church if you persist in this cruelty. Let me
write the letter. I believe I can convince John Campbell that
a year is not too long to wait. I don't think he'll be foolish
enough to defy the king's amnesty over the matter."

"The damned fox won't do it openly, Andrew; he'll bribe
his vulture friends to do it for him. I'll know better what to
do after I meet this niece of mine."

"She claims to be only a cousin."

"Her father was my sworn brother in youth, so I've
always considered her a niece, and from the sound of her, a
damned rebellious one."

"She's a MacDonald," Father Andrew murmured dryly.

Jolie's first formal meeting with the man who called himself her uncle took place at Carnock three days later—just
hours before Father Andrew left for Glengarry. While the
priest conferred with the MacDonald chief in the library,
Sister Jolie was given a tour of the beautiful home by Lady
MacDonald, who treated her guest with a respect that made
Jolie feel like a hypocrite. Even so, the house intrigued her.

Expecting the same tapestry-covered stone walls she'd
seen in Stair Castle, Kilchurn, and even in her grandfather's
chateau in Strasbourg, she was pleasantly surprised by the
wood paneling at Carnock and the delicately elegant French
furniture. But the numerous artifacts pointed out by the
proud hostess made Jolie nervous. These pieces were the
loot plundered during a hundred raids against their neighbors. She wondered sadly how many of them had once
belonged to Rorke's grandfather, whose estate had been
stripped and then destroyed. Had she known that the magnificent rings on eight of Lady MacDonald's fingers had also
been stolen, she would have felt even more alienated.

When Father Andrew emerged from the library, he drew
Jolie aside and whispered a terse warning. "Do as he tells
you, Sister, and don't argue with him. He can be childish
when he is in one of his moods."

Jolie's first impression of her courtesy uncle was of

height—lean, towering height, topped by a full head of white hair framing a tanned face and an extravagantly curled mustache. Rorke had been tall, Jolie remembered sadly, but still seven inches shorter than this overpowering giant. Resentful that her uncle seemed to use that height to intimidate her as he admitted her into another paneled room, she stepped away from him as quickly as she could. Before he could speak, she asked bluntly, "Was my father as tall as you, monsieur?"

"Nay, lass. Niall was tall enough, but he had the sense to stop growing a foot shorter and keep his brain intact. My head's been knocked about by every door lintel and low-hanging branch in the Highlands, but Niall ne'er took a blow. You have the look of him about the eyes, but I'll know better when I see your hair. Will you take your cowl off and humor an old man? Father Andrew said he'd convinced you not to shave your hair off."

"Only until spring, when I expect to be wearing official vestments, monsieur." More provoked with Father Andrew than with her uncle, Jolie removed the coif and waited. Annoyingly, MacIain only nodded before he introduced an entirely different topic.

"I've decided 'tis time you move to Kinvernach, lass, where you'll be safer. 'Twas your father's home, and his father's before him, and the croft folk about are eager for a permanent tacksman. You'll find the rent money and other such stored in the strongbox there, and I've kept a record so you'll know you've not been cheated."

Fearful that the word *safer* meant *inescapable*, Jolie protested, "I've promised Father Andrew that I'd remain at his home while he's in Glengarry."

"Aye, but your duty to your father's people is more important. Now, tell me about your first Campbell husband. I can't place his name with either the Breadalbanes or Argylls."

He has no intention of recognizing my vows, Jolie fumed silently. His words, *first Campbell husband*, implied all too clearly that in his mind there would soon be a second.

Ignoring Father Andrew's advice to avoid argument, she asserted boldly, "You should remember my husband's Argyll family, monsieur. The Glencoe MacDonalds destroyed his grandfather's estate forty-two years ago and killed everyone except his father."

"Then 'twas my father's doing, though I recall going on the raid as a young lad. They fought to stop us from crossing their land on the way to Glenorchy. We'd not have killed Argyll Campbells otherwise."

How casually unimportant he makes murder sound, Jolie reflected dismally. "My husband was a pauper because of that raid, monsieur," she reproached her uncle. "His mother was forced to ask the earl of Breadalbane for charity."

"She'd have found the devil a more generous lender," MacIain denounced harshly. "Andrew told me you were forced to wed the man in France."

"Yes," Jolie admitted.

"And you survived the marriage for a year or more."

"I was very happy. Rorke was a wonderful husband and the only man I'll ever love."

" 'Tis not the point, lass. You wed one Campbell against your will; now 'tis time you wed another. The priest was worried you'd be forced out of the church, but I'm thinking you're not as devoted to religion as you pretend. You didn't bat an eye or bend a knee when you passed that crucifix on the wall behind you."

"Neither did you, monsieur," Jolie snapped defensively.

" 'Twill be easier between us if you call me uncle. 'Tis not a prison sentence I'm wishing on you, lass."

"No, Uncle, not a prison sentence—a death sentence. I'm just not certain whose death it will be—mine or the *cochon* murderer you plan to make my husband."

Alasdair MacDonald stared long and earnestly at the woman the priest had called "resourceful," and his mind reverted to the distant past. Her father Niall had been the shorter, younger man, but not once had Alasdair bested him in a fight or argument. On one of the few times Niall had returned to Glencoe before he'd married the Frenchwoman,

he had announced his conversion to the Protestant faith and
his opposition to any future raids on other clans in front of
the congregation in Saint Munda's chapel. And no one in
the clan had dared challenge him on either issue! The
daughter had the same look of determined confidence that
only a fool would underrate. Better to risk Breadalbane's
anger about a year's delay than to expose the clan to
extermination if the woman carried out her threat to murder
the Campbell bridegroom.

Acknowledging still another defeat, MacIain nodded his
surrender. "You've your father's fighting spirit, lass. I'll
grant you the year's reprieve from marriage."

"In that case, Uncle, you'll call me by my title, Sister
Jolie, and you'll grant me permission to practice my profession of nursing."

God's wounds, she is a damnably stubborn woman,
MacIain fumed. But a moment later, he smiled with reluctant pride. She was also a fiery MacDonald who'd win her
share of battles, one way or another.

8

Jolie's fears that her inherited home, Kinvernach, would be located in the remote reaches of the valley, far removed from the accessible exit of Loch Leven, proved dismally accurate. The stone house was perched atop a low hill in front of the mountainous southern boundary of Glencoe, overlooking the village of Kinvernach. A mile and a quarter eastward on the same slopes was Achtriachton, the last settlement of the ten-mile valley, a sentinel village whose tacksmen maintained the eastern defenses of the MacDonald stronghold.

Driven to her new home in the sledge piled high with bundles and boxes taken from Carnock storehouses, and followed by another sledge carrying MacIain and his sons, Jolie underwent a formal introduction, first to the tacksmen of Glencoe, and then to the Kinvernach crofters from the village. In the manor house's main room, itself four times the size of a village cottage, she stood next to MacIain while he performed the lengthy introduction in Gaelic. Jolie had little idea what he said about her, but she knew from the expressions of the crofters nearest her that they were relieved there would be no Campbell tacksman dictating their lives for another year.

Afterward the elderly servants, who had maintained the house for twenty years during the absence of an owner, served a dinner to the forty guests that taught Jolie more about the lives of Glencoe people than all of Father Andrew's stern lectures. There was a democratic camaraderie from the youngest crofter to MacIain, and a capacity for usquebaugh and wine on all their parts that bespoke of frequent and expensive celebrations. There was also an exuberance about their merrymaking, from the wild music of the bagpipes to the athletic dancing of the men in solo or group performances.

As the only woman present, Jolie sat in lonely isolation next to MacIain at the head of the huge table that occupied a third of the room. Occasionally, the chieftain would speak in English to her, and during a lull in the entertainment, MacIain's oldest son, John, explained what her Kinvernach holdings were. She owned the home, the cattle meadow behind it, and all the land of the spread-out village. In Glencoe, John MacDonald said, only MacIain, his family, and his tacksmen could own the land; the crofters all paid rent to the owners. In her case, she'd also been paid rent for the use of her meadow.

Not until the next day, however, did Jolie learn the extent of her inherited wealth or understand completely why Breadalbane and his bastard son Tavis had schemed so villainously to acquire it. In an ancient strongbox bolted to the stone walls of Kinvernach's dank cellar, she found four chests amid a welter of yellowed parchment deeds to the various parts of her land holdings. The largest of the chests contained assorted sizes of silver plates, cups, and bowls, blackened by tarnish and embellished with the crests of a dozen different clans. Another one was full of silver coins, identified as rent money collected over a quarter of a century. In a much smaller chest, itself an ornate work of art, were gold coins, many of them dated a century earlier. The fourth and last was stuffed with a hodgepodge of jewelry—large silver brooches with Argyll and Breadalbane crests, ornate and ancient necklaces, rings of varying sizes and degrees of worth, and enameled cameos in gold filigree settings.

Her father may have declared his opposition to any

further raiding of Campbells, Ogilvies, MacGregors, and Camerons, Jolie reflected cynically, but not until after he and his ancestors had amassed enough booty to last the family for generations. Silently she vowed that none of this ill-gotten wealth would fall into the hands of Breadalbane and his murderous kin. If she were forced into marriage, the contents of these chests would be forever hidden in the vastness of the surrounding mountains.

It was to this end that she requested her head crofter to be her guide in an exploration of her land and the mountains immediately beyond. With his limited English and her few words of Gaelic, they communicated with a sufficient understanding as they snowshoed over her cattle pastures and then hiked up a narrow mountain trail to a small boxed-in canyon he called Coire Gabhail, the Hollow of Capture. Bitterly disappointed that she had not located an escape route out of Glencoe should the need arise, Jolie began the secretive task of moving her wealth in small parcels to the largest cave in the mountains surrounding Coire Gabhail, and hiding it in a pit she'd located among the broken rocks at the rear. Each morning she made her lonely pilgrimage until she knew the way even during a light snowstorm.

Driven by an urgency she could not explain even to herself, she continued her self-appointed task long after the chests from the strongbox had been emptied. Only now the bundles she carried had a more specific purpose—their contents would keep her alive if she were forced to flee from Kinvernach. They contained ancient furs from the trunks of stored clothing, small sacks of dried food from the large pantry, and two pots from the kitchen shelves.

Jolie knew that part of the compulsion that drove her was the need to be alone, to ease the grief she could not show to strangers, and to try to rebuild her shattered morale. The hatred that had sustained her during the escape from Kilchurn Castle did not lessen in intensity, but like her lonely grief over Rorke's death, it was an emotion she had to hide each day she returned from Coire Gabhail. The life of a MacDonald tacksman, she'd discovered the first afternoon after her introduction to her crofters, was not without responsibilities and administrative duties.

Alasdair MacIain had been stern in his admonishment to her. "You're to visit each crofter's home and learn to know your people. 'Tis the only way to build clan loyalty. They're your responsibility now, lass, and they'll look to you for guidance."

Since her protest that she knew nothing about Highland customs went unheeded, Jolie felt obliged to make at least a gesture of friendship. During those first afternoons, she trudged to each of the thirteen cottages in turn, with the head crofter as her guide and interpreter. After only one afternoon, she knew why these lesser MacDonalds were as eager for raiding as their masters. The cottages were larger than any of those she and Quinn had visited on Argyll Campbell land, and each one had shielings full of cattle and smaller animals. Although she saw no evidence of gold and silver inside the well-built stone houses, she noticed objects that indicated a wealth far greater than that of most Highland peasants.

The people, too, were better dressed than either Breadalbane or Argyll crofters—the men in leather trews and jackets, and the women in dresses more elaborate than homespun. Nor could Jolie find any signs of sickness among the numerous children—neither the flushed faces of lung illness nor the wizened look of undernourishment. At least the theft of cattle had benefited the children! The small oaten cakes Jolie was offered by anxious housewives were spread with butter and accompanied by cups of milk; not since Newcastle had she tasted either. But despite their obvious attempts to please her, Jolie felt alienated and hypocritical. They treated her with the same awed respect she suspected they had lavished only on Father Andrew prior to her arrival.

Not until the tenth morning of her residency at Kinvernach was she offered a gesture of genuine friendship. Just after she'd deposited an armful of furs on top of her goods in the cave at Coire Gabhail, she turned around to discover she had a silent audience of two men, both burdened with a load of peat fuel, a commodity she'd forgotten in her disorganized planning. While old Huw, the aged caretaker of Kinvernach Manor, rearranged her carelessly strewn stores and piled protective rocks over the sacks of food, her head crofter, Murray, spoke quietly to her in his mixture of Gaelic and English. To Jolie's almost tearful relief, he understood the reasons that had motivated her clandestine actions, and approved of them. As much as she did, he feared the prospect of a Breadalbane Campbell overlord. In a simple declaration of loyalty, he promised to help her avoid the threatened marriage if he could. Jolie no longer felt as alone or as isolated in her strange new world.

That warming sense of kinship was to be increased a hundredfold during the frantic days that followed Murray's and Huw's offer of support. Waiting for the three of them as they descended from Coire Gabhail was one of MacIain's gillies with a message that Jolie and Murray were to report immediately to Carnock. Vaguely irritated by the peremptory tone of the summons and hopeful that the occasion would not prove to be another celebration, Jolie was instantly chastened by the grim faces of the clan leaders already gathered in MacIain's library.

A message had arrived from a Glengarry MacDonald who'd been visiting his daughter in Ballachulish that a four-hundred-man Argyll regiment had been seen marching toward Fort William, twenty miles north of Glencoe, and that another contingent of equal size was reported headed for Ballachulish.

" 'Tis too many soldiers for that puny fort to hold," MacIain announced gravely. " 'Tis more likely the bulk of them will be quartered in Keppoch, Glengarry, and Glencoe. We all knew the parsimonious King William would not give amnesty without demanding payment. Very likely we'll be asked to house and feed a part of his army for the winter until he's certain he controls the Highlands."

MacIain paused in his recital to stare unhappily out the window overlooking the broad reaches of his ancestral land, which had never before been invaded by the Campbell enemy.

" 'Tis not a pleasant prospect, I grant you," he admitted reluctantly, "but if we're forced to play the host, we'll not surrender completely. You'll be leaving only your useless, rusted weapons on display; your good blue steel ones are to be hidden in peat stacks or beneath heaps of stones along the river banks. Aye, and hide your gold and valuables so you won't be robbed when they depart. Since royal armies consider all provender theirs for the taking, you'd best put aside some food stocks, lest you be caught short before the winter's through.

"Each of you will tell your crofters and gillies and see the work done as quickly as possible. But one more word of warning—let no man show his resentment! Not even the king's amnesty will be protection enow if any one of us draws sword."

In a final admonishment, MacIain turned toward Jolie. " 'Tis not likely you understand the necessity or know the way of it, lass. You'd best turn the task over to Murray, and give the women what comfort you can. 'Twill be their first time of meeting the enemy."

Even more than he'd underestimated her resistance to marriage, MacIain underestimated her understanding of the potential situation. Inexperienced about weaponry and a tacksman's duties she might be, but she knew more about the outside world than any of these insular clansmen did, their chieftain included. And she knew the stealthy methods employed by her personal enemies! If there were Argyll soldiers coming, Breadalbane's agents would be among them, and Tavis Campbell would not be far behind.

On the drive back to Kinvernach, Jolie and her croftsman, Murray, came to a ready agreement, their fears transcending all language barriers. It would take their combined strengths to prepare their people for the threatened ordeal. In one area, at least, Jolie had a distinct advantage: she knew how merciless Calvinist zealots could be about the artifacts of Catholic worship. Standing in front of the assembled villagers, she removed her cross and rosary and announced through Murray that she would keep everyone's sacred symbols as safe as she would her own. No other gesture could have won her a more instant loyalty. Despite the fact that some of the ornate crosses and carved icons the housewives brought her had been stolen from neighboring estates on some ancient clan raid, the MacDonald crofters were deeply religious people. One of the women handed her a magnificent breviary, yet Jolie was certain that no one in the village could read.

Within two days, Kinvernach people had carried out all of MacIain's orders, and Jolie's own hiding place in Coire Gabhail was well enough stocked to supply her for a year of hiding. But far from being calmed, her anxiety increased hourly. On her last climb up the steep trail to the hidden canyon, she looked around at the barren landscape, where the only other living creatures were a few cattle huddled near crude stone shielings, and shuddered uncontrollably. In the eight weeks since her abduction from Newcastle, her life had been one crisis after another, which she'd survived by cunning. But nothing she had learned from those bitter experiences could help her now, any more than the religious vows she had taken so impulsively. Broodingly, she thought about her last meeting with Tavis Campbell, when she had drugged his brandy and escaped from Kilchurn. She knew now that there could be no permanent escape from him until she was far away from Scotland, or until he was dead. This desolate canyon could only be a temporary sanctuary. Even if Tavis didn't discover its location, the isolation would drive her back to Kinvernach sooner or later.

Bleakly, Jolie wondered if she could ever deliberately take a human life, even one as despicable as Tavis Campbell's. It had been easy to convince herself that she was callous enough when she was arguing with MacIain and when she packed the jar of belladonna berries in her sack. At night, in the squalid hovels that had sheltered Quinn and her, she had brooded darkly about offering Rorke's murderer another bottle of brandy, this one laced with the ground-up powder of those berries. He had destroyed her happiness without mercy; why should he be spared? He wouldn't hesitate to kill her once he had acquired the money and power he craved, and she would be as helpless as Rorke had been against his hired assassins.

Not entirely helpless, Jolie reminded herself. There was more than one way to poison if she had no other weapons. Just the prick of a knife with a poisoned tip could kill if necessary. And self-defense was a necessity, Jolie thought grimly. She might not be capable of deliberate murder, but she was more than capable of fighting for her own life. Driven by an abrupt urgency, she began to run awkwardly across the snow-covered meadow, a feat she had not known was possible on snowshoes. Two hours later, in the dank and debris-filled corner of the cellar of her home, she rummaged through the piles of ancient weapons and broken pieces of armor discarded by her remote ancestors until she located what she sought—two rusty daggers still encased in their rotting leather holders. The smooth blades of the newer ones she had hidden beneath a peat stack would not hold enough belladonna paste to kill a man quickly, but the scaly patches of rust on these ancient weapons would.

In the privacy of her bedroom, she ground up the harmless-looking berries with the pestle and mortar she had found on a kitchen shelf, and added enough grease to make a paste. After smearing it evenly over six inches of each dagger blade, she buried the now-lethal weapons at the bottom of a chest of old clothing. That afternoon, as she and the crofter Murray visited with the anxious clansmen, she remembered her hidden weapons when she heard the latest rumor about the expected Campbell invasion. Two days later, those rumors turned into fact as two hundred Argyle soldiers marched into Glencoe Valley and asked for quarter.

Jolie learned of their presence hours after their arrival, when a messenger raced to Kinvernach with MacIain's orders that Campbell soldiers were to be quartered in every cottage and manor house in Glencoe. Despite the warning her crofters had received days earlier, none of them accepted the news calmly. Repressing her own churning fears, Jolie accompanied Murray to every cottage, nodding encouragement while he explained the necessity of a peaceful reception.

When the regimental contingent assigned to Kinvernach marched into the village, she stood silently alongside the crofters and shared their anger and apprehension. Not even the dragonades on the beach of the Rhine River had frightened her as badly. Perhaps it was the vainglorious uniforms these soldiers wore that made them seem so alien to the darker-clad MacDonalds. Dressed in bright red coats, yellow hose, and blue bonnets with the boar's head Argyll insignia on the side, they looked more like parade manikins than fighting men. But their muskets and pikes were expertly carried, and they marched with a precision cadence.

Within the hour, the efficient sergeant had quartered his men—three to the smaller cottages and five to the larger ones—and informed Jolie that he and four others would reside with her. At the supper table that night, he explained that only English-speaking Lowlanders had been assigned to her home in deference to her ignorance of Gaelic. They would, he assured her, be as little bother as possible and would in no way restrict her freedom or that of her villagers. On a more personal note, he admitted that he and his men were Calvinists, but that they would respect her Catholic office and call her Sister Jolie Annette as the Laird MacDonald had suggested.

Still cautious, but no longer so afraid, Jolie made an effort to ease the awkward tension still further. She told them about Rorke's five-year career of rescuing French Huguenots and about her own part in bringing the Reverend Abelard Darrell safely to Holland. At the mention of Darrell's name, one of the privates broke his silence.

"A muckin' busybody when he stayed at Edinburgh Castle winter last. He dinna like much of anything he saw and told us so from the pulpit every morning at chapel."

"He was not popular in France either, monsieur," Jolie murmured.

"Wasn't a one of us what didn't shout 'huzza' when the king sent for him," the soldier added with satisfaction.

As if nature approved of harmony among men, however strained it was, the next morning dawned warm and springlike—a rare phenomenon for early February in the Highlands. Within days, the snow was melted from the valley floor and a peaceful routine was established. During the morning hours, the village men went about their farm chores while their wives prepared the more extensive meals, and the Argyll soldiers drilled in the village meadows. But in the short afternoons, the Campbell Highlanders vied against the MacDonalds in the friendly competition of archery, sword dancing, wrestling, stone throwing, and pole tossing. Each victory was celebrated with toasts of usquebaugh, and the good-natured camaraderie continued in the cottages at night as the MacDonald hosts joined their Campbell guests in singing, gaming, and friendly exchanges of stories that avoided all mention of past animosities. While the women and children slept crowded into one room, the men gambled and played beneath the light of resinous pine candles or smokey mutton-fat lamps until they, too, retired to their pallets and slept through what was left of the night.

At Kinvernach Manor the festivities were more muted. Jolie ate her meals with the soldiers, but retired shortly after supper, leaving her guests with a plentiful supply of claret wine and usquebaugh. As Sergeant Cawley had promised, they didn't abuse her hospitality, and the relaxed conversations at the large table increased the general congeniality. Whatever strain her Catholic title of sister might have caused was eased by her admission that her religious duties were limited to nursing. When she admitted that had her Campbell husband not been killed, she would never have returned to her church at all, she achieved friendly rapport with the middle-aged Cawley. During the Commonwealth years, he admitted in return, his Catholic parents had been forced to convert to the stern Protestant faith of those repressive years. A career soldier, the veteran sergeant considered all churches to be little more than unnecessary irritants, and was accordingly more at ease with a medical nun than he would have been with a devoutly prayerful one. Jolie soon accepted his gruff companionship as she once had that of Rob Dunmore aboard the *Rijn Königen*, the Dutch ship that had carried her and Rorke from Mannheim to Holland so long ago.

But on the tenth day of the Argyll regiment's quartering at Glencoe, her fears returned in full strength. Prior to that, she had received only reassuring messages from MacIain, disclaiming any danger to her or to the clan. " 'Tis friends the Campbells have become, and our rivalry is now limited to games and drinking," he exulted in one hastily scrawled note.

That Alasdair MacDonald was childishly optimistic she learned on the day that Captain Robert Campbell of Glenlyon visited her. She was in the library, reading one of the French books left behind by her father, when the captain was ushered into the room by her nervous caretaker. At Stair Castle, during their previous meetings, she had been grateful for his friendly charm. At Kilchurn, though, Alanna Fairleigh had described him as the most devious of Breadalbane's tacksmen, a compulsive gambler and drinker, a consummate liar and actor, and a willing participant in John Campbell's most treacherous schemes. More important, he had lost his once wealthy estate partly over gaming tables, but mostly to MacDonald raiders from Glencoe.

Watching him as he strode into the library, his pale hair streaming over his shoulders and his lips stretched open with a smile that didn't reach his dark, staring eyes, Jolie felt a cold premonition. Why had a Breadalbane officer who had lost his fortune to the MacDonalds been chosen to lead the Argyll soldiers on this particular mission? Without giving her a chance to ask if Lieutenant Tavis Campbell had accompanied him, he boomed into jovial speech.

"I'd expected to see you long before this, Mistress Campbell. But 'tis understandable you stayed away, though I admit to shock at the odd way you sought to ease your grief. Still, MacIain tells me your penitence will last but a year, and you'll be Mistress Campbell again, instead of Sister Jolie Annette. Did you know that you and I are in very similar positions in this beautiful glen? You because 'tis still strange to find yourself a MacDonald after a lifetime of not knowing, and me because 'tis the first time I've been able to visit my niece Sarah and her husband, who's a younger son of your Uncle Alasdair. Sarah tells me she hasn't seen you yet."

"No," Jolie admitted. "I've met few people other than my villagers."

"That's your problem, lass. You shouldn't sit here like a recluse, brooding about a dead past, when there's a lively present to enjoy and a fine future ahead of you."

Repulsed by his loud voice and hypocritical advice, Jolie muttered in protest, "I'm not brooding, monsieur, and my future is already decided. I am returning to my profession of nursing."

" 'Tis no life for a pretty woman, mistress. You'll find 'twill not be a popular choice in Scotland."

"I plan to return to France, monsieur."

"Do you now? 'Twill be interesting to see how you will feel three months from now. Until then, the Highlands winter will hold you prisoner unless you grow the wings of one of your Catholic angels. But I didn't come to bedevil you, Sister Jolie Annette, only to bid you peace."

"Did you bring Tavis Campbell with you to bid me peace also, monsieur?" Jolie demanded dully.

"Aye, both he and Lieutenant Lindsey are here, but Tavis will not disturb you, mistress, until 'tis time. He was sore annoyed with you at Kilchurn, and none too happy about Lady Fairleigh's desertion to the Argylls. Aye," Glenlyon nodded when he noted Jolie's startled expression, "she left Kilchurn sometime after you, and took refuge with the Argyll tacksman she's since wed. The man did what your late husband was supposed to do; he claimed Alanna by handfast so he could adopt her son as his own. My Uncle John was none too pleased about losing control of Fairleigh Manor to the Argyll Campbells, but there's nought he can do. 'Tis stale news now, but of interest nonetheless. He'll want to know if the pair of you conspired or if the beauteous Alanna merely borrowed the idea from you. You seem to have developed quite a knack in the art of deception.''

"We did not conspire, monsieur," Jolie disavowed stiffly.

" 'Twill be noted to your credit, mistress. And since you came to Glencoe, where you were expected, there's no harm done. I'll leave you now. Did you know that in his youth, your father was as gifted a thief as Alasdair MacIain? I'd have thought his home would be more lavishly furnished, but 'tis of no importance. I imagine his wealth will be located in time. Farewell for now, Sister Jolie Annette. I'll see you again before I leave.''

Frozen to her chair for long minutes after Glenlyon's breezily dramatic departure, Jolie felt icy cold, despite the warmth of the fire. He was as clever a trickster as the earl of Breadalbane, she fumed desperately. In that boisterous, falsely jolly voice, he had stripped her defenses away and issued a warning that amounted to an ultimatum—she would not escape again! "Until 'tis time," he had proclaimed loudly when she had asked about Tavis Campbell. Time for what? A marriage at pistol point with Alasdair MacIain's willing cooperation? What a fool the Glencoe chieftain was if he trusted Robert Campbell of Glenlyon as much as his letter had claimed.

Mother of God, Jolie despaired, *without a miracle, I am trapped this time. Hiding in Coire Gabhail will just postpone the agony; there's no escape from that small valley any more than from Kinvernach. That clever devil today implied as much with his coarse humor. There'll be no wings of angels for me, but no one can prevent me from using Satan's weapons if I must. There's no one and nothing else to help me now.*

In her bedroom with the door barred shut a few minutes later, Jolie carefully removed her two poisoned daggers from the chest. Rummaging through the ancient garments, she located a velvet tunic with fabric thick enough to protect her own skin, and with the scissors, needle, and thread she had borrowed from the housekeeper days earlier, she fashioned a wide underbelt with stitched-in sheaths at each side for the daggers. By slashing open the sides of one of the heavy winter Sisters of Charity robes that had been the only wardrobe she had brought from Newcastle, she could reach the dagger hilts with a minimum of fumbling. Her only other preparation was to put her fur-lined boots and cloak on top of her snowshoes, next to the window in her bedroom.

Somehow, she survived the supper that night without alarming Sergeant Cawley or his soldiers, and endured the long hours the next day without panic. When the weather changed in early afternoon from a cloudless sky to one filled with the ominous forewarning of a winter storm, Jolie's mood darkened accordingly to a desperate determination. If the approaching snow were heavy enough, she'd leave no easy tracks to follow.

Isolated for two days from the world beyond her stone house, she didn't know until suppertime that the threatening storm had caused an upheaval throughout the glen. Habitually a phlegmatic, unemotional man, Sergeant Cawley arrived back at Kinvernach on that twelfth night in a mood as black as the darkest thundercloud gathering overhead. Throughout that awkward supper, Jolie and the confused soldiers carried on what disjointed conversation there was. Abruptly, after the housekeeper had replaced the food and bowls with the nightly crock of usquebaugh and pewter mugs, the sergeant rose to his feet.

"See to yer weapons, lads," he ordered heavily. "We'll be on patrol the night through."

As complaining as soldiers the world over when faced with a miserable assignment, the four men grumbled about the storm, about the fact that earlier night patrols had been only two hours long, and about missing their nightly ration of usquebaugh.

"Ye've five minutes to get yer gear and prime yer muskets. Now, get ye gone from this room," the sergeant snapped, his face distorted with a scowl that frightened Jolie more than his angry commands. But when he turned to face the woman who had been his hostess for twelve days, his voice held a note of pleading.

"If ye're brave enow to face the storm, Sister, ye'd best be gone from this house before daybreak."

Jolie stared at him in dawning horror. How could she have been self-centered enough to think she'd been the Campbell target? The whole MacDonald clan was the intended victim of the deadly, vindictive, play-acting Robert Campbell of Glenlyon.

"As soon as we reach the village," Sergeant Cawley admonished her gruffly, "ye're to leave by the back door and get as far away from this cursed glen as ye can. But ye're not to warn the villagers. 'Tis likely some of them already know."

"Know what?" Jolie asked in a shaken whisper.

"I canna tell ye, Sister. I'd be hanged for treason on the barracks gibbet if I play the traitor any more than I already have."

They both heard the pounding horse's hoofs in the stone courtyard, but before they could cross the room, the entry door was flung open, and a booted officer strode into the room, the Campbell tartan draped across his shoulder already dusted with snow.

"Get your men away, Sergeant," he ordered imperiously. "I'll keep Sister Jolie Annette entertained while you're carrying out your assigned duties. On your way to the village, tie my horse in a shieling and make certain it has feed. I don't want the beast damaged by the storm."

Conditioned by twenty years of obedience to Campbell officers, Sergeant Cawley walked mechanically toward the entry, turning briefly at the door to glance in Jolie's direction with a look of desolation stamped on his weathered features. Jolie understood the message, and her trembling fingers reached for the comforting hilt of one of the daggers fastened around her waist beneath the heavy, concealing robe.

As soon as the door closed behind the five departing soldiers, Tavis Campbell tossed off his swaddling tartan and

faced the woman who had eluded his control since he had
first met her, but who, he vowed, would never beat him
again.

"Aren't you going to offer me another cup of drugged
brandy, pretty Jolie?" he demanded sardonically.

"No, monsieur."

" 'Tis just as well; I'd force you to drink it instead of
me."

Taking a deep breath to ease her tension, Jolie murmured
shakily, "You're welcome to the usquebaugh, monsieur.
You didn't leave the sergeant and his men enough time to
drink their portions. The usquebaugh is untainted; I had no
reason to drug my guests."

"Why should I trust anything you say? You lied to me
and robbed my purse before you sneaked away from Kilchurn
like the thief you've become."

"I took only the amount the lawyer Carwhin stole from
me in Newcastle. I suggest you ask him for your money; I
have none left to give you."

"You'll learn soon not to take me for a fool. The
marriage contract 'twixt you and me has an accurate accounting of the dowry money you inherited from your
father. According to your Uncle Alasdair, 'tis all safely
locked in a strongbox in the cellar of this house."

"He is not an uncle, monsieur, only a cousin."

"He claimed you as a niece in the contract, so 'twill be
your legal status from now on."

"When was this contract arranged, monsieur? I was told
that MacIain did not leave Glencoe until after the holy days
of Christ Mass."

" 'Twas negotiated by letter long before, but 'tis legal and
binding all the same."

Struggling to control the sick churning of her stomach as
she tabulated the days such an exchange of letters would
have taken, Jolie experienced again the corroding acid of
hatred. Tavis may have planned the details of Rorke's
murder as he had claimed, but the earl of Breadalbane had
begun his negotiations with Alasdair MacDonald long be-

fore. Without raising her head to look at the man smiling at her with a caustic confidence, she articulated the words of denial in a lifeless voice.

"That contract will never bind me, Tavis Campbell. I've already taken the only vows I'll ever keep."

" 'Twill not matter so much if you don't keep the wedding vows, but you'll take them right enough."

"How? With a dagger at my back? Do you think even a minister like the Darrell will force a sworn nun against her will?"

Shrugging callously, Tavis mimicked her tone of voice. "Do you think my grandfather doesn't have a tame kirkman who'll do his bidding even if your hands are tied and your mouth taped shut? But 'tis foolish to waste the night away in talk about things already decided, when I've an appetite to see the gold your uncle promised me. Will you lead the way to the strongbox, mistress, or do I roust your servants from their beds?"

As she reached for one of the pine knot torches lighting the room, Jolie shuddered at the thought of walking again among the scurrying rats in the dank cellar, but she knew she'd be safer than her caretaker would be once Tavis saw the empty strongbox. He wouldn't dare kill her; not even a "tame" minister could force a dead woman to repeat the wedding vows.

Taking the torch from her hand, Tavis warned her sharply, "I'd be daft if I trusted any MacDonald with a lighted torch, much less one with your raw temper. I'd not trust you behind my back, either; 'tis needful we both survive this night."

Fifteen minutes later, though, Jolie didn't think she would survive another hour. Just after Tavis lifted the lid of the unlocked box, his doubled fist knocked her flat against the stone wall.

"You thieving bitch!" he screamed in fury.

Recovering her breath and her temper simultaneously, Jolie shrieked just as loudly, "What was I supposed to have stolen? The MacIain told *you* there was a fortune here; he didn't tell me. My father died more than twenty years ago, and since then, there's been no master at Kinvernach. Do you think that thieves like the MacDonalds are supposed to be would have overlooked an unguarded house in their own midst? I searched that box the first day I was here and found it as empty as you just did. If I'd possessed enough money to pay ship's passage to France, I'd have left this prison long ago.''

Because her impassioned protest echoed his own evaluation of the hated MacDonalds, Tavis demanded more calmly, ''What happened to the forty guineas you stole from me? You could have gotten back to England, at least.''

Knowing that she was already condemned as a liar a hundred times over, Jolie didn't hesitate. ''My relatives aren't the only thieves in Scotland. One of your grandfather's crofters stole that from me the first night after I left Kilchurn.''

''That man will hang if I find him. Did you mark the name of his village?''

''I don't understand Gaelic, and I didn't know one village from another. May we leave the cellar now? I do not like rats. Soeur Marguerite told me their bites are often as deadly as a poisonous snake's.''

''Spare me your childhood folklore; there's not a person alive who hasn't had a rat bite or two.''

But Jolie noted that he climbed the stairs well ahead of her, despite his distrust of having a MacDonald at his back. Stiffly she flexed her sore shoulder, injured when she'd landed against the wall, but she ignored the bruises on her jaw where his fist had struck. Her arms and legs still functioned without impediment, and her daggers were still secure about her waist.

As Tavis reached the dining table, he poured himself a full measure of usquebaugh and sniffed it only briefly before he downed it in rapid swallows. Twice he glanced at the oversized clock on the mantel shelf and scowled as he refilled his cup, but he didn't sit or cease his restless pacing.

Nervously, Jolie watched both him and the clock. Her

awareness of time was more critical than his. If he prevented her from leaving Kinvernach for another four hours, she could never reach the safety of Coire Gabhail before dawn. Tentatively she suggested that she be permitted to retire to her bedroom for the night, and she saw no reason he should not be blamed for her sudden indisposition.

"I have never been struck before, monsieur, and my head is aching. I would like to retire to my room."

"And be out of the window five minutes later? Nay, clever Jolie. Giles told me how you escaped his vigilance at the Edinburgh inn. Not that you'd get so far this time. 'Tis why I like Glencoe so much—'twill be easy to defend from enemies both in and out."

"Is Captain Giles Campbell here in Glencoe with you to silence any enemies you think you might have here?"

"Aye, but he's only a sergeant with the Argyllers. I left him at Achtriachton to take care of matters there."

"Is that where you've been hiding, monsieur? I had expected you to visit me long before this night."

"How did you know I was in Glencoe?"

"From your commander, Robert of Glenlyon. Who else could your grandfather trust to carry out his orders?"

"My grandfather arranged only our marriage, nothing else," Tavis contradicted her warily.

"Not according to the man he introduced me to as Sir John Dalrymple at Stair Castle. That conceited *cochon* considered me too stupid to understand what he was talking about. He does not like you much either," Jolie added slyly.

"Dalrymple's a bloody damn fool. He doesn't know the half of it."

In spite of her increasing fear, Jolie was tantalized by the confident conceit in Tavis's voice. His protest about Dalrymple had held no anger, only an amused contempt.

"What is the other half?" she asked cautiously.

"How much did my drunken relative actually tell you?"

Gambling with reckless desperation, Jolie blurted, "That Glencoe would not be a safe place for me tonight."

"You're a liar! Robert isn't the one who told you; he

received his final orders only this morning. And 'twas not any of your tame Lowland soldiers who warned you either; they weren't told until after they left here. So 'twas the sergeant who betrayed the command he was given just before sunset. I'll see him hanged for treason as soon as the deed is finished.''

Jolie wanted to scream the words, ''What deed?'' but her courage failed her; Tavis Campbell had become a frightening man. The usquebaugh he'd been drinking had not dulled his wits, as she had hoped; he'd been swift in his shrewd appraisal of her lie and in his accurate assumption about Sergeant Cawley. His pale eyes glittered with intense excitement, and his lips curved in a challenging smile. Lifting his cup to her in a mocking salute, he began to speak in a rush of words.

'' 'Tis safe now to end your torment and to tell you what the next few hours will accomplish for me. Six months ago our good King William proclaimed that all rebel Highlanders who did not agree to amnesty were to be punished to the extreme. 'Twas the opportunity the Campbells had awaited for twenty years—to destroy all thieving MacDonalds permanently. Glencoe will be first, then Glengarry, then Keppoch.''

Recalling what Father Andrew had told her, Jolie protested helplessly, ''But all the MacDonald leaders have signed the amnesty.''

''I'll admit as much, but only in private. Do you think Dalrymple and my grandfather stupid enough to let the bloody murderers escape justice this time, as they always have in the past? There'll be no proof left of the signing because their names were all erased from the record! And 'twill be eight hundred Argyll soldiers who'll carry out the king's order for extreme punishment, though 'tis doubtful King William intended it to be quite so extreme.''

Raising his cup in another salute, Tavis continued his jubilant narrative, ''Robert's assignment was Glencoe; there are others who'll destroy Glengarry and Keppoch as soon as we finish here. And that, my MacDonald wife-to-be, will be accomplished by midmorning, when every MacDonald except you lies dead in the glen. As the only relative of MacIain left, you'll be the only one with legal claim to the whole glen. And since I'm the one your uncle chose to be your husband, 'twill soon be mine to rule as I see fit. A pretty reward for the bastard son of the earl of Breadalbane, don't you think?''

Benumbed with horror, Jolie stared at the man whose red coat seemed already-stained with blood. ''The women and children, too?'' she asked in a hoarse whisper.

''Aye, every one of them, and by the same soldiers they've entertained for two weeks. 'Tis scheduled to begin at five o'clock, simultaneously in every cottage and manor. Those who escape will be killed by the soldiers on patrol. 'Tis a foolproof plan no one can spoil—not now. You and I have only to stay here and wait. Tomorrow, Robert and I will divide all the gold that's found—yours, too, as soon as you tell me where you've hidden it. Did you really think I believed your lies? The rest of the Campbells will divide the other spoils of war.''

''It's a massacre, not war!'' Jolie muttered.

''Undoubtedly, some narrow minds will consider it such. That's why Giles's and my names won't be listed on the regimental records, and why you'll be away from here before the news breaks. As far as the public is concerned, we'll be innocent bystanders shocked by the death of your family clan.''

The horror still engulfed Jolie, but her mind was no longer paralyzed and she prepared herself to snatch the first faint opportunity for escape. She listened with only scant attention as Tavis continued to talk. He told her he'd learned about his illegitimacy at the age of twelve, when his father had first promised him an estate equal to that of Breadalbane's legal heir. Only in the past two years, however, had Tavis developed ambitions beyond the expectation of wealth. With Glencoe in his possession, he'd have the means of acquiring power equal to that of his father, who ruled Glenorchy with absolute authority. Not once, Jolie noted bitterly, did he mention Rorke, whose murder had made his present delusions of grandeur possible.

As tensely as she'd waited for him to fall asleep at Kilchurn Castle, she now waited for him to relax his vigilance long enough for her to reach her bedroom and bar the door. In the minutes it would take him to break it open, she might be able to climb out the window and escape. So intense was her concentration, she didn't hear the stealthy sounds of footsteps in the hallway at the rear of the house until Tavis stopped talking abruptly and drew his sword with silent efficiency. Grabbing her arm with his other hand, he pulled her up from the chair and forcibly propelled her out of the room, past the torch-lit central corridor and into the darkened areas beyond.

What happened next was too swift for Jolie to prevent. She saw the flickering lamp being held by a shadowy figure ahead, but her belated scream of warning was seconds too late. Tavis dropped her arm and lunged, his sword striking its target once and then again with a lethal accuracy. As swiftly as he'd killed, he stooped to retrieve the lantern his victim was still clutching and to shine it in the dead man's face.

"Do you recognize the fool?" he demanded harshly. "'Tis not one of your servants. I was told you had but an old couple and their halfwit grandson."

Still shaken by the brief violence, Jolie recoiled in horror. "He was the head crofter of Kinvernach," she gasped weakly.

"Come to warn you, no doubt, like a faithful gillie to his overlady. 'Tis twice over your sergeant has earned a hanging. But 'tis not yet the time for discipline; 'tis still the time for action. I'll not be taken by surprise again. 'Twould have been easier for me to wait until the appointed hour, when I could have used pistols and finished the job more quickly than with my sword. Where are your servants quartered, mistress?" he asked without any discernible emotion.

Silently, Jolie pointed toward the brightly lighted entry hall, and watched with a pounding heart as Tavis set the

lantern down carefully on the stone floor. She, too, wanted
no surprises, and light was essential for a woman who had
never killed before. Making no protest, she submitted to
having her arm grabbed once again by a man who could
murder without remorse. But her other hand gripped the hilt
of one of her daggers which she hoped would be as lethal as
his sword. Seconds before he did, Jolie saw the shadowy face
of the caretaker in the doorway, staring at the bloody sword
in Tavis's hand. This time she made no outcry; she waited
mutely until her arm was dropped and Tavis stepped forward
to attack. Then she drew the dagger from its sheath and
moved silently toward him.

She plunged the rusty blade into his back with the
stored-up strength of desperation, and was still gripping the
hilt, even as he slumped to the floor without a sound. Jolie's
lips twisted into a grimace of revulsion as she realized she
hadn't needed the belladonna poison; her knowledge of
human anatomy had been sufficient. The dagger had pierced
his heart squarely, and his death had been instantaneous.

The dreaded walk across the meadow and the dangerous
climb up the steep trail during the snowstorm was not the
lonely escape Jolie had planned. Old Huw knew the way
better than she did, as he led his confused and terrified
grandson in advance of the two women who trudged along
behind. The aged caretaker had been equally resourceful in
the minutes following Jolie's violent action that had ended
the immediate threat to their lives. After issuing a sharp
order to his wife in Gaelic, he had tugged on Jolie's limp
arm and said, "Come, we take away," indicating the
red-coated body with a wave of his hand. Together they had
dragged the bodies of Tavis and the murdered crofter out the
rear door and across an expanse of new-fallen snow to a
spot behind the peat shieling. Silently, Jolie had watched as
Huw shoveled snow until the two corpses were covered.

Inside the house, his wife of fifty years had mopped the
floor clean of blood and assembled the bundles the couple
had prepared just after the head crofter had warned them. At

that time, both Huw and Murray had decided that the young Catholic nun should have an equal chance to survive the hideous night. Although Tavis had spoken only English, all but the halfwit grandson had understood the import of his loud boasts. Armed only with the heavy truncheons used in animal slaughter, Huw and the crofter had thought to create a diversion loud enough to lure the Campbell enemy into the hall. But when he'd emerged from the dining room and passed within striking distance of Huw's place of concealment, the caretaker had been unable to attack without endangering the woman whose life he was attempting to save. Helpless, the old man had witnessed the swift murder of his friend.

A MacDonald who had done his full share of fighting and raiding during his younger years, Huw had felt the fierce pride of one clansman for another as he had watched his mistress kill the hated intruder. Now, as he led the way into the safety of Coire Gabhail, he vowed her courageous deed would be long remembered by the villagers he knew were already in hiding there. As were other protected canyons in the mountains surrounding Glencoe, Coire Gabhail had long been designated as a place of refuge.

For a stunned and heartsick Jolie, there was no sense of victory. She had deliberately schemed to kill a man whose life she had once saved, and she felt as much a murderer as he had been. Not even the knowledge that she had avenged Rorke's death and saved the lives of her servants gave her any comfort as she huddled inside the dark cave now crowded with an unknown number of other silent refugees. Hours later, though, with the dawning of a day rendered white by the fury of the blizzard, Jolie's oppressive guilt was gradually replaced by horror.

Throughout the night, half-frozen MacDonalds had continued to arrive, their faces rigid with cold and terror. Women with half-naked babes and children were the most numerous and the neediest. With only one smoky peat fire at the rear of the cave, Jolie's stored supply of moldy furs was quickly exhausted, wrapped around the shivering bodies of small children. Her small hoards of crockery and cooking utensils were put to constant use in boiling gruel made from her salted and dried meats, oats and barley, and dried onions, peas and lentils. As soon as one potful had been fed to the whimpering children, the blackened pots were filled with snow and another measure of ingredients and replaced on the sluggish fire.

An hour after daybreak, order descended on the camp with the arrival of forty more fugitives led by John MacDonald, who quietly announced that he was now the clan MacIain. His father, Alasdair, had been the second man murdered in the bloody holocaust—shot from behind in his bedroom by Lieutenant Lindsey, who'd been his pampered guest for the twelve preceding days. Of the four tacksmen, two were known dead, one of them killed by Robert Campbell of Glenlyon himself.

Busy in the cave attending to the demanding nursing, Jolie heard the news in whispered snatches of Gaelic, which she understood imperfectly. She heard nothing from the new clan chieftain himself for three days, and she knew little about the decisions being made by the men crowded into one of the animal shielings—a crudely roofed stone shelter whose wide entrance allowed for little warmth. She didn't know that eight of the most skilled mountaineers had been dispatched to vantage points surrounding Glencoe Valley until they returned in the late afternoon. The news they brought to the one hundred and fifty survivors in Coire Gabhail renewed the terror and crushed all hope.

One of the men reported the early morning arrival of a second regiment of Argyll soldiers from Ballachulish. Another man described the midday approach of a four-hundred-strong army contingent from Fort William. This hard-driven force had reached the valley floor over the mountainous eastern route known as Devil's Staircase. Two others of the MacDonald observers told of the systematic looting and burning of every cottage and manor house. What had been thriving villages the day before were now only blackened piles of tumbled walls and rubble.

Long after dark, the last two of the reconnaissance patrols

returned to the encampment in a state of exhaustion. Theirs had been the most demanding assignment—to reach the Loch Leven entry to Glencoe and observe all activity there. The news they brought contained only one note of hope. All eight hundred of the Argyll soldiers had left the glen and boarded the small fleet of boats and barges waiting for them on the lake shores. Half of that motley fleet had headed north, and half had gone south. Crowded aboard the barges had been an estimated nine hundred head of MacDonald cattle, an equal number of sheep, goats, and pigs, and the two hundred horses that had been the proudest possession of the Glencoe clan.

John MacDonald had frowned when he had heard the tally, but he had held his peace. Every man in the shieling knew that there would be few if any animals left in the glen. Others of the departing barges had been piled high with bundles of food wrapped in hides, fleeces, and blankets stripped from the crofts and houses. Even the cooking utensils and dishes had been carried off by the army. The new MacIain didn't need to express his fears to the clansmen huddled in the cold shieling; all of them were aware of the fate that awaited them if there was no food left in the glen. Their escape from the bloody massacre no longer seemed miraculous; slow starvation would be a more torturous death for the survivors.

On the second morning of exile, most of the able-bodied men accompanied their new leader back into Glencoe on a burial detail. Returning with still more survivors in the late afternoon, they announced a tally of the dead, and the grim news that the vengeful enemy had located and stolen most of their hidden caches of food, weapons, and money. Repeatedly on successive days, the work details recovered the stocks of peat fuel that had not been burned, rounded up what animals were left, and buried still more of their dead—mostly women and children who had escaped the massacre, only to die of exposure during the blizzard. Not quite forty people, most of them men, had been murdered during the early morning hours of February 13, 1692, and twenty others known dead had perished in the storm—a combined total that numbered over a tenth of the Glencoe MacDonalds.

Crowded around the small camp fires at night, the men exchanged the stories of their individual survivals. The blizzard itself had been their main ally—Argyll soldiers had been unable to locate them in the blinding snow. But there had been many soldiers like the Kinvernach sergeant who had given subtle warning to their hosts. While they knew the MacDonalds deserved punishment for years of crimes against other clans, many Highlanders chose not to break the hospitality code; they were unable to murder the men and women who had been their companions for almost two weeks. Others of the survivors had given their own warnings— the warriors among them had become suspicious of the increased Argyll patrols the night before. One of the village bards, believed to be gifted with second sight, had alerted his neighbors by singing the traditional MacDonald song of alarm; and one old man had overheard an Argyll corporal talking to his squad.

Whatever the reason for their survival, the exiles in Coire Gabhail had small cause for rejoicing. Everyone had lost family and friends, and everyone knew the unrelenting cruelty of a Highlands winter. Without food and shelter, many more would die.

No one in the camp was more aware of the probability of death than Sister Jolie Annette. Two of the youngest children had already succumbed; and of the pathetic victims located the day after the massacre, three of the women were too lethargic to eat. Jolie felt particular pity for the widow of Alasdair MacDonald. She had been standing close to her husband when he had been shot. Her hands had been cruelly lacerated when her husband's murderer had ordered the rings stripped from her fingers, and she'd been left to die from the bitter cold. They would have been more merciful if they had shot her, Jolie thought as she watched Lady MacDonald's tenuous hold on life gradually fail.

Jolie's own personal ordeal, though, was just beginning.

Six weeks after the massacre, John MacIain received an official notice from King William. The lives of the remaining Glencoe MacDonalds would be spared only if they relinquished all claims to their land and agreed to long terms of indenture in the English colonies abroad. Knowing that she would be considered as much MacDonald as the other survivors, Jolie abandoned her last faint hope of escape. Unless the king relented his cruel edict, her fate would be the same as the proud, fierce clansmen, who would never submit to enslavement.

9

Although Jolie never joined the MacDonald clan spiritually, she quickly developed a deep respect for its new leader. Lacking his father's overbearing pride and dramatic appearance, John MacIain was a realistic man who wasted no time in cursing the enemy. Summoning Sister Jolie Annette to the shieling he'd marked as his headquarters on the fourth night at Coire Gabhail, he was bluntly factual in his appraisal of the situation.

" 'Tis not fair that you were trapped with the clan, Sister; you did nothing to deserve the fate the rest of us know we've earned. Your killing the man whom my father wrongfully condemned you to wed was self-defense, not murder. 'Tis about that matter that I wish to speak. I doubt you'll ever be blamed for the deed, even by Breadalbane himself, since his son's body and those of the four men we killed today will never be located. We found them searching the ruins of Kinvernach, and although they were no longer dressed as Argyllers, one of my men recognized their leader as Sergeant Giles Campbell, who had carried out the massacre at Achtriachton."

"He was a captain in Breadalbane's army," Jolie volunteered bitterly. "He and Tavis Campbell were the ones who murdered my husband."

"Then 'tis merciful for you they're dead, and merciful

for us that they left their weapons behind. But to more practical matters. The clan cannot return to Glencoe until we're certain the Argyllers will not come back to finish the killing. We'll be safe enough here, since a few men can hold off an army at the narrow, barricaded entry. But physical safety will be an empty victory if we are unable to purchase food from the Jacobite clans to the north and east. Unfortunately, you're the only one with the money to pay for it. A week ago your head crofter Murray reported to me privately that you were hiding everything of value here in the canyon. Had he told my father instead of me, you'd have been forced to return it. My father was a proud man who could not stand to have the promises he made broken.''

"He had no right to use me to save the clan from Breadalbane,'' Jolie demurred hotly. "That marriage contract was what made Tavis Campbell think he could claim the whole of Glencoe if I were the only MacDonald left alive.''

"'Twas a foolish conceit on his part. Robert Campbell made certain his niece Sarah and her sons were safe, and they would have had greater claim. To her everlasting discredit, 'twas not she who gave warning to my brother, Alasdair Og. 'Twas his own doing to lead her and his crofters to a safe canyon to the north while I came south to this one. I doubt that Robert was any too pleased when he learned that his plan to gain Glencoe failed so miserably.

"But 'tis already past history,'' John MacIain continued harshly. "'Tis survival now that's the important issue. To accomplish that, we'll be needing your money, but only the silver coins of it. If Robert thought he'd overlooked a fortune of gold, he'd be back, since he'd consider it his by right.''

Recalling the variety of clan crests that marked her inherited silver plate, Jolie smiled wanly. "You're welcome to the silver plate, too,'' she murmured. "But you'll have to melt it down first. I doubt there's a clan in Scotland that couldn't claim a piece of it.''

The new MacIain's humor was equal to hers. "Aye, but

we stole most of it from the Campbells, so 'twould seem you have their thieving ways to thank for part of your fortune.''

In the next breath, however, he was dourly serious again. ''We'll not be able to repay you for years, Sister Jolie Annette. Even if we regain our homes, there'll be little to support us, since I'll not countenance any more raiding abroad.''

''I don't expect any repayment,'' Jolie assured him. ''I won't be living in Glencoe anyway.''

''Will you be returning to your French family?''

''No, I have enemies there as vicious as the earl of Breadalbane.''

''Back to England, then?''

She recalled talking to Father Andrew about establishing an infirmary in one of the two French colonies she knew about, and vowed that if she lived through this winter, she would keep that promise. But it would be the tropical island, and not snowbound Canada.

''I'll stay in Newcastle until I can locate a ship to take me to the island of Martinique in the Caribbean.''

''Why would you go to so outlandish a place?''

''I own property there, and I could work as a Sister of Charity.''

''Then, why not stay in Glencoe?''

''You have too many widows already, John MacIain.''

''Aye, and fatherless children by the score. 'Tis why I need your help.''

''I'll help, but only until your clan is safe.''

'' 'Tis a generous offer, Sister Jolie, and in return, I'll see you safely away from Scotland. 'Twould not be safe for you to travel across Campbell land again. Even if the Grey Fox of Breadalbane never learns what happened to his bastard son, he'll not forgive you for the trouble you've caused him.''

''He caused his own trouble,'' Jolie muttered.

''Aye, and he and his fellow schemer, John Dalrymple, engineered the attack on Glencoe. Robert Campbell was only a tool, and the king would have chosen a more traditional punishment. So 'twill be that unholy pair who'll be blamed by the Highland clans, if I have my way with it. I'll make certain the earl of Argyll will be spared from suspicion; we'll be needing a friend in the enemy camp when all this is over. 'Twill be his soldiers I'll praise as the ones who gave us fair warning.''

"Don't name any of them," Jolie cautioned. "Before he died—before I killed him," she corrected herself hastily, "Tavis Campbell threatened to have Sergeant Cawley hanged. There could be other officers just as vindictive."

"Aye, I suppose you're right, but 'tis a shame that good men are rarely praised. Still, the mention of it without their names will be just as effective and will allow for some exaggeration."

He's a brighter man than his father, Jolie reflected, *and shrewd enough to put Breadalbane and Dalrymple on the defensive*. During the gloomy days that followed, her admiration for him increased steadily. He worked as hard physically as any of the men in winterizing their crude shelters with materials scrounged from the ruins of Glencoe. But he also organized the procurement of food by sending the most capable of his mountaineers to specified villages belonging to friendly clans. That her money was purchasing more than food, Jolie learned when the new MacIain showed her a supply of paper, quills, and ink that one of the men had brought back.

"Now we begin the work of regaining respectability," he informed her privately. On their next trip out of Coire Gabhail, the food procurers delivered letters from John MacIain to the chieftains of other clans, and returned with reciprocal messages. Thus the MacDonald survivors kept abreast of the news.

Within weeks they learned that Highland sympathy was in their favor, and that the Glencoe massacre had become an *affaire célèbre* in England and in France. Although Breadalbane and Dalrymple disclaimed responsibility, few men believed them; and an embarrassed King William ordered the remain-

der of the Argyll soldiers to report to Flanders. The only
one who admitted his part in the atrocity was Robert
Campbell of Glenlyon, and he claimed patriotic service to
the king as his defense. But not all of the news was good.
Six weeks after the massacre, the first official edict of
punishment arrived from the king.

John MacIain proved his capability for leadership on that
day as he read the royal message to the beleaguered remnants of his clan. Not a MacDonald there voted to accept
the king's offer of indenture in exchange for their lives, and
the news of their defiance was immediately dispatched to
the clan survivors hiding in the other canyons of safety
around Glencoe. Miraculously, during the months of grief
and hardship that followed, John MacIain held the clan
together and continued to write letters to friends, asking for
support.

For Jolie, those months were a grueling, heart-wrenching
period of hard work and little rest. Within days she'd
become a practicing surgeon, amputating toes turning black
from frostbite. Without medicine or proper instruments, she
treated the wounds of the fugitives who had been injured
during the escape. As the food supply dwindled to bare
subsistence, she watched helplessly as young children and
old people sickened and died. The graveyard at the remote
end of the canyon increased weekly in size.

By the time the spring thaw cleared the snow from Coire
Gabhail, the supply of domestic animals had been exhausted;
even the cows, ewes, and nanny goats had been slaughtered.
Although the wild deer had returned to the mountains, they
were no longer easy prey. Lacking powder and shot for their
muskets, the hunters were forced to use the less efficient,
makeshift bows and arrows. Even for the archery experts
who had competed against the Argyllers in early February,
the hunt could now take days instead of hours, and the meat
supply continued to be happenstance. The only reliable
supply of food was the sacks of meal and grain the hard-
pressed mountaineers continued to bring back from villages
three to six days' distant. Spring brought some relief in the

form of easily snared small animals emerging from their winter holes, but the hunger of the desperate clansmen was never fully assuaged. Everyone in camp was thin to the point of emaciation.

Since the first week of the ordeal, Jolie's main helpers in the arduous task of nursing the sick had been four widows who, like Jolie herself, had learned to bury their grief in work. The two youngest were childless brides whose husbands had been killed in the massacre; the third was the devoutly religious widow of one of the slain tacksmen; and the fourth was a long-widowed woman who had been a village midwife. Inevitably, the five nurses had formed a close bond. More than anyone else in the desolate canyon, they had monitored the suffering and been witness to the tragically frequent deaths.

Curiously, though, the four Glencoe women had never presumed a close friendship with Sister Jolie Annette. They treated her instead with a reverence very similar to the respect of a nurse for a doctor. Even the midwife had stood by in awe as Jolie officiated at a difficult childbirth and stopped the hemorrhaging with the last of the opium powder she had originally intended for her own use in case of injury. That Jolie had amputated gangrenous toes without an outward show of fear had established her as a being apart in the minds of the others, whose isolated lives had allowed them no access to modern medicine. The fact that her nun's robes were as worn and shabby as their motley dresses did not detract from her standing as both a Sister of Charity and a clan tackswoman.

Having never developed a need for women friends beyond her love for the dignified Soeur Charlotte and the stern Soeur Marguerite, Jolie was largely unaware of the veneration she inspired among her helpers. Thus, on the day they told her they wanted to become Sisters of Charity and to accompany her to the remote island she had talked about, she was astounded. It had never occurred to her that anyone but Frenchwomen would have such an ambition—not even devout Scottish Catholics.

Her first inclination was to refuse their request. She wasn't sure she could manage her own life in Martinique, much less that of four other women, three of whom spoke only Gaelic. Their reasons for choosing such a life, though, Jolie couldn't ignore; her own were too similar. Without husbands, the only life they could anticipate in Glencoe would be that of servants. Clan life revolved around men. Independence was not tolerated for lone women who lacked both children and money; they were at the mercy of the MacIain and his tacksmen. If there were men in need of wives, they were often coerced into marriages they did not want, much as Alasdair MacIain had tried to force Jolie. Just as Jolie herself could not tolerate the thought of marriage to any man other than the husband she'd lost, so couldn't the four Scotswomen. Although Jolie would have preferred establishing an infirmary on Martinique independent of church control, she knew that such an initiative on her part would never be allowed. Moreover, the other four women were as devoted to church service as they were to nursing.

In a curious way, Jolie's reluctant decision to accept their petition proved to be another turning point in her life; she no longer felt a hopeless prisoner in the squalid camp of fugitives. Her self-assigned task of nursing changed subtly to that of teacher in both medicine and language. Having acquired a workable command of Gaelic in four months, she was confident that her willing pupils could learn French in an equal length of time. By mutual consent, they agreed not to inform the other refugees of their plans until the future of the clan was decided.

By August, the Highland and English nobles who had labored hard to convince King William to abandon his cruel edict of indenture finally succeeded. The king granted the Glencoe MacDonalds permission to reclaim their valley, providing they swore unquestioning allegiance to him. Expressing his acceptance of conditions in humble words of unconditional surrender, John MacIain responded immediately and promised ''to live under His Majesty's royal protection in such a manner that the government shall not repent." Looking more like ragged beggars than a clan chieftain and aristocratic Scottish lords, the new MacIain and four tacksmen left Coire Gabhail the next day, bound for the Argyll stronghold of Inveraray to swear allegiance to the king.

Without considering the possibility that John MacIain might consider her insubordinate, Jolie promptly paid a clansman to carry a letter to Father Andrew in Glengarry. In addition to her request that he administer permanent vows to herself and the four novitiates, she asked that he bring bolts of gray wool cloth to Coire Gabhail so that she and the others would be more fittingly clad when they departed from Scotland.

Unaware that Sister Jolie Annette's request had not been approved by the new MacIain, the jubilant priest accompanied the messenger back to Coire Gabhail, bringing with him six Glengarry MacDonalds burdened with gifts of food and the gray cloth Jolie had ordered. Having agonized over the fate of his parishioners for six months, Father Andrew was amazed that so many had survived; the rumored number of clansmen killed in the massacre had been far greater than the actuality. In a mood of thankful celebration, the priest administered the vows to the five women applicants before he began the greater work of reorganizing his congregation. He was thus engaged when John MacDonald returned from Inveraray and ordered his clan to move back into Glencoe Valley.

Throughout the chaotic month that followed the descent of more than three hundred clansmen from the mountain retreats of Coire Gabhail and two others, Jolie had no opportunity to speak to the chieftain alone. As still more MacDonalds returned, mostly young men who had survived the February blizzard and reached the safety of Jacobite villages to the east, the tempo of rebuilding the destroyed Glencoe homes increased. Engrossed in the tremendous tasks of reorganization and in the negotiation of loans from

the MacDonald clans, John MacIain was too preoccupied to
worry about the lesser problems of religion and women.

On the September day he was confronted by Father
Andrew and five gray-uniformed nuns, his initial response
was one of annoyance—he didn't need a dispute with the
church to add to his other myriad problems. Too shrewd to
argue with the priest whose moral support he would need in
the months ahead, the MacIain listened with polite forbear-
ance to Father Andrew's proud announcement that the five
women were now servants of the church. Repressing his
irritation that he had not been consulted earlier, John asked
to speak privately with his tackswoman, Sister Jolie Annette,
stating only that he could not afford to lose any members of
his ravaged clan.

The priest was smiling as he led the other four nuns from
the half-finished house being built on Carnock's ruins. As
persuasive as John MacDonald had become during his
months as chieftain, Father Andrew reflected, he would be
no match for Sister Jolie. When he had first seen her after
an absence of six months, the priest had been appalled by
her gaunt appearance. He had barely recognized her as the
pretty girl who had outargued both himself and the indomitable old Alasdair MacIain. Her shadowed eyes and hollow
cheeks had made her seem years older, and he had thought
her spirit as weak as those of the pathetic clanswomen who
had wept brokenly when he approached them. How wrong
he had been!

The horror and hardships had only strengthened her
character and changed her into that rarest of women—a
leader whose courage inspired a respect that bordered on
reverence. God alone knew that it had taken courage for a
slender woman to kill one of the vicious Campbell marauders
when he had threatened her helpless servants! But she had
needed even more courage to perform the medical miracles
both men and women revealed to the priest. She had
changed in other respects, too, the priest concluded with a
satisfied pride. She no longer displayed the stubborn temper
that had annoyed him; she now stated her intentions with

calm assurance. Unless John MacIain intended to use force, Sister Jolie Annette and her followers would leave Glencoe within the week and begin their greater service to God and church.

John MacIain didn't want to lose the woman who had been his staunchest supporter during the months of unrelieved apprehension, or the other four women, who had contributed much to the clan's survival. Of more critical importance, he didn't want their unopposed departure to inspire others to leave the glen—especially the able-bodied men he needed so desperately. Having long ago dispensed with formalities, he addressed her as a trusted friend.

"Jolie, why can't you and the others serve in the same capacity here in Glencoe? God knows we're more in need of your help than are overfed colonials on a distant tropical island. You're a MacDonald now, lass, not a Frenchwoman. As for those foolish widows who want to follow you, they know nothing of the world outside this glen. I'd be doing them a grave disservice if I allowed them to leave the protection of the clan."

"What protection, John? The king's amnesty? It didn't protect your father from the Campbells. I've been told that the earl of Breadalbane is in hiding at Kilchurn Castle, but how long do you think it will be before he comes looking for the person who killed his son?"

"We'd not betray you, Jolie."

"John, everyone here and in Glengarry knows the story by this time, and one of them is certain to boast of it. I'd be a danger to you and the entire clan if I remained. You've no choice but to let me go, and you'd be just as foolish if you tried to detain the others. You've more widows than you can support as it is, and no men left for them to wed."

Far more than his father had been, John MacIain was a realistic man. He knew that the rumors about Sister Jolie Annette had already been circulated far beyond the glen, and it would be only a matter of time before the Grey Fox would learn the truth and seek his revenge. While the MacDonalds had been forced to pay for their crimes, John

Campbell had escaped all punishment for his. As his aggravatingly logical cousin Jolie had claimed, the clan would be safer without her. With a sigh, he glanced down at the roster of clan names and shuddered. She had been right about the number of widows, too—there were almost two of them to every man. God's blood, it would take a magician to feed and clothe the lot of them and to keep them from becoming quarrelsome crows!

"I can't allow clanswomen to go unescorted to England," he admitted in surrender. "Twould be a blacker mark against MacDonald honor than breaking the king's amnesty. I'll spare three men to give you protection."

"You'll not be sorry, John, if those escorts can be trusted to buy sheep and tools instead of horses and muskets. I've no use for the chest of jewels my ancestors stole from the Campbells. I doubt any goldsmith will find them of much value, but you're welcome to the lot."

" 'Tis another generous offer, Jolie, which I'd refuse if the need were not so great. And I'll send a tacksman with you to make certain the money is not misspent."

Father Andrew smiled widely as John MacIain and Sister Jolie Annette emerged from the house. On the appointed day of departure, he led a hundred ragged MacDonalds in prayer as five nuns and three men were rowed out to the small coastal sloop waiting for them on Loch Leven.

Two weeks later in Newcastle, Jolie spread the cache of brooches, chains, jeweled combs, necklets, rings, and assorted oddities she couldn't identify on the countinghouse table before the goldsmith, Nathan Morris, who courteously examined the lot before he spoke.

"Your Scot ancestors were sorry judges of value, Mistress Campbell. The silver pieces have small value, except as historic remembrances; and since they're obviously stolen, they'll need smelting into bars. The same is true of the crested gold pieces. I doubt there's an Englishman alive who would be seen in public wearing the Campbell crest; 'tis too infamous a name at present. Only the stones, providing they prove unblemished once they're removed, from their settings, will fetch a worthwhile price. But for now, mistress, we've more important business to discuss.''

Mutely, Jolie shook her head. She knew she would have to talk to him about Rorke's murder, but she had already broken down once when she had led her MacDonald friends into the infirmary she and Rorke had founded less than two years earlier. After months of an emotional void, she hadn't expected so violent a recurrence of grief. She wanted the business of money out of the way before she opened any more Pandora's boxes of painful emotions.

"Not yet, monsieur," she murmured. "First, I want to know the value of the gold coins in the other chest."

As indifferent as he'd been about the jewelry, the goldsmith was excited about the contents of the second small chest. While the coins, too, might have been stolen in ancient raids by savage Scottish Highlanders, they were untraceable collector's items of great value. Reverently he examined each coin. Three of them were over two centuries old, and fifty of them over a century. Even the more recently minted ones had seen no usage for forty years.

"They're worth a small fortune," he informed her gravely. "What do you want me to do with them?"

"Exchange them for money I can use, monsieur. I don't want to be reminded that my ancestors were thieves."

"Perhaps not all of them were stolen," the goldsmith countered judicially. "The early Scottish coins among them look more like kingly gifts than stolen plunder. I'll be delighted to buy them, and I'll not cheat you on the price. But I warn you, I'll make money on the trade; some of them may have doubled in value within two decades."

Jolie smiled wanly. To a woman who felt old and disillusioned a few weeks before her twenty-first birthday, twenty years seemed a lifetime away. "You're welcome to the profit, monsieur," she murmured. "I need only what ships' captains and the merchants in Martinique will accept. As soon as you've decided the worth of these things, I will take this money and the funds my husband and I left with you."

Uneasily, the goldsmith pushed his chair away from the table and left the counting room hurriedly, returning a minute later with a thick packet of letters. Holding them up for her to see, he spoke apologetically. "This is the important business I spoke of earlier. Two weeks after you were abducted, I received this first letter from Sir Colin Campbell of Carwhin, as did the other three goldsmiths in Newcastle. Although I sent no response to the lawyer, the others did, so I was deemed the guilty one. The letter claims that your late husband owed the earl of Breadalbane the totality of your money as payment for a debt."

Jolie sucked in her breath in a painful gasp. "That debt was paid by my grandfather in Amsterdam!" she exclaimed.

"Captain Huntington had already told me something of the matter, so I wrote to your grandfather immediately and received his reply two months later and a copy of the quitclaim the earl of Breadalbane had signed. When he arrived in Newcastle in late spring, Captain Huntington confirmed the fact. Before I could write to Carwhin that the earl's claim was fraudulent, I received a second communication from him, stating that you and—I think you should read this letter yourself, Mistress Campbell."

Apprehensively, Jolie shook her head. "I cannot understand written English so well, monsieur. Would you read the letter to me?"

"I have already read it several times, mistress. It states that you and Tavis Campbell were married in the Scottish town of Ballachulish on February 16 of this year, and that your entire fortune was the dowry promised to your new husband."

Staring at the embarrassed goldsmith with a hopeless resignation, Jolie asked dully, "Did you send the money as you'd been instructed, monsieur?"

"No, mistress. Again I consulted Captain Huntington. To my relief, he had in his possession a letter of instruction sent to him by your first husband a week before his untimely death. In the event you were threatened by the earl of Breadalbane, Huntington was to take possession of your money and keep it safe for you. But now I fear that protection may no longer be valid. The lawyer chose to ignore my letter that contained the information; instead, he continued to make threats of forcible repossession. Two weeks ago, I received this final letter, which states that a Flemish member of King William's privy council ruled that your money is now the responsibility of your new husband. I have been instructed to turn it over to the Lawyer Carwhin upon request.''

Jolie had listened to the tersely delivered report with fatalistic resignation—she was to be judged by an earthly court, instead of a heavenly one!

"Tavis Campbell will never receive it, monsieur. He was killed early in the morning of February 13. He was never my husband, and there was no wedding in Ballachulish on February 16.''

"God in heaven, mistress!''

"I hope *le bon dieu* is in heaven, monsieur, and that Captain Huntington is in Newcastle.''

"The captain has retired permanently to his home in Germany; his second son now manages his estate here in town. Can you prove that Tavis Campbell is indeed dead, and that you did not in fact wed him?''

"With a hundred witnesses, if need be; seven of them are with me in Newcastle.''

"Then I think you need help beyond my simple capabilities. I know of two men who will be more effective in dealing with the matter, since both of them are vitally interested in anything to do with the earl of Breadalbane. They're the fathers of the two young officers who were killed by the same brigands who murdered your husband.''

"Tavis Campbell was the one who paid those brigands.''

"Do not tell me any more, Mistress Campbell, until I can arrange for the two gentlemen to be present, and perhaps even for your own people to bear witness to what you say. I think young Huntington should also attend. Lord Mayhew and Sir Redmond are official Newcastle magistrates, as well as grieving fathers; so advise your people to be scrupulously

honest. In the meantime, I will send two of my guards to
escort you home, in case Mister Carwhin attempts to repeat
his earlier crime of abduction. Do not worry about your
money; at this point, I would not surrender it to the earl of
Breadalbane himself.''

At the infirmary, all Jolie told the anxious MacDonald
tacksman was that he would receive the money she had
promised John MacIain as soon as the goldsmith determined
the amount. As much to ease her own churning tension as to
pacify the other nuns and the restless MacDonald men, Jolie
put everyone to work under the direction of her faithful
caretakers. Within two days, the infirmary had been stripped,
and the home she had once loved, but which now held only
the poignant memories of heartbreak, had been returned to
the half-empty shell she and Rorke had leased. Everything
that had belonged to her and Rorke was divided into lots.
The equipment and medicine she would need in Martinique
were crated or packed into sea chests. The hospital pallets
and blankets, the pots and pans, and their clothing were
loaded into a wagon to be driven to Carlisle and then put
aboard a ship bound for Glencoe.

When the goldsmith arrived at the infirmary on the third
day, accompanied by the three men he had promised to
bring, all that was left in the near-empty rooms was the
furniture that belonged to the house. The goldsmith requested
that everyone be seated around the large Tudor table before
he turned the meeting over to the head magistrate, Lord
Mayhew. Coldly disapproving of the woman who had destroyed
his wife's reputation a year earlier, Mayhew addressed Jolie
as if she were a prisoner at the dock, demanding a description of her abduction and barely concealing his suspicion
that she might be guiltier than Colin Campbell of Carwhin.

''This lawyer, Carwhin, told you he was a MacDonald?''

''He said he represented Laird Alasdair MacDonald.''

''When did you first learn that he'd lied?''

''On the second night, when I asked a servant.''

''Did you tell Carwhin that you'd uncovered his real
identity?''

"Not until we reached Stair Castle."

His questions about Breadalbane and Dalrymple seemed endless to the woman whose memory of her last meeting with them still haunted her.

"Did the earl of Argyll seem as guilty as the other two about the death of your husband?"

"No, he was as suspicious as I was about Giles Campbell."

When she told about her captivity at Kilchurn Castle, she was interrupted only when she described Tavis's boast of arranging Rorke's murder.

"Did the villain admit to the murder of our sons as well?"

"He knew about their deaths because Giles Campbell had told him, but he never mentioned them either at Kilchurn or at my home in Glencoe."

"You claim that the cowardly scoundrel died just before the massacre began. Are you certain he could not have survived?"

"Very certain, Lord Mayhew," Jolie admitted dully. "I was the one who killed him."

The silence that followed her confession was broken when the MacDonald tacksman took over the narrative, and Jolie learned that her croftsman Murray had not been Tavis's first victim that night. On his way from Achtriachton to Kinvernach, he had killed another crofter and his two sons when he had caught them driving their cattle into a shieling. A neighbor had witnessed the killing and alerted other Achtriacton villagers. In a voice that shook with anger, the tacksman described the massacre, the subsequent killing of Giles Campbell, and the ordeal at Coire Gabhail. At the end of his description, he asked if any of the Campbells had been punished.

Lord Mayhew's response stopped just short of treason. The king, he commented pungently, tended to be myopic about the loss of English and Scottish lives. But the Campbell soldiers, he added, had already received their punishment. A month after they had arrived on the Flemish battlefields, the entire Argyll army had been treacherously surrendered to the enemy and were now languishing in a French prison. Sadly, Jolie thought of Sergeant Cawley and the other decent soldiers who had refused to take part in the massacre at Glencoe. As John MacIain had said, good men were rarely praised for their deeds. More cynically, she reflected that evil men frequently profited from theirs.

She was gratifyingly surprised when Lord Mayhew announced just the opposite. At least one of the minor conspirators would be severely punished, and two of the major ones would not rest easily in their beds for years to come.

" 'Tis doubtful we can bring Dalrymple or Breadalbane down completely. Dalrymple doesn't bother to deny his part, and the Grey Fox makes a religion of denying his guilt. But Glencoe is still a popular cause with the journalists. We'll see they receive the information you've given us with enough names to point the finger of guilt squarely at the two master villains. In Breadalbane's case, we'll add another penalty. If his lawyer, Carwhin, dares to push his claim that Sister Jolie Annette married a dead man, he will be fined to the extent of his personal fortune and be charged with fraud, criminal abduction, and harassment of Newcastle businessmen. Undoubtedly, he will have sufficient means to blackmail Breadalbane into paying that fine for him. At the moment, John Campbell is in no position to risk another scandal.

"In the meantime, 'tis necessary that all MacDonalds leave our city as quickly as possible. 'Tis one thing to sympathize with your plight; 'tis quite another to risk the antagonism your presence might arouse among our people. We do not wish to appear ungracious, but your religion and your reputation for causing trouble could destroy the public sympathy we hope to gain for you.

"Sister Jolie Annette is to be given the totality of her money, and then she and her associate nuns will board the Huntington ship currently in harbor and be taken to the French port of Le Havre. We are fortunate that the ship is German registered and will not be fired upon by the French. Her subsequent transportation to Martinique will be her own affair. Can all of you be ready to leave by tomorrow morning?"

Although she was angered by the blunt dismissal from a man who had once accused her of libeling the murderous William Somerton, Jolie forced herself to reply graciously, "Thank you, Lord Mayhew. We will leave as soon as I receive my money."

"Then I suggest you accompany Mr. Morris to his place of business immediately. I wouldn't like Carwhin to arrive in Newcastle while you are still here. He would demand the right to question you, and 'tis my experience that women make sorry witnesses in a court of law."

In the counting room at the goldsmith's shop, Nathan Morris tried to reassure his client about Lord Mayhew's lack of gallantry. "He and Sir Redmond are still bitter about the deaths of their sons; they feel that had the young officers not been traveling with your late husband, they might have been spared his fate. I regret being the one to tell you, but they have an additional reason for their distress. When they arrived at the place of ambush, they found the graves disturbed and the bodies missing."

Jolie closed her eyes to blot out the vision of this one last horror, recalling all too vividly the unmarked graves in Glencoe Valley and the weeping widows who mourned even more brokenly because they did not know which of the grassy mounds contained the bodies of their husbands. She had thought their concern foolish at the time; only now could she understand their desolation.

Listening in silence as the sympathetic goldsmith described the extent of her wealth, Jolie remembered the worry she had once had about her lack of money. Now that she possessed it in ample quantities, all she wanted to purchase with it was forgetfulness and peace of mind.

" 'Tis almost twenty thousand pounds, not including the value of your two pieces of colonial property—a formidable fortune for one so young. How much of it do you wish me to set aside for Laird MacDonald?"

"How much did the jewelry earn, monsieur?"

"Only four hundred pounds, mistress."

"And the gold coins?"

"I am offering you two thousand pounds for the collection."

"Then my gift to my clan will be half the combined amount—twelve hundred pounds."

"A generous contribution, mistress."

"They are a destitute people, Monsieur Morris."

"What do you want me to do with the money your husband left in trust for his mother?"

Repressing the guilt she experienced at having forgotten Edina's existence, Jolie shook her head. "I don't even know where she is."

"She is in Edinburgh, mistress. I have received four letters of complaint from her in nine months. It has been my experience that her kind always survives. Apparently, she has not yet been told of her son's death."

"Then don't tell her—she has little enough reason for happiness. If I leave the money with you, will you see that she receives it?"

"If that is what you wish, but your husband wanted you protected first. 'Twas the money he received from the late duke of Newcastle, and he said it should be yours by right as repayment for your generosity to him."

"His mother needs it more," Jolie said quietly, but the tears fell unnoticed down her cheeks as she left the gold-smith's shop. Even in death, Rorke had tried to protect her.

An hour past dawn the following morning, two wagons left the infirmary and were driven to the private dock, where a sleek Huntington ship was waiting. With respectful gallantry, the MacDonalds and the two caretakers helped the deckhands carry aboard the piles of medical crates and the eight sea chests rendered heavier by the gold coins hidden inside. As Jolie watched her sister nuns bid a tearful farewell to men they had known all their lives, she felt her eyes fill with unshed tears as she spoke her own farewell in Gaelic. She had shared almost a year of their lives, and never would she forget the heritage they bore in common.

* * *

The peppery-eyed woman seated behind her desk in the gloomy motherhouse in Paris that still functioned as a Sisters of Charity hospital, stared angrily at the spread-out papers in front of her. Not for the first time, her thoughts about the French hierarchy of the Holy Roman Church were as unholy as forty years of unrequited service could engender. Once again she had been outmaneuvered by priestly bigots who still considered her order of nuns undeserving of the praise they lavished on the Ursulines. Yet the Sisters of Charity, organized sixty-five years after the vaunted Ursulines, were already double in membership. The holy mother, Sister Agathe Vincentia, knew all the arguments the priests used to detract. Half the nuns were volunteers who took only limited vows, while others had been Huguenot women ordered to join in atonement for their earlier heresy. They underwent no official periods of novitiate training, they were allowed to move freely about in public, and they lacked the discipline of convent-bound nuns.

Such weaknesses had been the deliberate intention of the founder, St. Vincent de Paul, because he had wanted to bring the church closer to the common people. Although Sister Agathe agreed in principle with the ideal, she had worked for twenty years to make the order respectable and to stop priests and bishops from dumping problem women into her care and dictating their placement. Cynically, she knew that wealthy men often paid church officials to rid them of quarrelsome mothers, spinster sisters, widowed sisters-in-law, and dull-witted daughters.

In the past, the holy mother had borne the irritation and frequently dunned the male relatives of such women for annual donations to her order. Since few of these problem women were trainable as nurses or teachers, she had assigned them to menial positions in the laundries, sewing rooms, and kitchens. But the papers on the desk before her now posed no such simple problem. She had been commanded by two Franciscan bishops to approve the admission of five foreign widows. They were to be trained and outfitted in one month before they were shipped to Martinique to establish an infirmary there in a vacated Ursuline convent.

Horrified that she would have no personal control over these aliens, since she could never spare either the time or money for cross-Atlantic travel, the holy mother studied the Gaelic names resentfully. Automatically, she crossed out the oddly spelled words and substituted the appropriate French ones. Sister Annette, the woman the bishops had designated as the chapter head, became Soeur Anne, Moira became Marie, and the other unpronounceable names became Elizabeth, Jeanne, and Catherine. Except for the fact that all five women were lifelong Catholics and the one called Annette was a trained nurse, Agathe could find no justification for the bishops' enthusiasm or for such a faraway chapter, other than its financial independence. The woman they had chosen to head the infirmary had promised to support both it and her sister nuns.

Wearily, the holy mother glanced at the clock and shuddered with unpleasant anticipation. In a few moments, she would be forced to greet this newest contingent of Sisters of Charity. As they filed awkwardly into her office, her first impression was of disbelief. She had been told they were already uniformed, but these scarecrows were clad in heavy wool robes permitted only during winter travel. And the robes themselves were mockeries of the traditional habits— they were black gray instead of blue gray, inaccurate in cut, poorly sewn, and devoid of white linen undercoifs. On closer inspection, Agathe discovered more serious irregularities, as well. Only two of the women were wearing crosses, and all of them still had full heads of hair. Had the bishops not assured her that the women had already taken lifetime vows, the holy mother would have ordered them removed from her office.

"Which of you is Soeur Anne?" she demanded. When no one responded, she amended her question tartly, "Soeur Annette?"

The woman who stepped forward seemed the youngest of the lot, but her voice rang with a familiar, impudent authority.

"You have become forgetful, Holy Mother. I am Soeur Jolie. Annette is my christened name, but I do not like it."

For once, the head of the Sisters of Charity was almost silenced. "Mother of God," she gasped, "I did not recognize you."

"It has been a long time since you saw me, Holy Mother."

"What are you doing here, child? It cannot be as the bishops said—that they appointed you as sister superior. You are too young to qualify for such a position."

"I am of age, and I have been a nurse for seven years. But my other qualifications were more important to the bishops—I was wealthy enough to purchase the position. They wished to transfer a chapter of Ursulines from Martinique to Canada. I gave them the deed to some property I owned in Montreal, and I promised to support my people with another piece of property I own on Martinique. They asked for no other qualification."

"How was it you were able to contact Franciscan bishops so easily?"

"I didn't. Last January, Father Andrew had written to them telling of my intentions, and I had written to Soeur Charlotte in the Strasbourg infirmary. Just before I left Scotland, I wrote to her again, and her nephew, Paul Arnaud de Laurent, was waiting for me in Le Havre with the two bishops."

"Didn't Bishop Valerian challenge your claims of being Sisters of Charity? The robes you're wearing are abominations."

"He knew we'd been in Scotland and England, where Catholic robes are not popular. I will purchase enough correct ones before we leave France."

There had always been something intimidating about her, even as a child, Sister Agathe reflected sourly, but now there was a cynical ring in her voice and a glint of stubborn determination in her eyes. How in the world had a pauper foundling gained so much confidence in so short a time— and so much wealth?

"When last I heard of you, Soeur Jolie Anne, you had married a foreign doctor and left France."

"I am a widow now, holy mother."

"Your husband was a wealthy man?"

"I inherited my money from my parents and my *grandpère*. I was not a foundling, as I'd been told."

"Who were your parents, child?"

The probing question was softly asked, but Sister Agathe's shrewd old eyes glittered with an avid curiosity that made Jolie doubly cautious about revealing anything of her French family.

"My father was a Scottish aristocrat from Glencoe. Have you not yet read Father Andrew's letter?"

Irritated by the direct question, Agathe responded defensively, "I was about to read it when you came in." Actually, she had read the first paragraph and decided the author was another parish priest currying favor with his superiors by convincing problem women in his congregation to become nuns. Now, as her eyes focused on the second paragraph, she recognized the event described as one that had been highly publicized in the Parisian newspapers.

"You were a part of that horror, child?" she asked.

"All of us were, but it is something we wish to forget. Bishop Valerian said you would want to interview us separately. Since you have finished with me, I will leave you with the others and prepare the rooms we are to use while we're here. Just one more thing, Holy Mother. We will shave our heads when we reach Martinique, but not before. We have been told that winter storms at sea can be very cold."

During the following interviews, Agathe learned more about Jolie than she did about the other four women. In halting French, the two youngest nuns described Jolie's work in Coire Gabhail in reverent tones of praise that impressed the holy mother, despite her irritation. With a rare honesty, she admitted silently that Soeur Jolie had always been an excellent nurse, but now she sounded more qualified than Marguerite du Troyes.

It was during her interviews with the older women,

however, that Agathe Vincentia relaxed much of her vigilance. The one whose name had been changed from Elspeth to Elizabeth was the ideal recruit—a disciplined, unsentimental woman, experienced in midwifery and practical nursing. Her comment about Jolie was a simple admission: "She was more courageous than any of us there, except John MacIain. She is the reason I am here."

With the fourth neophyte nun, Agathe herself was on the defensive. Moira Dundee MacDonald, who gracefully accepted the title of Soeur Marie was an educated, aristocratic woman. The daughter of a Highlands chieftain, she had hated the clan violence of her youth and the twenty years of it she had endured as the wife of a MacDonald tacksman. After describing what had happened at Glencoe and Coire Gabhail, she launched into a defense of Jolie that silenced the older woman.

"You must not blame Soeur Jolie Anne because she does not seem as devout as you and I. She does the work of God even though she never speaks of it as such. If not for her courage and generosity, the rest of us would have remained in that valley of death and lived hopeless, useless lives. Because of her, I have a chance to work in a new world and to forget the ugliness of this one."

Soeur Agathe remained seated at her desk a long time after that final interview. Not for years had she remembered her own youthful ambition to create a better world. When she had been but a girl she had joined this wayward order of nuns because it had offered her more freedom, yet she had spent the last twenty years denying that freedom to others by insisting on foolish rules rather than by encouraging new ideas. Now, two years from her retirement, she was being given an opportunity to break out of the prison she had constructed and to lead her followers beyond the boundaries of a decaying, Inquisition-ridden France into the broader world beyond its boundaries. It was a moment of triumph for the tired old woman.

Three weeks later, the holy mother and two of her secretaries accompanied the five Martinique-bound nuns up the Seine River to Le Havre. Crowded into every corner of the riverboat were piles of luggage—almost double the amount the foreign women had brought from England. To the astonishment of her hard-worked staff, the old nun had broken every one of her own rules. She had been lavishly generous with expensive supplies of medicine; she had not insisted that the new chapter be burdened with the problem nuns who had proved useless in other infirmaries; she had overlooked inadequate training in chapel ritual; and she had ordered the best meals ever served at the Paris motherhouse. Most astounding of all, she had paid for the entire cost of the transatlantic transportation out of the traditionally hoarded general fund. When asked the reasons for the remarkable generosity by one of her bolder assistants, she replied with a cryptic boast, "I decided it was time for our order to become international. Someday there will be chapters of Sisters of Charity all over the world, and we will have been the ones to pioneer the movement."

Standing near the taffrail aboard ship looking toward land, Soeur Marie murmured to her companions, "Once she accepted the idea as her own, the holy mother was most gracious."

Smiling with residual disbelief, Jolie shook her head. Her old friends at the Strasbourg infirmary would never believe that Soeur Agathe Vincentia had actually kissed her good-bye and wished her Godspeed.

10

S tepping onto the stone ledge from the small boat he
had just tied to an outcropping, the tall, heavily
bearded man looked around him with the alert animal
caution he had developed during two years of involuntary
piracy. Even in the dim light that penetrated into the familiar
Rhine River cave, once used to harbor fleeing Huguenots,
he could see the broken remnants of the vandalized luggage
left behind four years earlier. Disciplined not to indulge in
sentimental recall during moments of potential danger, Captain James Rorke, the most recent of the several aliases he
had used over the past three years, seated himself facing the
cave's entrance and waited for nightfall. Unconscious of the
automatic gesture, he rested his hand on the hilt of his
cutlass.

At thirty-four, he was a changed man from the conscientious doctor who had left Newcastle, England, and his
knowledge of violent combat was a hundredfold greater than
it had been during his career in France. With a part of his
mind detached from his now-instinctive vigilance, Rorke
wondered how much he could safely tell his friends, Arnaud
and Paul de Laurent. They might wish that his reported

death had been real if they learned that he had helped a Dutch privateer-pirate capture six French ships.

Rorke's first glimpse of that Dutch captain three years before had been a reassuring sight after the hours he had been held captive by the ruthless gang of thugs who had ambushed him and the two young English army officers. Bound hand and foot when they had been dragged from the wagon and forced to stand on numbed legs inside a crude, lamplit shed, Rorke had stared at the two men seated at a table in front of him. In comparison to the brutish, vulpine features of the highway brigand whom Giles Campbell had called Scully, the Dutchman's bland, plump face had seemed that of an honest seagoing merchant. Until he had stood up to peer more closely at the prisoners, Rorke had expected him to have the short, rotund figure common among Holland businessmen. Instead, the man had been broadly muscular and well-armed with both cutlass and pistols.

Unerringly, he had pointed toward Rorke and demanded harshly in an English that bore only a scant trace of accent, "Is this one the doctor?"

"Aye, 'tis, and as ye ordered, he's not been damaged," Scully responded with pride.

"Then you'll be paid the price I offered."

"Hold on, Deventer. The three of them will cost ye more."

"You've still not learned your trade, Scully. The other two have the look of pampered aristocrats who would play havoc with common seamen. I've no use for such aboard my ship."

"They're officers in the king's army, Dutchman, and ye're not one to pass over good fighting men. 'Twas impossible to take the doctor without them."

Captain Deventer had shrugged indifferently. "Then you should have shoved them into burrows, as you've done with farm lads and mill hands who didn't survive the drugs you slipped into their pints at the alehouse."

"Damn ye, Deventer, 'twas just fool's luck I found ye the doctor ye said ye needed. A fighting man, ye said, when

every other doctor in fifty miles was fat with paunch and
doddering with age. If I hadn't known the murderous
Scotsman from years back, he'd have hired cutthroats for
the job, and ye'd be sailing without yer doctor aboard. But
I'll heave him and the others into the river before I'll let ye
cheat me.''

Again the Dutchman shrugged, but this time with the
subtle confidence of a man who knew he had won the
argument. "I'll give you swabbers' rates for the pair, and
you can count yourself fortunate to be rid of them so easily.
When they don't report for muster aboard a king's ship
tomorrow, there'll be a hundred soldiers combing the woods
for them. The offer is the only one I'll make you, Scully,
and you've no choice but to accept if you wish to avoid the
hangman's noose.''

That conversation had been Rorke's chilling introduction
to Captain Jan Deventer, an educated trickster whose letters
of marque had been issued by a youthful William of Orange
twenty years earlier. Only through the merciful intervention
of death was Rorke to escape his domination. For the first
six months aboard a ship as deceptive in appearance as its
captain, Rorke did not see land, although the *Indomeer* was
rarely more than two hundred miles offshore. Looking as
much like a lumbering cargo ship as artifice could contrive,
the *Indomeer* was in reality an efficient ship of war whose
only cargoes were multiple ships' crews and modern weaponry.
Its function was to capture ships for the Dutch East Indies
Company, whose spice trade had become a worldwide
monopoly during the past century.

In the Bay of Biscay west of the French port of Bordeaux,
Rorke had learned the harsh reason behind Captain Deventer's
insistence that every man of the five hundred crowded aboard,
including the ship's doctor, know how to use both sword
and side arms. For a month the *Indomeer* had been on the
prowl, searching for French or Spanish ships in the vast bay,
but only fishing boats had been spotted. On the day a larger
ship appeared on the eastern horizon, the *Indomeer*'s crew
needed no emergency orders to prepare for a well-rehearsed

action. While its sails were swiftly reefed, the ship's ensign was hoisted upside down on its mast in the international signal of distress. As the French ship reached clear telescope range, Deventer relayed a description to his crew.

"A privateer with twenty cannon and a company of marines already preparing to board us. She'll be a lively prize to take."

All too swiftly, it had seemed to Rorke, the French warship was within hailing distance, and Deventer returned the enemy captain's call in French as excellent as his English.

"Our rudder is fouled and we're taking on water. We need your assistance to reach port."

"Will you surrender your ship and cargo in return for your lives?"

"Aye, if we've no other choice, but we're naught but an unarmed merchantman."

Still cautious despite the reassurance, the French captain circled twice around the drifting *Indomeer*, until his lookouts reported no cannon in sight, then he ordered his ship into grappling position alongside. Even before the lines were completely secured, the French marines had begun boarding the Dutch ship. Jan Deventer waited calmly on the aft bridge until all of the enemy marines were aboard before he called out in a voice no longer conciliatory.

"If you'll look over the side, Captain, you'll see we've fifteen cannon trained on your ship at the water line. Order your marines to surrender or we'll sink you."

In contemptuous disbelief, the Frenchman bellowed the command for his men to kill every Dutchman who offered resistance. A minute later, he tried to recall his impulsive directive, but he was too late to prevent a brief and bloody skirmish. From scores of hiding places, the *Indomeer*'s defenders rushed out to engage the enemy. Their numbers were three times greater than the French attackers.

Having been standing near Deventer throughout the entire episode, Rorke had been forced to fight for his own life and Deventer's. Although the Dutchman had drawn his sword, he had made no attempt to use it, relying instead upon Rorke to defend him from two determined French marines. The battle lasted only a few minutes, but even so, a dozen men were killed and another twenty-odd wounded. Tending to the injured below decks for the next three hours, Rorke understood why a doctor was essential aboard any ship Jan Deventer captained, and he fumed silently that the Dutchman had been testing both his fighting ability and his loyalty during the fighting.

Rorke was summoned deckside in time to see the conclusion of the capture. Invited by Deventer to go aboard the French ship, Rorke saw the open cannon ports that lined the side of the *Indomeer*. He hadn't even known of their existence because their hatch covers had been all but invisible from the outside and because he had never been allowed the freedom to explore the *Indomeer*'s hidden defenses.

"Were you impressed by our subterfuge, Doctor?" Deventer asked companionably.

Cautiously, Rorke responded to the first friendly gesture the Dutch captain had made to him. "Except for the loss of life, 'twas very effective."

"So were you, Doctor; I'm told you saved a dozen lives in surgery."

"I lost another dozen, Captain."

"A reasonable number, Doctor, when you consider the excellence of the prize. Not everyone has your talent for disarming men during a sword fight; most of us prefer to kill our enemies."

"I didn't think their deaths necessary," Rorke defended himself stiffly.

"An interesting philosophy, but on occasion, a foolish one. Still and all, I was happy to note that you're no stranger to battle. Your friends were equally impressive. They'll be serving as marines aboard this captured ship on the homeward voyage."

Repressing the surge of excitement he felt, Rorke asked dryly, "Back to Holland?"

"Home is on the other half of the Dutch empire, a goodly

distance from here. You'll find the East Indies an interesting
contrast to your native Scotland, and you'll be given land
leave there. You can tell your friends they'll have the same
privilege if they continue to be cooperative.''

Rorke scarcely recognized the two officers who had been
his fellow victims; he hadn't seen them since their violent
capture. While he had been given decent clothing and a
private cabin, they had been forced to share the crew's lives
and quarters. Sensing their resentment, he delivered Deventer's
message without comment.

''Hell's fire, that's twelve thousand miles from England,''
Gordon Mayhew exploded. ''I would just as soon have been
one of the poor devils killed today. Did you know that a
third of the crew are Englishmen who were 'recruited' the
same way we were? And that some of them have been in
Deventer's service for over ten years?''

''The ones I talked to weren't complaining,'' George
Redmond countered thoughtfully. ''They said that after the
first enemy capture, they had been paid a fair share of the
prize money, and that's more than they would have earned if
they had been forced to serve in the royal navy. To tell the
truth, I think we've a better chance of surviving this kind of
war than we would the one in Flanders. If you remember,
Mayhew, our commanders there were a pack of fools. At
least this captain and his officers are damned successful at
what they do—and damned persuasive. I listened to Deventer
convince a score of the French swabbies to join his crew by
promising them a share in the profits from the sale of their
own ship. 'Tis possible we weren't so unlucky as 'twould
seem.''

Recalling the last time he had seen the pair of Englishmen
again, Rorke smiled; within a year, both had become officers aboard the captured French privateer and had boasted of
the fortunes they were amassing. Rorke hadn't mentioned
that he had been even better paid. As the *Indomeer*'s doctor,
his share of prize money equaled that of the first mate's. But
unlike the two aristocrats, who hadn't indicated any eagerness
to return to England, Rorke had remained steadfastly hopeful

of release. Ironically, his eventual escape was not the result of any action on his part; rather, the reverse. He had survived four extended voyages under Deventer's captaincy, and not once had there been even the slightest chance to put his own plans into action. During his brief leaves ashore on the half-savage East Indies islands, he had found himself as hopelessly confined as he was aboard the *Indomeer*, with no access to any ships other than the Dutch company ones.

But on the fifth voyage, Deventer made a mistake that was to prove a fatal one for him. Instead of returning to Holland or England to replace his supply of extra crews, he decided to recruit from among the native fishermen and merchants who were skilled in both seamanship and navigation in the South Pacific waters. Following his custom of crowding the *Indomeer* with enough sailors to man four ships, Deventer had been obliged to visit the less civilized islands to fill his self-imposed quota. At one of the native port towns on Sumatra, he and the rest of his shore party contracted malaria and were already fevered by the time they reboarded the *Indomeer*.

Had the ship's supply of cinchona bark been sufficient, Rorke might have saved their lives. But because of Deventer's refusal to return to Holland during the past two voyages, all medical supplies were critically low—the cinchona bark ironically so. Fifty years earlier, pioneers in the Dutch East Indies Company had transported the seeds of the cinchona trees from Peru to Java, where the species had flourished until the bark, with its precious supply of quinine, had become one of the company's major exports. During the *Indomeer*'s last layover in Jakarta, Rorke had repeatedly reminded Deventer of the lack, but the Dutch captain had refused to consider native diseases of any importance.

"First we obtain the crews," he had insisted, "then we worry about their health."

Like all tyrants, he had been too egotistical to consider any priorities other than his own. Despite his brilliance as a naval tactician and his generosity in sharing prize money, he had been a harshly obsessive leader. He had maintained

superb discipline through bribery and fear; he would sacrifice men unnecessarily during battle in order to keep the
targeted enemy ships undamaged; and he repressed all
leadership potential in his officers. He transferred any suspected
rebels among his crew immediately to the captured ships,
keeping only the best trained and most obedient men to
crew the *Indomeer*. Because he had insisted on having a
doctor aboard, Rorke had been his only exception.

When Rorke had pronounced Deventer dead after five
days of violent delirium, the crew had been stunned, and the
ship's doctor was the only one with the initiative to fill the
void. The competent, spiritless first mate had refused the
responsibility of captaincy. After putting all the native
crewmen ashore near their villages, Rorke had ordered the
Indomeer returned to European waters. Only through an
accident of fate did the veteran ship capture another prize in
the same Bay of Biscay where Deventer had taken the
French privateer. This time it was a coastal patrol ship that
pursued and overtook the fleeing *Indomeer*. Given no choice
but to fight, Rorke had employed the trickery he had learned
from the former captain. He had ordered the blue and
orange Dutch flag replaced by the white one of surrender,
and had waited until the French ship was within cannon
range on a tack that exposed its flank.

The battle that followed was of brief duration. As obedient
to him as they had been to Deventer, the *Indomeer*'s skilled
cannoneers primed their cannons before they opened the
concealing hatches. In their first volley of fire they demasted
the smaller, fleeter ship, and were preparing to fire again
when the enemy struck its colors and surrendered. More
merciful than Deventer had been, Rorke ordered the dis-
abled ship towed within sight of land before its crew was
put ashore in longboats. While he was still within hailing
distance, the French captain had asked the name of his
victorious counterpart.

"Captain James Rorke," one of the Englishmen among
the *Indomeer*'s exuberant crew had shouted back. For the
first time, the crewmen hadn't been forced to risk their lives

during the taking of a prize, but Rorke hadn't expected the name Jan Deventer had given him to become an item of international news. Before the French ship had attacked, his intention had been to sail the *Indomeer* up the west coasts of England and Scotland and to locate Jolie in the MacDonald Glencoe Valley. But such a venture was impossible with a demasted ship in tow. Reluctantly, he had ordered the route changed to the safe waters of the English Channel and endured the long weeks of slow progress to Amsterdam, arriving there in late spring. After both ships were safely docked, he learned that King William was still fighting in Flanders; and on the off chance that the single-minded monarch remembered that Dr. Campbell had never reported for duty as ordered, Rorke had decided that his new name would become a permanent one as soon as he resigned from the command of the *Indomeer*.

To his dismay, he quickly discovered that resignation from the Dutch East Indies Company was by no means a simple matter. Almost as powerful in Holland's government as they'd been in the distant island empire, the company's owners did not want to lose a competent command officer— even one whose services had never been voluntary. For weeks Rorke had been delayed by the slow legal process of deciding the ownership of the vessels. Because Jan Deventer had left no will and no record of any family, the lawyers eventually ruled that the company and the surviving crew would share ownership of the *Indomeer*. In addition to prize money for the recently captured French ship, the dead man's accumulated fortune stored in the ship's strongbox would also be awarded to the crew, according to established percentages.

Rorke was shocked when his portion was tabulated. All told, in three years of dangerous piracy, he had earned more money than he could have in three lifetimes of medical practice. At that friendlier meeting with the company directors, Rorke was also awarded something of even greater importance to him—a release from company service and the right to resume his interrupted life. Part of that victory was due to a timely intervention by the two stadholders who had helped Arnaud de Laurent four years earlier. It was from Stadholder Willem Vandergeben that Rorke heard the first mention of the Glencoe trouble.

When Vandergeben had asked about his immediate plans, Rorke had responded promptly, "Home to Scotland to locate my wife."

"You'll need royal permission," the stadholder had cautioned him. "The prince of Orange has become overvigilant about who enters and leaves his realms."

"I doubt he'd post guards on MacDonald land," Rorke had countered lightly. "Their clans are not noted for hospitality toward alien soldiers."

"The name MacDonald is a familiar one, Doctor. Several years ago it was often mentioned in the news," Vandergeben asserted. "If I remember rightly, the incident was not one of our mutual king's more glorious accomplishments."

The cold fear Rorke had experienced when he read the accumulated reports about the Glencoe massacre in the offices of the Amsterdam newspaper, *Oprechte Haarlemsche Courant*, did not relax its icy grip until he reached Wallmond Castle five weeks later. Forced to travel overland since French gunboats now patrolled the length of the Rhine River, Rorke wore out five horses in his desperation to reach the one man whom he was certain would know Jolie's fate. Rorke would never forget the baron's ebullient greeting.

"Your remarkable wife survived, old friend, and she rid the world of the bastard I should have killed four years ago."

As thoroughly as he had once recounted the details of his abduction of Tavis Campbell, the baron revealed everything he had learned from his son in Newcastle and from the captain who had taken Jolie to Le Havre. During the telling, Rorke's initial relief had gradually faded to renewed concern. How the devil was he to get a sworn nun away from a convent in a French colony? Even if he owned a ship as powerful as the *Indomeer*, he could never succeed in a frontal attack against an island he had heard described as a guarded French bastion. As a twice-condemned enemy of France—once as Dr. Rorke Campbell and more recently as Captain James Rorke, he could expect instant execution if he were captured.

In response to Wallmond's insistent questions about his escape from the murder planned for him, Rorke was brief. "I was sold to a Dutch pirate and was a well-paid prisoner for two years before I took over as captain."

Wallmond had smiled sardonically. "The only Dutch pirates I've ever encountered were royally mandated privateers working for the Dutch Indies companies. Was your captain one of those charming fellows?"

"According to company records, he was among the most successful, but he was still a pirate."

"Most privateers are. They were one of the reasons I never entered into colonial trade. For your information, England employs as many as Holland in both the Caribbean and South Pacific. They're cheaper than royal navies and far more enterprising. Regardless of their methods, they do their fair share in protecting us merchantmen from the brotherhood of pirates who claim no national origin. Did you meet any of that breed during your odyssey?"

"Two old Spanish galleons that were flying the pirate black in waters off North Africa. Their ships weren't worth the taking, but their cargo was Spanish gold accumulated over a ten-year reign of terror. They were trying to reach their stronghold on the Canary Islands. Before our captain hanged the half of them he did not induct into his own crew, he learned that their leaders had been part of the original crews who had tossed their captains and officers overboard."

"I know 'tis a foolish question, but is that the method you employed to gain control of your own ship?"

"There was a time I would have if I'd been able, but Captain Deventer died from malaria because he considered himself invincible."

"If Jan Deventer was your captain, you were luckier than the other Englishmen impressed into naval service. He was well known for having the most loyal crews in the business.

Did he pay you enough to buy the ship you'll need if you plan to go hunting for your wife in the Caribbean?''

"If she is in Martinique, as you said, I couldn't take a ship flying either a Dutch or English flag into its harbors.''

"Louis XIV isn't at war with Germany and hasn't been for three years, and the *Lorelei* is licensed to fly the German flag. I've retired from the sea, my friend, and I've no use for an idle ship and crew. Did you qualify for your master's papers?''

"I was offered a permanent captaincy with the Dutch East Indies Company, but I know little of a ship's operation other than battle tactics, and I couldn't navigate one safely out of the Zuider Zee.''

"I've a full slate of officers skilled in those tasks. 'Tis a command they'll lack without me at the helm, and I assume you filled that role with considerable success. How much fortune did you earn?''

"A little over ninety thousand Dutch guldens.''

Wallmond's lips had pursed in a silent whistle. "'Tis a wonder those Spanish galleons didn't sink from sheer weight,'' he murmured.

"I was awarded a share of Deventer's own fortune.''

"As I said before, you've been more fortunate than most; you have five times the amount needed to buy the *Lorelei* and to pay its crew for a year.''

Recalling the small size of the graceful ship, Rorke shook his head. His experience at sea was limited, but sufficient enough for him to know that the *Lorelei* would be no match for a heavily armed ship like the *Indomeer*.

"'Tis no ship for dangerous waters, Baron. She hasn't enough cannon to fight off an armed coastal brig or the smallest of the pirate corsairs.''

"I admit she's light on cannon, but there's deck space to add four more without slowing her down. 'Tis her light weight and speed that's to her advantage—you'll not find another ship on the Atlantic Ocean that can overtake her. And since she's a two-masted sloop, she requires only a third the crew you'd need to operate a heavily armed, three-masted frigate. I'll wager your Captain Deventer never captured any ship her equal.''

"He was always after bigger game. But you're right, the *Indomeer* was a slow ship that used trickery to lure its victims. Would your crew accept me as captain?''

''Aye, they're restless to leave the Rhine River far behind; the French gunboats are like a plague of locusts. And the navigator, in particular, is eager for the challenge of open sea.''

Again Rorke had hesitated. "I still have no idea if my wife ever reached Martinique or if she decided to go to Canada instead. I'd be on a fool's errand if she is really safe in France.''

'' 'Twill be dangerous for you to travel in France.''

"I'll have to risk Strasbourg, at least. I'll need Arnaud's and his daughter's help if I'm to convince my wife to break the damned vows she's taken.''

"She thought you dead, my friend,'' Wallmond reminded him gently.

The gloomy possibility that Jolie would refuse to accompany him, if by some miracle he were able to locate her, haunted Rorke during the arduous journey to Baden-Baden. He had no way of gauging her emotional reaction to the violence she had suffered or her gratitude to her church for offering her permanent safety. He had been victimized, but never to the extent of deliberate cruelty; his young, inexperienced wife had been trapped in a savage hell he could only imagine. While he had been forced to kill strangers in self-defense, she had been driven to kill a man whose life she had once saved. God knows what that experience alone had done to her! She might never want to return to the world of men again, or to a husband she might not even recognize. He looked more like a bearded buccaneer or an escaped convict now than a civilized doctor.

Then, too, there was the nagging problem of a safe destination if she did consent to rejoin him. Because of two temperamental kings and one vindictive, villainous Scottish

earl, the world they had known would no longer be safe for
them. Not even Germany could offer them permanent
sanctuary—King Louis's forces now landed frequently on
German soil. Rorke had seen no fewer than six patrols of
them camped along the German shores of the Rhine River
as he had made his cautious way south from Mannheim.

At the home of his friends in Baden-Baden, on the
southern reaches of the German Rhine, he learned that
Charlotte de Laurent Bourbon had died suddenly the year
before and that the infirmary had been closed. Ironically, the
son who had inherited her estate had been commissioned to
guard the border with Germany. When he had heard the
discouraging news, Rorke had almost returned to Mannheim.
Unless Jolie had written to her grandfather, he would be
risking his life needlessly without learning any more about
her whereabouts than he already knew. But he had crossed
the Rhine River anyway, bedeviled by the same compulsion
that had driven him to buy the *Lorelei* from Wallmond. Jolie
might have accepted her life as a nun and might even be
happier, but Rorke knew he would have no peace of mind or
any worthwhile purpose in life until he found her. While his
conscious mind may have retained only fragmentary memories of her face, his brief year with her had been the only
happy time of his life.

Rising from the floor of the cave with muscular flexibility
acquired from three years of strenuous exercise on the
rolling deck of a ship, he left the cave and climbed the rocky
ledge to the well-remembered path leading to the Chateau
de Laurent. Half an hour later he handed the startled
gatekeeper the letter he had written in Mannheim—a letter
signed with the same cryptic signature he had used during
his years in France. Tense minutes later he was admitted
into the dimly lit servants' entry by Jean Cheney, who still
monitored his master's affairs with unceasing vigilance.

The old man recognized him instantly. Paul Arnaud's
recognition was even more immediate; he had never believed
the hero of his youth dead. Having learned many of his own
remarkable survival skills from the Scottish doctor, he had

insisted that until the body was located, he would remain convinced Rorke had escaped the murder plot. Now, in the privacy of Jean Cheney's room, Paul spoke softly in warning.

"I'm sorry I can't offer you better quarters, but my cousin, the Chevalier Bourbon, has been visiting *Grandpère* for two days. And he's a better policeman than poor old Uncle Henri ever was! Now, tell me where you've been and why you're here, rather than in Martinique rescuing Jolie."

"How can she be in any danger locked in a convent?" Rorke demanded apprehensively.

"Since when did my cousin ever stay locked up? She can find trouble wherever she is; only in Martinique, I think she deliberately creates it."

"What the devil is she doing, Paul?"

"Irritating some doddering old bishop, as far as we can tell. We learned about that trouble from the lawyer she hired to tend to her business there. Since she couldn't tell the damned Scoville who's been managing the property there who she is, the lawyer wrote to us for the information. If only Jolie were more like my Aunt Charlotte was, and not such a fighter."

"I was sorry to hear about Charlotte's death, Paul. What was it?"

"Her heart. According to *Grandpère*, she died in the same way her mother did. When are you doctors going to learn your business?"

"The only medicine I've practiced recently has been patching up battle wounds. Has Jolie written to you at all?"

"A dozen letters to *Grandpère* and a couple to me."

"May I read at least one of those letters, Paul?"

"You can read them all—but later, after I've told you all the news. I saw Jolie two years ago when she arrived at Le Havre. The priest who had helped her in Scotland had written to *Grandpère* asking for our help in getting the holy mother's permission to open an infirmary on Martinique. We did better than that. In Paris, I contacted a pair of bishops I had known during my seminary years and persuaded them to come to Le Havre with me. Jolie did her own convincing once we got there.''

"How did she look?"

"About what you'd expect after what she'd been through, but much better than you do, even so. What in the devil happened to make you look like a criminal on the run, five jumps ahead of an executioner?''

Rorke laughed with quiet humor; like Jolie, Paul Arnaud had an unbridled tongue and a sharp humor. "That's probably what I'd be called in every country except Holland and Germany. The pirate I served under was no respecter of flags. Even though a third of us aboard were Englishmen or Scots, we still helped him take a British privateer that fired on us in the Indian Ocean. 'Tis a grim business, Paul.''

"It sounds more exciting than ironmongering, but I've no complaints. I travel enough around France to break the monotony. Tell me what your plans are once you have Jolie in tow.''

Rorke shook his head. "I don't know where we'll settle. The American colonies perhaps, if King William doesn't have too many of his spies there. Paul, did Jolie ever mention me in any of her letters?''

"You're her patron saint, Rorke—the only one she really believes in, or ever has, I think. In the one letter Soeur Marguerite has written so far—''

"Soeur Marguerite is with Jolie?" Rorke interrupted in surprise.

"She went to Martinique right after my aunt's death. She was convinced that Jolie would be happier outside a convent, but she wrote that Jolie had refused to consider any replacement for you. Don't look so grim, Rorke. Three years is a long time for a woman to mourn.''

"I was thinking that she might not want the trouble a husband would bring her—even me. Paul, could I read those letters now?''

"As soon as Jean brings us word that my cousin Michel is no longer talking with *Grandpère*. He's been a houseguest for the past two days.''

"If Arnaud is ill, perhaps 'twould be better not to disturb him."

"He's old and crippled and still mourning my aunt, but he'd flay the skin off my back if I didn't bring you to see him. Besides, he wouldn't allow me to take Jolie's letter out of his sight. He has six other grandchildren, but to hear him talk, Jolie puts the rest of us to shame. If I didn't agree with him, I'd be jealous. Michel thinks it's because Jolie is the only one our *grandpère* can't admit to having. He hates our mutual Aunt Joanna and Uncle Henri even more than I do."

"Have they threatened you or your grandfather in any way?"

"No, but I'll be glad when Jolie is safely within your keeping again."

"So will I, Paul."

Four hours later, Rorke left Chateau de Laurent as silently as he had arrived. He had learned everything he had wanted to know, and had renewed a friendship with one of the few men he had ever admired completely. Even though Arnaud de Laurent was enfeebled with age and infirmity, his mind was still incisively sharp and his wit unimpaired. Rorke had not really needed to read Jolie's letters, so accurately had her grandfather catalogued the contents, but he had anyway and had rejoiced with the old man that her spirit had not been broken and that she had not retreated from life. Her letters had sparkled with an undiminished fire of defiance or enthusiasm, depending on the subject. The one from Marguerite, however, had held an element of warning that lent wings to Rorke's feet as he ran across the courtyard. "Jolie was never meant to be a nun," the old woman had written about her former pupil. "She's as restless as a caged bird in spite of her stubborn clinging to a dead past, but she's too rebellious to listen to reason. Unless a miracle intervenes, I'm afraid she'll spend her life tilting useless windmills, as I've done, and become just as embittered."

Despite the gloominess of the words, Rorke's hopes soared. He prayed that the *Lorelei* was as swift a ship as its former owner had boasted. With the crusty old nun's help, it shouldn't take a miracle to persuade Jolie to leave her new life and resume the old.

From a small upstairs window overlooking the chateau courtyard, a disciplined young aristocrat watched the tall figure of a bearded man, barely visible in the waning moonlight, cross the paving below and disappear into the darkness beyond the iron gates. Chevalier Michel Bourbon smiled gently to himself. He'd kept the promise he had made to his dying mother to protect her beloved Jolie at all costs. Without any sense of disloyalty to his unforgiving king, Michel had decided that promise of protection should extend to the husband of the beautiful nun cousin he had never seen. Someday he would tell his grandfather that he had overheard part of the clandestine conversation between the old man and the remarkable Dr. Rorke Campbell, alias Captain James Rorke. Occasionally, Arnaud needed reminding that Paul was not the only grandson who loved him, or the only grandson who had been fiercely proud of his grandfather's courage in helping Huguenots. As powerful and omnipotent as the royal family was, Michel much preferred his membership in the humbler de Laurent one.

Three thousand miles away, on an island where the eternal summer was interrupted only rarely by hurricanes or the torrential rains of tropical storms, the youthful sister superior of the Sisters of Charity convent was frowning in irritated concern. The letter on the cluttered desk in front of her was an official announcement from the St. Pierre Cathedral secretary telling her that a new bishop would be arriving on the island within three months. In preparation for his assumption of control over the island diocese, the replacement prelate had demanded that he be given a complete accounting of the funds used by the convent during the past two years.

"While Bishop Villiers has tolerated your negligence," the secretary had written, "our new spiritual leader will not. It is therefore necessary that you send the report to me as quickly as possible."

"*Peste!*" Jolie exclaimed, almost as annoyed by the letter's address as by its contents. Despite the fact that everyone else connected to the convent called her Soeur Jolie, Bishop Villiers had insisted that her official name was the alien *Anne* that the holy mother had chosen for her in Paris. As she glared at the offending letter, her angry frustration mounted. Her expenditures were nobody's business but her own! Except for the passage money the holy mother had paid, Jolie's own money had supported the infirmary and the school, and she had kept no records of what she had spent. Now, because a new bishop was coming, she would have to undergo still another inquisition about the source of her income and her management of it.

Two years ago, the day after she and her four sister nuns had reached the port of St. Pierre, she had made certain that there would be an income even before she reported to Bishop Villiers at the cathedral or investigated the convent she had paid for with her Montreal property. Paul Arnaud had insisted that she take care of business first, that she know exactly how much income she had before she made any rash promises. In Paris, she had disregarded his advice and told the holy mother that the infirmary would be well-funded, but in Martinique, she was no longer as confident.

Armed with the deed to the Maison de Scoville and with the letter of introduction her grandfather had sent her, Jolie had gone alone to the warehouse, whose stone docks could moor three ships simultaneously, and asked to speak to the manager. The perspiring, middle-aged man engaged in supervising a dock crew had glanced irritably in her direction and kept her waiting for twenty minutes. That delay had been a shock to a woman who had never seen a Negro before and who had mistakenly believed that slavery was limited to the barbarous non-Christian countries of the world. In the space of five minutes, she counted six white men and fifty black ones. By asking one of the white workers who was momentarily idle, she learned that he and the other Frenchmen were related to the manager, while every Negro there was a slave, as was two-thirds of the population of the small island.

Minutes later, her introduction to Auguste Scoville was another shock. He claimed to have no knowledge of the transfer of deed, and suggested strongly that her claim was fraudulent.

"The date on this new deed is almost three years old, yet in all that time I have continued to send the profits to the same owner I have served for twenty-two years."

"If you'll reread the count de Laurent's letter, you'll find that he bought the property from his daughter, Joanna de Guise, and that he allowed her to keep the income until such time when I would need it."

Perspiring more freely as he followed her instructions, Auguste Scoville finally blurted, "We'll talk no more of the matter until I send for a lawyer, Soeur—"

"Soeur Jolie, monsieur."

Desperately grabbing at straws, he muttered, "The name on the deed is Annette Marguerite MacDonald Campbell."

"The first two names I have never used. The last ones belonged to my father and to my husband. Why do you doubt me, monsieur?"

"Why would a French count give such a valuable piece of property to a foreign nun?"

"That is not your concern, Monsieur Scoville. Are you related to Madame de Guise? I have been told that her grandfather was also a Scoville."

"We are only distantly related."

And even more distantly related to me, Jolie thought with abhorrence, grateful for her grandfather's insistence that she not claim any relationship to her mother. *As if I ever would*, she reflected gloomily. Thus far, she had found only four relatives she would even consider claiming—Soeur Charlotte, her grandfather, Paul Arnaud, and John MacDonald. She had disliked Rorke's mother and distrusted Alasdair MacDonald, just as she doubted the plump, swarthy manager of this warehouse. In Holland, her grandfather had assured her that he had sent letters of explanation to both Martinique and Montreal.

Suddenly curious about the reasons for Scoville's nervousness, Jolie reverted to the technique she had found effective with the merchants in Newcastle. She began to ask questions about the business and about the amounts of income she could expect. She learned that the exports were mainly the produce grown by the island's planters—sugar, cotton, tobacco, coffee, and rum—and that they represented the main source of income from the Martinique property. Only a small percentage was earned from the imports sent by the main branch of the company in France.

Thoroughly confused by the time the lawyer arrived, Jolie endured the introduction with scant patience until she noted the oddity of his name.

"Riveira is not a French name," she murmured.

"No, Soeur Jolie," he responded courteously, "it is Portuguese."

At least he isn't evasive, she concluded with a satisfaction that grew with each passing moment. He reminded her of Nathan Morris, the Newcastle goldsmith who had proved to be a good friend to her. She was particularly impressed when he asked the clerk about any prior communications from the Comte de Laurent.

"According to this letter, you were notified immediately after Comte de Laurent purchased his property from his daughter," Riveira stated with a firm insistence.

Nervously, the clerk left his stool and rummaged through a dusty ledger stored on a remote shelf. Silently, he handed the lawyer a letter whose seal had already been broken. Gravely, Riveira read the contents before he turned his attention to the manager.

"You were indeed notified of the transaction, Monsieur Scoville."

"I never saw that paper before," the manager sputtered.

"Yes, you did, Uncle Auguste, but you said it was of no importance, since it did not require any change in the accounting."

Before Scoville could explode in anger over his nephew's disloyalty, the lawyer intervened smoothly. "Your clerk is quite accurate, Monsieur Scoville. Such was the agreement the comte de Laurent made with his daughter, Madame de Guise, at that time. Now, of course, Soeur Jolie will receive the income since the deed is unquestionably valid. Is there any other service I can perform for you today?" he inquired politely.

Recalling the legal protection Colin Campbell of Carwhin had given the earl of Breadalbane, and knowing her own ignorance about the export-import business, Jolie was prompt in her response to the question.

"I would like to employ you as my lawyer, Monsieur Riveira."

"I am flattered by the offer, Soeur Jolie, but usually your church employs its own people."

"But this is not for the church, monsieur—it is for my personal affairs."

"In that case, I accept with pleasure," Riveira assured her, but his smile concealed the speculative look in his eyes. Two hours later, in his own office, he was duly impressed by the extent of her personal affairs. He was to make certain she received her due amount of profit from the Scoville company, and he was to be her adviser in all matters pertaining to her financial support of the infirmary.

"Have you discussed this matter with Bishop Villiers yet?" he asked sternly.

"No, monsieur, but I have permission from the head of my order of nuns. Soeur Agathe wants my income protected so that the infirmary is completely financed," Jolie lied glibly.

Fully aware that no head of an order of Catholic nuns would grant permission for an underling to defy a ranking priest, Riveira asked sardonically, "Is there anything else you have to tell me about this unusual situation, Soeur Jolie? A lawyer really should know everything about a client if he is to protect her fully."

Jolie took a deep breath and blurted, "Yes, there is.

Comte de Laurent is my grandfather, and Madame de Guise is my mother, but no one else is to know.''

"I think you had better tell me the whole story.''

Within the hour, Jacob Riveira was well-informed about his new client, and by nightfall, the fourteen thousand gold guineas remaining of the money Jolie had brought from Newcastle was safely locked in another goldsmith's vault. Of more practical concern, the lawyer's own clerk was already at work on the account books of the Maison de Scoville.

The next morning, the five weary nuns and the piled stacks of luggage and medical supplies were driven to the distant convent in wagons hired by the obliging lawyer. In the rush of converting what had been a staid boarding school for the young daughters of planters into a workable infirmary, Jolie did not once remember the required audience with the Martinique bishop. Until he summoned her a month later, she had almost forgotten that the infirmary was a part of the church. If gentle Soeur Marie had not conducted a brief chapel each evening and led in meal-time prayers, there would have been little religion practiced. Just how the news of the infirmary had spread so rapidly among the townspeople of Fort-de-France and the neighboring plantations, no one was certain. But even before the convent gates were open to the public, there had been a line of supplicants waiting outside, and the number of patients increased daily.

Jolie's "*ma foi*" became a commonplace exclamation of exasperation among the other four nuns as their winged white hats drooped from the perspiration engendered by unceasing work. From the start, an even more serious problem was evident. While no payment was asked of the desperately poor mothers with children, the obviously prosperous people were expected to pay. Yet most of them claimed to have no money even for the medicine. The techniques Jolie had employed to collect fees from the patients in Newcastle were inappropriate for nuns sworn to serve the people. Not until Soeur Elizabeth, the most experienced of Jolie's assistants, reported a still greater imposition, did the sister superior overcome her reluctance to return to St. Pierre and to her lawyer's office. Within the first weeks, large groups of slaves were being delivered to the infirmary in wagons driven by white or mulatto overseers. In every group, at least one or two of the Negroes were suffering from infected lash marks on their backs.

After listening to her complaints, Jacob Riveira nodded in understanding. "You are being swindled," he told her. "Martinique planters are wealthy men who can well afford to pay you for treating their injured slaves. So can most of the people who come from Fort-de-France, and even the poor villagers can pay you in produce from their gardens. What you need is a competent gatekeeper who will collect what payment he thinks the patients can afford to pay."

Jolie sighed tiredly. "I need a staff of servants, monsieur. The three who were there when we arrived are lazy, fat women who pretend they can't understand what we tell them to do."

"Unfortunately, there are many such servants on Martinique; you would do well to dismiss them. If you will trust me, I will locate some excellent workers who will earn their wages. The man I recommend to collect the payment for your patients has been well-trained in a similar position at one of my cousin's stores in the Negro ghetto of St. Pierre."

Jolie took a deep breath. "Is he a slave, monsieur?"

"We do not employ slaves, Soeur Jolie; nor do I think your church would permit you to own any. Sébastien is a mulatto whose French father was a shipper who transported slaves from Africa. During his young manhood, Sébastien served as a navigator aboard one of those ships. After his father's death, he became an assistant manager in my cousin's trade mart, but now he wishes to move his family into the country. Like most port cities, St. Pierre has its full share of problems."

Within a week, the convent's financial and domestic problems were solved. Sébastien was an articulate man who wore the simple white island costume with a dignified grace; he was also a heavily muscled giant almost as tall as

Alasdair MacDonald had been. He arrived at eight o'clock on the first morning of his employment with his mulatto wife, two daughters, and a son. In ten hours the convent was clean, and Sébastien had collected four times the amount of money he had requested in wages for himself and his family. Promptly at sunset, they departed for the home they had located a mile away. Only the French housekeeper and Negro cook whom Riveira had hired remained on the premises.

Shortly after Sébastien had taken charge, a messenger sent by the lawyer arrived, bearing a letter and a two-week allotment of Jolie's earnings from the Maison de Scoville. The amount was a stunning surprise for the new owner, whose one visit to the warehouse had been a bitter disappointment. Riveira's accompanying letter of explanation more than confirmed her suspicions—his clerk had discovered that Auguste Scoville had been systematically looting the profits for twenty years. But in the past two weeks, the lawyer reported sardonically, Scoville had become scrupulously honest.

When a sprucely robed Soeur Jolie responded to the bishop's summons, she was confident he would find no fault with her management of the infirmary. Old in years and deceptively benign in appearance, Bishop Villiers received her unattended in his office quarters of the impressively ornate cathedral. His opening reprimand that she should have reported to him immediately upon arrival in Martinique was muted by his praise of the excellent progress she had made, but his next question had shocked her.

"When do you intend to reopen the school? It has been four months since the Ursuline nuns departed, and a number of the landowners are eager for their daughters to resume their education."

"We are nurses, Your Eminence, not teachers, and there are only five of us," Jolie protested.

"Bishop Villiers will be sufficient in your address to me, and I think you will be less nervous if I call you Soeur Anne."

"I would prefer Soeur Jolie, Bishop Villiers."

Briefly, a frown destroyed the priest's serenity as he shook his head. "It is not one of the permissible names for a nun," he disclaimed tersely, continuing in a less censurious tone of voice, "The head of your order wrote to me that you are somewhat less experienced than is usual with a convent superior. She also wrote that she is sending an additional ten nuns to join you as soon as you are settled. In the meantime, I suggest you make accommodations for twenty-five young girls. Since they will be boarding at the convent, I'll see that you have a proper staff to help you with their physical needs."

As Jolie's shock subsided, she had recovered both her wits and her tongue. "Bishop Villiers, what you suggest is nonsense. The other four nuns are Scotswomen who are just learning to speak French, and none of us could teach any subject other than nursing. That is the only thing we were sent here to do. You say there are twenty-five pupils you wish to enroll; we have already treated twenty times that number of sick people. There is something else, Bishop. I do not as yet know if my income will be sufficient to support a school as well as an infirmary."

"But I was told that you are the owner of the Scoville export company."

"Only a branch here on Martinique. Didn't the Bishop Valerian inform you that I had already given the Montreal branch to the Ursuline nuns who will be working there?"

The frown that settled on the bishop's face was no longer slight. "What arrangements did your holy mother make to supplement your income?"

"None. Each chapter is expected to be self-sufficient, but I don't think the Martinique infirmary ever will be. Half the patients are too poor to pay in money, and the medicines they need are very expensive. Already we have been forced to keep twenty people overnight or longer in the hospital, and the food is also expensive. Unless the fathers of the pupils you wish enrolled are made to pay the entire cost of their daughters' education, the school will be even poorer."

Bishop Villiers sighed in pursed-lip irritation. If he hadn't been assured that there would be no cost to the church, he would never have permitted the Sisters of Charity to settle on his island. They were a troublesome lot, entirely too independent for women in or out of the church. In particular, he was annoyed at the prospect of having to become personally involved in the management of an unimportant nunnery, but quite obviously, this naive young woman was incompetent to function without his help.

"Very well, Soeur Anne," he informed her sternly, "I will postpone the opening of the school until I determine the extent of your income. To that end, I will have my people begin their investigations immediately."

"That will not be necessary, Bishop Villiers. I have already hired a lawyer."

"You cannot go outside the church in such matters. Who is the man you employed?"

"His name is Monsieur Riveira. He is Portuguese."

The old priest's lips were compressed with renewed anger. "I know who and what Jacob Riveira is, young woman. Forty years ago, three hundred of his people were driven out of Brazil because of their religion and allowed to settle on this island."

"But I thought Brazil was a Catholic colony, the same as Martinique."

"Brazil *is*, these people are *not*. They are Jews."

"That is impossible; King Louis would never permit it."

"Our beloved monarch was very young when he offered them asylum; now it is too late to rectify his mistake. Unfortunately, some of them have become essential to the island's prosperity. But I will not allow any of them to become involved in church affairs."

"Monsieur Riveira is not involved in church affairs, Bishop Villiers—only in my personal business. He is doing an excellent job of protecting my income, so I cannot dismiss him. I know nothing about the export business, and I don't think your priests would know much more. Monsieur Riveira has already learned that the manager cheated the former owner; but with a lawyer watching him, he will not cheat me.''

Suddenly aware that the bishop was regarding her with an expression similar to the one the holy mother had once worn, Jolie retreated into the appealing cajolery she had often used to placate dyspeptic patients.

''The money will not be tainted, Bishop,'' she wheedled, ''and I will need as large an income as possible if there is to be a school as well as an infirmary. The holy mother told me that your church is too poor to aid us financially, so I must do everything I can to make sure my funds are sufficient.''

For a moment, Bishop Villiers stared at her in sour disapproval. The idea of a nun being allowed to keep her fortune separate from the church, or for any woman to have control of money, infuriated him. At the moment, he wasn't certain they should be given even a rudimentary education— they lacked the moral sense to know right from wrong.

Still, he couldn't deny that this irritating nun was right in some of her allegations. His diocese was poor—deliberately so, since he'd been forced to send all but bare maintenance to the mother church in France at the king's insistence. The slyly insolent woman had also been right about the caliber of priests sent to help him; undoubtedly, a Jewish lawyer would be more competent in dealing with a dishonest businessman. Most certainly she was right about postponing the opening of a school. The landowners would be furious with the church if she were to become the only teacher for their impressionable young daughters. With her persuasive glibness of tongue and her impudent independence, she could destroy the moral fabric of the island social order that kept women restricted to their homes.

11

As Jolie reread the demanding letter, her lips compressed cynically at the church secretary's claim that Bishop Villiers had been overly tolerant in ignoring her frequent negligence. For a year after that first interview, he had found constant fault with her mangagement of the convent. He had criticized her lack of segregation among the women patients who remained overnight at the infirmary.

"You may not approve of the social order here on Martinique," he had warned her, "but you cannot treat white women as you do slaves and mulattoes."

When she had refused his request to send one of the nuns to a remote plantation to tend the owner's wife during the final weeks of pregnancy, Bishop Villiers had remonstrated angrily, "This woman is more deserving of your services than the slaves you insist on treating. She and her husband are among our most generous parishioners, yet you deny her any spiritual assistance during her difficult ordeal."

"The problem is not spiritual, Bishop, it is medical," Jolie had explained. "Only two of us are qualified midwives, and both Soeur Elizabeth and I are too busy to leave the infirmary for so long a period."

Prior to the reopening of the school, just after the additional Sisters of Charity had arrived from France, Jolie had turned the selection of applicants over to the experienced

Soeur Thérèse, who had administered a similar school in
Bordeaux. Because a parish priest from Fort-de-France had
conducted the opening ceremonies, the bishop learned about
Thérèse's democratic enrollment from the complaints of
wealthy parents. While their daughters were the only ones
who could afford to board at the school, they were outnumbered
two to one by daytime pupils from the families of tradesmen,
Fort-de-France soldiers, and other such lesser members of
the island's citizenry. Outraged that he had not been consulted
in advance, Villiers had reprimanded Jolie severely and
demanded that she expel the two mulatto girls who had been
included.

Having paid little attention to Soeur Thérèse's choice of
pupils, Jolie endured the reprimand, but refused the request
on principle. A week later, she returned voluntarily to the
bishop's office and informed him that the pupils in question
had been enrolled by two landowners who claimed them as
daughters. When faced by one of the uglier realities of
island life, the beleaguered bishop had withdrawn his objection. But he had not relaxed his vigilance over the convent
or the independent nun who supported it; nor did he cease
his efforts to gain control.

As he had promised earlier to supply a staff of women to
help in the school, he had sent half a dozen elderly and
infirm aristocrats, who had been promised the right to spend
their declining years in a convent. At Soeur Thérèse's
insistence, Jolie had returned all but one to their St. Pierre
homes; the others had been too irritably intolerant of the
nonsense of schoolgirls.

"The Ursuline nuns never refused this responsibility,"
Bishop Villiers had raged. "These women have earned the
right to a peaceful death through years of service to the
church."

"The Ursuline nuns never operated an infirmary," Jolie
had retorted, "and our school enrollment is three times the
size of theirs. Believe me, Bishop, there is very little peace
and quiet at the infirmary and no provisions for the care
these old women need, regardless of their deserving piety.

We would not have refused them had they been impoverished nuns, but these women have wealthy families who can provide for them.''

Until his own health had failed him eight months later, Bishop Villiers had continued his interference in the convent's affairs. The only aspect he had eventually ignored had been the financial one. That grudging oversight had not resulted from a lack of interest, but from Jacob Riveira's letter of warning that the church had no legal control over his client's private income. Since Jolie's share of the money from the Scoville company had been ample enough to support the convent and to provide for the necessary expansion of the facilities, she had not worried about her expenditures or kept any records. Nor had she thought about the lack until the arrival of this autocratic demand.

With abrupt determination, she rose from her desk and shoved the letter into her pocket. She knew of only one man who could help her resolve the problem of this latest of her confrontations with church officialdom. The increasing frustration she experienced as she was driven to her lawyer's office was multiple in origin. Not even the memory of her joyful reunion with Soeur Marguerite three months earlier could dispel her gloom. She hated the thought of having to adjust to another autocratic priest, who sounded more dictatorial than Bishop Villiers had been at his worst. Despite the physical beauty of the island and the blue seas surrounding it, she was depressed by the people who lived on it. The slaves who were brought to the infirmary were apathetic, frightened, or sullen; and their diseases were usually chronic recurrent fevers she knew nothing about and could not cure. Except for a few like Sébastien and his family, even the free mulattos were repressed and spiritless. Of the poorer French settlers she had met, only a small percentage possessed the resilient independence of the farm families she had known in Strasbourg, while the wealthy planters were more overbearing than the titled English aristocrats had been.

More than any other annoyance in her present life, however, Jolie hated the endless work of administration. How she wished she had inherited her Aunt Charlotte's calm temperament and multiple abilities; and how she wished she had been more observant and appreciative as a girl. While Soeur Marguerite had seemed the real heroine, Charlotte had maintained her ancestral vineyard, administered a convent larger and more complex than the one on Martinique, and still had time to mother a problem niece.

Although Jolie had delegated the responsibility for the school to Soeur Thérèse and the chapel functions to Soeur Marie, she had been forced to spend long, dull hours with merchants, builders, church officials, and the parents of the enrolled pupils. For a few months she had been challenged by the enormity of the necessary preparations and by the excitement of living on an exotic-looking island. But with the addition of the school, her administrative duties had tripled, and she had become increasingly resentful of the time she had had to spend away from the infirmary.

Bouncing along the rutted road in the poorly sprung coach she had purchased for the convent, Jolie contemplated the future with the honest evaluation she had avoided for months. She was bored with everything except her infirmary work, and she was critically unhappy with her performance as the sister superior. In spite of the reputation she had earned for decisive leadership, she knew she was a fraud. Her attitude toward religion had remained unchanged, and she hated the hypocrisy of pretense. How she longed for the freedom she had enjoyed in Newcastle, and how often she had to repress the corrosive bitterness she felt when she remembered her lost happiness.

Even in the infirmary, she was no longer the central figure of authority. Despite her crippled legs and age, Soeur Marguerite was still the more knowledgeable and masterful. From the first day of her residency at the Martinique convent, she had won the respect of the nurses and patients alike with her pharmaceutical knowledge. And the old nun still understood her former pupil better than Jolie herself did! Her greeting on the day she'd arrived had been a characteristic scolding.

"You haven't the temperament or the patience for a cloistered life, young Jolie. If I have my say, you'll leave this prison to those of us who have no other sanctuary, and you'll get back to where you belong."

"Where would I go if I left here? I can't return to France or Scotland or England, and I've learned that it's a dangerous world for a woman alone."

"You wouldn't need to be alone. You've enough money to buy yourself another doctor and the face to win his interest if you'd stop looking like a martyr on the cross. I know you loved Rorke Campbell, in spite of his gruffness to you, but he's been dead three years now, child. You've mourned him long enough."

"I've taken my holy vows, Soeur Marguerite."

"How absurd. You're no more holy than I am or than Charlotte was. The two of us made the best of the bad luck we suffered on the outside. Your aunt enjoyed the life, and medicine has been the only thing that ever interested me; but you'll age before your time if you've no other goal. Charlotte was the one who sent me here, Jolie. She worried about your happiness more than you'll ever realize."

Jolie had wept at the news of Charlotte's death and wished that she had known when she'd been a child that the nun was her aunt. But she had thought the rest of Marguerite's words cruel and unfeeling. No one could ever take Rorke's place. Jolie knew that she could never again be as happy as she'd been with him. But memories did not change reality, nor could Marguerite's optimistic advice that she find another man to love. The only home Jolie had left was the convent, and the only happiness possible for her was the satisfaction of nursing. Perhaps if she were able to concentrate on medicine, she would survive as well as Marguerite had.

The idea that had begun to form just after that conversation with her old teacher had slowly crystallized; the letter from the bishop's secretary had only accelerated her time schedule. Driven by the same powerful sense of self-preservation that had led her to seek Father Andrew's help in Glencoe, Jolie entered Jacob Riveira's office with a purposeful step.

"As soon as you read this letter," she announced in greeting, "I have two tasks I wish you to perform for me, monsieur."

Always the careful lawyer, and even more, a cautious man whose own self-preservation and that of his people depended upon his knowing what changes were taking place in his small island world, the letter's contents came as no surprise to Riveira.

"I had heard that Bishop Villiers was about to be replaced," he murmured. "I had hoped the new man would prove as manageable, but I rather doubt it from the tone of this letter. I suspect this new bishop intends to discipline the rebels among us. What do you want me to do for you, Soeur Jolie?"

"I haven't kept any records of the expenditures," Jolie confessed. "I am hoping you will be able to help me manufacture some."

Riveira chuckled softly. No wonder he liked Jolie so much—she faced a problem directly, without hiding behind excuses or feminine protestations of self-pity. His response was as practical as her request.

"It will be an interesting challenge. I'll have my clerk prepare a sheaf of papers so jumbled with complicated figures and explanations that even the most discerning of priests will have little complaint. And I'll make certain that this one does not learn there has been an unused surplus in your income. The old adage 'rob Peter to pay Paul' has had a remarkable history within the Catholic church, and I wouldn't like this new bishop to decide that he has the right to claim your excess for his own. You said you had two commissions for me today. What is the second one?"

Jolie took a deep breath. What she was about to do would change her life irrevocably once again. "I want you to transfer the deed to my Scoville property here on Martinique to the Sisters of Charity, and to send it to Soeur Agathe Vincentia in Paris. As I told you before, she is the holy mother of the order. In the explanation you write, I want it clearly understood that the money is to be used by the nuns here on Martinique."

Thoughtfully, Riveira regarded this most unusual of women. In two years he had found her to be both courageous and intelligent. She had successfully defied many of the established social laws of Martinique, and she had established a reputation for excellence in medicine that the Bishop Villiers had found impossible to belittle. But now she was proposing to relinquish the one certain guarantee she had of maintaining her independence from church domination.

"Would you mind telling me your reasons for this rather dramatic decision?" he asked mildly.

"I am resigning from my position as sister superior and recommending that the holy mother appoint Soeur Marie in my stead. It would not be fair to the others to have an underling nun control the money. Besides, this way, if something happens to me, the convent could still continue its work."

"Is there some special reason for your resignation? From what I've heard, you've been doing an excellent job." Riveira prodded subtly.

"I am tired of the work, and I am not talented in diplomacy. Soeur Marie is. Bishop Villiers would never have challenged her authority as he always did mine."

"What will you do?"

"I'll work under Soeur Marguerite in the infirmary, as I did in France."

"Then you are not planning to leave the order?"

"I have nowhere else to go, monsieur."

"Do you want me to transfer your other money, as well?"

"No, it is—" Jolie stopped abruptly when she realized that she had been about to add "my only means of escape."

Shrewdly, the lawyer completed the sentence, "Your personal security. I think you're wise to retain possession of it; the future is not always as predictable as we would like.

Are you still determined to relinquish your income from the Scoville company?''

"Yes."

"Then we'll take care of the matter today. One of the ships we employ will be sailing in a few days with letters to our associates in France. Have you written your resignation yet?''

Jolie hesitated a moment before she responded, "No, monsieur, I was hoping you would help me word it so that the holy mother will not refuse.''

Jacob Riveira chuckled gently. "It is what we lawyers do best.''

When Jolie left the office two hours later, she felt lighter in heart than she had for months. That night she informed the sisters—Marie, Thérèse, and Marguerite—that they were now the convent guardians.

The morning dawned clear and sun-filled, with few reminders of the rain that had lashed the island for the prior two days. Visible in the distant north, Mount Pelee rose above its sister peaks in symmetrical majesty, and the calm seas were vivid aquamarine in color. Inside the dormitories of the convent, the schoolgirls needed no prodding to leave their beds; today was to be one of the most memorable occasions in their lives. Everyone in the convent, even the servants, had been summoned to the convocation being held on the square in front of the St. Pierre Cathedral to watch the installation of the new bishop. Not for twenty years had such a momentous event disturbed the placid lives of the island residents. But while most of the citizens would be restricted to the fringes, the convent pupils and nuns would be positioned in a place of honor near the foot of the wide cathedral stairs.

Already assembled on the convent grounds were the flower-decorated wagons that would carry them into the city; and in the kitchen, festive picnic lunches were being prepared. Such was the degree of excited anticipation that the girls donned their best blue-gray cotton uniforms, snowy white aprons, and small white caplets without their usual complaints. Racing outside, they watched the parade of people already astir on the road that followed the shore between Fort-de-France and St. Pierre, and kept a zealous count as their daytime comrades arrived.

Almost as pleasantly excited, fourteen of the sixteen nuns dressed in their newest blue-gray habits, fluffed their white aprons until not a wrinkle showed, and fastened their crisply starched hats securely on their heads. Only Soeur Jolie and Soeur Marguerite dawdled over their preparations, even though they knew they had no choice but to accompany the others. While they could avoid the public ceremony if they chose, they could not ignore the private audience with the new bishop that they had been ordered to attend.

Jolie's reluctance was based on disappointment that she had not yet received an acceptance of her resignation from the holy mother. She hated the thought of attracting the attention of the new bishop, about whom she was already apprehensive. In the three months since her lawyer had sent the hastily made-up financial accounting to the cathedral secretary, along with the notification of her resignation, she had received three additional requests from the church official, asking for more detailed information. Pointedly, the letters had all been addressed to Sister Superior Anne rather than to her replacement. Her responses had been brief and noncommittal, referring the reader to the original accounting. The letter that had asked for the precise total of her two years of income from the Scoville company, she had turned over to Jacob Riveira. His comment had been a cautious speculation. "Perhaps I erred in not informing him that you no longer owned the property."

"Why didn't you?" Jolie had asked.

"I wanted to be sure there had been no mishap at sea in the event this new bishop decided that the property and its income could be better administered by local church authorities."

Today, as Jolie made one final inspection of the empty

infirmary, she shivered in aversion. The day could not pass quickly enough to suit her.

Marguerite's objections were far more complex—she hated the pretentious pomp of such ceremonies; she hated standing in the hot sun; and she was nagged with concern over a story that a recent patient had told her. The man had reported that a small company of cavalry soldiers had arrived in St. Pierre a few days earlier. It had been his description of their uniforms that had aroused Marguerite's suspicions. If they were the royal dragonades, their presence on Martinique could only mean one thing—the new bishop was bringing the Inquisition to the island! The old nun sighed with regret. She had hoped to spend her remaining years without any more reminders of King Louis's obsessive ambition to achieve religious solidarity in his empire. Not wanting to alarm the others unnecessarily, she kept silent, never mentioning her vague fears about those soldiers.

Riding in the coach with Jolie and the other two convent heads, Marguerite bided her time until they reached the cathedral square in advance of the beflowered wagons carrying the other nuns and the squealing schoolgirls. After Marie and Thérèse had dismounted to organize the pupils into orderly lines, Marguerite gripped Jolie's arm with an uncharacteristic display of weakness.

"Jolie, child," she murmured, "this sun is too much for me; I feel faint. Do you suppose your lawyer might be generous enough to offer me shelter for a few hours? I daresay he wasn't summoned to attend this pretty circus."

Instantly concerned for her friend's health, Jolie reached for the large bag at Marguerite's feet. "Did you bring some smelling salts?" she asked.

Pushing the bag away from Jolie's reach, the old nun retorted tartly, "It's shade I need, not smelling salts or any other folderol; and I'll need you to stay with me. You'll never be missed in that crush anyway; there are enough worshipful witnesses already there for a royal coronation." Marguerite didn't mention the white-uniformed soldiers she'd glimpsed, standing by their horses on a side street, or the apprehension the sight of them had aroused.

As she leaned forward, she spoke crisply to Sébastien, still waiting patiently on the driver's bench. "I don't suppose we'll find the lawyer at his office today, but I'm certain you know where his home is located. You'd better drive us out of here before we're hemmed in by traffic."

Sébastien obeyed the order with a speed that rattled the underpinnings of the coach, not because he thought Marguerite ill, but because he was curious. Twice during the past few days, she had asked him many questions about the lawyer and the other Jewish people in St. Pierre. He, too, had heard rumors about these new soldiers, and had noticed them as he had driven past the street. Unlike most of the insular people in Martinique, though, Sébastien knew what they were and how dangerous they could be. Years before, in French port cities, he had seen companies of them arrest frightened heretics who had been trying to leave France by ship. As he pulled the coach to a halt alongside a high wall that was unbroken except for a barred gate, he wondered if Soeur Marguerite had come to warn his old benefactors about the royal dragonades.

Dismounting from the coach, he walked to the gate and pulled the bell rope. The frightened maid who answered the summons relaxed visibly when she recognized the caller. A minute later, Sébastien returned to the coach and climbed aboard.

"Monsieur Riveira will see you at his office," he announced laconically, without revealing the rest of the servant's message that there had been thirty anxious people assembled in the house. Neither did he mention that he had been told to use the rear entry to the office, rather than the one that fronted on the main street. Within minutes after Riveira's arrival, Marguerite knew the reason behind that precaution. Showing no sign of the weakness she had complained about, she hobbled down the dark corridor in the lawyer's wake and asked to speak to him privately. When Jolie protested that the older woman should rest, Marguerite snorted in derision.

"I'm not ill. I needed an excuse to conduct some business without the others knowing. While you're waiting for me, you can read the letter I brought you from France. It's the last one your aunt wrote to you. She asked me to give it to you whenever I thought you would take her advice." With a flick of her strong wrists, the old nun pulled the sealed epistle from her bag and pushed it into Jolie's limp hand.

Inside the closed office, Marguerite addressed the lawyer with her customary bluntness. "I want you to store these three thousand gold livres with the rest of Jolie's money. Her Aunt Charlotte was afraid her niece had lost everything during the massacre in her father's village, but I knew she had more sense than that. Has Jolie told you much about her background?"

Without denying or confirming that Jolie's other money was in his safekeeping, Riveira commented blandly, "She has told me about her parentage, but not much else."

"Her life has been as unusual as she is, Monsieur Riveira. But at the moment, there are more important things we must discuss. Have you heard anything about the king's dragonades yet?"

"Their commander and the new bishop have already contacted me. Of the two, I found the priest a more reasonable man than his brother."

Marguerite closed her eyes briefly in tired resignation; the fear that had nagged her all week had been doubly justified. Not one, but both de Guise brothers had been sent to Martinique. Apprehensively, she asked, "Did either Bishop de Guise or the colonel mention Jolie?"

"No, their concern dealt only with my people and our future conduct. That is why I suggested you use the rear door. I was informed that my office would be under their surveillance."

"Monsieur Riveira, your life and those of your people

could be in danger with that pair of fanatics in charge of the island!"

"No, merely uncomfortable. They know our charter with King Louis is inviolate and that the landowners would not condone any violence against us. Because we frequently lend them money, we are part owners of many plantations."

Marguerite's eyebrow rose skeptically. "Why should such men protect you? If you were driven from the island, or worse, they would not have to repay their debts."

"We are not unaware of our precarious situation, Soeur Marguerite. The deeds and loans of such transactions are safely stored with our associates in France. Islanders much prefer us as their creditors, since we understand their problems and frequently wait until they can repay us. Now, tell me, what problem does Soeur Jolie have with the new bishop?"

By the time Marguerite concluded her terse narrative, the lawyer was frowning. "This Colonel de Guise does not know she is his wife's daughter?"

"No, and I'm afraid the despicable Joanna may not have told him that she sold her property here to her father four years ago."

"I believe you may be right. It would explain their presumptuous interest in Soeur Jolie's income. But surely they wouldn't dare accuse the comte de Laurent of fraud. I have been informed that he is highly respected and extremely wealthy."

"I'm afraid they will be far more direct. Will you defend Jolie if they resurrect those ancient charges against her?"

The lawyer shook his head. "I cannot even offer her asylum in my home. I was expressly forbidden to have anything more to do with the convent or its people."

"Then Jolie must leave the island as quickly as I can arrange for a ship. She will be safer in France with her grandfather than she is here. She said you had access to such a ship."

Again the lawyer shook his head. "The two we use are at sea, and I trust very few of the other captains. In the meantime, while I consult with my colleagues, I will make arrangements for her to remain hidden in the home of another mulatto friend. Sébastien can take her there immediately. She must not attend that meeting with the new bishop under any circumstances. As an added precaution, I suggest you show Bishop de Guise the letters I received from the comte de Laurent in response to my inquiries. They detail a complete record of her birth and of the inheritance he gave her.''

Outside the office, the waiting room was empty, and only Sébastien was aboard the coach. ''Soeur Jolie decided to walk to the cathedral. I'm to take you there whenever you're ready,'' he told Marguerite.

''Mother of God!'' she muttered.

Never before had Jolie felt so lacking in purpose or so indecisive about what she really wanted in life. As she had read her aunt's letter in the empty waiting room, she had experienced a restless need to be alone and away from Marguerite's domination, if only momentarily. Charlotte's loving advice had been so much more understanding.

''Don't ever lose your rare courage, my dearest niece, and don't ever let your spirit be crushed by circumstances. Life hasn't been kind to you thus far, but I am convinced there can be contentment ahead for you if you persevere. Remember, child, that you still have alternatives to the convent, should your present task prove unbearable.''

This morning, when Jolie had looked back at the well-maintained infirmary and school, and watched the nuns and their excited pupils climb aboard the wagons, she had been proud of her achievements here on Martinique. But she had been unhappily aware that she no longer felt a part of the convent life. Even more unhappily, she felt that she had failed to become a good nun. What had seemed to promise her a peaceful sanctuary throughout the grim months in Coire Gabhail and the final tense days in England now seemed as prisonlike as Breadalbane's Castle Kilchurn had been.

As she strode along the street overlooking the harbor, which was crowded with a dozen ships riding at anchor, she remembered Marguerite's blunt words: "You have enough money to buy yourself another doctor." With a doctor to give her respectability in another colony, she could open a small infirmary like the one in Newcastle. Rorke had once told her that there were poor medical students at Edinburgh University. Perhaps one could be tempted to accept her invitation to come to any one of the dozens of English colonies already established in the Caribbean and in the New World to the north. It would be exciting to work with a doctor again—not a husband, Jolie reflected sadly, but a man whose professional title would attract more challenging patients than the pathetic people who came to the infirmary only because they could not afford doctors. She would have the freedom to prescribe medicines and to perform operations without worrying about church restrictions.

Her steps slowed as she neared the cathedral. She hated to end the first free hours she had had in months, but the church bells were merciless in their tolling of the time. If she didn't report for the audience with the new bishop, Soeur Marie would be the one to suffer a reprimand. That she was already late, Jolie realized the instant she approached the nuns and schoolgirls already picnicking beneath a stand of jacaranda trees next to the square. Standing watchfully near them were two brown-robed priests. Jolie watched in surprise as the middle-aged Scottish midwife, Soeur Elizabeth, ran toward her.

"Soeur Marguerite said you were not to attend, that you were to go someplace with Sébastien right now!"

"Why?" Jolie demanded.

"Don't ask questions, just go!"

But that one question had already cost Jolie her chance to reach the waiting coach. The two priests converged on her, one to each side, and pinioned both her arms.

"The bishop is expecting you, Soeur Anne. He'll be none too pleased with your tardiness," one of them scolded her sternly.

"You did not attend the ceremonies," the other one accused her. "Where were you?"

"One of the nuns became ill," Jolie responded vaguely as her lips curved into a rebellious smile. What hours of lonely soul-searching had failed to accomplish, this latest display of arrogant church dominion had done for her. Soeur Anne would soon become Widow Jolie Campbell! Met by the agitated secretary, she responded readily to his fussy scolding, "I am not deliberately late, Father Patrice. I lost my way returning to the cathedral."

"You should not have been alone on city streets," he chided her. "In the future, you will follow the rules of conduct for a nun."

To a woman who had crossed half of Scotland on snow-shoes, the dictate seemed ridiculous, and Jolie was still pensively amused as she entered the familiar bishopric office as unobtrusively as possible. Relieved that her entry elicited no immediate comment, she kept her eyes downcast until she reached Soeur Marguerite's side and could hide her face behind Soeur Thérèse's large white hat. Listening to Soeur Marie's gently spoken description of the convent, she relaxed still further. Like her Aunt Charlotte, the aristocratic Scotswoman possessed an assured dignity that would impress the most irascible of bishops, Jolie reflected irreverently.

"Ours is a most fortunate chapter of our order of nuns," Soeur Moira MacDonald proclaimed triumphantly. "We were able to purchase the convent itself from our Ursuline sisters, and we have sufficient income to support our needs. I am certain Your Eminence will find us a most loyal and cooperative part of your diocese."

Expecting only a polite expression of approval from the new bishop, Jolie jerked angrily when his coldly authoritative words expressed only the reverse. But not until he called her by name did she recognize his voice; then, only the strong pressure of Marguerite's fingers on her arm kept her silent.

"I'm afraid I do not share your enthusiasm or confidence, Soeur Marie," he had begun his condemnation. "According to the records I have studied, the convent belongs to the Sisters of Charity only because of a questionable exchange of deeds. The income you boast of is not the property of the convent; for the past two years, it has been sent to one of your nuns who is still listed officially as the sister superior.''

"Not anymore," Marie volunteered earnestly. "Three months ago, our benefactress deeded her last holding in the Scoville company to our order of nuns and sent both the deed and her resignation as our superior to the holy mother, Soeur Agathe Vincentia, in Paris. Her only stipulation was that the income be used by our chapter. That income is the reason we may sound overconfident, Your Eminence.''

"It could also be the reason your convent may soon be in serious trouble, Soeur Marie. The Maison de Scoville company has been owned by one Scoville family member for the past twenty-four years. We could find no evidence that any part of it was sold to an adventuress of doubtful antecedents and integrity who calls herself Soeur Anne, but whose legal name is Annette Campbell.''

"You are wrong about her antecedents and integrity, Your Eminence," the middle-aged nun countered with the ingrained pride of her Scottish heritage. "Her father was one of the finest members of our MacDonald clan, and Soeur Anne has been his worthy heir, the bravest and most generous woman I have ever known.''

Surprised by the intensity of the defense and shrewdly aware that the speaker could not be easily cowed, the bishop attempted a more conciliatory approach. "I am not challenging your faith in her, Soeur Marie, or the fact that she may have earned your commendable loyalty. But there are irregularities in her possession of two deeds to Scoville property. Since there might even be criminality, I insisted she be here today to answer certain questions pertaining to the matter. In order to limit the scandal as much as possible, I ask that the others of you leave my office while I decide the issue of her innocence or guilt.''

Until Jolie and Marguerite broke formation and moved forward, neither of the other two nuns moved from their shielding positions. Jolie was the one who broke the tense silence.

"I insist that they remain, Your Eminence. The future of the convent is their responsibility, and they should be told about any attempt to destroy it. These deeds were given to me by the comte de Laurent four years ago, when he visited my husband and me in Holland. When I showed them to my lawyer here on Martinique, he assured me that my ownership of them was entirely legal."

"How would a lawyer on a remote island recognize the signature of Arnaud de Laurent? And since you conveniently rid yourself of the last deed prior to my arrival because you knew I *would* recognize the signature as a fraud, I have no recourse but to recommend that you be charged with theft until you can produce more convincing proof. Do you have such in your possession?"

"Jolie doesn't, but I do, François de Guise," Marguerite declared vigorously. "However, I agree with you that we should limit the scandal that could reach royal ears within months if you persist in this persecution. Before I left France, I placed a letter in Agathe Vincentia's safekeeping. I didn't write the letter—Charlotte Bourbon did several months prior to her death. Although she didn't tell me, I think she knew that you were slated to be sent here, and she wanted Jolie protected. That letter is to be delivered to Madame de Maintenon if Jolie's life or freedom is ever threatened."

Pausing to address the two nuns who had remained silent after the bishop had accused Jolie of theft, Marguerite's voice was sardonically cheerful. "Moira, you and Thérèse are responsible for getting that horde of girls safely home. Just tell Sébastien to wait for Jolie and me. We'll be safe enough here, since François and I are very old acquaintances."

Waiting only until the two women had reluctantly left his office, François de Guise exploded into furious speech.

"If you ever address me so again, Marguerite du Troyes, I will order you publicly flogged," he raged.

Ignoring the threat, Marguerite pushed Jolie toward one

of the elaborately carved chairs and seated herself in another. Looking up at the man glaring at her from behind his desk, she said wearily, "Sit down, François, and take that uncomfortable miter off. You'll have headache enough without that pretentious crown weighting you down. Before you say anything you might regret, I'm going to tell you what you've already committed in offenses against Jolie. You deliberately withheld your name from her, and you threatened her lawyer to keep him from defending her in court.

"I visited Jacob Riveira quite by accident earlier today. He was the one who revealed your identify and advised me to come prepared with proof of Jolie's claims. Two years ago, Jolie told him the complete story of her ownership of Scoville property, and, cautious lawyer that he is, he wrote to Arnaud de Laurent for written confirmation and received not one, but three letters in response. If, as you claimed, you can recognize his handwriting, you'll know that the contents of the letters are accurate in every detail. They concern the French half of Jolie's antecedents."

"May I read them first?" Jolie asked quietly.

"There's no time for any more delays, child, and you already know the truth about your mother."

As Jolie studied the averted face of the priest while he read the letters with intense concentration, she remembered the ironic part he had played in her life. If he hadn't forced her into marriage, she would never have had her one beautiful year of happiness; nothing he could do to her now could rob her of that memory. It really didn't matter what was in those letters; Jolie no longer had any real hope of escaping from this island prison, nor any real illusions about a happier future. Without Rorke, her life would be a make-do compromise wherever she was. She returned her attention to the present proceedings with little more than a spectator's interest; she even smiled faintly with sardonic irony when she met Bishop de Guise's intent eyes and heard the tacit admission of defeat in his voice.

"When I first saw you, I wondered why your face

disturbed me. Your coloring is different, but you inherited your mother's features.''

"That is all she did inherit from that woman," Marguerite intervened vindictively. "Joanna didn't *give* her those two deeds; she *sold* them to her father because she needed money. Are you satisfied now that it is the mother who is guilty and not the child?''

De Guise moved restlessly in his chair, his thoughts in a turmoil over the enormity of the danger to his own and his brother's reputations. In recent years, King Louis had become fanatically prudish about everyone's bastards but his own; and regardless of Joanna's marriage to the Scotsman, the daughter would still be labeled bastard. Even worse, Joanna's desertion of the child would destroy her friendship with Madame de Maintenon. The king's wife had once been a Huguenot herself and would never countenance such callous treatment of an innocent child. As the cursed Marguerite du Troyes had threatened, the scandal would destroy his brother's family completely, and eventually damage his own career.

"I suppose I must accept what is obviously the truth," he affirmed tonelessly.

"Will your brother Henri be as reasonable?" Marguerite persisted.

"I no longer have any control over my brother's actions; he has not had much success of late. When Joanna repurchased his commission in the dragonades—he lost it when he displeased the king over some trifling incident—Henri requested permission to accompany me on my assignment here. I didn't learn his reasons for the request until we were at sea. Two years ago, when the income from the Scoville branches here and in Montreal stopped abruptly, he wrote to the two managers and learned that an Annette MacDonald Campbell had claimed ownership and presented deeds as proof. The name meant nothing to Henri; I was the only one who knew her identity. Quite naturally, he assumed she was a clever adventuress, and he secured a warrant to return her to France for trial. From the records I had secured from Soeur

Agathe Vincentia, I learned that she had become a Sister of
Charity and that the money was supporting two convents.
But, like Henri, I believed her guilty of criminal fraud."

"And you agreed to be the one to serve that warrant,"
Marguerite accused him relentlessly.

"I am not a man of violence; I agreed only to investigate
the matter. If you recall, I saved her once before when he
threatened to take control of her life."

"You mean when the pair of you were fighting like alley
cats over her and her money!" Marguerite amended snidely.

Jolie stared at the two antagonists, realizing they had
forgotten she was even there. And Marguerite was so
preoccupied with her hatred for the priest, she had forgotten
that his brother was the more dangerous man. It had been
Henri who had threatened to murder Rorke in Strasbourg,
and François who had saved him. And it would be Henri de
Guise who would make certain she never reached France—
not with a convenient ocean between here and there.

"How will you save me this time, Bishop de Guise?" she
asked aloud, adding caustically, "If you recall, your brother
is a violent man."

Startled by her candor, the bishop responded with a rash
question. "Did you inherit your father's fortune, as Charlotte claimed you would? Perhaps if you were willing to
compensate Henri for his loss, he would be more reasonable."

Smiling with cynical contempt, Jolie retorted bluntly, "I
inherited a lovely home and several chests of stolen gold
and silver. The money was stolen from me during the
Glencoe massacre, and the home was burned."

"Then you have no money of your own?"

"None!"

"She has a small inheritance Charlotte left her," Marguerite intervened swiftly. "Just enough to get her safely away
from this island, providing I can locate a trustworthy captain."

"You won't find any such captain in St. Pierre harbor,"
de Guise volunteered heavily. "Henri has spent this past
week warning each one of them that he will be charged with
a felony if he helps her escape."

Far from being silenced by the grim news, the old nun rose from her chair in renewed fury. "In that case, François, you can give your brother this message. Tell him that even if he succeeds in silencing every one of us here on the island who knows of his wife's perfidious treachery, he can never silence Arnaud de Laurent or Soeur Agathe Vincentia or Madame de Maintenon. Come along, Jolie, I have already made arrangements for your immediate safety."

The two women had reached the door before the bishop stopped them. "I cannot permit Soeur Anne to leave the cathedral. Henri's dragoons are posted at every entrance with orders to arrest her when she emerges. She will have to remain in sanctuary here."

"King Louis has forbidden the use of sanctuary," Marguerite challenged.

"Only for heretics and traitors; it is still permitted for men charged with lesser crimes."

"When has it ever been permitted for women?"

"I have the authority to make an exception in the case of a sworn nun."

"In that case, I'll remain with her to prevent your de Guise pride from overwhelming your priestly conscience later on today or tonight."

"As you like, Soeur Marguerite, but I cannot arrange for a ship, and I cannot predict how long Henri will permit me to keep Soeur Anne in sanctuary. Not even a bishop can countermand an order given by a colonel of the king's dragonades."

"Very well, François, but I will be here every day to tend her needs. Where will she be?"

"In one of the traditional cells near the choir. I have been informed that the last tenant was a pirate."

Marguerite's farewell to Jolie was an admonition not to attempt to escape. "Henri de Guise will be even more dangerous once he learns the truth about his wife," she warned.

Left alone with the bishop, who now seemed little more to her than a tired and worried man, Jolie experienced a curious relief. She was free of all responsibility, even for her own fate; whatever was to be would take place without any volition on her part. Nor would she ever again be forced to assume a pious expression in deference to the schoolgirls who had made her their special heroine. Smiling at the solemn church prelate who was escorting her to her latest prison, she asked lightly, "How much do you intend to tell your brother?"

"Only what you told me yourself," the bishop responded. "That you acquired the deeds honestly from the comte de Laurent. You didn't mention your mother, nor shall I; but I do admit to some curiosity. Surely you can have no affection for her."

"I consider her the same as I did the young Scottish aristocrat you allowed my husband and me to remove from Strasbourg."

"Was he really the grandson of a Scottish earl?"

"He was the earl's son."

"Whatever happened to him?"

Jolie smiled again; her guilt about Tavis Campbell had long since been expiated. "He died quite violently at Glencoe." In her present reckless mood, she would have answered the question with detailed honesty had she not wanted more substantial food than a penitent's bread and water.

Until Rorke had spent ten frustrating days in Martinique waters, he had thought that Jan Deventer's hatred of small, populated islands had been merely a personal idiosyncrasy. When Rorke had first studied the nautical charts of the island during his weeks of preparation in Amsterdam, he had been pleasantly surprised that it was only twenty miles wide and forty-three long. At the most, he had reasoned, it would take only a day to locate a convent in so small an area. Unfortunately, the sparsely populated Atlantic coastline had been too poorly marked on the charts for safe exploration, and the island's interior too mountainous for easy traversing. Even more unfortunately, the inhabitants were not simple island natives who could be pacified with gifts; they were alert Frenchmen who had good cause to be suspicious of all ships approaching their shores.

Warned by a captain in the Dutch East Indies Company that the two cities on the island's west coast had been heavily refortified after an attempted English invasion two years earlier, Rorke had decided to use a stratagem he had learned from Deventer. He anchored offshore along a barren stretch of beach protected from sight by high bluffs. Taking with him the four marines who spoke French fluently enough to avoid attracting attention, he had gone ashore and spent the day in a discouraging reconnaissance of Fort-de-France and its large, protected bay. The only ships in the harbor had been French, and the extensive waterfront had been well patrolled by soldiers. Dressed more like the French sailors they had seen in the crude waterfront inns, they had returned on two successive days, amassing enough knowledge about the island's defenses to make Rorke doubly cautious.

The highway that connected Fort-de-France to the larger city of St. Pierre was defended by frequent cannon emplacements, which overlooked a coastline devoid of concealing harborage for unauthorized ships. Rorke and his men listened to the roistering of French sailors and learned that several of the ships in the harbor had come from other French Caribbean colonies. Their passengers had been priests and civic notables determined to witness the installation of a new bishop whose diocese included their own islands. Because the hotel accommodations in St. Pierre, where the festivities were to be held, were overcrowded, these visitors were being housed with the military in Fort-de-France.

Disappointed by his inability to learn anything about the location of the convent, but grateful that he had not made the mistake of sailing directly north, past the batteries of shore cannon, Rorke ordered the *Lorelei* taken the long way around the island. A full day later, a few miles north of St. Pierre, the ship was anchored in another cove, protected by mountainous cliffs. Gambling that a ship's captain would have better access to information than a common seaman, especially in a sophisticated French city, Rorke left the *Lorelei* at dawn and remained in St. Pierre until dusk. With his beard trimmed in the prevailing style favored by French businessmen, he attracted no attention along the crowded embarcadero and the tree-shaded boulevards of the central city. From the workmen scrubbing the cathedral stairs, he learned that the religious ceremony was scheduled three days distant, and that every islander of importance was due to attend. Hiring a driver whose light open chaise allowed him an unobstructed view, Rorke toured the outer city, memorizing the routes that led to the southbound highway and listening as his guide pointed out the cannon fortifications that guarded the harbor. To his relief, he noted that two of the ships anchored in the harbor were flying a Spanish flag, and a third one was Portuguese in origin. While a German flag had probably never been seen in these remote waters, it was possible that the *Lorelei* might be equally welcome.

Rorke's caution about exposing the *Lorelei* to the Martinique port authorities was not the result of cowardice, but of experience. Three weeks earlier, on the English colony island of Barbados, the *Lorelei* had been fired on by shore batteries when it had entered Bridgetown harbor with a captured pirate ship. Although both vessels were flying the Union Jack at the time, the pirate ship had been recognized as the marauder that had raided the harbor on several occasions, looted storehouses, and taken prisoners. If an English patrol ship hadn't intervened, the *Lorelei* and its captive prize might have been sunk. On the French island of Martinique, which was even better defended than Barbados, Rorke was determined to avoid a similar reception.

That he was able to do so was the result of a fortunate happenstance. Nearing the end of his tour of St. Pierre, the driver took him past the crowded, bustling warehouses strung out along the commercial embarcadero. Just by chance, Rorke recognized the name of one of them—the Maison de Scoville. Until that moment, he had not remembered the name of the Martinique property Arnaud de Laurent had

given Jolie. Rorke was smiling as he asked the driver to take
him to the harbormaster; he now had a legitimate reason for
being in Martinique. Introducing himself as Baron Wallmond,
he requested permission to bring the *Lorelei* into port for the
purpose of conducting his business with the Scoville company.
The business, he announced with a glib mendacity, was a
partnership arrangement with the comte de Laurent of
Strasbourg, whereby Rhine Valley products could be traded
in Martinique. His current cargo was German wine, he
confessed confidentially.

"A cargo of good wine," Jan Deventer had once told
him, "will make you welcome in any port in the uncivilized
half of the world." In Amsterdam, Rorke had purchased the
finest available at the same time he had installed additional
cannon on the *Lorelei* and hired twenty seasoned marines
from the *Indomeer*'s old crew. He smiled with amusement at
the speed with which the harbormaster granted him port
liberty. Rorke was still smiling as he ordered the chaise
driver to return him to the Maison de Scoville and wait for
him. He saw no reason for returning on foot to the small
beach, where a longboat and four oarsmen were safely
hidden. With official papers giving him the freedom of the
island, both he and his crew could move about without
arousing suspicion in the immediate future.

His ballooning optimism was crushed minutes after he
met Auguste Scoville. Using the same alias he had given the
official, Rorke asked the manager how he could contact the
owner, whom he claimed the harbormaster had identified as
a Sisters of Charity nun.

"You'll find her sitting ten miles south of here in a
convent she stole, the same as she did this company,"
Scoville rasped with vindictive triumph. "If you want to
transact any import or export business with the Scoville
company, you'll do it with me or with the husband of the
real owner."

Typical of undisciplined men who impulsively reveal
more than is prudent, the manager stopped talking abruptly
when he realized his mistake. But Rorke had learned what

he wanted to know—far more than he'd expected, and most of it alarming. He returned to the waiting chaise and paid the driver a bonus in gold coin to take him to the distant beach in record time. On the way, he learned that although the man had not seen any royal dragonades in St. Pierre, he had heard rumors that a company of them had arrived with the new bishop. Rorke's jaw was grimly set as he asked how many men had been in that "rumored" company.

"Couldn't have been more than twenty—at least, that was the number of horses I heard were brought ashore and taken to pasture," the driver responded promptly.

"What about the island's regular soldiers? Will they be attending the bishop's installation?"

"They attend every ceremony in St. Pierre. This one will be the most important."

Rorke's thoughts were in a whirl as he was rowed out to his ship; there was no longer any room for error. The *Lorelei* could not remain in St. Pierre harbor, as he had planned, while he conducted a relaxed search for Jolie. A German baron would attract instant attention, and the attention of one man in particular would be instantly fatal. François de Guise could recognize him! Every man aboard the *Lorelei* would be in danger if such a catastrophe occurred, and he would be executed. But de Guise would not be able to take any official action, either against Jolie or himself, until after he was installed as bishop. Nor would his more dangerous brother dare to make arrests without the bishop's permission. Moreover, Henri de Guise had not been conscious when Rorke had examined him in Strasbourg. Without his older brother's prompting, he could not know what Rorke Campbell, a condemned enemy spy, looked like.

Rorke's plan, when he finalized it, was a relatively simple one. The *Lorelei* would return to Fort-de-France and anchor within the port itself. The papers the St. Pierre harbormaster had issued to Baron Wallmond would serve as well there as here. To avoid any confrontation with the Fort-de-France military that might result if he paraded his

marines through the fortified town, Rorke would bide his
time until the French soldiers had departed for St. Pierre on
the morning of the public installation of the new bishop.
Then he and his twenty marines would locate the convent
and wait for the nuns to return from St. Pierre. The faint
hope that Jolie would refuse to attend and remain at the
convent on that day died quickly. As a Catholic official
herself, she would be duty bound to swear an oath of
loyalty; such ritualistic protocol was mandatory in a church
based on hierarchy. Not so easily dismissed was the fear that
the de Guise brothers would take action against Jolie the
same day. But Rorke gradually concluded that François de
Guise was too astute a politician to risk the antagonism of
an entire convent on the first day of his administration.

More quickly resolved was the choice of route. While the
short voyage south to Fort-de-France could be accomplished
in a few hours, there was still no guarantee that the shore
cannon would not open fire on an alien ship in sensitive
waters. Not even the friendly harbormaster could identify
the *Lorelei*. With a decisive authority, Rorke ordered the
sleek ship underway to the north as soon as he boarded. It
was a decision he would regret a hundredfold for two and a
half days.

The winds that had been briskly cooperative on the
voyage to St. Pierre were unpredictable on the reverse
journey. Wildly turbulent gales alternated with dead calm
seas as heavy rains flattened the ocean's surface and soaked
the limp sails. Instead of one day to traverse the hundred-
mile distance, it took three nights and two days to reach
Fort-de-France and another frustrating two hours to locate
the assistant harbormaster in the almost deserted town. By
the time Rorke persuaded an irascible innkeeper to rent him
a delivery wagon and driver at ten times the expected rate,
the day was half gone, and they still had ten miles to travel.
Accompanied by his twenty marines, Rorke endured the
slow pace of two plodding horses with impatient anxiety.
But when they reached the narrow, dusty lane leading to the
convent itself, he was relieved that he had not attempted to

walk the distance. So concealed were the buildings behind
thick shrubbery and trees that he would have walked past
without seeing them.

Admitting himself and the others onto the parklike grounds
through an unlocked gate, Rorke strode toward the largest of
the stone and wood structures and pulled the bell rope.
When no one answered his third summons, he walked
around the sprawling complex, experiencing a momentary
gratitude for the emergency that would force Jolie to leave
Martinique, regardless of her attachment to this peaceful
place. Only the square, two-story central building had paned
windows; the obviously new classrooms and the infirmary
extension had nothing but storm shutters to keep out the
elements. Having practiced medicine for two years in the
fetid hold of a ship where the stench of wounded men had
been overpowering, Rorke envied the windswept openness
of the operating room and wondered if Jolie had been the
architect. Someday, perhaps, he would resume his own
interrupted career in medicine, providing he and Jolie could
work unhurriedly, in pleasant facilities such as these.

Rorke heard the commotion minutes later at the rear of
the convent, when the wagonloads of tired, giggling young
girls were driven onto the grounds. He reached his men in
time to prevent hysteria. Not once had Rorke considered
what the sight of a small army of battle-hardened marines
would do to naive nuns and frightened schoolchildren—
particularly, foreign-speaking marines. As the pupils were
hustled inside, Rorke was confronted by two middle-aged
nuns who demanded to know the reason for his intrusion
onto private property.

"I'm here to see your superior, Soeur Jolie. Where is
she?" Rorke demanded aggressively.

"Soeur Jolie is no longer our superior; she resigned three
months ago. I am Soeur Marie, her replacement, and this is
Soeur Thérèse, the head of our school. What is your
business with Soeur Jolie?"

"I am a friend of her grandfather, and I—"

"Her grandfather is French, but you are not, monsieur," Soeur Thérèse interrupted shrewdly.

"My ship and most of its crew are German, and we have official permission to be here. The former owner was Baron Wallmond, who is also a friend of Soeur Jolie," Rorke replied with ill-concealed impatience. "Now, tell me where she is."

"She remained in St. Pierre with Soeur Marguerite," Marie began. "We expect both of them to—"

Rorke's heart was pounding with a dull sense of failure. "Where in St. Pierre?" he asked heavily.

"We left her and Marguerite with Bishop—"

"François de Guise," he completed her sentence angrily. "Do you know him?"

"I know him. What did he want with Jolie?"

"He was under the mistaken impression that she did not have clear title to the property that supports our convent, but Soeur Marguerite insisted he was wrong. And she and the bishop are old friends."

"Where did you hear that?"

"From Marguerite herself. That is why we felt it safe enough to leave them there—and, of course, Sébastien is with them."

"Who is he?"

"Our most reliable worker, monsieur. He is very resourceful."

"He'd be one man against twenty," Rorke exploded. "Did either of you notice a company of royal dragonades at today's ceremony?"

"I did," Thérèse admitted, "and I wondered what Inquisition soldiers were doing on Martinique. Is Jolie in trouble with them?"

"Yes," Rorke responded briefly. "Is the coast road the only one to St. Pierre from here?"

Marie nodded thoughtfully. "You would not be able to use it until everyone has returned to Fort-de-France. You said you had a ship?"

"I don't want it exposed to shore batteries."

"That will be no problem," Thérèse asserted quickly. "I will accompany you to Fort-de-France and speak with the commander. His two daughters are pupils here. But first, monsieur, you will tell me who you are and why you are so concerned about Jolie. If she is in trouble, as you claim, I think you will need our help. And I think we should remain right here until she and Marguerite return."

"What if they don't return?" Rorke demanded.

"Sébastien will give us warning. Now, tell us why an Englishman is here in a French colony when England and France are at war. Your accent is not German, monsieur."

As aggressive as Thérèse sounded, Marie became openly antagonistic in her accusation; her ears had detected an even more accurate evaluation of Rorke's nationality. "He is not an Englishman, Thérèse; he is Scottish. If he is a Breadalbane Campbell, he could be more dangerous to Jolie than the worst of the Inquisition soldiers."

Rorke sighed heavily in surrender. "My real name is Campbell," he admitted reluctantly, "and at one time I considered myself a Breadalbane clansman. But I was not one of those who attacked Glencoe. I am Jolie's husband."

"Holy Mother of God," Moira MacDonald murmured in English.

12

At Marguerite's frantic insistence when she had discovered Jolie missing from his waiting room, Jacob Riveira had remained in his office, but he had not been idle. He had dispatched his driver on three errands and written two letters to the owners of fishing boats. Although he had enjoyed having a young Catholic nun as a client, his industry on her behalf was due to expediency rather than to sentiment. As long as Soeur Jolie remained on the island, his own safety and that of his people would be threatened. Had the Inquisition dragonades been impersonal watchdogs of King Louis's demand for religious uniformity, Riveira would not have felt endangered. He and his people had been granted immunity from persecution under normal circumstances. But Colonel Henri de Guise was not motivated either by religious fervor or by loyalty to his king. He was in Martinique to reclaim a valuable piece of property and to silence the woman he accused of the theft. Once he learned the truth, as he would if his bishop brother showed him Arnaud de Laurent's letters, the younger de Guise would have even more reason to silence Soeur Jolie and everyone else who knew the truth about his wife.

If Soeur Jolie were not available, however, and if the scandal did not become public knowledge, Colonel de Guise might be persuaded that any further investigation would damage his own reputation. It was an uneasy hope at best, the practical lawyer realized, but it was the only way he could devise to protect both his client and himself. When a desperate Marguerite returned to his office, he was fully prepared to help her.

The news that Soeur Jolie was being held at the cathedral under the questionable protection of the bishop was a setback he hadn't anticipated, but even the problem of getting her safely out of sanctuary was not insurmountable.

"If you or Soeur Jolie are willing to pay a large number of the idle sailors in port at the present to start a riot on the square, you could take her out through a rear entry of the cathedral and drive her to Fort-de-France in a wagon that Sébastien would have waiting. There are only sixteen dragonades under the colonel's command, and I doubt they'd be foolish enough to do anything to the sailors except knock a few heads about. Many of the captains who frequent this port have engaged in battles at sea and are well able to take revenge if their crewmen are badly injured or killed. I have a client who could organize such a riot if he were well paid to do so."

"How long would it take him?" Marguerite demanded.

"I imagine he could be ready in three days. In the meantime, you could prepare everything else."

"Did you locate a ship?"

"Two possibles, both fishing craft, but fully capable of interisland travel. Since one of my associates is part owner of the vessels, I believe both fishermen would readily agree, again for a price, to take you and Soeur Jolie to a nearby English island. They would, however, require Sébastien's services as navigator; he has often performed in such a capacity for us, so he knows the safest routes."

"I will not be leaving the island," Marguerite said quietly. "This is the last day you can be safely involved with this problem, Monsieur Riveira, and someone will have to remain here to blackmail Henri de Guise into silence. If he is vicious enough to attempt violence, the father of every convent pupil will be notified of the entire scandal. Now, about practical considerations. Jolie will need to take all of her money with her.''

The lawyer smiled; the old nun was as decisively direct as the young one had been. ''I have already sent for her funds,'' he murmured as he indicated the chest next to his desk.

''She will also need clothing and a wig. A Catholic nun would be as welcome as a black plague carrier on an English isle.''

Again the lawyer smiled. ''I sent my driver to fetch the keys to two of our stores. Sébastien will know how to locate the merchandise you require. My only request is that you do your shopping today. My people have decided that for a few weeks, we will remain in seclusion.''

It was Marguerite's turn to smile. Within those few ''secluded'' weeks, the commerce of the island would come to a halt, and the governor would be forced to discipline the royal dragonades and their commander. Abruptly, her thoughts reverted to the immediate emergency. Even a week might be too late to help Jolie. In a mood darkened by suspicion and worry, she rushed through an hour of shopping, grateful for Sébastien's help in locating a wig—the wrong color, but adequate for the purpose—a chest of the loose cotton dresses worn by island women, and the few articles of feminine grooming that Marguerite could remember.

On the long drive back to the convent, she gnawed her lower lip with frustration over the straggling groups of pedestrians crowding the road and necessitating frequent stops. When Sébastien finally headed the coach into the convent driveway and pulled to a halt, the old nun shrieked with alarm and exhaustion as a lantern was shone in her face and a man's voice demanded, ''Where is Soeur Jolie?''

Nearby, the sister superior's voice sounded in a mild reprimand. ''We'll wait until Marguerite catches her breath before we ask any more questions, Captain. Sébastien, will you carry her so that she does not stumble in the dark?''

''Don't be a fool, Moira; I've been stumbling around on these crippled legs more years than Sébastien is old,''

Marguerite snapped crisply. "Now, tell me about the man who accosted me so rudely a moment ago."

As the procession moved slowly toward the lighted dining pavilion, Moira MacDonald smiled broadly. In the six months she had known the venerable French nun, she hadn't won a single argument.

"He's a friend," she murmured in response, "a good friend."

"Well, *bon ami*, whatever your name is," Marguerite addressed the man she sensed was walking by her side, "Jolie is in sanctuary at the cathedral."

"With your *good* friend François de Guise?" Rorke demanded caustically.

"What imbecile told you that hypocrite was my friend?"

"I did," Soeur Marie admitted defensively. "You said so just before Thérèse and I left Jolie and you in his office."

"The word I used was *acquaintance*, Moira. I'm certain that even in your own language, there's a difference. I've hated François de Guise for twenty years."

"Then, why in the devil did you leave Jolie in his power?" Rorke rasped angrily.

Pausing just inside the lamplit dining area, Marguerite turned to stare at the tall man following her, shaking her head in irritation when she failed to recognize his bearded face.

"I left her in sanctuary to protect her from Henri de Guise, who was waiting outside to arrest her for theft," she retorted irritably.

"Does anyone else know she's there?"

"I told four priests before I left the cathedral. I'm a medical nun, not some ignorant novitiate who believes in miracles or in—" Marguerite's acrimonious rasp faded in a gasp of shock, and she sat down on one of the dining benches, as if her legs had failed her. She hadn't recognized his voice or face, but she knew the strong, flexible surgeon's hands he'd spread on the table as he'd leaned impatiently toward her.

"Holy mother of God!" she whispered harshly. "You're alive!"

Taken aback by the totality of her shock, Rorke asked curiously, "How did you know? You didn't recognize me a minute ago."

"Your hands. I watched you work in my infirmary in Strasbourg some years back. Why didn't you get here two days ago?"

"Would to God I had, Marguerite du Troyes. Now, tell me about this sanctuary. The last I heard, it was no longer possible—at least, it never was available to Huguenots."

Having regained her mental equilibrium, the old nun smiled sardonically. "It is no longer allowed for major crimes like heresy—only for the minor ones of murder and piracy, and for innocent nuns who might embarrass the bishop's family."

"Can you get Jolie out of the cathedral without his permission?"

"Sanctuary is voluntary; François would have no right to hold her. The problem will be getting her past Henri's sixteen dragoons."

"Is that all he has?"

"According to Jolie's lawyer. He was the one who helped us arrange for her escape from the island."

"How did he plan to get her safely away from the cathedral?"

"He has a friend who'll organize a riot of drunken sailors in the square. While Henri's men are subduing them, Sébastien and I will be waiting to take Jolie out through a courtyard gate. Monsieur Riveira didn't think Henri would order his men to fire on unarmed sailors."

"Four years ago, I watched Henri's men fire into a crowd of unarmed bystanders and kill five of them. And if you remember, the courageous Colonel de Guise ordered his soldiers to kill me, my cousin, Jolie, and Paul Arnaud on sight when we were leaving France."

"How did you learn about that incident, Dr. Campbell?"

"I no longer use the name of Campbell, Soeur Marguerite.

I learned about that near miss when I went to see Arnaud de Laurent to find out where Jolie was. I wish now I'd asked where the de Guise brothers were.''

"Arnaud wouldn't have known. François himself didn't know his brother's intention until they were at sea.''

"Do either of the bas—either of the devils know about Jolie's mother?''

"Yes, I showed François the letter the lawyer had given me. He said it was the one certain way to prove Jolie's innocence. That information was the only reason François offered her sanctuary; otherwise, Jolie would have been arrested when she walked out of the cathedral.''

"Do you trust him to keep his word?''

"Not even a bishop can deny sanctuary once it's been granted. I am more worried about Henri forcibly removing her. That is why I'll be staying with Jolie once Sébastien and I arrange for the fishing boats to take her to an English island.''

"Whose idea was it to use a fishing boat?''

"There are no ships available. Henri has warned every captain in St. Pierre harbor not to help her.''

"There isn't a fishing boat in either harbor that could have survived the storm that battered us yesterday and the day before. We'll use my ship, and we'll remove Jolie from the cathedral tomorrow. But I'll need your help and the help of one of those fishermen to serve as navigator aboard the *Lorelei* to sail us safely from Fort-de-France to St. Pierre and to take us in and out of that harbor at full speed.''

"Sébastien was going to be the navigator for the fisherman. That was his profession for many years.''

"Would he be willing to help me?''

At the sound of the deep, rumbling response, "I will help,'' Rorke spun around to stare at the speaker whose height made him seem a giant, but whose educated speech seemed at odds with his light brown skin coloring and laborer's clothing.

"How much experience in navigation have you had?'' Rorke asked skeptically.

Again the deep-toned, fluent speech startled the Scotsman. "I was navigator for ten years aboard one of my father's ships. I know the South Atlantic waters and the southern Caribbean."

"Do you know the St. Pierre harbor channels well enough to take us in and out under full sail if we have to run for it?"

Sébastien smiled faintly. "I do if your crew can respond to orders quickly enough."

"Can you help my navigator plot the fastest course to the Dutch island of Curaçao?"

Again the mulatto smiled. "I can if your navigator will take orders from a man of color."

"He'll be grateful for your assistance. He's never been in these waters before, and one island looks very much like another to beginners. Monsieur Sébastien, do you have any idea how Colonel de Guise warned those captains in St. Pierre? Did he go aboard their ships, or summon them ashore?"

"Usually, the harbormaster and his cargo inspectors are the only ones to board the ships until the cargo has been cleared and the crew inspected for contagious diseases."

"How do we go about getting that service as quickly as possible so that we can dock?"

"The captain and his officers are allowed ashore to talk to the harbormaster. What cargo are you carrying?" Sébastien demanded.

"German wine and Dutch spices."

"You'll have no trouble; they are both in short supply on the island."

"One more question, Sébastien. Was the lawyer accurate in his estimate of the number of royal dragonades?"

"Monsieur Riveira is almost always correct; today I counted the same number as he said—sixteen, not including the colonel. Will you be needing wagons and drivers tomorrow? If I were you, I would not trust the driver you hired today."

"I'll need two. Do you know where we can find both wagons and drivers?"

"The wagons are already here, and I have two friends who are expert."

"Good. Tell them they'll be well paid."

"Dr. Campbell, or whatever you're calling yourself these days," Marguerite interrupted the conversation impatiently. "What is it—?"

"I use the name of Captain James Rorke, but tomorrow I'll be posing as Baron Ransford Wallmond, the name I gave the St. Pierre harbormaster four days ago. Now, about the plan I think will work. Sébastien, you and I will return to Fort-de-France tonight, providing you can navigate as well on land as at sea. We can notify your family and friends along the way. My men will remain here at the convent, if Soeur Marie grants permission. Early tomorrow morning—"

Two hours later, after the plans had been finalized and everyone had eaten supper, Rorke and Sébastien loaded all of Jolie's possessions, except for her nun's robes, aboard the rented wagon. Underway a few minutes later, Captain James Rorke was smiling with ironic humor. He owed one more debt of gratitude to the dead Dutchman, Jan Deventer. Two years ago, in the Portuguese colony of Mozambique, Deventer had secured the release of the entire crew of a Dutch East Indies Company ship by a stratagem similar to the plan Rorke and the others would use tomorrow. His smile broadened when he remembered that on the way out of that port, the *Indomeer* had retaken that captured ship and stolen one of the Portuguese corsairs for good measure.

François de Guise had spent an uneasy night. Offering sanctuary to a woman on his first day of administration had been a sorry mistake; the resident priests and secular scholars had been sullenly resentful of the intrusion. Since the meddlesome Marguerite du Troyes had made certain they were informed, François had been coerced into making the announcement officially. The bishop's main perturbation, though, had been more personal—he had been forced to deny his brother access to the cathedral. Not even a bishop could betray sanctuary once it had been sanctioned.

Initially, he had been irritated by the woman herself; she possessed the disconcerting confidence all the de Laurents had and a peppery intuition that surpassed theirs. While the du Troyes woman had assumed François would tell Henri the whole story, the younger nun had known he wouldn't. When he had questioned her about her life in England and Scotland, she had revealed a hardened sophistication beyond her years. Most annoying of all had been her casual request for dinner, as if sanctuary guaranteed the luxuries of an inn instead of mere physical safety.

As he had escorted her personally to the remote cell, rather than turn the task over to an underling as custom dictated, the newly installed bishop had been as irritated with himself as he was with her. Even robed in the ridiculous peasant costume the Sisters of Charity had adopted, there was no disguising the fact that Soeur Jolie had developed a mature beauty that was more intriguing than her mother's. Yet she seemed to have no awareness of her power to make even an ambitious prelate of the church long for a return of his own youth. Only one other woman had affected him so intensely—the haughty, unattainable Charlotte de Laurent, and she had not been beautiful or even pretty. It disturbed him that he had resented her death, as if a part of his own life had ended.

His resentment, however, had shriveled when he had learned that her estate had reverted to her older son instead of to the church. After thirteen years of supporting a convent, she had proved to be humanly fallible after all. In contrast, her enigmatic niece had already generously donated to the church, and that generosity puzzled François. Why should a young woman, whose devotion to the church was minimal at most, give the remains of her fortune to two convents? If she had retained her position as superior, such extreme munificence could have been due to an ambition to become head of her entire order of nuns eventually. Bishop de Guise knew all too well that many of the exalted

positions within the church had been purchased. Lacking
that necessary wealth, he had gained his lowliest of dioceses
only because none of those affluent prelates had wanted it.
Ironically, the woman he was taking to the uncertain protection of sanctuary had already increased his own prestige. A
self-sufficient, active convent always reflected favorably on
the diocesan bishop.

It was unfortunate that the money she had used was the
same that Henri was counting on so desperately. When
François had told his brother that the deeds had been
honestly obtained, Henri had been stubbornly argumentative.

"Why would Arnaud favor some misbegotten foundling
over Joanna?" he had demanded.

"Since your wife sold him the property when she needed
money, your father-by-marriage had the right to do what he
wanted with the deeds. Perhaps by giving them to a nun, he
felt he was expiating his former disloyalty to the church."

"The woman wasn't a nun when he gave them to her; she
was the wife of a criminal mercenary. But whatever she
was, Arnaud had no legal right to those deeds. Since I had
not given Joanna permission, the original sale was illegal,
and the nun is still guilty of theft and fraud."

"Don't be a fool, Henri. You'd have to name Arnaud and
your wife as co-defendants if you made any such charge.
You can't afford the scandal of a public trial."

"If the nun were dead, there'd be no trial, and Joanna
could reclaim the property here on Martinique, at least."

The words *if the nun were dead* preyed on François's
mind throughout the night. Henri had always been unreason-
able, but now he was illogical, as well, and reckless to the
point of danger. In his obsession to regain the de Guise titles
and fortune, he had been goaded to rash lengths that had
damaged his reputation beyond repair and cost much of
Joanna's remaining fortune. Unlike François, who had abandoned all such ambition after Henri's dismal failure in
Strasbourg, Henri had persisted until he was shunned by
every aristocrat in Versailles. Only Joanna's friendship with
Madame du Maintenon had prevented a complete disgrace.

On a Flanders battlefield against William of Orange, Henri had been relieved of command for needlessly risking the lives of his men. At Versailles, he had earned the king's displeasure by challenging men to duels over imagined insults, and he had antagonized the duc d'Orleans by threatening Charlotte's sons. François had been the one who had apologized to the king's brother and announced from the pulpit that the personable and successful young Bourbon chevaliers were above suspicion.

Desperate to get her husband away from Versailles and out of France, Joanna had purchased this minor command over a token force of dragonades as a last resort. Foolishly, she had gambled that the daughter she had deserted would have no interest in so remote an inheritance. François could not really blame her for lacking the courage to tell her husband about the existence of a daughter; Henri had always possessed an overweening pride and a violent temper.

Now the older brother was trapped dead center in a miserable situation that could complete the destruction of the entire de Guise family. Soeur Jolie was a formidable threat who could not be hidden for long. Even if he could convince Henri that neither the property nor the income from the Scoville company could be recovered, he knew his brother would eventually ferret out the rest of the ugly story. Despite his lack of success in other fields, Henri could be diligently persistent once his suspicions were aroused, as they had been over this particular nun.

And he could be ruthless! François shuddered when he recalled Henri's threats to the lawyer Riveira. Merciful God, he had sounded like a prosecutor at a medieval Inquisition trial. François had warned his brother that the church had granted special dispensation to this Jewish colony, but Henri had ignored the warning. If he ever discovered that the knowledge of his wife's past was shared by any number of people on this small, isolated island, he could bring the wrath of the entire population down on both their heads. Again the words *if the nun were dead* returned to tantalize François's fevered brain as he lay fretfully awake. Gradually, the thought gained a firm foothold. Neither he nor Henri would be held responsible; the senile old Bishop Villiers had left enough notes behind about "the upstart nun" to justify the charge of heresy. Toward morning the new bishop slept more soundly. If all else failed, he was confident that he now possessed the means to resolve the problem.

The Baron Ransford Wallmond who welcomed the St. Pierre harbormaster aboard the *Lorelei* early the following afternoon had subtly changed from the discreetly dressed man of a few days earlier. While not ostentatious, the wig he wore and the cream-colored satin suit bespoke of wealth, as did the captain's quarters aboard ship. The costly artifacts and furniture stored in the hold had been uncrated and returned to their original places, and six tuns of fine wine were conspicuously visible on the floor.

Just as Rorke's costume was different, so was his conversation. Rather than a merchant interested in trade, he was an aristocrat seeking a favor.

"When I spoke to you last," he confided with the companionable condescension he had learned from the Dutch privateer, "I'd forgotten my second reason for coming to Martinique. My partner, the comte de Laurent, had asked me to check on his granddaughter while I was here. Since the woman is only a nun, I had understandably forgotten her existence until I visited the Maison de Scoville just after I left you. It would seem that being a nun does not always guarantee a moral existence. The manager accused her of theft—quite extensive theft, as a matter of fact. Late yesterday when I went to the convent, I learned the young woman has taken refuge in the cathedral to avoid arrest, and I was also told that the unpleasant affair is already public gossip. Have you heard any rumors of it?"

Plainly embarrassed, the official admitted to hearing far more than rumor. "Colonel de Guise made extensive accusations and warned all shippers against helping the nun escape from the island," he confessed.

Rorke sighed artfully. "I was afraid of something like

that, but naturally, I cannot permit my friend's granddaughter
to undergo a public trial, even if she's earned the punishment.
I'm asking for your help in preventing such an embarrassment
to all concerned. If the nun is not guilty, then the reputation
of an entire convent would be needlessly compromised.
Moreover, the comte de Laurent can be a vindictive man,
and he's wealthy enough to wield power, even on this
remote outpost. What I want you to do is to deliver a letter
to this Colonel de Guise and persuade him to accept my
offer. If he will turn the nun over to me, I will give him my
entire cargo of wine, lacking only those six tuns that are a
gift to you. Are we agreed, monsieur?''

Although he nodded vigorously, the harbormaster counseled thoughtfully, "You could be wasting your money
needlessly, Baron Wallmond. Not many of us believe that
Soeur Jolie is guilty of anything, and Colonel de Guise has
already made many enemies in the city."

"I can't permit her to face a trial under any circumstances; I prefer to let comte de Laurent settle his own score
with the colonel. Incidentally, you're not to mention that the
count is the woman's grandfather. I believe there is some
secrecy in that respect."

The letter the harbormaster delivered to Henri de Guise
was written on vellum parchment embossed with the Wallmond
crest, and was deliberately light in tone. "*Noblesse oblige*,"
it began. "As an aristocrat yourself, you must know that
scandal is best avoided at our level of society." It ended
with the assurance that the *Lorelei*'s cargo would more than
compensate for any financial loss suffered at the hands of an
errant nun.

Two hours later the port official returned, accompanied by
Henri de Guise and six dragoons. A smiling "Baron
Wallmond" greeted them urbanely and waited until the
harbormaster had departed with his wine before he addressed
the stiffly suspicious colonel.

"I imagine you'll want to inspect the cargo before we
discuss the business at hand," Rorke suggested blandly. "If
you'll follow me—"

"Not until I know why a German aristocrat is interested in a thieving French nun," Henri snapped.

Shrugging indifferently, Rorke countered with an arrogant brevity. "I'm not, but my French partner is."

"Arnaud de Laurent is your partner?"

"We have collaborated in business for ten years, Colonel. When he approached me about establishing trade with the Caribbean colonies, I agreed."

"Arnaud has always used the Scoville export company before."

"So he said, but the Scoville company can deal only with French colonies. As a German, I have access to all European colonies in the New World."

"Why did you choose to make Martinique your first contact?"

"Arnaud asked that I deliver a packet of letters to the nun in question. I learned she was in trouble when I visited the convent yesterday."

"Why is Arnaud interested in the woman?"

"He promised his daughter Charlotte to look out for her. I am merely acting as his deputy in the matter. Are you interested in the offer I made you or not?"

"What will you do with the woman if I agree?"

"Remove her from your island. Since I'm not a policeman, I will allow her to choose her own destination. According to Arnaud, she has relatives in Scotland."

"You're willing to sacrifice an entire cargo for a woman you don't know?"

"If I didn't, I might lose Arnaud as a partner."

"Will you give me your word that you will not return her to France or leave her in another French colony?"

"An odd request, but if that is the only way I can secure her release, I agree."

"Very well, Baron Wallmond, I accept your offer, providing the wine is suitable in quality and ample enough in quantity to repay me for my loss of income. My men will accompany me to the hold of your ship."

"As you wish, Colonel," Rorke murmured suavely.

Within fifteen minutes a furious Henri de Guise and his six dragoons had been disarmed and locked in the iron-barred cell in the *Lorelei*'s cargo hold.

Ashore, on the outskirts of the cathedral square, two separate groups of people had waited patiently until Colonel de Guise and six of his men had ridden off in the direction of the embarcadero before they began their separate assignments. Six identically dressed nuns, led by the three who had visited the bishop the day before, walked past the dragonades remaining on duty in front of the cathedral stairs. Admitted by the custodian priest, Soeur Marie and Soeur Thérèse requested an immediate audience with the bishop, while Soeur Marguerite and the other three nuns walked purposefully toward the nave of the church.

In the anteroom of the bishop's office, the secretary priest refused adamantly to disturb Bishop de Guise, until the usually patient Sister Marie lost her temper.

"Tell him," she declared aggressively, "that if he refuses to hear our complaint, we will go directly to the governor."

A minute later, they were escorted into the office of the haggardly irritable bishop, who greeted them with a sharp reprimand. "I do not tolerate idle threats, Soeur Marie, and I do not permit subordinates in my diocese to discuss church affairs with the civil authorities."

"My threat is not an idle one, Bishop de Guise. Last night Soeur Marguerite returned to the convent without Soeur Jolie. Before she collapsed in a state of exhaustion and illness, Marguerite muttered some nonsense about sanctuary. We're here to find out what you have done with Soeur Jolie."

With his annoyance replaced by abrupt interest, the bishop asked brusquely, "Didn't Soeur Marguerite explain the circumstances to you?"

"I just told you that she was too distraught to tell us much of anything. Why would Soeur Anne Jolie ask you for sanctuary? Yesterday, Marguerite told you that she had absolute proof that Jolie was innocent of the charges you made against her."

"Marguerite's proof was insufficient to convince my brother, and Marguerite du Troyes herself is not above suspicion, according to Henri's records. Did she accompany you today?"

"Against my advice, she came to give Jolie—Sister Anne—what encouragement she could."

Both of the nuns noted the fleeting expression of satisfaction that flashed across François's face, but neither of them made any comment. Instead, Soeur Thérèse announced implacably, "We are not leaving this office, Bishop de Guise, until you have explained to our satisfaction exactly what evidence your brother has to support his charges."

After almost thirty years of maintaining a precarious balance between his professional and personal ambitions, François had become expert at manipulating facts to suit his purpose.

"The charge of theft has become a minor one," he began. "Four years ago, before she became a nun, Soeur Anne committed acts of heresy against the church with Soeur Marguerite's full cooperation. At that time, I saved them from public exposure, despite my brother's objections. To my horror when I arrived in Martinique, I discovered that Bishop Villiers, without knowing anything of Soeur Anne's earlier guilt, had already registered another charge of heresy against her, based on her actions here on the island. In desperation, I took the only means I had to protect her. Because sanctuary is not possible for accused heretics, I offered her sanctuary on the charge of theft."

As complete as François thought his explanation was, Soeur Thérèse questioned him with a schoolteacher's thoroughness, and finally elicited the admission that Soeur Marguerite had also been offered sanctuary and that Bishop de Guise planned to do everything within his power to save both women from his brother and from church prosecution. When the two nuns rose from their chairs exactly twenty minutes after they had entered the office, François breathed a sigh of relief and bid them a solicitous farewell. After retiring immediately to his bedchamber for a much-needed rest, he was rudely awakened two hours later by a smiling man he had thought long dead.

Marguerite's first intimation of trouble was her discovery that the sanctuary cell had become a prison, locked from the outside rather than the reverse. Her second was the warning delivered by the priest on guard duty that she would be the only one allowed to visit the prisoner.

"Your friends," he declared sternly, indicating the three nun-clad figures standing twenty feet away with their faces carefully averted, "will remain in the nave." As he unlocked the cell door—a skillfully hidden one that appeared to be a part of the wood paneling—he added less aggressively, "I am only following the bishop's commands, Soeur Marguerite. He was most precise in his instructions to me."

Had Marguerite been standing in front of the door when the priest slid the panel open, she too might have been shoved to the floor when Jolie erupted from the cell in a desperate attempt to gain her freedom. As unexpected and swift as her action had been, the events of the next seconds were swifter. Within moments, the priest's protest had been muffled by a large hand clamped over his mouth as he was dragged inside the cell by the berobed marines who had accompanied Marguerite.

"They're friends," the crippled old nun explained hastily to the startled young woman, who seemed immobilized by the sight of the frightened priest being stripped of his robes. "They're from the ship that will take you safely away from Martinique. Now, tell me quickly what happened here."

"Early this morning, Bishop de Guise and Father Matthieu came to the cell, and I was told that old Bishop Villiers had accused me of heresy, and that I was being imprisoned until the charge could be investigated. You were to be locked in here with me, and Father Matthieu was to monitor our conversation."

"Then we'll give him something of importance to report to his fellow priests. If and when he is released, he can tell them that François and Henri de Guise are liars. You can untie his hands, monsieurs, and remove the gag from his mouth. I'm certain that Father Matthieu will find these letters from Arnaud de Laurent of great interest. He might even realize that Bishop de Guise and not Bishop Villiers is the one who manufactured the heresy charges.''

The abused and half-naked priest was still engrossed in studying the documents Marguerite had shown to the bishop the preceding day when four nuns followed a Jesuit-robed marine through the cathedral. This time there were no royal dragonades to question their actions as they climbed aboard a wagon waiting for them on the street next to the square. The capture of ten bored and inattentive soldiers had been an easy chore for seventeen veteran marines trained by a pirate-privateer—Jan Deventer—who had captured more than fifty ships during his career.

Two of Rorke's French-speaking marines had driven a large wagon around the cathedral, and had stopped at the five sentry posts and told the dragonades on duty that Colonel de Guise had ordered them to report to the embarcadero to help unload a cargo of wine. Relieved to be freed from a monotonous duty assignment, the dragoons had climbed aboard without suspicion. Only when the wagon was driven into the empty stable yard several blocks from the cathedral did any of them reach for their weapons. But at the sight of fifteen cocked pistols pointed at their heads, they surrendered without violence. At a quietly spoken order, they exchanged their distinctive white-and-blue uniforms for the coarse canvas garb of common seamen. Only then did their captors restrain them with bonds and gags and return them to the wagon.

Less encumbered with human cargo, the second wagon to leave the vicinity of the cathedral made two stops. At the first one, Marguerite dismounted awkwardly and hobbled a short distance down the street to board the convent coach waiting for her. A block farther on, the wagon was driven into the cathedral stable yard, where the priestly robed marine left the others and walked briskly toward the embarcadero and the waiting *Lorelei*. Minutes later, the two wagons, with the human load evenly distributed, headed south along the coastal highway.

Throughout the long, slow-paced ride to the appointed place of rendezvous five miles south of St. Pierre, Jolie sat huddled in the miserable silence of self-condemnation. Seated on the bench beside the driver, she reflected bitterly that she had gained her freedom only at the sacrifice of her oldest and best friend. Soeur Marguerite would now face alone the jeopardy Jolie had just escaped. When the old nun had insisted on rejoining Soeur Marie and Soeur Thérèse, Jolie had been dumbfounded, but her arguments had gone unheeded.

"Don't talk nonsense, child," Marguerite had scoffed. "I'm in no danger, and you have a life of your own to lead from now on."

"Not without you!"

"You need a man, not a worn-out old nun to tie you down to worn-out old loyalties. I've a task to finish here, and I intend to do just that before I retire. As for you, I hope you have the sense to take what happiness you're offered and to write to me occasionally if such a thing is possible in a world run by idiots."

Marguerite's final words of farewell, though, had been directed to the marine wearing the stolen priest's robes. "Tell your captain that the older brother is more treacherous than the younger one. He'll know what to do."

Dull-witted after a sleepless night and terrifying morning, Jolie had paid little attention to the cryptic message. Her mind was still morosely preoccupied with fear for an indomitable old woman who would now be at the mercy of a pallid-faced bishop ruthless enough to condemn a woman to death without remorse or conscience.

While the abduction of Henri de Guise and his dragonades had been a necessary part of the plan from the beginning, Rorke had not contemplated a similar fate for the Bishop de Guise. Experience had taught him the dreary lesson that religious zealots of any faith were problem passengers aboard ship. Moreover, the Dutch West Indies Company

headquartered on Curaçao Island might well refuse to accept
a prelate of the Catholic church under any circumstances.
Such a man would be of small commercial value to merchants
and sea captains intent on profit; his only use would be as a
hostage in a prisoner-of-war exchange. Unfortunately, after
the news of his most recent villainy reached official ears in
France, it was doubtful if even his own church would want a
disgraced bishop returned. But after hearing the report
delivered by the marine who had helped Jolie escape, Rorke
knew he had no other choice. He could not leave Marguerite
du Troyes or the other nuns who had risked their lives to
help Jolie at the mercy of François de Guise.

Hastily summoning his officers and Sébastien to his
quarters, he explained the last-minute change of plans and
asked the mulatto navigator to choose still another point of
rendezvous, this one only a mile south of St. Pierre.
Ordering a longboat lowered over the side, he assigned the
third mate the task of accompanying four of the best
oarsmen to the chosen rendezvous to await his arrival. The
remainder of Rorke's preparation was accomplished in a few
minutes, and he left the ship accompanied by the one
marine and two muscular sailors. Still dressed in their
disguises—Rorke in the elegant attire of Baron Wallmond,
and the brawny marine in the brown Jesuit robes—the two
men walked rapidly toward the cathedral, followed by the
sailors aboard a wagon driven by its cautious owner. While
the wagon was halted beside the walled cathedral courtyard,
the marine led Rorke through the gate he had left unlocked
earlier. Twenty feet into the enclosure, he paused to point
out the window Marguerite had identified as belonging to
the bishop's personal quarters. Within the cathedral itself,
the interlopers walked unnoticed through the ornately dignified nave, past the candlelit altar, and into the recessed choir
section. Rorke unlocked the cell where the unhappy priest
was still imprisoned and ordered the marine to return the
robe.

"Had you known the nun Soeur Anne before Bishop de

Guise accused her of heresy?'' he asked the frightened priest casually.

"Everyone on the cathedral staff knew her; she was not an ordinary nun."

"Had you ever had any reason to suspect her of heresy before?"

"She often annoyed Bishop Villiers, but there was never any question of her loyalty to the church."

"Bishop Villiers never publicly accused her?"

"Never."

"Then how did Bishop de Guise convince you that she had suddenly become a heretic?"

"He told me that Bishop Villiers had left a written accusation behind, stating that she openly consorted with heretics here in Martinique, and that in France, she had helped criminal Huguenots and was Huguenot herself."

"Do you still believe those charges?"

"Not after reading the letters her grandfather wrote to Jacob Riveira."

"How would you feel if Bishop de Guise were to desert his post and leave the island?"

The priest hesitated only briefly before he responded, "Most of the cathedral staff would be relieved. We've never had an Inquisitionist on the island before."

"Even if he didn't leave voluntarily?"

"I cannot condone violence to his person."

"I intend him no physical harm, but I won't leave him here to punish the innocent nuns who helped Soeur Anne escape."

"Most of us know her as Soeur Jolie, and her friends would not be the only ones the bishop would punish. There are many islanders who are already afraid of him and his brother."

"Then, will you help me?"

"I cannot be partner to a crime or a lie!"

"I want you to be partner to the truth and to send copies of those letters to your church in France and to the governor here on the island. I also ask that you tell them about Soeur

Jolie's imprisonment on false charges of theft and heresy. Bishop de Guise will be in no position to deny your charges against him, nor will his brother or any of the royal dragonades. They are already securely restrained aboard my ship. If you make no mention of my part in the business, the authorities will accept the rumor that the bishop and Colonel de Guise resigned and left the island rather than face public outrage and disgrace."

Thoughtfully, the priest studied the cold blue eyes of the tall foreigner and shrugged. "When the church learns that the bishop abused the laws of sanctuary for personal reasons, he might have been forced to resign anyway. And since I do not know your name or your exact intentions, I will have little to report about the bishop's disappearance."

"Then I thank you for your courtesy, Father Matthieu. I would have hated to commit a sacrilege in your cathedral. I'll bid you good day now and leave the cell unlocked."

Almost casually, the priest murmured, "I will continue my meditations here until vespers. By that time I trust our spiritual home will have regained its serenity. You might watch out for the bishop's secretary. Father Patrice is inclined to be overly diligent on the bishop's behalf."

The removal of François de Guise from the cathedral was accomplished within the hour and without interference. He was limply unconscious when Rorke shoved him out of the bedchamber window into the waiting arms of the marine. The chiming of the cathedral bells was a pleasant accompaniment to the clandestine activity of the skillful kidnappers. As the body of the bishop, now clad in demeaning seaman's clothing, was laid on the bed of the wagon, Rorke announced tersely to the watchful driver, "This man is one of my crew who collapsed while he was visiting the cathedral. Since he may have contracted smallpox at our last port of call, I want to place him in quarantine aboard my ship before the disease spreads to your islanders."

While there were few observers along the way to clock the wagon's speed, the drive to the rendezvous spot a mile south of the city undoubtedly broke all existing records. Asking no questions about the location of a ship along the deserted stretch of beach, the driver waited only until his passengers were unloaded before he drove off at even a faster pace. Rorke smiled with sardonic amusement as the body of the sleeping bishop was stowed aboard the longboat that had been hidden behind an outcropping of shore rock. Not for the first time had the mention of quarantine proved to be an effective means of avoiding suspicion—almost as effective a means as the ruse employed to lure the overly diligent Father Patrice from the anterooms of the bishop's quarters.

Speaking in his native Flemish French, the marine had walked into the outer office and announced that he had been sent by his captain to warn the bishop that Colonel de Guise had laid claim to a chest of gold coin belonging to the church.

"I cannot disturb the bishop—he is resting," the secretary had disclaimed fussily.

"Then go yourself, Father. The captain does not want to be held responsible if the gold is stolen. We've carried it a long way from the cathedral in Bordeaux."

"Where in the harbor is your ship located?"

"We're docked behind the Scoville company north of town, but we'll be leaving port at sunset."

Rorke smiled as he recalled the speed with which Father Patrice was driven away from the cathedral a few minutes later, never having noticed the elegantly dressed man who had entered the deserted office. "Human greed is the only infallible lure," Jan Deventer had often remarked. "It is what makes a profession like mine highly profitable." In this instance, Rorke reflected cynically, it had removed a potential witness and made it possible for priests like Father Matthieu to claim the bishop had left the island voluntarily because of scandal.

Greed, however, had played no part in the easy capture of Bishop de Guise; medicine had been the trickery used in that instance. There had been no need for violence; the bishop had awakened briefly when a hollow bamboo needle had pricked his arm and been held in place until the measured dose of a soporific opiate had been expelled. In South Pacific ports of call, Rorke had amassed a wealth of knowledge about the use of exotic drugs that had abounded in the Orient for centuries. While European criminals and doctors still resorted to unpredictable dosages of adulterated wine, Oriental practitioners had developed delicately precise instruments. François had fallen peacefully asleep within minutes and would not awaken for ten hours. The task of removing his layered robes of office and replacing them with loose-legged canvas breeches and a shapeless shirt had been swiftly accomplished, and the departure through the window even swifter.

Seated midsection in the longboat only half filled by the ten silent men, Rorke was first to glimpse the familiar sails of the *Lorelei* as the ship bore steadily north, silhouetted by the rays of the setting sun. At that moment, had he not been a practical man of science, he might have been tempted to believe in the superstition of destiny. By happenstance, more than four years earlier, he had married the only woman capable of inspiring his love; today, by sheer luck, he had rescued her from the same pair of villains who had threatened her in the beginning. His lips curved into a smile of anticipation as he ordered his crewmen to begin rowing toward the *Lorelei*, still a mile away.

13

S eated apart from the marines and captive dragonades
on a sandy stretch of beach, Jolie felt as inert as the
rock she was leaning against, her restlessness of the
past months forgotten. The freedom she had longed for only
yesterday no longer seemed like a beckoning adventure; it
had been too dearly purchased at the expense of others. In
her earlier flights from danger and entrapment, Jolie had
taken her own risks and made her own decisions. This time,
everything had been decided for her. She was to go wherever the ship just now coming into view on the northwestern
horizon took her. Although Marguerite had assured her that
she would not be returned to France or Scotland or England,
Jolie wondered if any of the unknown countries would be
any happier for her. Thus far, she had been discontent in
every place she had chosen for herself. Listlessly, she
watched the ship sail closer to shore and reef its sails as
three small boats were lowered over the side. Only when
she recognized Sébastien in the lead boat did she experience
a painful rebirth of emotion; even he could be in danger
because of her.

After walking to the water's edge to greet him, she told
him sadly, "Soeur Marguerite refused to come with me.
Now she'll be the one who's punished."

"There is no longer any danger, Soeur Jolie. All the

villains have been removed from Martinique. Life will go on as before," her loyal servant of two years informed her proudly.

"Even the Bishop de Guise?" Jolie asked in disbelief.

"Even the priest, Soeur Jolie. Everyone, I think, will be happier to have him gone. He was a bad priest who would have made trouble for your friends and for Monsieur Riveira."

Not until Jolie clambered up the swaying rope ladder onto the deck of the *Lorelei* did she realize that she, too, could have remained safely on Martinique. Now that it was too late to return, she felt no regrets—not even that Marguerite had stayed behind. As the depression that had gripped her for a full night and day dissipated, she took a deep breath of relief and smiled faintly at the man who walked across the deck to greet her. As he returned her smile with cheerful friendliness, she stared at the plump, round face in vague recognition.

"I cannot recall your name, monsieur," she murmured.

His smile broadened into a chuckle as he responded crisply in English, " 'Tis Chapman, mistress, and 'tis sharp eyes you have to know me at all. When last we met in Newcastle, I was butterball fat, what with working only half a year for Captain Huntington—the old captain, not the young one."

Sighing in relief, Jolie looked around the ship she remembered only vaguely. She had not been rescued by strangers! "Is Captain Huntington aboard, Monsieur Chapman?"

"Nay, lass—or is it the grand title of *sister* you're still wanting to be called?" the man who had served as first mate aboard the *Lorelei* for twenty years asked easily with a democratic impudence.

Jolie shook her head and smiled. Three years of nunhood had eliminated all traces of her earlier need for special recognition. "I am no longer a nun, monsieur. What happened to Captain Huntington?"

"He retired permanently to his castle on the Rhine as Baron Wallmond. He's not liked England since the death of

his old friend. His second son has taken over the family
business there.''

"I remember his son very well,'' Jolie admitted. "He
was the one who helped my friends and me leave England.''

"Aye, that's how we learned about the sorry trouble you
suffered in Scotland.''

"Is Manfred Huntington aboard, monsieur?''

"Nay, he prefers the safer waters 'twixt Newcastle and
Amsterdam.''

Vaguely disappointed, Jolie murmured a muted, "Oh.''

"You'll find the new captain a livelier sort than the
cautious Manfred,'' Chapman chided her lightly. "He thought
you might enjoy a bit of luxury while you're aboard, so he's
offered you the use of his own quarters. Come along, I'll
show you. 'Twill be a more cheerful sight than watching
prisoners being stowed below deck.''

Jolie's first impression of the large cabin was one of
awe—the furnishings were as opulent as the duke of
Newcastle's had been. Even the built-in chart desk was
finely carved, and the dining table gleamed with a mirror
shine. Smaller in size, but equally elegant, the adjoining
cabin contained a full-sized bed covered with a velvet
counterpane. But it was the array of feminine attire spread
on top that captivated her attention—a golden-haired wig, a
pretty cotton dress the bright blue of a sunlit Caribbean sea,
and the almost forgotten gold medallions her grandfather
and the duke of Newcastle had given her.

"Was it Soeur Marguerite who brought these things?''
she asked softly.

"Aye, the captain said she had packed all your belongings. Your money's stored in the ship's strongbox, and your
other frocks are in that chest yonder. Captain said you'd be
needing the wig until your own hair grows out. 'Tis not as
bright a color as your own, if I remember rightly, but 'twill
keep you from looking as bald as the likes of me. Come
along, lass, there's still more magic to be seen aboard this
rich man's ship.''

As he slid the last door open, Jolie gasped in shock,

feeling as if she had stepped into a scene from the *Arabian Nights*. As incredible as a copper bathtub aboard ship was, the mirror above the washbasin was more so. It was the sight of her own image in that mirror that brought her crashing back to reality. The once crisply starched wings of her hat drooped in soggy disarray, and her face was streaked with dirt.

"I look like a scarecrow," she gasped.

"Aye," her amused escort agreed, "but 'tis nothing a warm bath won't mend. And that's another of the *Lorelei*'s marvels. On the deck above is a barrel of sun-warmed water with a pipe that lets you fill the tub. When you're finished, you pull that cork from its hole and the water is piped into the sea. 'Twas Captain Huntington's idea, and the envy of every other ship's master in Newcastle. I'll leave you now, lass. If you need me, my quarters are just across the companionway."

As much as she would have enjoyed soaking endlessly in the warm water, the memory of her image in the mirror drove her to scrub with efficient speed. She looked so oddly changed since the last time she had studied her face in a mirror at her house in Glencoe before the horror. Her eyes seemed larger and her cheekbones more visible. *I look so much older*, she thought in dismay. *Marguerite was right when she said I'd age before my time if I stayed in Martinique. I wonder if that's the reason convents are not allowed to have mirrors, so we won't worry about our appearances.*

Standing in front of the mirror as she adjusted the fitted bodice of her dress, Jolie remembered Soeur Catherine, the youngest of the widows from Glencoe, who had gained forty pounds in Martinique, but who had looked much the same as the others in her nun's habit. For a moment, Jolie felt a glow of pride that her own figure was still as slender and supple as it had been during her girlhood in Strasbourg. The addition of the wig, though, ended her self-recognition. The gold curls that tumbled down over her shoulders made her look a stranger—a woman who held little in common

with the often stern and overworked nun she had been for
three years.

On the dining table in the outermost cabin, she found her
dinner waiting—a hearty meal of cold lobster, fresh fruit,
wine, and cheese. Last night she had been given a bowl of
tasteless stew and a slice of dried bread. As she relished the
delicious food before her now, she recalled Chapman's
descriptive words—"a rich man's ship." Looking around at
the contents of the room, she wondered if it had been
Captain Huntington or the new owner who had surrounded
himself with such luxury.

Curious about the identity of the unknown captain who
had gone to such remarkable lengths to rescue her and to
provide her with accommodations far beyond her expectation,
she began to search the cabin, aimlessly at first, and then
with serious intent. At the elongated desk, she studied the
charts pinned to the surface, noting the shape of Martinique
and the depths of the water surrounding it, and the carefully
inked lines that traced the route from Amsterdam westward.
Pausing a moment, she stared at the handwriting of the
notations that accompanied the compass headings. Without
any real purpose in mind, she pulled another chart from the
shelf—one that marked the route from the Rhine River in
Germany to Newcastle in England. The handwriting was
notably different, and the identifying initials were R. H.
instead of the J. R. on the Atlantic and Caribbean chart. The
vague suspicion that had begun to form as she stared at the
later handwriting intensified into a wild disbelief when she
opened the most current of the ship's logs and read the
sprawling signature of the author—Captain James Rorke.

Her heart was pounding as she raced back into the
bedchamber and pulled open the lids of the sea chests lashed
to the bulkhead. The smallest one contained other dresses
similar to the one she had on, and the next three were full of
men's clothing, but nowhere could she find the one garment
she was seeking with a desperate hope—a doctor's long
black robe. Sick with disappointment, she opened the remaining
chest and sank to the floor as tears gushed to her eyes. That

chest was packed with familiar surgical instruments and carefully labeled jars of medicine. This time, Jolie recognized the handwriting.

Shaking with an emotion so powerful she could barely walk, and all but blinded by tears, she left the suite of captain's cabins and crossed the companionway to knock on the door legended *First Mate*.

"Where is your captain?" she asked hollowly, and her voice broke.

The tears were streaming down her face when Chapman took her arm and led her back into the cabin she had just left. "I warned Rorke you'd best be told before you ferreted out the truth for yourself, but for the life of me, lass, I was afraid to be the one to tell you. He expected to be here to greet you himself, until Hals returned with the news that the priest would have to be dealt with same as the soldiers, else your convent friends would face the punishment the devil ordered for you."

"Why didn't Soeur Marguerite tell me?" Even as she asked the question, Jolie knew the answer Chapman would make.

"None of them dared tell you before you were safe, lass. 'Twas a complicated plot Rorke devised to get you away from the cathedral, and he didn't want you too upset to do your part. I suspect he didn't want to be upset himself when he went to fetch the priest."

"He went alone into St. Pierre?"

"Nay, lass, Hals was with him. Between the pair of them, there's not much they don't know about so simple an undertaking. We'll be reaching the point of rendezvous within the half hour."

"But it will be dark by then!" Jolie exclaimed in distress.

"Aye, 'twas part of the plan. Best not to have folk ashore asking questions about a longboat headed out to sea at sunset."

"That was how we came aboard."

"'Twas no one along that stretch of beach to see—Sébastien knew every inch of shore in these parts. The captain's waiting just south of the city, within sight of shore cannon. 'Twas not safe traveling any farther on the road— not with a trussed-up bishop in the wagon. You needn't fear they'll miss finding the *Lorelei*; the third mate and four of the best oarsmen will bring your husband safely aboard.''

Struggling to keep her voice steady, Jolie asked the question that had been tormenting her. "When did you learn he was alive, monsieur?"

"Not quite a year ago, he arrived at Wallmond's castle on the Rhine River. Like everyone else, we thought he'd been killed—murdered by a foul pair of Campbell relatives. 'Tis one of the reasons he vows never to use that name again. From the baron—Captain Huntington—he learned that you'd survived the savagery committed against your Scot village and that you were a nun, mayhap in Martinique. When he found out for certain where you were from your grandfather, he bought the *Lorelei* from the baron so he could fetch you.''

The tears in Jolie's eyes were replaced by shock. "My husband bought this ship?"

"Aye, that he did. He hired the lot of us as crew and still another twenty in Holland."

"How, monsieur? What had he done to earn that much money?"

"Well, now, that's something 'tis best you learn from your husband. I'd not like to be the one to tell you false."

"Will you at least tell me what happened to him in England and why he never let me know he was still alive?"

"Aye, at least I can ease your mind on those points. The men hired to kill him sold him to a ship's captain instead, and he spent two years at sea on the other side of the world."

"As a prisoner?" Jolie persisted.

"Every man aboard a ship is a prisoner of sorts, lass— even those of us who volunteered for the life. I expect your husband found the life bearable after a while."

A few probing questions later, Jolie had learned almost the entirety of Rorke's activities of the past three years.

Engrossed in easing the shock for a tearful young wife, Chapman revealed far more than he had intended, even to the extent of warning her that she would find her husband a changed man.

"He's more sea captain now than doctor, and the best in the business. Wasn't a one of us who didn't want him deep-sixed during those first six weeks at sea, when he forced us to deck drill like a crew of green farm lads. But he had the right of it when we reached Caribbean waters. Except for the Dutch marines he hired in Amsterdam, there wasn't a one of us who'd ever seen a pirate until one of them waylaid us north of Martinique. We could have outrun the scurvy devil, but the captain didn't want it dogging our heels while we were figuring out how to get you off a French island. 'Twas masterful the means he used to lure the villains in close enough for him and his marines to capture their ship without losing a man."

"What happened to the pirates?"

"Hanged in Barbados, where we sold the ship and returned the English prisoners whom those lawless scoundrels had kidnapped two months earlier. The *Lorelei* crew made more money in that transaction than we'd earn in a dozen years of wages, what with the price of the ship and the stolen cargo in its hold."

"Is that what will happen to the French dragonades and the bishop?" Jolie asked fearfully.

"Nay, your husband's not that much changed. We'll be turning them over to the Dutch authorities on Curaçao as prisoners of war. 'Tis unlikely they'll be returned to Martinique until they learn a new trade. Now, mistress, 'tis time for me to return to work, and 'tis time for you to dry your tears. You've but a few hours left of widowhood, and you're to spend them here in the cabin. 'Twould be unsafe on deck for a landlubber after dark, since we'll be running without a light showing once the captain's aboard."

Left alone in a cabin now as dark as the windowless sanctuary cell had been the night before, Jolie saw nothing of the activity on deck when the sails were reefed and the ship anchored long enough to permit a boarding. Standing before an open transom window, she listened tensely to the muted sounds of the anchor being winched aboard and felt the ship surge forward minutes later as the unfurled sails filled with wind. But she heard none of the low-spoken orders issued by Captain James Rorke when he took command of his ship. A half hour into her lonely vigil, she jerked in nervous anticipation when a soft knock sounded on the door. Groping her way across the unfamiliar room, she opened the door and stared in bitter disappointment at the shadowy figure of the first mate, lighted only by a shaded lantern.

"I've come to ease your fears, mistress, and to tell you all's well."

"Does my husband know I'm aboard, Monsieur Chapman?" she blurted in frustration.

" 'Tis a foolish question, mistress, after he's come three thousand miles for you. A ship is not a toy, lass, that can be set aside after you're finished playing with it. Until we clear these waters and learn whether or not a French patrol corsair is following us, the captain's the only one with command experience enough to fend it off in case of attack. Since there's naught you can do until the danger's past, 'tis best you get some sleep and forget the upsetting day you've had."

Embarrassed by the bland scolding she realized she'd deserved, Jolie did as she had been told; but instead of tossing fitfully about as she had the night before, she fell asleep as if she had swallowed a dose of Soeur Marguerite's poppy powder. Her last rueful thought was that Rorke hadn't changed as much as Chapman had claimed. He was still the preoccupied leader who had ignored her in Baden-Baden and aboard the *Rijn Köningen* while he'd tended Huguenot refugees.

Jolie awakened in the gray light of predawn to find what looked like a bearded stranger sleeping next to her in bed. She hadn't stirred when he had joined her hours before, as exhausted as she'd been after two days of unrelieved tension. Easing herself from the bed, she studied his gaunt face until she located the familiar features beneath the beard. Until that moment, she had believed in his miraculous return from the dead without really believing. For three years, since the bleak moment in the library of Stair Castle when she had been handed a letter that announced Rorke's death, Jolie had not thought in terms of happiness, only of bearable survival. But as she looked down on the face of the only person in her life who had belonged to her, tears of joy blurred her vision. The taut bands of steely determination that had kept her from despair in Coire Gabhail and from dispirited surrender in Martinique broke, and the fiery passion of her youth coursed unrestrained through her trembling body. She felt as young as she had when she had raced down the Mannheim dock and flung herself into his arms.

When she rejoined him in bed, it was her arms that encircled him and her joyous giggle that greeted him as he roused from sleep. For a moment, they lay quiescently facing each other, smiling with a happy recognition despite his beard and her shaved head, and savoring the intense pleasure of being together. When Jolie would have spoken, Rorke stilled her lips with a kiss that began as a gentle salute to their reunion, until the chemistry of love altered its purpose. Jolie was the first to break free of restraint, the first to move her body sinuously in invitation. Even three years of separation had not dulled her memory of their last days together in Newcastle, when she had been the aggressor in the crowded home of the duke of Newcastle. As he had then, Rorke accepted her invitation with a passionate response that quickly overwhelmed her senses.

What had been the endearment of remembered love became a throbbing need for fulfillment, a compelling drive toward repossession. With a swift dexterity, his hands explored her trembling, straining body only briefly before he pulled her to him without any pretense of seductive artistry. The turbulence that followed was blindly instinctive as their bodies meshed together in the pulsing rhythm of mating that ended for both of them in a climax of hypnotic ecstasy, leaving them panting with momentary exhaustion. Recovering his breath at the same time he did his humor, Rorke chuckled softly as he rolled over, taking her with him.

"I should have taken you away the first day I arrived on Martinique."

Vaguely hurt, Jolie demanded, "Why didn't you?"

"I was afraid you might have become a real nun and refused to leave your convent."

"*Ma foi*, I was a terrible nun!"

"Not according to Marguerite. She said you'd become as good an administrator as your Aunt Charlotte had been, and that everyone treated you like a heroine. Did you design those additions to the original buildings?"

"I did not wish to be imprisoned again, and the odors in the infirmary were terrible without windows," Jolie admitted defensively, adding a rueful confession, "Bishop Villiers said they were heretically pagan, and he ordered me to have them torn down."

"But you disobeyed him."

"*Ma foi*, yes! I told him that fresh air was necessary to cure island diseases, and that the schoolgirls did not fall asleep as often. Did you not like those rooms?"

"For this climate, they looked ideal. There were times when I wanted to blow holes in the side of the ship to get fresh air into the hospital ward."

"There is a hospital aboard this ship?" Jolie asked eagerly.

"Nay, the *Lorelei* is not a ship of war, and we've been lucky so far on this voyage. 'Twould be impossible for me to spend much time in a ship's infirmary now."

Jolie's voice was tinged with disappointment as she absorbed the meaning of his words. "Then it is true what Monsieur Chapman said—that you no longer wish to be a doctor?"

" 'Tis a full-time job being captain of a ship, my critical wife. And as long as the *Lorelei* is the only safe home we have, 'tis Captain James Rorke I have to be. In truth, sweet Jolie, with you aboard, 'twill be a happier life than tending men mutilated by senseless warfare. With you aboard, I've little enough to complain about, unless you insist on talking when I've other things in mind. I was relieved to note you'd not forgotten the way of it, but now 'tis time to test your staying power.''

That their earlier reunion had been merely an introduction and that her husband had become a domineering man, Jolie learned within minutes. His lovemaking this second time was laced with a humor he hadn't displayed so openly since their long ago sojourn in the Utrecht house in Holland, and his possessive caresses were bolder and more intimate than she remembered. By the time his lips and hands had erased all awareness of their intervening dialogue, Jolie felt consumed. Not since their first time together had Rorke been so completely in control, so thorough in his skillful titillation of her throbbing senses, and so deliberately slow to consummate their union. Twice when she tried to pull him into position, he had shaken his head in refusal and smiled at her with knowing humor. When he finally thrust into her melting body with a strength that penetrated completely, she was already in the throes of an ecstasy that endured throughout the violence of mating and overlapped his as he collapsed on top of her. Neither of them moved as they lay panting with exhaustion and their perspiration-soaked bodies cooled, but still Rorke's humor persisted.

Nuzzling her ear with his lips, he demanded softly, ''Any regrets, my shave-pated siren?''

''No,'' Jolie responded tremulously, ''except that your beard tickles. I'll be happy to shave it for you so we'll be more of a matched pair.''

''We're matched well enough as 'tis. The beard stays to remind you that at sea, 'tis the ship's captain who calls the tune and not the captain's wife.''

Jolie's lessons in being a captain's wife were just beginning. While she remained contented and drowsy in bed, Rorke arose swiftly with a purposeful determination and walked into the fanciful washroom. After what seemed only a minute or two later to the half-asleep woman, he emerged in his working clothes, and Jolie met Captain James Rorke formally for the first time. Uniformed in an open-throated white shirt, fitted buff-colored trousers, and burnished brown boots, he wore both cutlass and pistols around his trim waist, and his voice was crisply commanding.

"Wake up, sweetheart. No one is allowed to ignore routine aboard ship. You'll have to be washed and dressed within the half hour so the cabin boy can bring our breakfast and clean the room. I'll tell you the rest of shipboard rules while we're eating."

Even as she was protesting that neither of them had been subjected to repressive rules when they'd been passengers aboard the *Rijn Königen* or the ship that had taken them to England, Rorke pulled the covers off and lifted her into his arms. Sweeping her slender, struggling body with his eyes, he lowered her slowly to her feet.

"I haven't forgotten that your hair is red and that you've a temper to match," he scolded her with a broad grin, "but this time, there are rules you'll have to obey whether you approve of them or not."

When Jolie entered the outer cabin the thirty specified minutes later, however, those shipboard rules were instantly reduced to one—she was to remain secluded in their quarters until Curaçao. Rorke stared at her in appreciation and pursed his lips in a silent whistle. In the blond wig and feminine blue dress, he admitted to himself, she would destroy crew morale. Even if he escorted her on deck as he had intended, he knew that she would play havoc with men who hadn't been given extended shore leave in six months. But not even a nun's robe would guarantee her safety today; there was an incandescent glow in her eyes that the most obtuse swabbie would recognize. God's wounds, he swore in silent acknowledgment, she'd become more beautiful than he remembered, and the subtle air of assured authority stamped on her proud features made her doubly challenging.

Chapman had tried to warn him last night, he recalled belatedly, but he had foolishly assured the first-mate that Jolie was an experienced nurse who had treated men pa-

tients successfully for years. Rorke felt no such reassurance
now. In bed this morning, even without the concealing
allure of the wig, she had roused a storm in him. No wonder
two successive bishops had tried to break her spirit. At the
reminder that one of those vindictive churchmen was a
prisoner in the hold of his ship, Rorke's resolve hardened.

"Jolie, sweet," he began, "the *Lorelei* has never had a
woman aboard before, and sailors are a superstitious lot.
Until we reach Curaçao, you'll have to remain in these
cabins."

"That's nonsense, Rorke. I had no problems with any of
your men yesterday."

"Yesterday you were a nun," he reminded her pointedly,
"and according to Chapman, an unhappy one with a dirty
face. Today you're my wife, and I don't want to discipline
some unlucky sailor who forgets his place. 'Twill only be
for five or six days, and I'll see you're not too bored."

As a matter of record, Jolie had no time for boredom; she
had formulated a goal more imperious than any she had ever
set before. The prospect of being a cosseted wife imprisoned
uselessly in ornately elegant cabins aboard a ship that
roamed aimlessly from port to port appalled her. "As long
as the *Lorelei* is the only safe home we have, 'tis Captain
James Rorke I have to be," her husband had warned her.
But he had made no mention of seeking a safe homeland,
Jolie remembered with a cynical conviction that Captain
James Rorke was already overfond of a footloose life. With
the same determined scholarship she had once applied only
to medical books, she began her search in the charts
overflowing the locker. Almost as quickly as she discarded
those of European waters, she laid aside the ones of Caribbean islands. She wanted a life more challenging than the
limited, stagnant existence of island life, where slaves
outnumbered their complacent, arrogant masters.

Tucked in a drawer with their seals still unbroken were
the critical charts she sought—charts of a land where she
would have been sent with all the other Glencoe MacDonalds,
had King William not relented. With a keen interest, she

studied the names that dotted the coast of the American
colonies, frustrated that the nautical charts gave no information about any of them except water depths and harborage.
But one of those ten, she vowed, would become the safe
home she and Rorke would adopt as their own. Lacking any
other resource of information, Jolie waylaid Chapman when
he emerged from his cabin.

As sympathetic as he had been the night before, the first
mate answered her questions with a blunt honesty, but the
only American colonies he knew anything about, he detested.
"Worse than Oliver Cromwell at his worst," he declared
succinctly. "Religious fanatics who interpret the Bible to
suit themselves and who outlaw those of us with broader
views." Grateful for his revealing candor, Jolie scratched
out the names of Massachusetts and Connecticut; she wanted
no more church dictatorship in her life. For the same reason,
she eliminated the tiny colony of Rhode Island. It was
surrounded by Puritan neighbors, and Jolie knew from
experience that church leaders often resorted to force in
stamping out all religions contrary to their own.

On the night Rorke invited three of his officers to share
their dinner, she ruled out the southernmost colonies—the
two Carolinas and Virginia. According to the second-mate
navigator, the wealthy farmers there depended on slave
labor. In her two years on Martinique, Jolie had learned to
hate the ugly undercurrents of such a society.

Ironically, it was on the Dutch island of Curaçao that
Jolie's and Rorke's ultimate destination was decided—not
by either of them, but through an odd series of circumstances. Six days after leaving Martinique, the *Lorelei* sailed
into the magnificent port of Willemstadt, the heavily fortified
trade center of the Dutch West Indies Company. Within an
hour of anchoring in the crowded harbor, the ship was
boarded by a trio of Dutch officials, accompanied by six
armed guards. Thorough in their inspection of the ship,
crew, and cargo, the officials retired to the captain's quarters
to announce their findings.

The German wine was readily admitted, but the stocks of

East Indian spices were declared a monopoly of the combined Dutch companies and refused. Even more uncompromising was the official decision about the human cargo.
While the sixteen French dragoons were named valid prisoners
of war who would serve their periods of captivity as
crewmen aboard company ships, the Dutch officials declined to take responsibility for the de Guise brothers.
Among the reasons they listed, in addition to the absence of
prison facilities on Curaçao, were the de Guises' lack of
commercial value and their potential for troublemaking. In
the case of the bishop, the objection was more precise—the
residents of the Dutch island did not want any trouble with
their Spanish and Portuguese neighbors on the Catholic
mainland of South America.

Seated next to Rorke throughout the gloomy proceedings,
Jolie had understood little of the Dutch language being
spoken; but it was her whispered question to her husband
that reopened the discussion.

"Rorke, did you ever tell the bishop or his brother what
could happen to them if they returned to France?"

For a brief moment, Rorke shook his head in barely
concealed annoyance at the interruption, then turned to her
with a smile of understanding. In rapidly spoken Dutch, he
ordered Hals Wister, the marine who had assisted in Jolie's
rescue and had accompanied him back to the cathedral, to
bring the disputed prisoners to the cabin. Rorke's explanation to the Dutch officials was that while the de Guise
brothers might be unwelcome in the Dutch West Indies
Company, they could prove of value to the Dutch East
Indies Company, providing they agreed to accept the necessary discipline. In that assumption, Rorke held a distinct
advantage over the Curaçao inspectors—he knew more about
the Dutch East Indies than they did. While educated, literate
men in Holland did not object to traveling four thousand
miles to the Caribbean, they were reluctant to accept jobs on
the more oppressive and dangerous islands twelve thousand
miles distant. The French colonel at least, Rorke explained,
had a rudimentary knowledge of the Dutch language and

could undoubtedly keep accurate records of company profits. As for the priest, he added, there was little mischief he could do among East Indian natives who were largely Mohammedan in their religion.

Still obdurately skeptical, the three officials remained silent throughout the unique and antagonistic scene that ensued after François and Henri de Guise were led into the room and seated in chairs facing their accusers. Having already been informed of the reasons the two men had been kidnapped, the Dutchmen evinced little interest in Hals Wister's laborious interpretation of the French dialogue that followed.

Prior to Rorke's concise recounting of the separate steps he and Marguerite du Troyes had taken to destroy the de Guise reputations on Martinique and in France, there had only been one word spoken. When he had first seen Jolie, Bishop de Guise had muttered "Jezebel" in contemptuous tones, but Jolie had been too startled by the changed appearance of the two men who had been her vicious enemies a week earlier to pay any attention to the insult. She hardly recognized Henri de Guise; without the elegance of a pretentious uniform to support it, his haughty expression of command seemed ludicrous. The bishop, she thought almost with pity, looked like a tired old man who had already realized that his thirty-year career as a priest had ended in disgrace. François listened to Rorke's cold accusations with a fatalistic calm; it was his less disciplined brother who exploded into speech when Rorke revealed the name of Jolie's mother.

"My wife was untouched when I wed her," he rasped hotly. "This blond thief does not even resemble her."

François shook his head. "Joanna lied to you, Henri; the woman is her daughter. Had the secret not been deliberately kept from you, we could have dealt with the annoying problem years ago. Now you and I will pay the penalty for your wife's cowardice and sins," he said in a tired voice devoid of expression.

"The sins you'll be paying for are your own," Rorke

countered harshly, "and I'll make certain the payment matches the crime you planned to commit against my wife. Since our Dutch hosts have refused to accept you as prisoners of war, I'll be the one to decide your fate. As soon as I am certain the reports Father Matthieu and Marguerite du Troyes are sending to France have accomplished their purpose, you will be transferred to a French ship and returned to your country to face charges of abuse of office and attempted murder of two innocent nuns."

Whatever else François and Henri de Guise were, they were not stupid; nor did either of them possess a martyr's courage. Henri was the first to address the Curaçao officials with a demand for asylum. In a vehement harangue spoken in a confusing mixture of Dutch and French, he denounced the charges against him and his brother, accused Rorke of criminal abduction, and demanded safe asylum in Curaçao. When he received no response from his impassive audience, his pleading became an impassioned recounting of the conspiracy that had destroyed the de Guise family—a conspiracy that named King Louis XIV and Comte Arnaud de Laurent as perpetrators, with small regard for logic or fact. Sharply reprimanded by his shrewdly observant brother, Henri concluded his tirade less aggressively by admitting that they could not be safely returned to France and by repeating his request for asylum.

Except for her fervent hope that Rorke would be spared any further responsibility for the two men, Jolie felt only a cold detachment as she listened to the impassioned outpouring of bitter recriminations. Any sympathy their desperate plight might have engendered had vanished when François laid all the blame on a woman whose only sin had been the desertion of a child twenty-four years earlier. For a fleeting moment, Jolie remembered Tavis Campbell and the lack of conscience with which he had ordered Rorke's death. Like François and Henri de Guise, he had never felt either guilt or remorse for his criminal actions. Glancing up at her husband's set face, Jolie experienced deep gratitude. Rorke had risked his own life to protect a convent of nuns, but now she was certain he would have to pay a penalty for that gallantry. She didn't understand many of the words one of the officials was saying, but she knew they were meant for Rorke, not for the prisoners.

Pushing his chair away from the table, the perspiring Dutchman declared, "If this were Amsterdam, the request for asylum would be granted easily enough; but there are problems in Curaçao that make it difficult."

"But not impossible," Rorke prompted patiently. Halfway through Henri's verbal catharsis, Rorke had watched the Dutchmen exchange glances with each other and nod imperceptibly as they agreed on a solution to the problem. Knowing that such company agents never indulged in unprofitable charity, he waited cynically for them to name the price he would have to pay to have the de Guise brothers shipped to the South Pacific.

"Not impossible, but expensive. These men would not be safe on Curaçao. In Jakarta, yes, but not here. And it will cost money to take them there."

"I'll pay the price if 'tis a fair one," Rorke volunteered readily, but he knew the negotiations were just beginning. There was a speculative gleam in the spokesman's eyes that denoted far more than mere money.

"An exchange is what we have in mind. Do you know the English colony Pennstadt on the American coast?"

"No, but I believe the colony you're referring to is called *Pennsylvania*. What about it?"

As she recognized the name of one of the four places she had been studying on the charts, Jolie leaned forward with renewed interest. She felt the same sense of fate as she had the day she had learned that Glencoe was only twenty miles away from Kilchurn Castle. Nudging her husband's arm, she whispered urgently, "Ask him about this Pennsylvania." At the knowing look Rorke gave her, she stiffened defensively; he had been monitoring her search for a home without telling her.

The Dutchman's explanation, however, contained no information about the colony; it was, instead, a bluntly worded business proposal. "Two months ago," he began, "one of our patrol ships came across an English ship that was foundering in heavy seas. The captain transferred the crew and passengers to his own ship and brought them to Curaçao."

"Did the English ship sink?" Rorke asked dryly.

Annoyed by the interruption, the official shook his head. "It was a derelict when our captain retrieved it," he admitted reluctantly. It was also an old Dutch privateering trick to force a crew to leave a distressed ship so that it could qualify as a derelict and be claimed as a prize, Rorke reflected sardonically.

"What is it you want me to do?" he asked aloud.

"We cannot deliver these people to this Pennstadt, but you can," the Dutchman declared curtly.

"Good God, man—the *Lorelei* is a small ship. How many people?"

"Not so many now. The crew volunteered to work for us, so there are only the officers and fifty-some-odd passengers. They have already paid for their grant of land in Pennstadt, and they have enough money left for their transportation. We will give you safe escort to the coast of North America, and the voyage is not a long one."

Had Rorke not known through experience that the laws that made Holland a free country did not apply to Dutch commercial shipping, he would have refused the proposition. But the *Lorelei* was no match for a fully armed privateer. Grimly, he settled to the task of gaining the best possible terms.

"I will accept only if you provision my ship at your expense and promise to leave my crew alone."

"The provisions we will supply, but some of your Dutch marines have already requested transfer to our privateers. Now, Captain Rorke, it is time to dock your ship." Turning abruptly toward the almost forgotten prisoners, the Dutch official added brusquely, "You will have the asylum you requested, but first you will be given a bath and clothing so you will not look like the criminals you are."

Jolie moved protectively closer to her husband when she intercepted the silent glares of hatred in the eyes of François and Henri de Guise, and she breathed easily only after they'd been taken from the cabin. She wondered bleakly why the world seemed to be more easily ruled by hatred than by happiness. She felt no triumph at having been the cause of their downfall.

By the time the *Lorelei* cleared Willemstadt harbor, Captain James Rorke was fully prepared to renounce a life at sea. He had lost sixteen of his marines and twelve crewmen to persuasive Dutch privateers whose need for trained seamen was never-ending. He had watched helplessly as fifteen more German Anabaptists than the Dutch officials had promised were crowded into limited quarters. And he and his navigator had plotted a fifteen-hundred-mile voyage to the distant colony of Pennsylvania with little knowledge of the navigational hazards along the way. An hour before sailing, Chapman had returned with four drunken crew members who had not reported for muster, and just before the gangplank was raised, Dutch soldiers had marched ten additional passengers aboard. Rorke had scowled in irritation with himself over that incident; he had forgotten the English captain and officers whose own ship had been confiscated by an enterprising Dutch privateer months earlier.

For the beleaguered *Lorelei* captain, the week in port had been too frustratingly busy to allow him enough recreational time with the wife he had traveled thousands of miles to reclaim. More often than not, it had been Chapman who had escorted Jolie on her daily excursions into the bustling city, while Rorke had been obliged to meet with officials of the Dutch West Indies Company. As ponderously slow as their East Indies Company counterparts in Amsterdam had been over the disposition of the *Indomeer*, they had insisted that Rorke be party to the negotiations of the sale of his wine cargo and of the agreed-on restocking of the *Lorelei*'s stores.

As soon as the officials learned of Rorke's career in the

eastern company from his erstwhile marines, he was treated as a confederate rather than a foreigner, and the requested meetings became more social than business. Unfortunately, the island's socializing was as exclusively male as its commerce; and on the day Rorke was introduced to the privateer captains assigned to escort the *Lorelei* through Caribbean waters, his disenchantment with life at sea became a revulsion. Like Jan Deventer, these men were vagabonds whose lives held little purpose beyond the capture of the next ship or cargo. Rorke was appalled at the prospect of becoming a permanent member of their isolated, single-minded brotherhood.

Thus while Jolie was left to her own devices during the days, and the *Lorelei*'s officers divided the chores of preparing the ship, Rorke fretted with increasing annoyance. On the last night in port, he arrived back on dock in time to discover that his wife had been busier than he had during the week in Curaçao. When he found her missing from their quarters, he learned from Chapman that she was below decks with the passengers.

"You needn't fret about her safety, Captain," the first mate assured him readily. "She's spent the better part of the week with them."

"Did anyone think to tell those Protestant zealots that she's Catholic?" Rorke demanded.

"Aye, but they're not zealots like your Scottish Covenanters, and they appreciate her skill as a nurse the same as our crew lads do."

"You allowed her to doctor the crew? Belay that question, Chapman. I know my wife frequently fails to ask permission. What was wrong with our men?"

" 'Twas the first time in a tropical port for most of them, and a few of the brawlers among them overmatched themselves in fighting." The first mate paused long enough to chuckle before he continued, "There was no need for discipline when she finished patching them up. She may look a delicate woman, but there's a steel edge to her tongue that made every one of them stand up straighter."

"What about the passengers?"

"A durable lot who are used to hardship."

"Any disease?"

"The lass delivered one of their babes three days ago, and there's a child or two who's ailing, but the others are well enough."

"How the devil did she get to know them? She doesn't speak German or Dutch."

"King William kept them waiting in Liverpool for two years before he gave them permission to emigrate to Pennsylvania."

"Are they all aboard now?"

"Aye, and settled down without complaint."

"What about the crew?"

"Still a dozen of them on shore leave."

"Were you able to stow enough cargo aboard to offset some of the loss we'll be taking on this damnable out-of-the-way voyage?"

Again Chapman chuckled softly. "Aye, and with a cargo guaranteed to earn a profit in Pennsylvania."

"How would you know that? No one I've asked knew anything about that colony," Rorke declared skeptically.

"The Dutchies won't admit it," Chapman confided smugly, "but they've reason enough to steer clear of the port of Philadelphia. Years ago, 'twas some of their own company men who started a colony there, but those lads traitorously joined with the Swedes and Welsh and English settlers to begin their own trade. Now there are almost as many Pennsylvania privateers as there are Caribbean Dutch, and the competition is lively."

"I'll be damned; I heard 'twas a Quaker colony started less than fifteen years ago," Rorke protested mildy.

"Aye, the Quakers were forty years behind the first colonists, and now they're in the privateer trade, same as the others. However, our cargo won't be competing with theirs; we'll be selling what they can't buy on these islands."

"I'd have thought rum and sugar would be the most profitable."

"Aye, I thought the same thing until your wife said different. Two of our passengers had lived in Pennsylvania for five years before they went to Germany to fetch their families and friends. She asked them about trade cargoes, and they told her that tea and rice were in short supply because the English shippers charged more than the Dutch."

"Those are our only cargoes?"

"Nay, we've our own spices, and the South Sea medicines she said you'd be needing."

"My wife has been damned busy," Rorke muttered as he headed toward the companionway leading to the below decks area he entered only rarely. Since his last dismal stint as a working doctor aboard the *Indomeer*, he had avoided all such closed-in spaces, just as he had ignored the profession he had once enjoyed. Jolie emerged from the entry while he was still several feet away, and he stared at her in shock. Her wigless head was wrapped Caribbean-slave style in a white cloth, and she was wearing her cut-down nun's robe.

"What the devil!" he exploded as he noted the gleam of perspiration on her face reflected in the lantern light. "You look like a kitchen slavey!"

"I feel like one," she retorted tartly. "One of your men just—"

"Why the devil did you start playing healing angel to drunken sailors? Now every time one of them stubs his toe, he'll come running to you. And why in hell did you think it necessary to pamper fifty religious refugees? I thought you'd learned enough with the last ones we—"

"There are sixty-eight of them, and they don't expect any pampering!"

"Christ!"

These last words were exchanged inside their cabin just before Jolie fled into the inner room, leaving a frustrated husband behind. Angrier with himself than with her, Rorke sat down heavily and stared unseeing at the charts spread out on the table in front of him. By the time she emerged, wearing her wig and a flowing, light-colored robe he had never seen before, Rorke's unreasoning anger had been replaced by the heavy calm of decision.

"Sit down, Jolie, 'tis time we settled our future. I've decided that we'll return to England. I've enough money so that neither of us will have to work. We'll buy a home in some city where we won't be bored, but where life is regulated by law and order. I'm tired to death of shipboard emergencies, and I'm not cut out to live in a savage wilderness ruled by religious bigots of any kind."

"Pennsylvania is governed by the same laws as England," Jolie declared defensively, "and it's no longer a wilderness. Philadelphia has seven thousand people who have the freedom to belong to any church they want. All you need to become a citizen is enough money to purchase land and to support yourself. I don't want to live in England, where a king can send you anywhere he wants and where his *cochon* lords and earls have the power to—"

"We'd have the same king in any English colony, Jolie."

"But he'd be too far away to run our lives. He didn't send one single colonial to fight in his useless war. *Ma foi*, Rorke Campbell, I thought you'd want to be free after what you've been through. And don't tell me that you've been free on this Dutch island. Monsieur Chapman has been afraid they would steal your boat as they did the English one."

As Jolie spoke, her tempo had become more rapid and her accented English more infused with French words. Rorke was smiling long before she finished, and his memories of their former life together were far more accurate. Her ability to express her opinions with a pungent candor had remained unimpaired, and her independence still bordered on disobedience.

"Let's go to bed, my determined firebrand. Tomorrow's going to be another busy day," he suggested good-naturedly, his humor restored.

Rorke's prophecy proved to be a hopelessly optimistic understatement compared to what happened that first day at sea. With three longboats already in towing position when the English captain and his officers were deposited aboard, Rorke and his entire crew were too preoccupied with the mechanics of getting the *Lorelei* underway to greet the newcomers. That task fell to the captain's wife, who led them into the main cabin. An hour later, just after the longboats were hauled aboard and the *Lorelei* began moving under its own wind-driven sail power, Jolie and the stocky English captain emerged from the cabin and located Rorke on the bridge.

"Rorke," she announced quietly, "Captain Edwards has something to say, and I think you should listen to him."

Without waiting for permission, the Englishman launched into terse speech. " 'Tis my opinion you'll lose your ship to the Dutch jackals once they have you boxed within cannon range."

Rorke shook his head. "I've been promised safe escort by the company directors," he countered sharply.

"Aye, by the same fat hypocrites who promised to return my ship. They'll not be the ones to decide your fate; 'twill be those tricksters waiting for you yonder. Think, man, they'll not pass over a prize ship like yours. You've had enough experience with their breed of pirates to know they'll wait a day or more before they attack."

"They wouldn't dare bring the *Lorelei* back to Curaçao," Rorke insisted stubbornly.

"More likely they'll steal your crew and put the rest of us ashore on some uninhabited island, then proceed with your ship to Cartagena on the mainland, where there are fleets of the skull-and-crossbones brotherhood that would buy this ship and cargo with no questions asked. I checked the route you marked on the chart, and 'tis not the one that's used, except by fools or by mariners new to the Caribbean. Do you gamble, Captain Rorke, or do you let me help you get your ship safely to Pennsylvania? You've not enough cannon to outgun them should the need arise; but there's enough hull speed in this graceful dancer to outrun them before they can guess your intentions."

It took Rorke only seconds to recall his own gloomy

suspicions of a week ago and to offer the brusque Englishman a shared command of the *Lorelei*. The decision was one he'd never regret. Had Captain Edwards not known the storm paths of the Northern Caribbean, the ship would have foundered a dozen times over. And had the *Lorelei* not been far at sea when it passed the deadly Hatteras Cape off the Carolina coast, it would have been pounded to flotsam by the storm-driven seas. Again in the treacherous roadstead of the Delaware River leading to the port of Philadelphia, only a navigator familiar with the shifting channel could have guided the ship to safe anchorage. After four weeks of turbulent weather, Rorke no longer pretended even partial command of his own ship, and the long-time navigator of the *Lorelei* admitted he had failed to plot a safe course along the uneven shores of the unknown continent. Halfway through the voyage, Rorke had hired Captain Edwards as his permanent replacement.

Standing with his arm around Jolie as the *Lorelei*'s cargo and weary passengers were loaded into tender boats for the short haul to the city-length embarcadero that fronted Philadelphia, Rorke experienced the relief of homecoming. Regardless of what lay ahead in the New World, he was confident that the troubles that had plagued him in Europe and England hadn't polluted this brave new colony. But still he was not yet willing to admit to his glowing wife that he had capitulated completely.

"I repeat what I said about England, Jolie. We've enough money for a leisurely life, and I've no intention of working as hard as we did in Newcastle."

"Neither do I," Jolie murmured contentedly. "That is why I instructed Captain Edwards to hire two young doctors from Edinburgh University on his first trip to England. They will tend all the routine patients while we choose only those that interest us." Trying out for the first time the colorful English contractions that marked her husband's speech, Jolie added with a self-conscious giggle, " 'Tis what I intended to do before you rescued me from Martinique.

Now 'twill be even more glorious to share my plans with you.''

Looking down on the slim woman who had become the lodestar of his life, more essential to his happiness and peace of mind than life itself, Rorke surrendered without protest to her skillful manipulation of their future. In the past, her predictions had been more accurate than his. She had been right about the danger they had faced in Edinburgh and about the need for an infirmary in Newcastle. Had he listened to her when danger again threatened them in Newcastle and agreed to her suggestion to hire a smuggler as they had in Holland, the three years of desolate separation would have been avoided. Unless it proved an oppressive city, Philadelphia, in the burgeoning new colony of Pennsylvania, would become their permanent home. Rorke did wonder briefly, however, if the city, ostentatiously based on brotherly love, would be tolerant enough to accept a red-haired woman who had yet to learn the cardinal canon of organized society—that men were the natural and ordained planners and leaders.

Smiling with an abruptly wayward humor, Rorke studied the symmetrical rows of brick houses that stretched out along the distant shoreline almost as far as the eye could see. He didn't really want Jolie to become another of the obedient homebodies he had heard colonial women were. She had conquered every other place she had lived in; why not Philadelphia? Even the proud MacDonald Scots, who had bowed their stubborn heads to no woman other than the long-dead Queen Mary, had respectfully revered their own red-haired nun; the pupils and other nuns on Martinique had adored her; and the stiff-necked Anabaptist Germans had obeyed her orders as readily as they had his. When the settlers of this American city met their first retired Sister of Charity superior, their first professional nurse with the skill of a physician, and their first outspoken Scottish-French aristocrat of the female persuasion, they, too, would accept her for what she was—a unique woman, destined as much as they had been to become a pioneer in a new, unspoiled world.

Until the next morning, though, when they would go ashore to fulfill that destiny, Rorke wanted her conquering magnetism concentrated solely on him in the privacy of their cabin bedroom. Tomorrow would be soon enough to begin the adventure of building a new home and a new life.